RITA BRADSHAW

The Colours of Love

PAN BOOKS

First published 2015 by Macmillan

This edition published in paperback 2015 by Pan Books
an imprint of Pan Macmillan
The Smithson, 6 Briset Street, London EC1M 5NR
EU representative: Macmillan Publishers Ireland Ltd, 1st Floor,
The Liffey Trust Centre, 117-126 Sheriff Street, Upper
Dublin 1, D01 YC43
Associated companies throughout the world
www.panmacmillan.com

ISBN 978-1-4472-7158-1

9 8

A CIP catalogue record for this book is available from the British Library.

Typeset by Ellipsis Digital Limited, Glasgow
Printed and bound by CPI Group (UK) Ltd, Croydon, CR0 4YY

Visit **www.panmacmillan.com** to read more about all our books
and to buy them. You will also find features, author interviews and
news of any author events, and you can sign up for e-newsletters
so that you're always first to hear about our new releases.

For our precious and beloved granddaughter, Chloe Elizabeth Bradshaw, born 14 May 2014; cherished baby daughter for Ben and Lizzi and beautiful little sister for Reece; adored new cousin for Sam and Connor, Georgia and Emily, and Lydia. You are the most exquisite little baby in the world, darling one, with your big brown eyes and wide smile. Daddy is going to have to fight the boys off in droves when you get older!

We praise the Lord for your safe arrival in the world (and so quick, Lizzi!) and give thanks to God for His treasured gift. He truly does do all things well – alleluia to the King of kings and Lord of lords.

Though I speak with the tongues of men and of angels, but have not love, I have become sounding brass or a clanging cymbal. And though I have the gift of prophecy, and understand all mysteries and all knowledge, and though I have all faith, so that I could remove mountains, but have not love, I am nothing. And though I bestow all my goods to feed the poor, and though I give my body to be burned, but have not love, it profits me nothing. Love suffers long and is kind; love does not envy; love does not parade itself, is not arrogant; does not behave rudely, does not seek its own, is not provoked, thinks no evil; does not rejoice in iniquity, but rejoices in the truth; bears all things, hopes all things, endures all things.

Love never fails.

1 Corinthians 13, v.1–8

Author's Note

This is a story I have wanted to write for years, and I must thank my lovely editor, Wayne Brookes, for trusting me to do it sensitively. Having said that, I think I have wrestled with disgust and horror at man's inhumanity to man more during the time of writing *The Colours of Love* than at any other point in my life. My research threw up horrible facts and figures about the slave trade, the English oppression of the Irish during the potato famine, and much more. It is ironic that in America during the 1850s the black populace, who hated the Irish even more than the average white American did, were the first to call the Irish 'white niggers'. Throughout the book, incidentally, I have not used this offensive term – not because of issues of political correctness (I always aim to be factual about an era that I'm writing about, however unpleasant the subject), but because I couldn't bear to put the word on the printed page. My darling son-in-law, Roy, has come in for abuse on the football field and that word has been used, and on the few occasions I was there, I wanted to take the perpetrator by the throat.

Several great Americans who didn't agree with the oppression of any peoples – be they slaves brought by force to the United States, or immigrants like the Irish, Jews, Slavs and Italians – predicted a change in future thinking. Orestes Brownson, a celebrated convert to Catholicism, stated in 1850: 'Out of these narrow lanes, dirty streets, damp cellars, and suffocating garrets, will come forth some of the noblest sons of our country, whom she will delight to own and honour.' And in little more than a century his prophecy came true: Irish-Americans had moved from the position of the despised to the Oval Office. And now, in the twenty-first century, there is a black President in the White House. This is encouraging and is not to be underestimated, even though the world is in such a terrible state, with countries, cultures, religions and individuals fighting each other.

In my story, it is love that overcomes prejudice and fear and hatred; love between a man and a woman, and the love of a family, and steadfast friends. In the real world I truly believe love is the only answer, too.

Contents

PART ONE

Two Mothers

1923

Chapter One

She was whimpering – she could hear herself. Or perhaps it was Harriet making the animal-like sound? No, it *was* her. The occasional tortured moan came from Harriet, but she seemed better able to manage the unspeakable pain they were both enduring.

She hoped she died; she hoped the baby died too, because death would be preferable to having the baby given to the nuns at the Catholic orphanage. Her grandmother had told her enough stories, about her own terrible childhood in one of those loveless places, for her to be sure of that. She couldn't bear the thought of her own and Michael's precious child suffering such cruel treatment; far better that they went together now, and then she could hold her baby safe for all eternity.

Ruth Flaggerty raised her head to glance across at the woman in the other bed that the room held. She hadn't known Harriet Wynford before they had boarded the passenger ship bound for England, but the fact that they were both with child had drawn them together on the journey from America. Then had come the severe storm, which had blown the ship off-course and finally onto rocks close to a little fishing village somewhere along the Welsh coast. She didn't know exactly where, and she didn't care, for the trauma of the shipwreck had brought on her confinement, and Harriet's too. Several people had been injured; and three, including Harriet's personal maid, had lost their lives whilst attempting to reach safety. Once on the shore, she and Harriet had been carried to the village inn and an old crone of a midwife summoned, a near-toothless hag who stank of gin and was clearly ine-briated. The woman was at present snoring loudly in the chair she'd positioned earlier between the two beds.

'She's been like that for the last little while,' Harriet whispered weakly, as their eyes met. 'She's as drunk as a lord, dreadful woman, but we'll see this through together, you and I. Are your pains very bad, Ruth?'

Ruth nodded. Another contraction was coming and her body tensed against it. 'I can't bear much more, Harriet,' she gasped. 'Really, I can't.'

'It will soon be over.'

She didn't think it would ever be over; there was noth-ing in the world but this grinding, relentless agony, which went on and on. Ruth twisted on the hard straw mat-tress, tears trickling from her eyes. *Michael, oh Michael.* If only her family had let them get wed, this would be so different. She wanted his baby more than anything, but not like this. And they hadn't even let her say goodbye to him. Her father and two brothers had woken her in the dead of night and pulled her from her bed, and her mother had stood over her while she had dressed. When she had protested, they'd gagged and bound her and carried her to the waiting carriage, along with the valise and bags that her mother had packed. And the 'companion' they had hired to accompany her, Miss Casey, was nothing more than a gaoler; she even looked the part, with her big, beefy body and hard, flat face.

In the midst of her pain Ruth heard the chair creaking as the midwife lumbered to her feet, and then the woman was talking to Harriet, her voice slurred and her sing-song Welsh accent strong. 'Come on now, you've had babies before, so you know what to do. It's time to push.'

What a horrible old witch. In the midst of her distress, Ruth wanted to shout at the midwife. Fancy throwing Harriet's previous history of umpteen miscarriages into her face at a time like this. And Harriet so brave too, and so kind. When they had sat together on the deck of the ship, muffled up against the keen, salty wind and with thick blankets over their knees, they had whispered confidences to each other when they could be sure Miss Casey wasn't within earshot, and a strong bond had been forged between them. Apart from her family and Miss Casey, Harriet was the only person who knew Ruth wasn't married to the father of her baby, although she hadn't explained further than saying that her family deemed Michael unsuitable, and Harriet hadn't once made her feel wicked or immoral. And, in turn, Harriet had divulged that, after many miscarriages, the doctors had told her this pregnancy must be her last, and she was desperate to present her husband with a live child.

Ruth didn't think she liked the sound of Harriet's husband. She pictured him in her mind. Theobald Wynford seemed the antithesis of his sweet, well-bred wife and she couldn't imagine why Harriet had married him in the first place, but then she supposed opposites attract? And Harriet had never said a word against him, but then that was Harriet all over: loyal and good and uncomplaining.

She was tired now, so tired. It had been twilight when they'd been carried to the inn, and the agonizing night had seemed endless. It was still dark outside, the icy rain lashing against the small leaded window and the pain unremitting. If only she could sleep, escape into the land of dreams, where she met Michael and they held each other close for long, stolen moments. They had planned to run away and start a new life together, far from anyone who knew them, and had been only days from leaving, when her mother had heard her being sick on consecutive mornings and had put two and two together.

Ruth tried to shut her mind to the scene that had followed, when her mother had seemed to go mad, demanding that she name the man and then becoming hysterical when Ruth had done so. She had been locked in her room, and not even the maids had been allowed to see her; her mother had brought her all her meals on a tray. Her father had come once on that first morning, and it was as well her mother had accompanied him. Ruth's hand went involuntarily to her throat. If her mother hadn't pulled her father off her, he would have succeeded in strangling her for sure. As it was, the marks of his fingers had taken some time to fade completely.

The pain had become unbearable again and she whimpered against it, before clamping her lips together. If Harriet could bear this torture over and over again, to give her husband the child he wanted, then she could suffer it without complaint too. But oh, how she wanted Michael . . .

How much later it was when Ruth felt the nature of the spasms racking her body begin to change, she didn't know, but with the urge to push came a strength that she would have sworn moments before she didn't have. She knew Harriet's baby still hadn't made an appearance, from the sounds from the other bed and the midwife's monologue of 'Push, push!', which seemed to have been going on for hours. At one point she had managed to raise herself and glance at Harriet, only to see her friend's contorted body heaving, and the midwife standing looking down at her while she swigged the contents of a gin bottle that she had clearly brought with her.

As Ruth began to grunt and strain with the dictates of her body, she became aware of the midwife moving to her side.

'That's it, dear, you do your job, an' I can do mine,' the dreadful woman crooned. 'Not like this other one,' she added, as if to herself. 'Not got the strength of a kitten. Same with all the old wives. If the babbie don't slip out, then it's done for. You need youth on your side for this work. Damned men – they have it easy. Sow their seed an' have their pleasure, an' to hell with it.' She continued to mumble and then, as Harriet gave a terrible long howl, there was a scurry followed by the midwife crooning, 'All right, m'dear, all right. 'Tis as expected. Rest now.'

Harriet's baby wasn't crying. Didn't all babies cry when they came into the world? Why wasn't it crying? Ruth's fevered mind asked the question, even as her body got on with the job in hand. The contractions were tumbling one on top of the other now; as one ended, the next one was already upon her, and with each came the primal urge to bear down.

The sweat was pouring off her, her back arching and, at the moment the child left her body, she called out, '*Michael!*' – his name ringing from the rafters. And, as if in answer, the baby yelled, a loud, lusty cry full of life and vigour.

Chapter Two

Harriet stared at Ruth. Right up to this moment of time she had thought of Ruth as a young girl; a good girl, but one who had fallen in love and had been tempted, and who was now paying a terrible price for that weakness. But the girl had become a woman, and the proof of it was in the words she was speaking now. The midwife had lurched drunkenly from the room a few minutes ago with an armful of soiled bedding, telling them she would return shortly, and immediately she had gone, Ruth had come to sit on the side of her bed, taking her hand and saying softly, 'I'm so sorry about your baby, Harriet. So very sorry. Listen, I have an idea, but if it is to work we must act quickly. You say your husband is desperate for a child, and I don't want Miss Casey to hand my baby over to the nuns. You take her. Pretend she is yours. I'll . . . I'll say my baby was stillborn.'

Harriet made an enormous effort to pull herself together. She had been bereft when her last hopes had died, along with her baby, although in truth she had been expecting it. Expecting it, but still hoping God would answer her prayers and end her barrenness. But the baby had come too early, like all the ones before it, and she didn't think the shipwreck had really been the cause. She had been feeling unwell before the storm came. Wiping her eyes, she whispered, 'You can't give me your baby, Ruth.'

'I can. She would have a life with you; parents who love her, and a future. With the nuns' – she swallowed hard – 'her childhood would be unbearable. I know. I know what those places are like.'

'But . . . but the midwife?'

'She's so drunk she can barely walk, and I dare say she's having another drink right now. She won't remember which baby is which and, even if she does, it's our word against hers. But she'll just take her payment for services rendered and buy more gin; and we'll be gone from this place soon.'

'It wouldn't work.' Fear of Theobald warred with a hundred other emotions. 'People – Theobald – would know.'

'*No one* would know, not if we act now, before your husband comes, or anyone else. She . . . she's beautiful, Harriet. Look at how beautiful she is.' Ruth slid off the bed and went to the foot of her own bed, where the baby was lying in a makeshift crib of a wicker basket, making little mewing sounds. The other basket, at the foot of Harriet's bed, was still and silent, the child it contained hidden under the coverlet.

Ruth bent and tenderly lifted the small infant swaddled in a rough blanket, gazing down into the minute face for a long moment, and then carried the baby over to Harriet and placed her in the other woman's arms.

Harriet gazed down at the perfect, fragile features and fell instantly in love. The little girl *was* beautiful, she thought wonderingly – exquisite, her porcelain skin thrown into greater contrast against the mop of black hair above it. 'She . . . she's got such a lot of hair.'

'I know. You could plait it already.' Ruth gave a little sob of a laugh.

Harriet looked up from the baby, seeing Ruth's tears. 'You can't give her away – you're her mother.'

'I want the best for her, and you're the best, Harriet. You will love her as she deserves to be loved.'

'But your parents might change their minds when they see her.'

'They won't see her. Miss Casey has strict instructions to dispose of the baby before we return home. But even if they did see her, they wouldn't change their minds. You don't know what they're like, Harriet. They'll never forgive me for what I've done, and if the evidence of my wickedness was in front of them . . . ' She shook her head. 'You don't know them,' she repeated fearfully.

'Oh, my dear, you're not wicked,' said Harriet gently, feeling immensely sorry for the girl who, at fifteen years of age, was twenty years younger than herself. 'You simply fell in love, and if the young man in question wanted to marry you?'

'He did.'

'Then the fault is theirs as much as yours.' Harriet looked at the child in her arms. Because the parents did not consider Ruth's young man good enough for their daughter, Ruth would be deprived of her baby. It was wrong and cruel, but Ruth wasn't the first to experience such bigotry, and she wouldn't be the last.

'Will you take her, Harriet? Please?'

'But what if you change your mind?'

'I won't, I promise. This is for the best. I know that.'

The baby stirred, one tiny hand escaping the blanket. Harriet studied the minute fingers and felt such a surge of maternal love it made her breathless. She had been dreading Theobald's fury when he discovered he'd been thwarted of an heir yet again – and that was the way he would view the baby's death. He'd blamed each miscarriage and stillbirth on her delicate constitution, saying that he should have married a wife who was stronger and healthier. It had been on the tip of her tongue many times to ask him why he hadn't, but, of course, she knew the answer to that. Theobald was a wealthy landowner and local magistrate in the north-east of England, with a gift for business that he'd inherited from his father, a man who had risen from relative obscurity to great wealth during his lifetime. But Theobald had desired the prestige and standing that marrying a daughter of the aristocracy could give him. She was the third daughter of a lord and, unlike her sisters, was plain and awkward and shy. She had felt she was on the shelf, at over twenty years old, and when Theobald had offered her the chance of ending her spinster existence, she had taken it. It had been a marriage of convenience on both sides, but she had lived to regret her foolishness. Bitterly.

Would things have deteriorated so badly between them if she had given him, earlier in their marriage, the heir he craved? Perhaps Theobald would have been content to leave her alone then. As it was, his increasingly frenzied efforts to make her body bear his child had resulted in Harriet hating him. He was worse than a wild beast in the bedroom, tearing at her, month after month; her only respite occurred during the months she carried a baby in her womb.

'Harriet?' Ruth touched her arm. 'The midwife will be back soon with the fresh bedding.'

'Are you sure, my dear? That you want to give her up?'

'It's her only chance of a good life. *Please* take her.'

Harriet began to tremble, as hope mingled with the grief and despair she'd been feeling since the midwife had taken the limp little body from between her legs. She hadn't asked to see the baby; she'd seen so many in recent years that she'd felt she couldn't bear it again, but now she murmured, 'I want to see it, Ruth. To say goodbye.'

Understanding immediately, Ruth took her baby from Harriet and then fetched the other basket to her. Harriet took a deep breath and then, very gently, slowly folded back the coverlet. It had been a boy and he was much smaller than Harriet's child, his head and body the length of her hand and his limbs matchstick-thin. But he was perfect, and he was beautiful. Her precious, sweet baby son. 'I love you,' she breathed softly. 'I love you so much. Forgive me. It doesn't mean I love you any the less, please understand that, my darling.' She stroked the doll-like face with the tip of her finger, her tears falling on the bald little head. He was already cold.

Ruth, her face awash, murmured, 'You're in a better place, little baby, safe and warm in the Almighty's arms.'

'Do you believe that?' Harriet looked up. 'Really believe it?'

'Of course. Don't you?'

'I did once.' Before her heart had been ripped out by the roots, over and over again.

'Believe it, Harriet. You'll see him again one day.'

Harriet said nothing for a few moments, then carefully replaced the coverlet and handed the basket to Ruth. 'Put him at the end of your bed.'

It was decided.

Theobald Wynford was not a big man, being only an inch or so taller than his wife, but what he lacked in height he made up for in presence. Broad and compact, with an olive complexion and thick, grizzled hair, he radiated energy and life. His eyes were such a dark brown as to be almost black, and his nose, a large curving protru–sion, hinted at Jewish blood somewhere in his ancestry, although it would be a brave man indeed who suggested this out loud. Intolerant and opinionated, he demanded respect and subservience from those beneath him, including his wife. Having broken his right leg in two places when the ship had been driven onto the rocks, he'd drunk himself insensible to dull the pain, on reaching the inn. The nearest town that boasted a doctor was some distance away and, due to the inclement weather and the fact it was nightfall, it had been decided to wait for morning before someone was dispatched to fetch him.

It was this same doctor who was now telling Theobald that he had a daughter. 'A beautiful child.' The doctor smiled, his voice hearty. 'Bit on the small side, but none the worse for it. Your good wife tells me this is the news you have been waiting for, Mr Wynford?'

Theobald nodded, his teeth gritted against the pain as the doctor strapped up his injured leg. He would have preferred a son, but beggars can't be choosers, and his dried-up stick of a wife wouldn't be dropping any more bairns. The damned doctors had made that plain when this last pregnancy had been confirmed.

'It will be two weeks or so before your wife's fit to travel, but I dare say that won't bother you too much, in view of your good news.' Having finished his ministrations, the doctor straightened. 'I'm sure they will make you as comfortable as possible here – they're good folk.'

Good folk? Theobald's face spoke volumes. This was a wretched, grubby little inn in a wretched, grubby little village where the stink of fish permeated everything. His wife and the young girl who was also expecting a baby had been given the only spare room in the place. Where was he expected to sleep?

The doctor had no trouble discerning his patient's thoughts, and his voice held a note of warning when he said, 'Two weeks, Mr Wynford – unless you want to put your wife's life and that of your daughter in jeopardy. Do I make myself clear?'

'Quite clear.' *Jumped-up little upstart!*

'Good. Your wife has been through quite an ordeal, Mr Wynford.'

So had he! Theobald adjusted his aching leg. 'I understand arrangements have been made to transport the remaining passengers and crew out of here later today, and I intend to avail myself of that. I shall find a hotel in the nearest town and wait there until my wife and child are able to leave.'

'As you wish.' Theobald's voice had been curt, and the doctor's was equally so. He glanced round the crowded room of the small inn, where folk were sitting or standing as best they could. Apart from a few broken bones and two cases of mild concussion, the only serious injuries seemed to be an elderly lady who had damaged her back and a young man who had been unconscious for hours. The innkeeper and his wife had given up their own bedroom to the old lady, and the young man was stretched out on a settle on the other side of the room, where a couple of the passengers were keeping an eye on him. It hadn't escaped the doctor's notice that Theobald had the best chair in the place, positioned close to the warmth of the fire, even though several ladies – one of whom had a broken ankle – had need of a seat.

Bringing his gaze back to Theobald, the doctor said shortly, 'I shall return tomorrow to examine Mrs Wynford. Here is my card. Once you are established in the town, let me know and I'll visit with an update on your wife, Mr Wynford. And I can check that leg while I'm about it.'

No doubt, and charge a pretty penny for his services too, Theobald thought. Damned doctors cost a fortune. Quacks and charlatans, the lot of 'em. Keeping his thoughts to himself, he merely inclined his head.

'I presume you would like to see your daughter before you leave? I will see that she is brought to you. It would be difficult for you to negotiate the narrow stairs to your wife's room with that leg. And now, if you will excuse me, there are other people needing my attention.'

Theobald's gaze followed the doctor as the man made his way across the room, but his thoughts were elsewhere. A child – a daughter. So Harriet had finally managed it. He had waited long enough, damn her. He had willed her to go full-term with this one; had willed her bony, unattractive body to provide him with an heir, a son in his own image. But she hadn't gone full-term and the child wasn't a boy, but a girl. He raised his hand to his face, touching his nose. The Wynford appendage didn't sit too well on the female of the species; his two sisters had been proof of that. His mother had been a pretty woman, but he and his sisters had taken after his father; the Wynford

genes were strong. Still, no matter. His father had virtually bought husbands for Amanda and Susannah,
providing them with dowries that had proved sufficiently
enticing. He could do the same with his daughter, but in
her case there would be a stipulation to the man who
took her as wife: he must take her name also, and relin-
quish his own, if he wanted to inherit the estate. The
Wynford name would carry on – nothing mattered more
than that.

At this point in his thinking he checked himself. The
child wasn't yet twenty-four hours old and was small
into the bargain, coming early, as it had. It might yet still
go the same way as the others, if it was sickly.

And then, as if in answer to the fear that had beset
him, he became aware of the buxom figure of the innkeeper's wife at his elbow. 'You wanted to see the baby,
sir? Here she is, and a prettier little one you couldn't
wish for.'

She bent down, depositing in his lap the tightly
wrapped bundle she was holding. His arms instinctively
closed around the cocoon and he stared down into the
tiny face, which was all that was visible. He had had no
real experience of babies, but if he'd had to voice an
opinion about them, it would be that to him they all
looked the same – usually bald and unattractive. He had
never understood the female mind that cooed and twit-
tered about how sweet and charming infants were; and
his sisters' children had been positively ugly. But this
one . . . He examined the minute features under a shock

of black hair. This one was actually pretty. Amazing! He smiled to himself. Especially in view of her parents. But perhaps she would take after his mother? Whether she did or didn't, he wasn't sorry she had escaped the Wynford nose.

The baby gave a yawn, revealing pink little gums, and then opened her eyes as she wriggled against the constrictions of the blanket. One small hand forced its way out of the folds of material and then caught hold of one of Theobald's fingers, in a surprisingly firm grip. 'She's strong,' he breathed, almost to himself.

'Oh yes, sir, she might be small, but she's a survivor, this one.' The innkeeper's wife nodded cheerily. 'Makes all the difference if they're a fighter, when they're born before time.'

The baby was looking at him, and he could swear her great eyes were filled with curiosity and interest. Now that she was awake she seemed very alert, but peaceful, not squawking as his sisters' babies seemed to do constantly. He felt a thrill of ownership shoot down his spine.

'Shall I give your wife a message, sir?' the woman said, bending down and picking up the baby again.

Theobald considered his reply. He was disappointed the child was not a boy, but, having seen the infant, he was pleased enough with the look of her and, as the innkeeper's wife had said, she seemed a fighter. Harriet could have done worse. 'Tell my wife I want the child named Esther, after my mother, and give her my good wishes for a speedy recovery.'

The innkeeper's wife looked somewhat askance. 'And the little one?' she pressed. 'What shall I say you think about her?'

Theobald settled back in his chair and reached for the tankard of ale at his elbow. 'Say that she'll do,' he said shortly.

Chapter Three

Harriet and Ruth were to look back and see the two weeks that followed Esther's birth as a time of bittersweet joy. Harriet was grieving the loss of her tiny baby son, but was filled with thankfulness at the gift Ruth had given her; and for her part, Ruth begrudged even an hour spent in sleep, because she needed to cherish every moment with her daughter, before she was taken away to her new life. The two women often talked long into the night, but although Ruth told Harriet about her family, and the pride they felt at having risen from rags to riches, after her grandparents had emigrated to America from Ireland at the height of the potato famine in 1850, she said nothing about Michael. Harriet, fearing the subject was too painful, asked no questions, but wondered much. It was clear the two young people had loved each other, and it seemed too cruel to deny them their happiness. But through their misfortune she had been given a pearl beyond price: her precious baby girl.

The weather added to the sense that the three of them

were removed from the real world. Since the day of the shipwreck, wild November storms had battered the Welsh coast unmercifully, the days dark and gloomy, with unremitting rain and sleet. The wind howled like a banshee, shaking the little leaded panes of glass in the windows of the inn until the women felt sure they would shatter. But inside their room, all was snug and warm. The fire sent flickering shadows over the beamed ceiling and illuminated their faces as they tended to the baby, each of the women wishing these days could last forever. But all too soon the time came when they had to depart – Harriet bound for the north-east of England with Theobald, and Ruth back to America.

The weather had turned colder in the last day or two, and on the day of departure they awoke to a hard frost, the window so thick with ice they could not see out. Before they had finished breakfast the odd desultory snow-flake was wafting in the air, but neither Ruth nor Harriet was concerned with the weather. Both women had slept fitfully, and in the middle of the night Harriet had heard Ruth trying to stifle the sobs that were shaking her body, and she had got up and gone to her. After that there had been no sleep for either of them and it had been a relief that Esther, being so small, demanded feeding every two hours.

Now they were dressed for the journey, and Harriet was giving Esther her last feed before the carriage was due to arrive. Miss Casey had been staying at a bed-and-breakfast just outside the town where Theobald had resided, and was due to arrive later in the morning.

Ruth watched Harriet, with her own breasts aching, although they had been tightly bound to dry up the milk for the last days and had stopped leaking moisture now. But the ache was in her heart.

Once she had finished feeding the baby, and without asking Ruth, Harriet placed the infant in the other woman's arms. They had both been dreading this day, and Harriet felt wretched at Ruth's distress.

Tears trickling down her face, Ruth touched with her lips the baby's eyes, her mouth, her cheeks, her little hands, kissing each tiny finger and then stroking her silky black hair. 'I love you,' she whispered softly to her. 'I'll always love you – always – although I can't be with you. Forgive me for letting you go, but it's the only way.' A sob caught in her throat and she looked up at Harriet, who was crying too. 'How am I going to bear it?' she whispered brokenly. 'Oh, Harriet, what am I going to do?'

Harriet sat down beside her then and took Ruth in her arms, the two of them swaying in an agony of shared grief above the sleeping baby in her mother's embrace. Harriet didn't try to speak, for there were no words to say after all. Nothing could make this easier for Ruth.

'Will . . . will you let her second name be Joy?' Ruth murmured after a while. 'That's what I want to give her, in placing her in your care: joy.'

'Of course.' Harriet hugged her. 'And I'll make sure she

knows nothing but love and happiness, Ruth. I promise.'

'I know.' Ruth rested her head on Harriet's shoulder for a moment and then, as they heard footsteps on the stairs outside the room, she stiffened.

The innkeeper's wife poked her head round the door after knocking. 'Your husband's here, dear,' she said to Harriet.

'Tell him I'm coming in a minute.'

'Right you are.'

Alone again, they stood up, Ruth smothering the sleeping baby in kisses and beginning to sob uncontrollably.

'I can't leave you like this,' Harriet said through her own tears.

'You can. You must.' Ruth wrapped the baby's blanket more securely around her tiny shape, and then thrust the little cocoon at Harriet. 'Take her, now, while I can still do this. Please, Harriet, help me do what's right for her.'

They embraced one last time and then Harriet walked to the door with the baby cradled in her arms, opening it and leaving the room without looking back. Ruth felt her heart being torn from her soul with a pain so intense she had to ram her fist into her mouth to stop herself from screaming, and she began to panic. She couldn't do it – she couldn't let her baby go. She would run away from them all, grab her baby and disappear somewhere. *Michael, oh Michael, why aren't you here? Why didn't you follow me and find me somehow?*

Choking on her tears, she paced the room, wringing

her hands together, before opening the door and going onto the landing. She wouldn't run after Harriet and her baby, she knew that, but in the last moments something had broken and torn deep inside her and it would never heal, no matter how many years she continued to live.

She couldn't see the main room of the inn from the small square of landing, but she could hear voices, and suddenly the panic was strong again. She had to have one last glimpse of her baby; she had to see her go.

She ran back into the room and began to struggle to force the frost-rimed window open, pushing with all her might until at last the ice splintered and the window sprang wide. Peering out, she saw Harriet being helped into the waiting carriage by the coachman, and caught a glimpse of Theobald inside as he leaned forward to take the baby. And then the horses' hooves were clattering on the cobbles and the carriage moved out of sight, and there was only the snow falling thickly now out of a laden sky . . .

Immediately she was settled in the carriage with a thick rug over her knees, Harriet reached for the baby, smoothing the blanket from her little face. She glanced at Theobald and saw that his gaze was fixed on the child in her arms. 'She's a bonny little thing,' he said softly. 'I'd forgotten how bonny.'

'Yes, she is.' The observation unnerved her; it was as though he was questioning the baby's parentage, but Harriet knew it was her guilty conscience putting a hidden meaning in his voice, and this was confirmed when he said with evident pride, 'She takes after my mother. Can you see the resemblance?'

She had never met Theobald's parents, for they had both died some years before he had married her, but there was a large portrait of them in the hall at home, and her husband was the very image of his father. Taking a deep, steadying breath and trying to keep the tremor out of her voice, she said, 'It was the first thing I noticed about her.'

Gratified, Theobald leaned back in his seat, his injured leg stretched out in front of him. After a moment or two he cleared his throat. 'I meant to ask before, what did – what was her name? Mrs Flaggerty? – what did she have?'

'Ruth Flaggerty, yes. She had a little boy.' Harriet didn't know if he had been told about the stillbirth, but was banking on the fact that he hadn't bothered to ask about Ruth. Self-centred to the core, Theobald rarely concerned himself with anything that didn't directly impinge on him, and in this instance it would work to her advantage. If he knew one of the babies had died, he might begin to wonder.

Theobald nodded. 'Damned funny time for her to come and visit relatives in England, wasn't it? And that companion of hers – a grim-looking woman.'

'I understand the visit had been arranged for some time.'

'Still damned funny, and her husband not accompanying her seems fishy to me. Did she say anything about him?'

'Only that she loved him very much and was missing him.'

Theobald had lost interest in the conversation. Adjusting his position on the hard seat, he muttered, 'This leg is giving me gyp. Can't sleep for more than a couple of hours, even with the pills the quack gave me. Why we ever made the damned trip to see your sister, I don't know. I won't be gallivanting abroad again, I can tell you. And them Americans – damned funny ideas some of 'em have got. No, give me England every time.'

Harriet could have said that she had never wanted to travel halfway across the world in the first place, and that she knew full well why Theobald had insisted on making the trip. One of her sisters had married an English earl and the other, Bernice, had bagged a very wealthy and influential American senator. In the past Theobald had been somewhat dismissive of the latter, affecting an air of snobbish condescension and belittling his brother-in-law's venture into politics, but when the US President, Warren G. Harding, had died suddenly of a massive stroke in August, and his successor – the taciturn Calvin Coolidge – had turned out to be a good friend (a very good friend) of Bernice's husband, Theobald had suddenly seen the potential of having someone in the family who rubbed shoulders with the President of the United States. They had spent three months with her sister, and Theobald had been ecstatic when they had been invited to dinner at the

White House. For herself, she didn't like her brother-in-law, and she had found that she disliked President Coolidge even more, and it had sickened her the way Theobald had ingratiated himself with them both.

Making no comment, she looked out of the window into the swirling snow, her thoughts back at the inn with Ruth. Part of her – a part she was deeply ashamed of – had been glad to leave the American girl. She had wanted to put some distance between them. The giving-over of the baby had seemed too good to be true, too miraculous a gift when she had thought all was lost, and the fear that the gift would be snatched back and that Ruth would change her mind had been with Harriet night and day, however hard she battled against it. But now she was safe. She looked down into the small, sweet face that had become her world. She could be Esther's mother in reality. The danger was over. But, having lost babies of her own, she knew what Ruth was feeling.

'I've made arrangements for a nanny to be in place at home when we return,' Theobald said some time later, when they had sat in silence. 'And Mrs Norton is also seeing to setting up some interviews for a new lady's maid for you.'

Harriet would have preferred to choose her own nanny for Esther, but she made no comment on this. Inclining her head, she murmured, 'Poor Atkinson.' She had barely given her maid's untimely death a thought in the last two weeks, with all that had happened. Her guilty conscience prompted her to say, 'Atkinson had a widowed mother who was completely dependent on her. I would like to settle a sum of money on the woman, so that she is not destitute. There will be no help from any other quarter.'

Theobald frowned. 'Surely that is not necessary?'

'Nevertheless, I would like it. We have been given so much, Theobald' – she looked down at the baby in her arms – 'can't we afford to be generous?'

She thought he was going to refuse, but after a moment he nodded. 'If it would please you, I will see to it that she receives a monthly allowance for as long as she is alive,' he said magnanimously. 'Will that do?'

'Thank you.' Harriet was in no doubt that his current benevolence was due solely to the child in her arms. Nor did she fool herself that his good mood would last. He would think nothing of spending a small fortune on a thoroughbred stallion in order to impress their social set in the local hunt, but he was far from being a generous man. With this in mind, she pressed, 'And it will be enough for her to live comfortably?'

'Yes, yes, enough to keep her out of the workhouse, if that is what you are asking,' he said irritably.

And Theobald knew all about the horrors of the workhouse, being on the board of the Workhouse Guardians. But to hear him talk, every poor soul incarcerated in that hellish place was there because of their own delinquency, Harriet thought, glancing at his hard face. She had accompanied him to the workhouse just once in the early days of their marriage, when he had insisted that she acquaint herself with the 'duties' expected of her as his wife. From the moment they had passed through the high, forbidding gates into a big yard surrounded by brick walls, she had felt the terror of the building. The principle that those who sought relief in the workhouse should be divided into groups was a flawed one, in Harriet's opinion. Men were separated from women, thus breaking up families; and both groups were again divided into the able-bodied, the aged and children. However, no proper provision was made for the sick and the mentally ill, and vagrants were totally ignored. The austere uniform, the workhouse diet – the staples of which were coarse bread, cheese, gruel and potatoes – the rigid discipline and harsh punishments had left her shocked and sickened.

She had asked Theobald why the hair of both the little boys and girls was severely cropped, and why the adult inmates had their hair cut in a standard rough-and-ready manner, to which he had replied shortly, 'Hygiene.' He had also given this as the reason for the severe workhouse clothing, although she had suspected (and rightly) that it was more for reasons of economy, and as a badge of pauperism.

When she had objected to the biblical text over the door of the dining hall – 'If any would not work, neither should he eat' – saying that the workhouse had taken St Paul's words out of context, Theobald had been furious with her, and they had had their first disagreement on the way home in the carriage. 'Poverty is a necessary

and indispensable ingredient in society,' he had growled
at her. 'Without it there would be no labour, and without
labour no riches, no refinement and no benefit to those
possessed of wealth. There is a section of the poor who
have always been poor, and will always remain so; everyone has the ability to work and take themselves out of
the mire, but some choose to remain there. It is indi-
gence, and not poverty, that is the evil; the poor should
always be reminded of this, and thus motivated to work
for their living. It was work that took my father from
mediocrity to great wealth in his lifetime.'

That and Lady Fortune smiling on him, Harriet
thought, saying out loud, 'And when the poor sink so
deep into poverty, despite all their efforts, and are unable
to support themselves, what then? There are many who
try and fail.'

'Then there is the workhouse for those who have not
worked hard enough, and they should be damned glad of
it, because it's more than they deserve.'

She had known then that she couldn't reason with
him, and also, with terrifying clarity, that she had made
the biggest mistake of her life in marrying Theobald Wynford. She'd confided this to her mother when they had
next been in London and had received short shrift from
that aristocratic matron, who had not hidden her relief
when a man had been found who was prepared to take
her plain, nondescript daughter off her hands.

'You married Mr Wynford of your own free will,
Harriet,' her mother had said grimly. 'You will not bring

disgrace on the family name by being anything less than an obedient and dutiful wife. I do not wish to speak of this again.' And that had been that.

Now Harriet gazed at the cold, barren world outside the coach. Her life with Theobald had been like that, but no longer. She had a child; at long last she had a child. The future was bright.

The journey upcountry to the north-east was a long and tiring one, and not for the first time Harriet wished Theobald would put aside his aversion to automobiles. His farm manager and several of their friends and acquaintances had tried to persuade him that motorized vehicles were the way of the future, but her husband was stubborn to the hilt and refused to have anything to do with what he called 'mechanical monsters'. Bernice had her own car – the latest model of the Austin Tourer – and, whilst they had been staying with her sister, the two of them had gone out for a spin several times when the men were otherwise engaged.

Through the doctor she had earlier sent a message to Theobald asking him if they might make the journey home by train, which would have been so much quicker, but he wouldn't agree to that either, insisting that he wanted Purves, their coachman, to come and fetch them, in view of his injured leg. In the event, Theobald felt every pothole and bump in the roads and spent the entire journey swearing under his breath.

It had been dark for hours when they finally drove

through the open gates of the estate. It was situated to the west of the town of Chester-le-Street, in the centre of the Durham and Northumberland coalfield, and the township had doubled since the turn of the century, the population now having reached 16,000 men and women. Theobald made it his business to have his thumb in many pies in the town, including shares in an engine works and a rope-making works, among other ventures. The Wynford family had reserved seats in the parish church of St Mary & St Cuthbert, in the gentry's gallery. Such niceties were important to Theobald.

The wide drive was bordered by ornamental privet hedges, beyond which stretched manicured gardens; and the house itself, along with the high walls that surrounded the grounds, was made of mellowed stone. At the back of the house were the stables and a massive courtyard, the kitchen garden and greenhouses, and a large orchard that led to an area of woodland. This shielded the house from the view of the farmland beyond, and the fields of grazing cattle. The sprawling farmhouse was occupied by Theobald's farm manager – Neil Harley – and his family, and at the side of it ran a row of labourers' cottages. Beyond these were the byres and barns, a number of pig-sties, the hen coops and a purpose-built and relatively new dairy, the old dairy having lost its roof in a bad storm a few winters ago.

Under Neil Harley's management the farm ran like clockwork and made a good profit each year; and the gamekeeper, who had his own cottage on the very edge of the estate, provided the big house with fresh game birds and venison when required, along with rabbits and wood pigeons for the labourers' tables and the servants' hall.

It was generally acknowledged, by the estate workers and the servants in the big house itself, that the master – although an exacting and strict employer – was, on the whole, a fair one. True, he kept their wages low and expected them to work from dawn to dusk without complaining, but they were well fed and adequately housed, and as long as they didn't express any progressive views or socialist ideas, he let them alone. The one or two unfortunates in the past who had made the mistake of wanting to 'better themselves' had been turned out on their ear, before you could say 'Jack Robinson'.

When the carriage reached the pebbled forecourt in front of the house, lights were shining from the downstairs windows; and even before the horses had come to a stop, the wide front doors had been opened and a footman and two housemaids came hurrying towards them, followed by a small uniformed woman that Harriet took to be the new nanny. In a flurry of activity the coachman and footman assisted Theobald up the steps that led to the stone terrace fronting the doors, and there the butler, Osborne, took over from the coachman. With a quiet 'May I, ma'am?' the nanny reached for the baby, leaving the maids to look after Harriet. And she was glad of their help, Harriet acknowledged, as they each took an arm.

She was feeling weak and wobbly, and not at all like herself.

She must have looked as exhausted as she felt because Mrs Norton, who had been waiting on the top step beside Osborne, murmured, 'Your room is aired, ma'am, and there are hot-water bottles warming the bed. Bridget and Elsie will help you upstairs and assist you to retire. I'll bring a dinner tray shortly, when you are ready. I've ordered a light meal, ma'am. Soup and one of cook's soufflés.'

'Thank you, Mrs Norton.' Then, as Esther began to grizzle, Harriet glanced at the nanny. 'She's hungry. Follow us.'

'I can give her a bottle, ma'am.'

'No – no bottles.' Realizing she'd been a little abrupt, Harriet smiled as she said, 'What is your name?'

'Rose Brown, ma'am.'

'Well, Nanny Brown, my daughter was born early and is small, as you can see. She requires feeding every two hours or so, and I happen to believe a mother's milk is best. Night or day, I wish her brought to me. Is that clear?'

'Of course, ma'am.' Rose hid her surprise. Well-to-do ladies often had wet-nurses or told the nanny or nursemaid to use pap-bottles, particularly during the night hours when they didn't want to be disturbed. Mrs Wynford was obviously a devoted mother.

Theobald had been muttering and cursing as he hobbled across the hall on the arm of the butler. Now he brushed the man irritably away, leaning against the drawing-room door as he growled orders. 'A bottle of my best malt whisky, Osborne. And I'll have my meal in here.' With a cursory glance at his wife, he added, 'Get to bed and stay there till Dr Martin calls.'

Harriet couldn't have argued if she'd wanted to. She felt so shaky that the stairs seemed a Herculean trial. But she was home now, and she had Esther. She was safe. And the baby *did* carry a passing resemblance to Theobald's mother, funnily enough. She glanced at the gold-framed portrait of her husband's parents hanging on the opposite wall, and at the woman who stared un-smilingly back from the painting, jet-black curls piled high on her head and her dark eyes set in creamy olive skin. She could easily have been Esther's grandmother.

Once in her bedroom suite, the maids helped Harriet disrobe and wash. When she was settled comfortably in bed, propped against thick, soft pillows and with a hot-water bottle at her feet, Rose placed the baby in her arms. Snuggled at the breast, the baby immediately stopped her fretful squawking and began to feed with gusto. Harriet smiled as she stroked the child's soft cheek. The doctor in Wales had remarked that many pre-mature infants experienced difficulty in feeding, but Esther wasn't one of them. Of course, she wasn't as pre-mature as the doctor had been led to believe. Ruth had only been three weeks away from giving birth, whereas Harriet had had two months to go.

'She's beautiful, ma'am, if you don't mind me saying,' Rose murmured when the maids had left the room.

Harriet looked at the nanny and liked what she saw. They smiled at each other, before Harriet said, 'Come and sit down and tell me about yourself, and the families you have worked for. How old are you, incidentally?'

'I'm coming up for forty in a week or so, ma'am, and you could say I've been responsible for little ones all my life, because I was the eldest in a family of twelve. My poor mother was never well, and so caring for my brothers and sisters fell mostly to me from an early age. Not that I minded that. I've always loved children.'

They smiled at each other again as the fire crackled in the grate, and the baby made little contented grunts every now and again.

'I started as nursery maid to Reverend and Mrs Fallow's first child, when I was fifteen years old, and they had two more – all boys. When the youngest, Master Stephen, went off to boarding school, I applied for the post of nanny to Colonel and Mrs Smith's twin daughters, and I was with the family until now. I have good references, ma'am, as you'll see.'

'I'm sure you have.'

'Thank you, ma'am.' Rose hesitated. It was a bit early to bring it up, but nevertheless . . . 'When Mrs Norton engaged me, she said it was on a temporary basis as you hadn't seen me. She said you would decide by the end of the month, ma'am?'

Harriet hadn't known about this stipulation. It had

been thoughtful of the housekeeper, but she found that she thoroughly approved Mrs Norton's choice of nanny. There was a warmth about the woman that bode well. Having been brought up herself by a nanny who was every bit as cold and stiff as her parents, Harriet didn't want that for her daughter. And Esther *was* her daughter now; the worry was over. 'I'm sure you will suit,' she said quietly.

'Thank you, ma'am, and I can assure you I will devote myself to the baby's needs.' Rose had been on tenter-hooks, but now she felt herself relaxing. Mrs Wynford was lovely, and that made all the difference in this job.

Esther squirmed away from the breast and gave a very loud and unladylike burp, and Harriet laughed. 'I think you can take her now. She's full, and I might have a nap before dinner.' She was barely conscious of the nanny leaving the room, as thick billows of sleep drew her down into the softness of the bed, and her last thought was not of Rose or Esther, or even of Ruth. It was of Theobald. With deep thankfulness she knew he had fully accepted that the baby was his. The future was set now, she told herself, golden with promise and fulfilment – the years stretching out like an ever-growing tapestry, full of the happiness that only a child can bring.

PART TWO

Esther

1942

Chapter Four

It was a beautiful day for a wedding. Esther Wynford breathed deeply of the warm morning air as she leaned out of her bedroom window. The July sky was as blue as cornflowers, without even the merest wisp of cloud marring its expanse, and somewhere in the near-distance a fox barked as it made its way back after a night's hunting. It was wonderful to be home again, even if only for a short while, before she returned to her work as a Land Girl and Monty went back to the air force.

Monty . . . Esther smiled dreamily, inhaling the heady scent of the climbing roses covering the walls of the house. Montgomery Grant, only son of Brigadier and Mrs Clarissa Grant of Edinburgh. The most handsome, dashing, *thrilling* man in the whole of creation, and soon to be her husband, in – Esther consulted the jewelled watch on her wrist – seven hours. She shivered in delicious anticipation. At one o'clock they were to be married in her parish church, and she couldn't wait.

A missel thrush, on an early-morning mission to find

breakfast, called a warning as it caught sight of her, and a blackbird shrilled petulantly in reply. Esther turned back to the room, and to the sight of her wedding dress hanging on the wardrobe door. In these days of everyone doing their bit for the war effort, she had been prepared to get wed in a smart frock, as so many girls were doing, and forgo the traditional white wedding; but her mother had had her own wedding dress altered as a surprise, and there it was, a vision of ivory lace and satin. She had tried it on when she got home last night from the farm in Yorkshire, and it fitted perfectly. *Perfectly.* All of a sudden she twirled round and round in an ecstasy of joy until, giddy and breathless, she collapsed on the bed.

Was it wrong to be so happy, when the world was in such a horrible mess? The thought sobered her and she sat up, flicking back the thick mass of curly black hair from her shoulders. It wasn't that she didn't care, especially when in the newspapers last week it was reported that the Nazis had murdered more than one million Jews to date. It had said that in Poland the Nazis weren't bothering to send the Jews to concentration camps; instead they had special vans fitted as poisonous gas chambers, and they would herd up to ninety men, women and children into them, while other Jewish men would dig the graves. It was unbelievable, but true. And in the Warsaw ghetto, where 600,000 people were dying from starvation and disease, medical supplies were being denied to children under five. How would their poor mothers cope with such inhumane treatment? It would send you mad.

She shut her eyes, and other dreadful stories – like the Nazis' slaughter of a whole Czech village, in reprisal for two members of the Free Czech forces killing Reinhard Heydrich, the Hangman of Europe and architect of the Final Solution – crowded her mind. But she didn't want to think of such things today, not on this one special day.

Jumping up again, she walked over to the dress, fingering the folds of lace and satin and imagining Monty's face when he saw her walking down the aisle. She loved him so much, and with life being so precarious – especially for him, as a fighter pilot – she longed to be his wife. They would make the most of his leave and the one-week holiday she was allowed from the farm. Her work-roughened hands caught on the soft material, and she grimaced as she looked at her red skin and broken nails. The work that she, as a volunteer in the Women's Land Army, had to tackle was as varied as agriculture itself. Hand-milking cows, lifting potatoes, helping with land reclamation and drainage, operating heavy earth-moving machinery or driving a tractor, mucking out pigs, thatching ricks, hedging, hay-making, harvesting, planting, weeding, muck-spreading – she had done it all, and would no doubt do so again. It was a far cry from the country-house parties and tennis tournaments, the London Season and delightful social whirl that would have been her lot, had Adolf Hitler not forced Britain to declare war on Germany on a sunny September Sunday three years ago.

But – and she couldn't have discussed this with anyone, not even Monty, close though they were – she was glad she had been removed from the life she would have been expected to live, as the daughter of her parents. Not glad about the war; *never* that. She shuddered. But glad that she could actually *do* something: be useful, productive – not just a fancy adornment on a man's arm. Even her darling Monty's arm.

Oh, what was she thinking? She shook her head at herself. This was her trouble: thinking too much. Her dear mother had always said so. And it was certainly this attribute that had caused her to be at loggerheads with her father, from as long ago as she could remember. They'd had a blazing row on her seventeenth birthday when she'd declared that, now she was old enough, she was joining the Women's Land Army. She had read an article in the newspaper stating that two decades of rural depopulation, followed by an intensive army recruitment campaign in the spring of 1939 and then by conscription, had left a deficit of more than 50,000 farm workers. Once they were over twenty-one, farm workers were considered to be in a reserved occupation and were thus exempt from conscription, but the 20,000 who had joined the Territorial Army were nevertheless called up. The paper had also declared that the priority to increase the production of food crops by ploughing up permanent pasture meant that the number of farm workers required was increasing, rather than remaining the same, and that it was time for women to play their part in the war and get 'breeched, booted and cropped', as they had done in the First World War. She'd known immediately that's what she wanted to do.

Her father had been furious that a daughter of his could consider what he called 'menial work', rather than something in an office or the WAAF, or other occupations suitable for a refined young lady, and had been adamant that Esther would not join the WLA. She had been just as adamant that she would. After two weeks of bitter arguments, she had gone over his head and attended an interview, whereupon she had found that the WLA couldn't get enough people and there was no training at all – there simply wasn't time for it.

'You'll get all the experience you need on the job,' a sturdy matron had told her. 'Just remember the golden rule: don't fraternize with anyone; and remember that noisy or flirtatious behaviour brings discredit on the uniform and the whole Women's Land Army.' Esther had been issued with a pair of jodhpurs, two green jerseys, five beige T-shirts, a green tie, four pairs of dungarees of the bib-and-brace type, two pairs of heavy shoes that she could hardly walk in at first, a pair of wellington boots and several pairs of Boy-Scout style, knee-length socks, and dispatched to a farm in Yorkshire within the week.

Her father hadn't talked to her during the days before she left, which had actually been bliss, Esther thought now, deciding that she could do nothing with her hands and would have to try to keep them hidden under her bouquet for the walk up the aisle. Of course, once he had heard that Lady Rosaleen Hammond's daughter (the Hammonds were connected to her mother's family in some way) had joined the WLA, along with other socialites of the first order, his attitude had changed; and when Monty had proposed to her last year she had become the favoured daughter again. The Grants were *very* well connected.

Esther raised her chin, her large liquid-brown eyes with their thick fringe of long lashes narrowing as her full mouth curled in contempt. She had long since stopped feeling guilty that she didn't like her own father – probably about the time she was ten or eleven years old and was able to perceive that her mother didn't like him, either. He was a hateful man: belligerent and arrogant and so, so superior, when really he had nothing to be snobbish about. She remembered that in one of their more fiery arguments before she had left home, when he had criticized one of her friends, saying that the girl was beneath Esther because the family wasn't in their own social circle, she had flung at him that all the breeding in *their* family was on her mother's side, and not his. He had gone berserk, so much so that she had run to her bedroom and locked the door, which he had then proceeded to try and batter down with his bare fists.

But from this day forth she would be a married woman and no longer living under her father's roof. She wouldn't be living under her husband's, either, come to that, she acknowledged with a rueful smile. But at least they would have a little time together before they had to part. Monty had taken care of the arrangements for a short honeymoon at a hotel in Hartlepool overlooking the bay, promising that they'd have a few weeks travelling around Europe once the war was over. She didn't care about Europe; she just wanted the war over, and Monty to be safe. She was constantly tormented by reports of the carnage in the skies and of all the young men who would never see another dawn.

She continued to sit and muse until, an hour later, Rose tapped on the door and entered with Esther's morning cup of tea. She adored Rose. That her mother did too had become evident when Esther had grown too old to warrant a nanny, whereupon Harriet had decided that, as her personal maid was in the process of leaving to get married, Rose would take that position and also be available to act as a personal maid for Esther, if the circumstances required it.

The three of them – her mother, Rose and herself – were very close, but she and her mother were careful to give no inkling of this to her father. He would have been furious that a 'mere servant' could be considered in any other light than as a paid menial, and would have been quite capable of dismissing Rose to teach them a lesson.

Now Esther sprang off the bed and, after taking the tea and putting it on the bedside cabinet, twirled Rose around the room, just as she'd danced earlier herself. 'I'm going to be married, Rose! I'm going to be Mrs Grant and live happily ever after,' she sang as she jigged.

Laughing, Rose extricated herself from the embrace of the girl she loved as a daughter, and sank down on a chair. 'Enough, Miss Esther. I'm not as young as I used to be and I can't cope with your shenanigans,' she panted. 'And you're a young lady now, don't forget.'

'A young lady who can drive a tractor and spread dung, and pull swedes or mangolds and load them. There's not much clean or light work on a farm, Rose.'

'Aye, and to my mind it's all wrong you doing them sort of jobs, but you know what I think.'

Esther grinned. 'Yes, I know what you think, but don't forget the wonderful pay, Rose. Thirty-nine shillings and eightpence a week!'

Rose snorted. 'Don't get me started on that, Miss Esther. Disgusting, it is. And you working sixty or seventy hours a week.'

Esther shrugged. 'There's no fixed hours; we all work like mad till everything's done – that's the way it is. But Farmer Holden's all right, Rose, and his wife's lovely. We're lots better off there than some of the girls on other farms. We've got one of the farm cottages, so we don't have to bike miles every morning; some girls in the WLA are billeted miles away in awful digs, and are forever hungry. We get fed with the family, and Farmer Holden sees to it that we've always got plenty of logs for the fire, so the cottage's warm even in the worst of the winter. It makes all the difference at the end of a long day, believe me.' The last three winters had been exceptionally cold ones, with temperatures far below the average.

'I still call it slave labour, but as long as you're happy, Miss Esther.'

Esther smiled. 'Yes, I am, Rose. I am happy.' Even in the winter when there had been five feet of snow and the water bowls in the cow stalls had been frozen solid every morning, and she'd had to take a horse and cart with eight churns onto a frozen pond, break three inches of ice to fill the churns with water and then struggle back to the farm, she hadn't regretted joining the Land Army. The work was incredibly tough and tiring, but she and the other girls found time for fun, and food had never tasted so good. Her favourite meal was breakfast. Having been up since five o'clock to see to the milking, by six-thirty, when they all trooped into the huge farmhouse kitchen, she was always ready for Mrs Holden's feast of three home-cured rashers, a one-inch-thick slice of fried bread with two duck eggs on top, mushrooms in season and any potatoes left over from the previous day; plus cereal or porridge to start, toast and home-made marmalade or jam to finish – all washed down with gallons of steaming hot tea. She had never thought much about food before she joined the WLA; it was something that appeared on the table at home, served by the housemaids, who were overseen by the watchful figure of Osborne, the butler. Within days of living on the farm, however, the hard outdoor work had increased her appetite to the point where each mealtime had been anticipated with a watering mouth and a growling stomach.

'Your mother misses you, Miss Esther.'

The words were soft, and Esther answered just as softly, 'I know, Rose. I know.' And because she knew Rose would understand, she whispered, 'But I could never have come back under his roof, even if Monty hadn't asked me to marry him and the war was finished.'

Rose nodded, the memory of the awful rows between father and daughter, which had increased with each year that the girl had grown, vivid in her mind. And it wasn't altogether the master's fault, she thought sadly. If only Miss Esther could sidestep the occasional confrontation with her father; but no, she would challenge him at every turn. It had always been that way. It wasn't in her nature to avoid or evade him when he was being difficult, as the rest of the household did. In a nutshell, Miss Esther wasn't frightened of him like everyone else; and much as she admired the girl for her bravery, it would have made for a much more peaceful existence over the years if Miss Esther had been a little more like her mother. But then she wouldn't be Miss Esther, Rose told herself, and in truth she wouldn't want to change a hair of her head.

Standing up, Rose took one of Esther's hands between her own, stroking it as she said quietly, 'Whatever he says or does today – and he might say or do nothing untoward, of course – whatever happens, will you try to let it pass, for your mother's sake? She deserves a happy day, Miss Esther.'

Impulsively now, in one of the bursts of emotion that had been evident since she was a small child, Esther leaned forward and, dropping her head on Rose's shoulder, murmured, 'I promise, Rose. He can do his worst, and I'll be a perfect angel of sweetness and light. Really, I mean it.'

'Oh, Miss Esther.' They were both laughing now, but tears were only a breath away as they clung together for a moment. Then Rose straightened, patting Esther's cheek softly as she whispered, 'Be happy. That's all your mother wants for you: to be happy.'

'I know.'

'Now drink your tea and I'll see to it that a nice hot bath is waiting for you, with some of that rose essence you like so much, by the time you've finished.'

'A scented bath before breakfast? How decadent, Rose. The only perfume I'm used to these days is the delicate essence of cow dung.'

'Oh, Miss Esther, don't let your father hear you say anything like that.' Rose was smiling as she bustled out of the room, but there had been a note of admonition in her voice, and Esther's own smile faded once she was alone. She knew that Rose disapproved of her joining the WLA almost as much as her father had done. Rose was old-school; and to her mind, well-brought-up young ladies didn't dirty their hands doing physical work, especially not the sort of work expected of a farmhand. What Rose would say if she ever visited Yew Tree Farm, Esther didn't dare contemplate. Especially the farmhouse, for it was nothing like the one on her father's estate, which had been modernized in recent years.

Esther pictured the old Yorkshire farmhouse, which dated back to the thirteenth century. There were rough, uneven brick floors in all the ground rooms, with steps down into the enormous dairy, which still housed all the old equipment, such as big pans for making cream. The cottage where she and the other four Land Girls lived was equally primitive, but perhaps the most remarkable thing that she'd had to get used to was the garden privy, which was in a massive hollow yew tree. All Farmer Holden had done years before was cover the top with wood, put in a big square box with a seat, and fix a door to the front. When you sat in the privy at night, you could see the stars twinkling through the gaps in the wood, and chickens and owls roosting in the branches above. In summer it could be, if not exactly charming, then droll and somewhat whimsical. In winter it was a different kettle of fish.

But she had spoken the truth when she had said she was happy. Esther nodded mentally at the thought. Land Girls came from all classes – among their five was the Honourable Priscilla Crisford, the daughter of a viscount, who spoke with a plum in her mouth and had arrived at the farm in four-inch heels and wearing bright crimson nail-varnish, but who'd soon won the respect of everyone when Big Billy, the bull, had got free and she had single-handedly persuaded the huge animal back into its pen. Then there was Beryl Ash, a vicar's daughter, who wasn't

nearly as prim and proper as you'd expect; and Vera
Porter and Lydia Hutchinson, who had been born in the
slums of London's East End and could tell stories to
make your hair curl. But the five of them got on like a
house on fire most of the time, and had a special camaraderie that Esther had never experienced before, having
no siblings. They'd all cried together when Vera's whole
family had been wiped out by a German bomb falling
directly on their house; and when Beryl had caught ring-
worm from the cattle, they'd kept her spirits up, along
with watching that she didn't scratch the circular itchy
patches and make them worse.

Walking over to her portmanteau in a corner of the
bedroom, Esther opened it and took out the card and
present the girls had given her, with strict instructions
that she open it on the morning of her wedding. The card
was handmade and featured a drawing of her in her
Land Army uniform with an incongruous floaty veil,
hanging on the arm of – presumably – Monty, who was
in his RAF uniform. Inside it read:

> Back to the land, we must all lend a hand,
> To the farms and the fields we go.
> There's a job to be done,
> Though we can't fire a gun,
> We can still do our bit with a hoe.
> And Esther our bride, true, tested and tried,
> Is marrying the love of her life.
> The honeymoon's short,

But she's a jolly good sort,
And at least she'll come back a wife!

Written in Priscilla's flowing hand, which was all extravagant curls and loops, this was followed by: 'Have a wonderful wedding, old girl, and don't spare us poor workers a thought! Do everything we'd do and more, and we expect you to come back thoroughly exhausted!' Each of them had signed their name, with lots of love.

Giggling to herself, Esther placed the card on her bedside cabinet and opened the present wrapped in brown paper. A pair of real silk stockings and a positively risqué suspender belt and set of lingerie were inside, naughty enough to bring a hot blush to her cheeks. *Priscilla!* Esther knew who'd organized the thoroughly improper undies, even before she read the little note, which said: 'Give him something to remember that will keep him warm when he's back at base. We dare you! Or I do, at least. Priscilla.' Beryl had written: 'Nothing to do with me, Est – all Cilla's idea', and Vera and Lydia had put: 'We've had our eyes opened to what you society girls get up to, believe me!'

How on earth had Priscilla got hold of these? The wisps of satin and black lace were tiny, but Esther could imagine they'd cost a fortune. And silk stockings! For the last few months the five of them had been putting gravy browning over their legs, and then one of them would stand behind another and mark a seam on bare legs with a black pen or eyebrow pencil. Of course this fooled no one at the village dances they went to – the only entertainment that came their way. Children would amuse themselves by shouting, 'Hello, Oxo-legs!' and if it was raining when they left the church hall – as it often was in Yorkshire – the dogs for miles around would come sniffing their legs.

The silk stockings might have come from the GIs on the nearby American base, of course. They'd arrived in the spring, much to the disgust of the local lads, who found the village dances entirely different affairs once the American servicemen with their stylishly tailored uniforms and endless supply of forgotten luxuries descended. And Priscilla had been bowled over by the Yanks, Esther thought, declaring to all and sundry that the exuberant GIs had brought a much-needed splash of glamour to the quiet Yorkshire countryside, and making the most of her single status by dating one after another of the snazzy strangers in their midst. In fact Farmer Holden, worried by the British male's over-exercised and rueful joke about the GIs being 'overpaid, oversexed and over here', had had a cautionary word with Priscilla, who had listened dutifully and then carried on exactly as before.

Dear Priscilla. Esther stroked the satin and lace and decided there and then that she would take Priscilla's dare. She would be a married woman after all, so why not? Smiling to herself, she imagined Monty's face when he saw her in the wickedly provocative scraps of material. He had been very proper and respectful during their engagement, but more than once in a close embrace his body had made it clear that he was all man. And she wanted to make him happy. More than anything else she wanted their marriage to be one of trust and love and happiness – as different from that of her parents as it was possible to be.

The thought brought her mother to mind and, after gulping down her tea, she pulled her robe over her nightdress and slipped on her fluffy mules. She would go and have a few minutes with her mother before her bath, before the day began properly and the machinery of the wedding took over. She felt she needed to make it clear, in words as well as actions, that nothing would alter the special bond they shared, and that she knew she had the dearest, kindest, most precious mother in all the world.

Chapter Five

Harriet heard Esther as she came along the landing. She had always been so finely tuned to her daughter that it was as if she sensed her presence rather than heard it. Her daughter: the bright, beautiful, strong girl who had filled her life with joy and happiness beyond anything she could ever have imagined. And as well as everything Esther was to her, her daughter had also been the means by which Rose had come into her life. Not having been close to her mother and sisters, Harriet had never known what it was to share her thoughts and feelings with a member of her own sex before she'd met Rose. They understood each other in a manner that did away with the formal standing of mistress and maid, and she didn't care that they were miles apart in class and social equality. Rose was dearer to her than anyone, apart from Esther, of course. Rose took care of her when her heart was causing problems – something that had begun after her last pregnancy and confinement, but that had got much worse in the last year or two; a fact they both, by mutual agreement, kept from Esther. But not even Rose, dear sister that she had become, knew the true circumstances of Esther's birth.

Harriet worried at her bottom lip with her teeth. She had dreamed of Ruth last night, for the first time in years. When she had first brought Esther home, all those many years ago, she had thought about Ruth constantly. Her fear that somehow the baby's real mother would turn up and demand her child back had manifested itself in terrible nightmares, and it had been a double blessing when Theobald had made it plain, on the morning of their return to the estate, that he would not be visiting her chambers at night in future. Her duty was done, he'd said in his ponderous way, and 'that' side of things was over between them.

She had never been so glad of anything in her whole life, and his suite of rooms was sufficiently distant from her own for him not to be disturbed by her night-time terrors.

Eventually, as the weeks and months and years had slipped by, the dreams had faded and then disappeared altogether, and she hadn't given Ruth a thought for a long time. Until last night. Then Ruth had stood at the end of her bed, and she had stared into the young face, which looked exactly the same as it had done that last day at the inn. 'Tell her the truth, Harriet,' the apparition had whispered urgently. 'Tell her about me, and how it all came to pass that you took my baby. She will understand, if you tell her now.'

'No, no, *I'm* her mother,' she had whispered back. 'I'm the one who has looked after her and brought her up. She's mine – my daughter.'

'But not by blood. You know that; you know it's true.'

'I don't care about that. You gave her to me; you begged me to take her, and there's no reason for her to ever know the truth. She's happy. What could be accomplished by upsetting her now?'

'She'll know one day. Better it's now.'

Ruth had begun to come towards her, hands held out entreatingly, and she had stiffened in denial, shouting that Ruth was cruel and wicked to demand such a thing; and then she had woken up, bathed in perspiration and shaking.

As Esther opened the bedroom door now and peeped around it, all bright eyes and dancing curls, Harriet thought, *It was just a dream, that's all, brought on by the wedding*. But the dread that Ruth might one day appear in the flesh had come to the surface again for the first time in years, and she found it hard to respond naturally when Esther came quickly to her side, throwing her arms round her mother as she knelt by the bed.

'I've just been looking at the dress again, and it's so beautiful. Thank you so much, darling. I love you more than the stars and the moon – you know that, don't you?'

The old phrase from Esther's childhood, which had come into being when the child was trying to express just how much she adored her mother, and which she hadn't used in years, melted Harriet's ball of fear and enabled her to hug her daughter to her as she murmured, 'But I love you more', which had always been the stock reply.

They laughed together, and as Esther rose and sat on the edge of the bed holding her mother's hand, she smiled into the dear face. Touching her mother's hair with her other hand, she said softly, 'I just want you to know that even when I'm old and grey, I will love you just as much as I ever have. Getting married, and being with Monty, doesn't change anything and it never will. You're the best mother in the world.'

Harriet's eyes filled with tears. 'And I feel my life began when I had you. Be happy with your Monty, sweetheart.'

'I will. I know I will.' Esther paused, wrinkling her nose. 'But I shall make sure we don't live too close to his parents. They really are the most awful snobs, especially his mother. In almost every conversation you have with her, she is dropping names of this person and that. And I know she thinks Monty could have made a better match than me, although of course she's never said so.'

'You're not marrying his parents, darling.' Harriet squeezed Esther's hand. 'And I know your father is hoping that Monty will come into business with him and make it a real family affair. After the war, of course. It would mean you would live near us, which would be nice.'

This last was said rather wistfully, and checked Esther's reply that she had no wish to be near her father, either. She still hadn't forgiven him for suggesting – or, according to Monty, virtually demanding – that Monty take her maiden name, when he had gone to see Theobald to formally ask for her hand in marriage. Monty had left her father's study extremely perturbed. There was no possibility of such a thing happening, he had told Esther. She had agreed with him, and had been furious with her father for suggesting such a notion; and even more angry that he hadn't spoken to her about it first. Eventually – and Esther still had no real idea how it had come about, except that Monty seemed to want to placate her father – it had been agreed that their married name would be Wynford-Grant, and with this her father had deemed himself content.

Squeezing her daughter's hand again, Harriet said, 'Tell me about the farm and those wonderful girls you work with. How's Priscilla? Is she still seeing that rather brash GI you wrote about?'

Esther grinned. 'Which one? Cilla seems to have a different beau each week. But the Americans are generous, I'll say that for them. They're always hosting parties at the base for the local children, and giving them such rarities as ice cream and chocolate bars. Oh, and peanut butter, of course. That's been an instant hit, although I can't see the appeal myself. I must bring you a jar to try – it's like nothing you've ever tasted before . . . '

As Esther chattered on, Harriet sat back against her pillows, content to watch her daughter's expressive face and to hear her beloved voice. She had been silly to think of the dream as some sort of warning, she told herself. It meant nothing, and was probably just the result of eating too much cheese the night before. Her secret was safe, and would remain so. If they could all just get through this terrible war unscathed, then the future – with grand-children and family times full of fun and laughter – looked bright. She and Theobald had a good understanding now. He had his beloved business to occupy his mind, and his present mistress (one of many during the last years) to satisfy his bodily needs. She had her home and her friends and, most importantly, Esther, and wanted noth-ing more. Life was good, in spite of Hitler and his evil horde. She had faith in Mr Churchill and in his promise of ultimate victory, and now the Americans were in the war they couldn't lose. Everyone said so. Yes, she had been silly to let a ghost from the past cast a shadow over such a wonderful day . . .

Montgomery Grant turned to look at his bride as the organ announced her arrival, and his breath caught in his throat at the beauty of her. She was exquisite, he thought wonderingly, as the ethereal figure floated up the aisle on Theobald's arm, and at his side his best man whispered, 'You're a lucky bounder, old man, but you know that, don't you?'

Yes, he knew it. He had first set eyes on Esther at a Christmas ball that some mutual friends had thrown, when she had recently turned sixteen. He had known then she was the girl he wanted to marry. He had been a young and fancy-free man of twenty-three at the time, and with war having been declared some four months earlier in September, he had had no intention of falling in love. He had recently completed his training to become a fighter pilot and knew how precarious life might be, but even the threat of death at the hands of the Luftwaffe hadn't been enough to stop him declaring his feelings before the holiday had finished.

And, miracle of miracles, Esther had been as mad about him as he was about her, and had said so in no uncertain terms. He loved that about her: her frankness and lack of coyness. Esther was one of the few women he knew who was as straight as any man.

Of course their courtship had been far from easy, but then everyone was in the same boat these days. And he was sure it was Esther's love that had protected him during the Battle of Britain. So many of the laughing Spitfire pilots who had walked with him across their sunlit aerodrome, hair and scarves blowing in the summer breeze, had never come home, their lives ending in blood and pain and burning. All his close friends, apart from Dennis beside him, were gone, and Dennis's scars were a result of one rabid dogfight in the skies, when he had been shot down in flames. But he himself had remained unscathed thus far, and believed he would continue to do so. You had to believe that; had to believe that, when the Luftwaffe came at you like a flock of crows or a swarm of fat black flies in a big rectangular pack of Heinkels with their escorts of ME 110s and 109s, they wouldn't win, wouldn't touch you. It was the only way.

Esther was nearly at his side now and he could just make out her face beneath the swathes of veil, and she was smiling. His heart leapt and then raced like a mad thing. Theobald, beside her, looked like a rather grotesque goblin by comparison. Beauty and the Beast, he thought wryly. How Esther had come from Theobald and Harriet, he didn't know, but he thanked God that she bore little resemblance to either of them.

And then she was standing by him and the minister was beginning to speak, and as her veil was lifted back, her eyes danced at him. 'This is all so silly,' her eyes said. 'We should have run away and eloped, like I suggested in the first place, and weathered the storm of disapproval when our parents found out what we'd done. It could have been just the two of us, with everything how *we* wanted.'

But he didn't mind sharing her, for this one day at least; and he knew that a wedding in Esther's parish church had meant a great deal to her parents, and his own would have been beside themselves if things weren't done properly. His mother, in particular, was a stickler for the proprieties. It would go a long way to placate her, over his determination to marry Esther, that his bride was in virginal white and the wedding was an elaborate affair. When Esther had argued that in these days of austerity a white wedding with all the trimmings was wrong, he had agreed with her in part. Consequently the wedding list had been halved and then halved again, and the reception at the Wynford estate was relatively simple in comparison to what it might have been, had Hitler not reared his head. Nevertheless, it was a far more showy undertaking than either he or Esther had wanted – his mother had made sure of that. She was a formidable woman, his mother. And difficult. Very difficult.

'Do you, Montgomery Hubert Charles Grant, take . . . '

The minister's solemn voice brought his mind fully to the matter in hand and, as he gazed down into Esther's glowing face, he forgot everyone else as he made his vows.

The service and then the reception were voted a resounding success by all those present. Montgomery's mother even complimented Esther on her dress and was quite fulsome in her praise; she had been convinced that Esther would walk down the aisle in one of those awful suits girls were making do with these days, and had prepared herself for the worst. Instead, for once Esther looked a fit companion for her son. Her beautiful son, who could have had any girl he wanted as his bride, but who had chosen a virtual nobody.

Clarissa Grant's thin mouth tightened. Lord Bainsby's daughter, Annabella, a dear sweet girl with impeccable breeding, had made it clear that she liked Montgomery on more than one occasion; and Sir Rudolph Shelton had indicated to Hubert two summers ago that he would have no objection if Montgomery paid court to his eldest daughter. And there had been others – all far more suitable than Esther Wynford.

Clarissa glanced at her husband, who was sitting next to Harriet on the curved top table, where they all faced the assembled guests. She could tell by the silly smile on his face that Hubert had already drunk too much wine, but at least he merely became more and more comatose when he was intoxicated, unlike Theobald Wynford. Seated next to Esther's father, as she was, she'd had to endure his close proximity for hours, and with each glass of wine he tipped down his throat he became louder. Ghastly little man. How someone with the background of Esther's mother could have so far forgotten herself as to marry such an individual, she didn't know. Of course rumour had it that no one else had asked for Harriet all those years ago, and that Wynford had been her only hope of ending her spinsterhood.

Clarissa's bony chin lifted. She knew what she would have done in the same circumstances.

She stiffened as the master of ceremonies called their attention to the fact that the speeches were about to begin. Goodness only knew what Theobald Wynford would come out with, but at least this charade would soon be over and they could leave for home. Esther's parents had extended an invitation that they were very welcome to stay with them for a few days, but she had made it plain to Hubert that she would rather be hanged, drawn and quartered than stay one night under their roof. Not that the house and grounds weren't beautiful; they were, and far better maintained than their own home, which was in a state of disrepair. But that was by the by. Esther's father was everything she disliked about 'new' money, and she had no intention of suffering his company one minute longer than was necessary for the sake of appearances. She had already intimated to Montgomery that in the future he would do well to exert his authority as Esther's husband and see to it that the girl drew away from her parents – subtly of course, but consistently. She herself would not be averse to taking the girl under her wing, as it were, and instilling the finer facets of high society into her. But that would have to wait until the war was over, of course. And perhaps it might not be necessary; maybe the unpleasant and sometimes dangerous conditions that the Land Girls were experiencing would take their toll. Only last week the newspapers had been full of the death of a Land Girl who had fallen into a threshing machine; and the month before there had been a report that, apart from the perils of working machinery they weren't built for, the girls had to dodge the danger of bombs being unloaded by German aircraft as the planes made their way home after a city raid.

Clarissa's pale-blue eyes narrowed as Theobald rose ponderously to his feet, and she mentally braced herself for what was to come, stifling a sigh. A couple of hours more and they could be on their way, and it couldn't come a minute too soon.

'So, Mrs Wynford-Grant, how does it feel to be a wife?' Montgomery smiled at his bride as he drove his little sports car – a twenty-first present from his parents some years before – along the country lane leading from the estate, where their guests had just waved the happy couple off minutes before. It was approaching twilight, and the towering elms and oaks cast faint shadows over the leaf-bound lane, the air heavy with the perfume of eglantine, the wild briar, and the flowers without number that starred the verges.

Esther smiled back at him, thinking it was hard to remember there was a war going on, on such a heavenly day. And it had been heavenly, all of it. And now they were man and wife. At last. She glanced down at the gold band next to her diamond engagement ring. It felt strangely heavy, but nice – very nice. Softly she said, 'Stop the car a minute. I want you to kiss me, properly.'

'Yes, ma'am.' Monty grinned at her, pulling swiftly onto the grass verge and taking her into his arms even before the noise of the engine had died away. The kiss was fierce and urgent and never-ending, and they were both gasping when Monty raised his head. 'You're mine,' he murmured, a note of wonder in his voice. 'I've been terrified that something – I don't know what, but something – would stop us becoming man and wife.'

'Me too.' But in her case, Esther thought, she knew exactly what she had been frightened of, and it wasn't the war. Monty's mother was the sort of woman who was capable of anything.

'Really? You love me that much?'

'You know I do.' Smiling, she raised her hand to his face, feeling the stubble of his jaw under her fingers with a little thrill of pleasure. 'Come for a walk,' she said suddenly. 'Just for a little while.'

'Now?' He looked at her in surprise. 'But don't you want to get to the hotel and settle in before it starts to get dark?'

'We've bags of time.' She reached up and kissed him. 'And we haven't had a chance to be together all day. I know that sounds ridiculous, but that's how I feel. And it's such a lovely evening. There's the moor not far ahead. We could park and take a little walk, couldn't we?'

'Of course we could,' he agreed, starting the engine while she snuggled into him, her head on his shoulder.

They pulled off the road onto a thin dirt track when they reached the moor, parking the car on a small incline. The still air was scented with the sweetness of the dog-rose bushes at the edge of the track, and the sky echoed with the cries of swallows as they wheeled above the wild briar, skimming the air with graceful movements as they hawked hundreds of airborne insects.

'This is lovely,' Esther breathed, holding Monty's hand as they wandered towards a fallen tree, whereupon he lifted her onto the warm trunk and then stood with his arm around her as they watched the peacock butterflies sunning themselves in the evening sun and then flitting from bloom to bloom seeking the nectar. 'Just us, and no one else in the whole world.'

'*You're* lovely.' His voice was thick and husky, and when he took her in his arms again she returned his kiss with all her heart. The grass was dry and hay-like as he lowered her onto the ground, with foxgloves – tall and magnificent with their dappled bells – providing a natural screen to their hiding place. Esther didn't feel shy as he undressed her and then himself, knowing that she wanted their first time to be here, alone in the open, with only the birds and butterflies and the odd little shrew witnessing their coming together.

In spite of his desire, he kissed and touched her for a long time, and when he finally entered her, the brief discomfort was soon forgotten in her readiness for him.

When they finally sat up her face was aglow, her long curly hair tumbling about her slim shoulders, having come loose from the elaborate style she had worn for the wedding. Monty put out his hand and touched her flushed face, his voice soft as he said, 'I didn't hurt you?'

Funnily enough, in view of the intimacies they had just shared, the question made her feel shy. 'No, you didn't hurt me. It . . . it was wonderful.'

'And we have a whole week ahead of us.'

Esther smiled and then, high in the blue sky above them, they caught the low drone of aircraft. She felt a cold shiver snake down her spine. This war, this wretched war – how she hated Hitler and his Nazis. But Monty had come through the Battle of Britain, and he would come through the rest of the war. She had to believe that, along with Churchill's promises that right would triumph over might.

Her face must have revealed what she was thinking,

because Monty's hand covered hers. 'Don't worry.'

'No, no, I won't,' she lied, giving herself a mental shake. 'And, like you said, we have a whole week together. That's a lifetime, and we must make the most of every moment.'

'Well, we've certainly made a good start.' He grinned at her and, ridiculously, she blushed. 'I'd planned a romantic dinner and champagne and roses to seduce you, not an al-fresco romp in the altogether. Not that I've any complaints, I hasten to add, except . . . '

'What?'

'This took me by surprise. I wasn't prepared.'

'Prepared?' And then she realized what he meant. 'Oh, everyone knows a girl can't fall for a baby the first time,' she said blithely. 'And we'll be careful from now on.' They both wanted children, but only when the war was over and the world was safe.

He pulled her to him, kissing her long and lingeringly, before standing up and pulling her up with him. 'Get dressed, wench,' he said ruefully, 'before the temptation again proves too much.' But, as she turned away, he swung her round, kissing her again and murmuring, 'I shall love you to the day I die, and beyond – I can promise you that, in this uncertain world. You're everything I ever dreamed of, and more, my darling.'

He said such wonderful things and she was so lucky. The luckiest girl in the world.

Chapter Six

'There's no doubt, m'dear, no doubt at all.' Dr Boyce surveyed Esther over the top of his glasses. 'You're expecting a baby and, from the dates you've given me, you can expect the happy arrival any time from the middle of April. One can never be too sure of the exact day – babies come when they are ready.'

Esther stared at the smiling face of the village doctor. She'd suspected for a while that she might be pregnant, but had held onto the faint hope that the constant tiredness and absence of her monthlies could be put down to the hay-making, which had begun on the day she'd returned from her honeymoon, followed a few weeks later by the harvest. It had been an exhausting time. 'But I haven't felt sick once, Doctor.'

'Not everyone does.'

'But . . . ' She stopped, faintly embarrassed.

'Yes?'

'We only did it once without . . . without taking precautions.'

'Once is enough, m'dear, more than enough.' Dr Boyce paused. He understood this young woman's husband was a fighter pilot, and the RAF was taking a hell of a hammering in this damned war. Gently he said, 'You are young and healthy, and a baby is always a blessing, child.'

Esther nodded, but in truth she didn't know whether to laugh or cry. She wanted Monty's babies, of course she did, but they had thought children would be in the future – not now. Not when they were apart and Monty was in constant danger, and a madman was centre-stage in the world. *But a new life was growing inside her.* A little thrill, deep inside, caused her heart to race. Part of her, and part of Monty; a unique little being, their own tiny miracle. Her hand covered her stomach protectively as she murmured, 'It's just not a good time to bring a baby into the world.'

'Our twin girls were born a few months after I left for France in 1914,' Dr Boyce said quietly, 'and my wife felt exactly as you are feeling now. But our girls proved to be a great comfort to her, as this baby will be to you. The older one becomes, the more one realizes that life doesn't come in neat packages wrapped exactly the way we'd wish. I was badly injured in France and there were to be no more children for us, so our twins were a double blessing. One we've thanked God for every day. Don't try and understand or predict the future, Mrs Wynford-Grant. Take what you are given, and be grateful for it.'

It was exactly what she needed to hear. Esther's eyes

filled with tears. 'Thank you. Thank you so much, Doctor.'

Priscilla was waiting for her when she came out of the doctor's house, where he held his daily surgery in the front room. 'Well?' she asked, as Esther made her way out of the front garden along the thin concrete path, which had neat rows of vegetables on either side of it. These had replaced the flowers that had formerly been the doctor's wife's pride and joy, but this same lady had taken 'Dig for victory' to heart. 'What did he say?'

Esther opened the wooden gate and joined her friend. 'You were right,' she said quietly, taking her bicycle from Priscilla. 'I'm expecting a baby.' It had been the worldly-wise Priscilla who had urged her to go and see the doctor, when the time for Esther's second monthly had come and gone with no bleeding.

They walked a few yards pushing their bicycles, before Priscilla said softly, 'I know it wasn't what you and Monty had planned right now, but it'll work out for the best, Est.'

'That's what Dr Boyce said too.' Now that it was sinking in, she wanted this baby desperately.

'What are you going to do? I mean, about carrying on here? When I think what we did during the hay-making and harvest . . . ' Priscilla shook her head. 'That baby must be very firmly entrenched and determined to stay put, that's all I can say.' In the agricultural year, hay-making occurs before the harvest and is even more of a nail-biter. When Farmer Holden had said that a weather-window of dry, breezy and sunny days had made it perfect for hay-making, Esther and the others, and three Italian prisoners-of-war who had been 'borrowed' from a neighbouring farm, had worked from eight in the morning until late twilight, to make good hay. Due to the lack of petrol because of the war, Farmer Holden had gone back to basics, with a couple of the men scything a swathe all around the outside of a field of standing grass, and then two horses harnessed to the mowing machine taking over.

Esther nodded. 'And that hateful mowing machine during the hay-making, too.' The girls had all taken a turn with the mowing machine, and it had been a bone-shaking job sitting on the seat; there were no springs and certainly no cushions, simply a hessian bag folded and laid in the big metal 'pan' seat. The continual jolting had been almost unbearable, and the girls had had to keep their wits about them every moment, and the horses on the move at the right pace. Fortunately old Dora and Barney – Farmer Holden's horses – were placid, docile creatures, which was just as well, because at the corners of the fields there was a particular manoeuvre that involved reining back, and without the horses' cooperation, the girls would never have managed it.

It hadn't helped that Farmer Holden had been adamant about not letting the Italian prisoners-of-war on the mowing machine, saying that he didn't trust them. As Priscilla had said, what on earth did he expect the men to do, for goodness' sake! Gallop away into the sunset on the horrible thing? All the girls had agreed that handing the Italians the fearsome scythes with their lethal blades was far more of a danger, but the farmer hadn't seen it that way, and so the mowing machine had had to be endured.

Then there had been the laborious process of turning the hay by hand during the field-drying part of the work, after which (when Farmer Holden was happy it was sufficiently dry) they had piled it up into haycocks, which were then loaded onto carts and taken off to be made into hayricks. The business of getting the hay into the cart, and from the cart up onto the stack, by means of pitchforks was a strenuous one, and required a certain amount of brawn as well as skill. Esther and the other girls had fallen into bed without washing or getting undressed, night after night, too exhausted even to say goodnight to each other.

And her baby had survived all that, Esther thought now with a thread of wonder. It was meant to be, Dr Boyce was right. *Thank you, God, I didn't lose it*, she prayed silently. *Thank you for sparing me such heartache.*

'So, what are you going to do?' Priscilla asked again as they climbed on their bicycles. 'You could leave straight away, you know, in your condition.'

'I don't want to leave.' Esther was sure about that. She had no wish whatsoever to go home and be under her father's roof; and her in-laws were even worse. 'Do you think Farmer Holden would let me stay? I'm sure there are things I could do to help. There's the dairy work, for example. I could help Mrs Holden with that, and other things. It's only really heavy work that might be a problem. But having said that, I managed the hay-making and then the harvest too.' The corn harvest hadn't exactly been a walk in the park, either. Before she had become a Land Girl she'd always thought the fields of golden corn one of the quintessential English sights, but in the last couple of years she had learned that although England had one of the best climates for growing crops, it had one of the worse for harvesting them. The deep-blue sun-lit skies could be notoriously fickle.

'The hay-making and harvest were different – you didn't know about the baby then.'

Priscilla was right, Esther thought, as they began to pedal away from the village. She wouldn't dare risk her own and Monty's baby by undertaking anything like that now.

'Have a word with Mrs Holden first, before you tell him,' Priscilla said, after a minute or two. 'You know how she loves having us around, with them never having had children, and she's a motherly sort. She'll like being able to fuss over you a bit – you mark my words. Get her on your side and you'll be home and dry, old bean.'

'Do you think so?' She would have to leave sooner or later, she knew that, but she didn't want to go until she absolutely had to. The five of them – herself, Priscilla, Beryl, Vera and Lydia – had formed a bond that was precious, all the more so now that she knew her time with them was short.

Coming to a halt at the top of the hill that led down to the village, Esther gazed across the fields rolling away in the distance, most of which were newly ploughed. It was September already, she thought; the summer was all but over, even though the last few days had been unseasonably hot. The winter was in front of them, and in the spring her child would be born – her baby. She would be a mother, and Monty would be a father, and they were bringing a child into a world of terrible turmoil. And all because of a walk on their wedding day, which had ended in them making love under a blue sky with the scent of roses in the air.

It seemed to Monty that he'd hardly put on his pyjamas and lain down before the harsh shrill of the telephone had rung throughout the hut that night. Discipline had overcome the longing to turn over and bury his head under his pillow, and he'd been sitting up in bed when the orderly who'd answered the telephone had come running in, shouting for them to scramble.

There had been much cursing and swearing as everyone had climbed into their flying kit, half-asleep, fatigue clogging their exhausted brains, but then they'd poured out into the airfield and had run towards their planes, going through on autopilot the ritual of getting strapped in and starting the engine. As night turned to dawn, one by one they roared into the clouds. And now here they were, searching out the enemy, as they had countless times before.

It was a hell of a way to start a day, Monty thought wryly. But then, as the plane emerged from cloud at 10,000 feet and he found that the night had departed and a new day had arrived in light washed blue at the higher altitude, the thrill of flying took over.

This was what he had been born for, he thought, not for the first time. From a small boy he'd had an avid interest in aeroplanes, much to the disappointment of his father, who had made no bones about the fact that he had expected his only son to follow in his footsteps and join the army, as his father and his father's father before him had done. But it had been the Royal Air Force that had excited Monty, which had led to many acrimonious and tense conversations with his parents as he had got older. Public school followed by university had not dimmed his determination to fly, and when he had discovered at university that free RAF training was available to anyone who could pass the rigorous medical examination for admission to the university air squadron, he had somehow persuaded his father to sign the parental-authority papers that would enable him to fly.

He had taken to flying like a duck to water, and with his parents finally having admitted defeat about the army idea, he had literally found his wings. Because the university air squadrons were intended to do two things – encourage undergraduates to take up the Royal Air Force as a career, and create a reserve of partially trained officer pilots, who could quickly be brought to operational standards in the event of war – once Hitler had marched on

Poland, Monty had received his call-up papers. Then it had been off to the newly opened Aircrew Receiving Centre at Hastings, the Sussex seaside holiday resort, where he had joined several hundred other human products of Oxford, Cambridge and London universities, all resplendent in new officers' uniforms bought with Air Ministry allowances.

Monty smiled to himself. The Air Ministry had requisitioned all the suitable hotels and apartment blocks to lodge their charges in, and to knock their wet-behind-the-ears flock into shape for the dispersed flying schools they were to attend, but it had been no holiday. The NCO physical-training and drill instructors assigned to each squad had seen to that. They hadn't bothered to hide their contempt for the new commissioned breed, but really – looking back – Monty couldn't blame them. Most of the greenhorns, like him, had left the protective shelter of wealth and a privileged upbringing for the first time and barely knew their left feet from their elbows. But they'd learned fast. They'd had to.

He smiled again, somewhat grimly this time, as he thought back to the sarcasm, insults and sheer physical torture of the parade ground that they'd endured, each diatribe by one of the instructors ending with the regulation acknowledgement of the King's commission.

'When I say march, I mean Air Force march, not some fancy university shuffle . . . SIR!'

'Right turn, *right* – don't you know your damned left from your right, for crying out loud . . . ? SIR!'

'Put some backbone into those press-ups, you're not taking tea with Lord and Lady Muck now . . . SIR!'

But they'd survived; postings to flying schools had been announced, and with twenty-five other airmen Monty had made the train journey to RAF Cranwell on an over-cast, grey day, arriving at Sleaford station on a coal-black evening that the blackout did little to alleviate. And, in the Christmas break, he had met Esther. Sweet, passion-ate, wonderful Esther.

Suddenly the reason for the scramble to the skies became clear, as a twin-engined Junkers 88 dived out of the cloud layer above. Now there was nothing on his mind but chasing his quarry, along with his comrades ahead and to one side of him. They tore after the enemy plane, which, realizing its mistake, was diving towards the haven of cloud layer some distance below. Machine guns rattled, there was smoke, and then the German plane was spiralling out of control, and their squadron leader, Salty Fiennes, called over the R/T, confirming the hit and ordering them to return to base.

'Roger, Blue one,' Monty drawled. 'Wish they could all be as straightforward as that one.'

'You'll be wanting jam on your toast next, Blue three.'

Monty grinned. Salty was the sort of man you would want with you in a tight spot. He was a brilliant fighter pilot with a wicked sense of humour and a reassuring air of maturity about him, probably due to his shock of prematurely grey hair, which had earned him his nick-name.

Where the second German plane materialized from, he was never sure. It came out of the blue like a predatory bird, and Salty's aircraft was suddenly engulfed in smoke and orange flames.

At the same time as the controller's voice came sharply to his ears, asking what was going on, Monty realized that the Junkers 88 had made a mistake. In its eagerness to attack Salty, it had dived too close and become a target itself.

Monty didn't hesitate, keeping the firing button pressed until comparative silence, and the hiss of escaping air, told him that his ammunition was expended, but that was all right. The German plane had become a burning funeral pyre, and it went some way towards satisfying the anger and shock he felt at the suddenness of Salty's end. He didn't know why he felt such fury; he'd seen so many of his friends and colleagues die, after all, but somehow this was different. Maybe it had just been one too many, he didn't know; but he had wanted the enemy pilot dead, wanted him to burn in hell, and the force of his feeling was still causing his hands to tremble. If he could have killed the man with his bare hands, he would have done so and taken joy over it.

Sick to his stomach, he forced himself to concentrate on flying the plane, but inside he was asking, 'What am I turning into? Dear God, what's happening to me?'

Some time later, physically tired and mentally drained, Monty arrived back at the fighter squadron at Horsham

St Faith airport, near Norwich, where he had been
posted from flying school. He taxied back to the disper-
sal pen, still shocked at the pleasure that had coursed
through him when he had destroyed the enemy pilot, and
knowing that something had changed in him that day.
He had shot down and disabled other planes in his time,
but none of those fights had been personal. Then he had
been doing his duty for King and country against a face-
less foe that, if it was not stopped, would take over
England's green and pleasant land and commit the same
atrocities that were happening elsewhere. It had been
simple and clear-cut. But today . . . today he felt like a
murderer.

Once back in his hut, he sat on the bed and looked at
Salty's empty bunk. The others had gone for breakfast,
but he hadn't felt like eating.

He would give the world for Esther to be here right
now. Just to be able to talk to her, to hold her, to confess
what he was feeling inside. She wouldn't judge him, he
knew that. If he told her that he had enjoyed killing
another human being, that he had felt such a surge of
fierce, primitive joy when he had turned a plane into a
fireball – knowing that death was coming in burning
agony for those inside – she wouldn't understand, but
she wouldn't condemn him, either. Not his Esther.

With his elbows on his knees, he put his head in his
hands and pressed his little fingers against his eyeballs.
Had he sold his soul to the Devil? Was that it? But then,
whatever it took, Hitler and his Nazis had to be stopped,

even if it meant legalized murder. Look at the slaughter of those poor blighters in the Warsaw ghetto just days ago. German SS troops had mounted a major operation to 'clear' its Jewish ghetto, the newspapers had reported, killing more than 50,000 men, women and children with grenades and flame-throwers; and the ones who'd survived had either been executed or penned like animals and sent to the concentration camps. It was unbelievable that such barbarity was happening in a civilized world; but it was, and it would continue to be so, unless Hitler and Himmler and the rest of the madmen were killed. And if, in so doing, he and others like him became brutalized to some extent, maybe that was the price that had to be paid?

He raised his head, staring at Salty's bunk. He didn't know what was right and what was wrong any more.

When the door to the hut opened, it wasn't one of the friends he'd flown with that morning, but the station medical officer who stood there. Like most of his breed, the SMO kept a professional mask in place most of the time and rarely let his feelings show, but he had been a good friend of Salty's since before the war. Quietly he said, 'They told me you were in here. Come and get something to eat, man.'

'Not hungry.'

'Nevertheless, come and get something down you. That's an order.'

Monty stared at him. 'Do you ever wonder if this war is a sick nightmare from which you'll wake up?'

The SMO said nothing for a moment, then slowly walked to Salty's bunk and sat down, reaching out and touching the photograph of Salty's wife and child. Softly he said, 'She's a good woman, and a good wife. Salty thought the world of her. And Amelia, their kid, looks just like Maria. She's half-Italian, Maria. Did you know that?'

Monty shook his head.

'No, well, Salty didn't broadcast the fact, what with the war and all. Maria was born in England, and she's as English as you and I, but her parents' little restaurant's been daubed with paint and some of the local brats posted dog-dung through their letterbox. Maria's father – he's a Birmingham man – went mental when he caught one of 'em at it. He fought in the First World War, and to have dog-mess in his hall simply because he fell in love with an Italian woman umpteen years ago was beyond the pale. So he pushed the kid's nose in it. That's all; didn't clip him round the ear or knock him about, just sent him away with a dirty face. And the kid's father torched their place the next night, with them in it.' The SMO looked at him. 'So if you're asking about nightmares, I think plenty of us have them. The world's gone mad, that's for sure, and it's sending good people crazy with it. Neighbour turning against neighbour, and doing things they'd never have dreamed of before. But I know one thing, and so do you, and so did Salty. The only way to stamp out the madness is to win this war. Whatever it takes.'

'I enjoyed – *really* enjoyed – destroying Salty's killer.'

'Your friend was killed in front of you, and you settled the score, okay? You're not a perfect human being, Monty, and you never will be. Learn to live with it. Personally' – the SMO stood to his feet – 'I'd give you a medal.'

A weak smile touched Monty's face. 'That's all right then.'

'You can't afford yourself the luxury of remorse or regret or pity – it's distracting and worthless. If that enemy plane could have taken you, it would have. Any of us who survive this war will have to put the feelings connected with it in a box and keep the lid shut down, and the way you're feeling now is a perfect example. It doesn't matter what you felt when you shot the plane down – only that you did it.'

Monty was shocked. 'Do you really mean that?'

'I'm a medical officer, and I was a GP before the war. I'm no psychiatrist, I admit, but for what it's worth, this navel-gazing isn't an option. You can do all the forgiving – and whatnot – you want after we've won the war, for now you take the so-an'-sos down at every opportunity you get, and to hell with your motives. All right?'

Strangely, it helped. Monty stood up, wiping his hand tiredly across his face before he said, 'I could do with some of Lionel's burnt sausages and overcooked eggs.'

'Don't forget his cindered toast. It's an art form to get it that way.' The SMO grinned and then his face sobered. 'There'll be those who come through this, Monty –

believe you are one of them. You're married, aren't you? Any kids?'

'No. We decided we'd wait until we knew what we were bringing them into.'

'Well, for your future kids, believe you're invincible, and that you are the good guy. And for what it's worth, I think you are.'

Esther's letter came in that morning's post. He was lying with some companions on the grass at the edge of the airfield, listening to the nearby song of birds as the drugging effects of sleep took hold. The sun was high in a cloudless blue sky, and on the perimeter of his consciousness he could hear the others talking about the morning's raid, but he was deep in the pleasant land of inertia.

The screeching brake-drums of the tea wagon intruded on his drowsiness, and he was dimly aware of willing figures jumping up to help unload the heavy thermos flasks of tea and plates of elevenses, courtesy of the much-maligned Lionel and his kitchen staff. Rolling over onto his stomach, Monty shielded his eyes from the sun as someone called, 'Letters here for Croft, Lee and Grant.' He and Esther had agreed that 'Wynford-Grant' was for civilian life rather than the RAF.

Hoping the letter was from Esther rather than from his mother or friends, he raised his hand, shouting, 'Grant.'

It was her handwriting. He smiled, sitting up and slitting the envelope open as his heart raced. Just seeing the familiar, somewhat untidy scrawl was balm to his soul. As someone passed him a mug of tea he took it automatically, unfolding the contents of the envelope and smoothing the paper out:

Dear Monty,

I so wish I could tell you this in person, my darling, but needs must. Remember our first time on the moor, with the perfume of summer in the air and the birds and bees for company? Well, the birds and bees must have worked their magic, because I'm expecting our baby. I know it wasn't what we had planned, and it will be a surprise – if not a shock – but I hope you will be pleased. Perhaps there is no right time to become parents, my beloved? Perhaps these things happen when they should, and are for a purpose. I love you and I already love our baby, so very much.

I'm staying on at the farm, but Mrs Holden is seeing to it that I have light work; in fact she is clucking around me like a mother hen, which is rather nice, truth be told! The girls are being wonderful too, although Farmer Holden tutted a bit and would have had me shipped home, if it wasn't for his wife. I would have hated that, Monty: months of my father being around, although I know I'll have to go home before the baby is born. My mother would expect it, and it will be nice to be with her at such a time.

I'll write to my parents, and could you put yours in the picture? The baby's due in April. It would be lovely

if you could get leave arranged for then? I love you
more than words can say, my darling. Us – parents!

Your Esther

He raised his head from the letter in his hand, staring
into the distance where a heat haze shimmered over the
airfield.

A baby! The flood of elation took him by surprise.
There were a thousand reasons why this was the worst
time to think of bringing new life into the world, but
somehow it didn't matter. He was going to be a father,
and the next time he flew against the enemy, it wasn't
going to be merely for him and Esther and England, but
for the future of his child. His son or daughter.

'You all right, Monty?'

He came back to his surroundings to find his companions eyeing him anxiously. Bad news was a common
occurrence these days. He nodded dazedly. 'I'm going to
be a father,' he said weakly. 'Esther's in the family way.'

Cheering and ribald comments as to his prowess, and
having his hand almost shaken off, ensued, and when
one of the men produced a silver hip-flask full of brandy,
everyone held out their mugs for a dollop. Suddenly the
atmosphere had changed.

Monty stared round at the men who had become his
friends, as his news provoked talk about their wives and
children and sweethearts, and – for the unattached
and fancy-free among them – girls in general. Victor, a
long, lanky individual with a drooping moustache, was

describing the attributes of a barmaid he'd successfully wooed the night before; and Doug, a cheerful northern lad whose wife had just presented him with twin boys, brought out his photographs of the babies and was trying to press them on the others for the umpteenth time.

'Ugly little so-an'-sos, aren't they, Doug?' one of the airmen commented, with a wink at the others.

'Take after their father, poor little blighters,' another man chimed in. 'Nearly bald, with faces like smacked backsides.'

Doug grinned, every inch the besotted father. He'd heard it all before.

Monty swallowed the rest of his tea, the brandy sending a warm glow into his stomach, and stretched out on the thick green grass, his hands behind his head and the sun hot on his face. He was back on track again.

Chapter Seven

It had snowed heavily all day and now it felt as though the whole of the world was asleep under its blanket of white. Esther sat at her bedroom window looking out into the moonlit night, her hands resting on her swollen belly.

She couldn't sleep. She was so big now – as big as a house, she'd complained grumpily to her mother that morning – and getting comfortable in her soft bed at home had been an increasing problem, whereas in the farm cottage the hard beds had seemed to suit her condition. But at the end of January her mother and father had actually come to collect her, after she had made one excuse after another to delay her departure from Yorkshire. Now it was the middle of a bitterly cold April and, apart from the fact it had been snowing for weeks on and off, she supposed her time at home hadn't been *too* bad. Esther wrinkled her nose as her thoughts meandered on. If it wasn't for the constant worry at the back of her mind about Monty, she could have relaxed and enjoyed the time with her mother and Rose, both of whom had been thrilled to have her home.

The baby in her stomach kicked hard, as it was apt to do most of the night – another reason she found it hard to settle – and she smiled as she rested her fingers against the vigorous life inside her. 'It's all very well for Churchill to say your daddy and the rest of the RAF carry doom to tyrants,' she murmured, 'but I want him *here*, with us.'

Monty had managed to wangle a three-day leave at Christmas and had turned up at the farm unannounced, but Mrs Holden had made him very welcome. He'd had to sleep in the hay loft – Esther and the rest of the girls were packed into the tiny, two-bedroomed labourer's cottage like sardines – but every evening she had crept out and joined him in his fragrant bed, climbing the ladder that led to the platform above the barn, where they had held each other close and made delicious love for half the night.

And then, all too soon, Christmas was over and she had waved him goodbye, trying to be brave, but terrified she would never see him again. The farm didn't possess the luxury of a wireless or any modern conveniences, but every so often one of them would bring back a news-paper from the village and she would read with dread the reports of the RAF's bombing raids. In January the RAF's Mosquito fighters had launched two daring day-light raids on Berlin, just as the Reich Marshal, Hermann Goering, was to deliver a broadcast celebrating ten years of the Nazi regime; and later in the afternoon, at the time the enemy's propaganda minister, Joseph Goebbels, was broadcasting. In March she read about the RAF's bombing raids on Germany's industrial heartland, which aimed to destroy more than 2,000 factories and a million tons of steel, along with engineering shops and coal production, whilst still keeping up the destruction of Berlin.

She sighed. Her father had been triumphant about reports that the fires in Germany could be seen 200 miles away and had rejoiced at the devastation, but all she'd thought about were the men who would never return home to their loved ones. She ached to hear from Monty, but as soon as one letter arrived, she began worrying as to whether there would be another.

Esther turned as one of the logs in her bedroom fireplace spat and crackled briefly before dying in a shower of sparks. She ought to put more logs on the fire, but she felt too tired to move – not that she had done much for weeks. It was just that with the difficulty in sleeping, especially now she was so huge, and the mental strain of worrying about Monty day and night, she felt constantly exhausted, but in a different way from when she'd been working all hours at the farm. She missed Priscilla and the others so much, and although they wrote to her religiously each week without fail, it wasn't the same. She missed the camaraderie, the conviviality of having friends her own age, the sheer *fun* they'd had, and the laughs. Oh, the laughs. There had been times when her sides had ached with laughing.

A smile touched her lips and then, as the wind blew a

swirl of fat snowflakes against the window, she shivered. She must try to sleep; the baby was due any day, and after that she might not get much rest. She had made it clear to her parents, and Rose, that she intended to look after the baby herself and breastfeed too; she wanted to immerse herself in motherhood for the first few months. And after that? She bit her lip. A home of her own with Monty and their child was her dream, but life in the RAF was so precarious. There was talk that, with the threat of invasion lifted and the country's church bells ringing regularly once again, victory was in sight, but who really knew? So much propaganda went on. One minute the Russians were liberating cities held by the Nazis in the Soviet Union, and the Americans were driving the Germans back in Tunisia; the next minute the former Cabinet minister Lord Hankey was calling the anti-U-boat campaign a terrible failure. Who knew what to believe?

Slowly she manoeuvred her cumbersome body out of the chair and climbed into bed. She had left the curtains open, and the white world outside the window and the flickering fire provided enough light for her to see that her small bedside clock showed two o'clock.

At three o'clock Esther awoke as a pain – similar to that she'd felt when she'd eaten too many of Farmer Holden's barely ripe Victoria plums in the summer – gripped her. But this was no over-indulgence on green fruit, she thought, as gradually the pain lessened until it disappeared altogether. It was another ten minutes before the pain came again, and so it continued at regular intervals until seven o'clock, when she decided to get up and sit in the chair again. She had no sooner slid out of bed and stood up than a trickle of water down her legs told her that her waters had broken and the baby really was on its way.

After sorting herself out in the bathroom, she brought a thick towel into the bedroom and folded it, to sit on in the chair. The pains were still far apart and she saw no point in calling her mother and Rose yet. They would both be rising shortly – time enough then to tell them that her labour had begun.

At eight o'clock Rose gently opened the door and poked her head round, to see if Esther was sleeping, knowing that she had bad nights and sometimes slept in. She didn't notice the towel at first, but once Esther told her the situation, Rose ran for Harriet, who immediately insisted on Dr Martin being sent for, despite Esther's objections.

The good doctor, now stooped and white-haired, had come out of semi-retirement when his son, who'd taken over the practice from him, had gone into the army as a medical officer at the outbreak of war. He confirmed Esther's prognosis. The baby was still a long way from being born and the contractions could continue for some time. He would call back that evening, unless he was summoned in the meantime, but would send the midwife attached to the practice later that morning. And, with that, Harriet and Rose had to be content, in spite of all their fluttering anxiety. Esther, on the other hand, was as cool as a cucumber now that the time had come.

The day progressed slowly. The snowstorm continued, the midwife arrived and was soon comfortably ensconced with Esther, and the baby made it clear it was in no hurry to leave its warm, comfortable place inside its mother. Because her waters had broken, the midwife insisted that Esther stay in bed, because of the risk of infection. Esther didn't mind too much. She chatted with the midwife, who had six children of her own, the youngest of whom was a young man of eighteen; and the woman regaled her with the escapades of her family, and what they were all doing in the war. One in particular, a girl of twenty-one who had made the most of the changes to women's status brought about by the war, as the incursions into pub life and the grudging acceptance of this by men had taken place, was a constant worry to her poor mother.

The girl, Cathleen, was apparently having the time of her life and, as she earned good money in a munitions factory, saw nothing wrong in spending most of it with her friends and having a knees-up every night in the local pub.

'Now, I'm broad-minded,' the midwife said with a censorious sniff, 'but it isn't as if she and her friends have soft drinks, or just the one beer or short. There's music, and it's gay and lively, and all the military men get in there, and they're after one thing. Her da and me went to visit her last weekend, and do you know what she said to me, when I said we hadn't brought her up to behave like that? Prudish, she called me. *Me!* She said women are doing just as much in this war as the men, and why should people like me turn up their noses and act all Victorian because she walks into a pub in trousers and orders a beer or a whisky?'

The midwife took a breath, self-righteous anger mottling her face. 'But the thing is, Mrs Wynford-Grant, everyone knows there's a certain type who goes into pubs to pick up men. Get what they can, sort of thing. And sometimes they get more than they'd bargained for, when they go with the Yanks. Disease-ridden, half of them GIs are – everyone knows that. I said that to our Cathleen, and she said I was talking like we were still in the Dark Ages, *and*' – here the midwife's voice rose an octave – 'she said she'd been out with a GI or two and they were perfect gentlemen. I ask you. And then she said what did I think our Edward and Herbert and Wilbur were doing – all sailors, my lads are – if not making the most of their time ashore wherever they might be?'

The midwife sank back in her chair, clearly exhausted by her tale. Weakly she added, 'I mean, men have always sown their wild oats, haven't they? Nowt wrong with that. But nice girls behave themselves.'

Esther found all her sympathies were with the wayward Cathleen, but didn't think it prudent to say so. 'I'm sure Cathleen is a good girl, Mrs Shaw. At heart.'

'We're a respectable family. Her da'll kill her, if she gets into trouble.' The midwife stared at her with mournful eyes. 'Such a bonny little lass she was, and as good as gold, before she started all this feminism stuff. I blame Hitler. Who'd have thought, before the war, that my Cathleen would be dancing the jitterbug, or whatever it's called, with GIs – and goodness knows what else besides. It's not right, and some of them' – here Mrs Shaw's voice lowered to a whisper – 'are, you know, not like us.'

'Not like us?'

'In colour.'

'Oh. Oh, I see.' Esther knew the black American servicemen were something of an exotic prize as a dancing partner; Priscilla had told her so. Apparently they were segregated from the white American servicemen, but still expected to give their all for their country. She hadn't understood this anomaly, and neither had Priscilla. But then, as Priscilla had said at the time, such onerous distinctions were made by men, and it was their sex that had started every war since the beginning of time. She, herself, had never seen a black person until the GIs had arrived, and it appeared that she wasn't alone. Priscilla had confided that her latest boyfriend, a black GI, had told her – with exquisite irony – that he'd felt like 'Livingstone in the heart of Africa', when practically the whole village in Yorkshire had turned out to watch him post a letter. He and Priscilla had laughed about it; but now, faced with Mrs Shaw, Esther wasn't sure it was a laughing matter. Quietly she said, 'What does the colour of someone's skin have to do with anything, Mrs Shaw?'

The midwife stared at her. 'Well, it stands to reason.'

'Does it?'

'They're different.'

'And different is . . . '

Mrs Shaw was bristling. 'Different is different – that's all I have to say on the matter.' And then, as Esther's face screwed up with pain, her attitude changed into one of strict professionalism. 'This one is a strong one, is it? Just breathe, like I told you; it'll pass. You've been having contractions for some little while. They'll step up now, but all is as it should be, and you are progressing well.'

It might be all as it should be, but it was getting more and more painful and Esther felt so tired. Her mother and Rose had remained with her for most of the day, but her mother had been persuaded to take an afternoon nap over an hour ago, and Rose had been busying herself with this and that. Now, as they entered her room, Esther had to admit she was glad to see them. The pain had suddenly become more brutal.

Esther's baby was born just before midnight and it was a girl. Even in the midst of her exhaustion Esther smiled as she heard the loud wailing that signified all was well. Her mother and Rose were with her, holding her hands and encouraging her on, as the midwife delivered the child with the doctor looking on. He had decided to stay when things had become drawn out, but in the event Esther hadn't needed any assistance.

For a few moments, tired as she was, she was unaware of the silence that had fallen over the room once the baby stopped crying. She lifted her head slightly and saw the midwife busily wrapping the baby up to hand to her, but all of them – her mother and Rose and the doctor – had strange looks on their faces, which made her suddenly afraid. 'What's wrong?' Her voice was panicky. 'I heard her cry – she's all right, isn't she?'

'She's fine, Mrs Wynford-Grant,' said the midwife as she brought the baby to her, but the same expression was reflected on her countenance, and her voice held a shred of something Esther couldn't place.

She reached eagerly for the little cocoon, her arms going instinctively around her baby as she cradled her daughter to her. Through partly closed, sleepy lids, two dark eyes stared at her and then the baby yawned widely, showing tiny pink gums. But it wasn't this that had captured Esther's attention, or the mass of black hair falling over the little brow. It was the colour of the baby's skin, which was undeniably a deep brown.

She stared back into the small, sweet face, her surprise so great that it tied her tongue for some moments. And then she murmured what they were all thinking, 'But she's not white . . . ' She raised her head to the doctor, who was standing at the foot of the bed. 'How can she be this colour? I don't understand.'

Dr Martin cleared his throat twice, but still didn't speak, because for once in his life he didn't know what to say. He had known Esther all her life, watched her grow from a delightful, if somewhat headstrong little girl into a lovely woman, and he would have sworn she wasn't the type of person to be unfaithful to her husband. But here was the proof, and there was no getting away from it. It was this damned war, he thought with a thread of pity. It made folk go crazy, and all the normal morals and principles had gone out of the window. But there was no doubting the fact that Esther had gone with a black GI; and what her father would say when he saw the child, he didn't dare imagine. With this in mind, he turned to Harriet, who was standing with her hands pressed against her mouth and Rose's arm round her. 'I suggest you let Esther have a good night's sleep before Theobald sees the child,' he said softly. 'And I'll be back early in the morning to check on her and the baby.'

'But . . . ' Esther looked at each of them in turn. 'How could Monty and I have a baby with this colour of skin?'

'You couldn't,' the midwife said grimly, earning herself a sharp 'Mrs Shaw, *please*,' from Dr Martin.

The baby yawned again, one tiny hand extricating itself from the blanket and plucking at Esther's finger. A flood of love banished the puzzlement for a moment, and Esther's heart soared as she gazed down at her daughter. She was beautiful, she thought wonderingly, so beautiful.

'I sent a message to the base this morning to say the baby was on the way,' Dr Martin said to Harriet, his meaning clear in his voice. 'Monty could be here soon, as I understand they've granted him a few days' compassionate leave?'

'Yes, yes, that's right.' Harriet had to force the words out through numb lips.

'So you will see to it that he is prepared before . . . '

'What? Oh, yes. Yes.'

It was some minutes before the tight-lipped midwife left the room after finishing administering to her patient, but as the door closed behind her and Dr Martin, Rose said weakly, 'Oh, Miss Esther, how could you? What will Mr Monty say?'

'What?' For a moment Esther didn't understand.

'Was it one of the GIs from the base near the village? Does he know about the baby?'

Finally the penny dropped, and the reason for the hushed silence and the midwife's barely concealed contempt became clear. Horrified, Esther looked at them both. 'The baby is Monty's. How could you think I would even look at another man? She is his; of course she is his.'

'Miss Esther, she can't be.' Rose was near tears. 'And what's your father going to say?'

Bewildered and hurt, and utterly at a loss, Esther said again, 'She's Monty's baby,' before looking at her mother. 'I promise: she's his. I've never gone with anyone else. I wouldn't do that to Monty.'

'I believe you.' Harriet sank down at the end of the bed and, as Rose went to speak, she said softly, 'Be quiet, Rose. Please, not another word.'

'Oh, ma'am, you look ill. The shock . . . Shall I fetch your pills?'

'Pills?' Even in the midst of her distress, Esther was concerned. 'Are you ill?'

'It's nothing.' Harriet waved away the enquiry with a shake of her head. 'Esther, listen to me.' She rose and came to sit close to Esther, putting her arm around her so that the three of them – herself, Esther and the baby, who was now fast asleep in her mother's arms – were entwined. 'I have something to tell you; something I probably should have told you when you were old enough to understand, but which I thought was best kept a secret, for your sake as well as mine. Your father' – she paused – 'my husband is a man who is capable of anything, and for all our sakes I thought . . . ' She shook her head. 'I'm sorry, I'm not making any sense,' she added, reaching out and stroking the baby's tiny brow.

'What is it?' Esther began, just as a knock came at the bedroom door and Theobald's voice said, 'That old fool Martin told me to wait till morning to see my granddaughter, but I'm not having that.' He had already opened the door, but had not entered, as he added, 'Are you decent, Esther?' from the landing.

Esther saw her mother blanch, and it was this that made her call out, 'Can you give me a minute?' before she said urgently, 'What is it?' And then to Rose, as her mother's colour changed yet again to a pasty grey, 'Get those pills, Rose.'

'What's going on?' In typical fashion and without waiting for permission, Theobald barged his way into the bedroom, glancing first at his wife, who appeared to be half-swooning, then at Esther, who was attempting to hold the baby and support her mother at the same time, as Rose dashed past him for the pills.

'She's not well,' Esther said desperately.

'She's never well.'

'Help her.'

Swearing under his breath, Theobald lifted a chair close to the bed and plonked his wife in it, holding her up until Rose appeared with a small bottle of pills and a glass of water. When Harriet had swallowed the pills and Rose was assisting her mistress, Theobald straightened and bent over the bed, saying, 'Let's have a look at her then', as he folded back the blanket wrapped around the baby.

For a moment he remained perfectly still, frozen in a somewhat ludicrous stance. The only sound in the room was his wife's laboured breathing as she struggled to draw air into her lungs, and Rose murmuring, 'It's all right, ma'am, it's all right.' Theobald's eyes were riveted on the bundle in Esther's arms, which she had drawn protectively closer, but he didn't move or speak. Red colour stained his face and neck until his countenance had a purple tinge, and then he slowly straightened and seemed to swell as he gazed down at Esther.

It was clear to everyone that if it had been in Theobald's power to strike her dead, he would have done so. His rage was a tangible thing, and deadly. If there had been a knife to hand, he would have used it.

When he spoke, the words came up from the depths of him in a throaty growl. 'You whore!'

When his arm swung out, his hand bunched into a fist, Rose sprang up and hung onto him as she shouted, 'No, Mr Wynford, no.' And she continued to hang onto him as he tried to shake her off, spitting obscenities. Esther had bent over her daughter, shielding her with her own body, and it was into this mayhem that Monty walked.

For a moment he stood in the doorway to the bedroom, unable to take in the scene in front of him. When Osborne had answered the door to his knock, the butler had informed him that the rest of the staff were in bed, but the master and Mrs Wynford and Rose were with Esther and the little one, and all was well. Dr Martin had suggested that the master leave seeing the baby until morning, Osborne had added, as Miss Esther was exhausted, but the master hadn't been able to wait.

Monty had taken the stairs two at a time, his heart thumping with excitement, but as he'd reached the landing he had heard Rose shout.

Monty rarely raised his voice, for he had been brought up by a nanny who considered it the height of bad manners, but now he positively bellowed, 'What the hell is going on here?' as he leapt across the room and manhandled his father-in-law away from the bed. 'Have you gone mad? She's just had a baby – she doesn't need this.'

'Oh, she's had a baby all right.' Theobald seemed to have lost his senses. He was shaking with anger. 'But whose? That's the question.'

'Whose? Mine, of course.' Monty was still holding his father-in-law, who seemed to have had some kind of brainstorm. He could feel the man's fury through his fingers, which were gripping Theobald's upper arms.

'Yours?' Theobald gave a bark of a laugh. 'Look at it. *Look at it* and tell me if you think it's yours.'

'Monty . . . ' Harriet's voice was a thin thread, and as he glanced her way he was horrified at her condition. She looked as though she was dying. 'It's not Esther's fault.'

'Esther's fault?' His wife's words seemed to reignite Theobald's rage. 'Damned right it's not her fault. I blame you as much as her. From when she was born you've given in to her every whim and fancy, and spoiled her rotten. Many a time I've wanted to give her a good hiding, but no, you said – she's a girl, and you don't take a belt to a girl. But what's the result? *That!*' He shook off Monty's hands and wiped the sweat from his brow, his face murderous. 'A bastard. We're going to be a laughing stock, you know that, don't you? They'll all be at it, gossiping behind their hands and enjoying every minute. Oh yes, I know what our fine, dear friends will do.'

He stopped, gasping for breath, and as he did so Monty slowly approached the bed, where Esther was still bent protectively over the baby. 'What's wrong with it?' he murmured, unable to make head or tail of what was going on.

Esther raised her head, tears running down her face. 'Nothing is wrong with her, and she *is* your daughter. I swear it.'

Monty looked down at the little bundle as Esther showed the child to him, his eyes widening; and Theobald, seeing his son-in-law's expression, growled, 'You see? Now do you see?'

'Monty!' Again Harriet attempted to speak, her voice a little stronger now. 'Esther is telling the truth: the baby is your daughter. It is me who has lived a lie for years; Esther's done nothing wrong.' She took a gasping breath, her eyes beseeching Esther now as she said, 'You *are* my daughter, my darling, in every way except through blood. Someone . . . someone else gave birth to you.'

'You lying—'

As Theobald snarled at his wife, Monty cut off the other man's voice with an upraised hand as he said ferociously, '*Shut up!*' and such was the tone that Theobald fell silent. 'Tell me,' said Monty to the woman he had always privately thought didn't have the gumption to say boo to a goose.

'When . . . when Esther was born, there were two of us giving birth after the shipwreck.' Monty nodded; he knew the story. He'd heard it from Esther, who had always delighted in the fact that she'd survived against the odds. 'But my . . . my baby was stillborn. The other child, Esther, was small but healthy, and her mother was going to put her in an orphanage because the family in America didn't consider the father suitable. That was all I knew; and when Ruth – Esther's natural mother – begged me to take her baby and raise her as my own, with all the benefits that would bring, we . . . we swapped babies.'

'So . . . so you are saying . . . '

'The father, Ruth's young man, must have been black.

That's why the baby is the colour she is, but she is your daughter, Monty. Your flesh and blood.'

'But' – Monty was grappling to understand – 'Esther is white.' He looked at her, and for the first time the honey tint to her skin and the darkness of her eyes and hair took on a new significance. 'She looks white,' he said faintly.

'That's why I never suspected . . . ' Harriet's voice died away as she looked at Esther's face. 'I didn't know.'

'You're not my mother?' Esther felt faint and sick, whether from the birth or the enormity of what she was hearing, she wasn't sure.

'I am – I am your mother, in every way that matters.'

Theobald took them all by surprise as he lunged at Harriet, and it was only Rose flinging herself in front of her mistress that deflected the blow. As it was, Rose was hit with enough force to send her spinning to the floor; and then Theobald was on his wife, his hands around her throat, and Monty was yelling for Osborne to help him as he grappled with Theobald, who seemed to have the strength of ten men, in his rage.

Sheer pandemonium ensued, with Esther's and Rose's screams and the shouts of the men raising the whole house and sending more servants running to the room.

When Monty and Osborne finally managed to pull Theobald off his wife, Harriet appeared to be senseless and in a bad way. Rose was hysterical, and Esther was screaming at Theobald, 'Get out! Get out of here!' as she knelt in the bed clutching the baby, who was now adding her own high-pitched cries to the melee.

It took Monty, Osborne and the footman who had appeared in his nightclothes to force Theobald from the room, and once on the landing they manhandled him down the stairs, the four of them nearly going from top to bottom several times, before they finally managed to get him into his study. 'Stay with him,' Monty ordered Osborne and the footman, before dashing up the stairs again, convinced his mother-in-law had probably breathed her last, but as he entered the room, Harriet was coughing and spluttering as the housekeeper held a vial of smelling salts under her nose.

'Shall I call the doctor, sir?' One of the housemaids, who had been standing with her hands pressed to her mouth as he entered the room, now turned to Monty for guidance.

'Yes, yes, do that. And, Mrs Norton, if I carry Mrs Wynford to her bedroom, can you and Rose stay with her until Dr Martin arrives? I don't want her left alone – do you understand me? I want the two of you to stay with her.' He wouldn't put it past Theobald to try to attack Harriet again. 'And you,' he said to the other housemaid, who, like the first, was clad only in her nightdress and dressing gown, 'stay here until I get back.'

Harriet was still barely conscious when he deposited her on her bed, but she clutched his hand as he was about to leave, whispering, 'She . . . loves you.'

Monty couldn't reply. At this moment he felt some

affinity with Theobald towards the woman who had ruined all their lives. Esther wasn't who he thought she was. *Nothing* was as he had thought. And his mother . . . He groaned inwardly. Hell and damnation – his mother. What was she going to say?

After everyone but the housemaid had left the room, Esther lay back against the pillows, willing the feeling of faintness and light-headedness to pass. The baby had stopped crying and was now nestled against her again, apparently fast asleep; but then, as Esther opened her eyes and looked down at her daughter, two bright eyes stared back at her.

'Can I do anything for you, ma'am?'

The housemaid was hovering, clearly out of her depth at everything that had occurred, and suddenly Esther wanted nothing more than to be alone. 'A cup of tea would be nice,' she said quietly. 'I'll be perfectly all right while you fetch it.'

'But Mr Grant said . . . '

'I'll be fine. Go on, you won't get into trouble.'

Once the door had closed behind the girl, Esther touched the baby's smooth velvet brow with the tip of a finger as she whispered, 'You're mine and I'll keep you safe.' Who would have thought such a tiny little being would have the effect of one of Hitler's bombs in their lives? And why did she feel strangely numb about her mother's revelation? She ought to be beside herself, but after the first shock, a peculiar calm had settled on her.

Perhaps it was because she had to concentrate on her daughter right now? Her daughter, and Monty's. Everything else – the fact that her mother wasn't her mother, and her father wasn't her father – had to come second. Her head was swimming with exhaustion and her limbs felt like lead, and although the knowledge of what her mother had said was at the back of her mind, it was as though it was all about someone else.

The baby stirred, her tiny hands flailing for a second, before one gripped Esther's finger again. It was a firm grip and surprisingly strong, and as Esther gazed down into the small face, the baby yawned again, almost smacking her lips in the process. In spite of herself, Esther smiled, and it was at this moment that Monty walked back into the room.

He stared at her, at the woman he had loved from the first moment he had set eyes on her and who had been everything he had wanted in a wife, and it took all his control not to shout at her to wipe the smile off her face. That she could smile like that, after what had been revealed in this room! He was in turmoil – a turmoil worse than anything he'd endured after Salty's death – and Esther could smile. It felt as though she had just punched him in the stomach.

'Monty.' She looked up and saw him standing there. 'How is she? My mother?'

'Resting.' His voice was flat and cold.

'She'll be all right?'

He didn't answer this, nor did he come towards her

when she held out her hand. Instead he walked to the small fireplace and stood looking down into the glowing embers, with his back towards her as he said, 'She did a terrible thing. You do understand what she said?'

Esther stared at him. His back was rigid and his hands were thrust into his pockets. She had imagined he would come hurrying back to comfort her, to tell her nothing mattered but that she and the baby were all right; and then he would hold his daughter, like any new father. Her heart began to thump hard. 'She did what she thought was for the best.'

'For whom?' He swung round to face her. 'She took someone else's child, without knowing anything about the background of the parents, and then further compounded her crime by continuing the deception for years.'

'Crime?'

'What else would you call it?'

Please, please don't be like this. Don't look at me like this. I need kindness. I need you to put your arms round me and tell me that you love me. The words were in her head, but she didn't voice them, staring at him as she read what was in his face. 'I know it's a shock,' she said at last. 'Imagine how I feel. But it doesn't make any difference to us. To what we have. Does it?' He didn't answer, not until Esther repeated in a small voice, 'Monty, does it?'

'You have to understand how this will look to people.

The baby, it's . . . it's so different. My mother would never accept it. You know what she's like.'

'She's a *her*, not an it. Your daughter. And what's your mother got to do with anything?'

'She's old-school, Esther. You know that.'

Pain was tearing at her now, but she kept her voice from wobbling as she said, 'What happened to that love you said would last till the end of time, and beyond? I'm the same girl you married less than a year ago. I haven't changed.'

His head was lowered now as he muttered, 'I know, I know.'

'But?' When he didn't answer, she said again, '*But?*'

'I . . . I need time. It's a lot to take in.'

A lot to take in. She had just had a baby and in the same breath been told that her mother wasn't her mother, and everything she had ever known was built on sinking sand, and he said it was a lot to take in? The strange but welcome bubble of calm that had cushioned her was dissolving. Shakily she said, 'You'd better go then,' never dreaming that he would actually leave her at a time when she had never needed him more.

'I'll come back tomorrow.'

His face screwed up in protest as she suddenly screamed at him, '*Don't bother! If you're ashamed of us, don't bother.*' It was only as she said the words that she knew she had hit the nail on the head, as Monty scurried from the room without saying anything more.

Alone, Esther stared down at the sleeping baby. She

was so tiny and helpless. She hugged her daughter to her so fiercely that the baby awoke with a protesting cry. And when her tiny mouth opened wide, so did Esther's, tears gushing from her eyes and down her nose, as she moaned her anguish into the terrible emptiness that had opened up and engulfed her.

Chapter Eight

'There, there, Miss Esther, don't take on so.'

At what point in her storm of weeping Rose came into the room, Esther didn't know, but when her old nanny gently took the baby from her and settled her in the crib that had been placed in readiness at the end of the bed, Esther was too spent to protest.

Rose came and put her arms round Esther once the baby was quiet, cuddling her as though she was a little girl again, and murmuring comforting words that were meaningless in the circumstances. 'It will all come right, you'll see. Don't cry, lass. Everything will sort itself out in time – it always does. There, there, Miss Esther. Don't make yourself ill.'

They sat, rocking slightly to and fro, for some minutes before Esther could pull herself together and, when she could speak, she choked out, 'He's gone, Rose. Monty's gone.'

'He'll be back, Miss Esther, never fear. He loves you,

you know that. It's just been a shock for him, that's all. For all of us.'

'You – you didn't know?'

'No one knew.'

'All . . . ' Esther gulped, swallowing hard. 'All these years I thought she was my mother.'

'She *is* your mother. In every way that matters she is your mother, all right? Now you listen to me, lass.' Rose took her by the shoulders, staring into the drowned eyes. 'No one could love you more than she does. You've been her sun, moon and stars from the minute you were born, you know that. At heart you know that, don't you?'

Esther nodded, blowing her nose on the handkerchief Rose handed her. Yes, she knew that, but . . . 'I feel I don't know who I am, Rose,' she whispered, thereby contradicting what she had just said to Monty. She *was* the same Esther, but she wasn't. 'My real mother, I know nothing about her; and my father, who was he? How did they meet? America have treated their black people so appallingly, haven't they? Priscilla told me her GI isn't even allowed to sit with white people on the buses. It's awful. And . . . and she kept the truth from me, Rose.'

'Your mother wants to talk to you and explain, as far as she can; she's beside herself. Dr Martin's just left, and she mustn't leave her bed. Do you think, if I helped you, you could come to her room, Miss Esther?'

'Is *he* there?'

'Your father? No, he's not there.' Rose didn't add that Theobald was drinking himself senseless in his study, or that when Dr Martin had tried to talk to him and explain how seriously ill his wife was, he had slammed the door in the good doctor's face, nearly doing Dr Martin an injury in the process.

Esther looked at Rose. At the word 'father' a bolt of feeling – she didn't know if it was relief or elation or hatred, or a mixture of all three – had shot through her. 'He's not my father. I am nothing to do with him, and I'm glad. He's a vile, horrible man, Rose,' she said softly, 'I'm so glad I'm not his.'

'Come and see your mother, Miss Esther. I'll bring the baby, and you can lean on my arm.'

'I'm not ill, Rose. I've had a baby, that's all.' Nevertheless, when she put her feet to the floor and stood up, Esther was glad of Rose's support, as the room swam and dipped.

Harriet's eyes were on the door as they entered her room and immediately she said to the housekeeper, who was sitting in a chair by the bed, 'Would you fetch us a pot of tea, Mrs Norton?'

The housekeeper got to her feet and, as she passed them, she glanced at the baby in Rose's arms, and Esther read the same expression that had been evident on the midwife's face. For a moment she wanted to spring on the woman and slap her, but she restrained herself, going across to her mother and sinking into the chair that the housekeeper had vacated, while Rose stood with the baby at the end of the bed.

Harriet hadn't known what to expect; she hadn't even been sure Esther would come and see her. And so now, when Esther took her mother's thin hand and pressed it between her own, the flood of relief brought tears.

'It's all right, Mama. Don't cry,' Esther murmured, her own face wet, but her use of the old affectionate term, rather than the more formal 'Mother' that she'd adopted as she'd got older, caused Harriet to lose control completely.

It was a little while before Harriet could compose herself, and in the meantime Mrs Norton had brought a tray of tea and been told to go to bed by Rose, who now settled herself in a chair by the window with the sleeping baby as Harriet began to speak. 'I need to tell you all of it, Esther, or as much as I know. But before I do, I want you to understand I love you as my own child – more, if anything, and your mother loved you too. She let you go for your sake, not hers. You must believe that. She was desperate to save you from the orphanage.'

Esther listened as her mother talked and, when Harriet later paused for breath, she said quietly, 'So my parents *did* love each other? They wanted to be together?'

'Oh yes. Just as you were born she called his name. I've never forgotten it. Yes, Ruth loved him, and she believed he loved her. It was her parents who separated them.'

Esther nodded. 'And her name was Flaggerty. Where in America was she from?'

Harriet's brow wrinkled. 'I'm not sure exactly. I know

Ruth told me the family settled in New York when they first arrived in America, and they survived in a kind of shanty town. She had been brought up on stories of what both sets of her grandparents had endured, and how fiercely proud they were that sheer hard work and determination had elevated them to high society, but I think Ruth's family were in Cincinnati, or was it Albany? I don't remember. She said her family were politically minded and ambitious. I believe her father was something big in the Democratic Party and had been elected to the city council; there was even talk of the mayor's office itself in the future. Nothing could stand in the way of their ambition, she said, and with some bitterness.'

Harriet lay back against the stack of pillows behind her, her hand going to her chest as the pain that had gripped her earlier came again.

'This is too much for you – we'll talk tomorrow.'

'No.' She caught at Esther's hand again. 'No, stay, child. I need you to understand. We both loved you, your mother and I.'

'I do understand.' It was true. Esther could see how it had all come about, and it went some way to soothing the hurt and sense of – what? she asked herself – betrayal? Desolation? Bewilderment? All that, and more.

'I should have told you a long time ago. I see that now, but I was frightened it would spoil what we had.' Harriet's voice had the catch of tears in it. 'I'm sorry, I'm so, so sorry, my darling.' Her gaze went to the child. 'Can I hold her?'

At Esther's nod, Rose brought the baby and positioned her in Harriet's arms. She was still sleeping, her full rosebud mouth pursed and making little sucking movements now and again. 'I had no idea,' Harriet murmured, as though to herself. 'Ruth never even hinted that it was because Michael was black . . . '

'Would it have made any difference? If you had known?'

Harriet looked into the beloved face and knew she had to lie as she had never lied before. 'Not for a moment,' she said softly. 'I wanted you with all my heart and soul, and mind and body.' And that was true enough. But would she have taken Ruth's baby, knowing what might happen in the future? The very thing that *had* happened, with all of the complications that would ensue and the prejudice Esther and the baby would now have to endure? Harriet knew she wasn't a brave person, for she would have left Theobald years ago if she was.

But she hadn't known. And she was glad she hadn't, she told herself fiercely. Her life had been enriched beyond measure because of Ruth's deception, which had only been done out of love and wanting the best for her child.

Esther moved to sit on the bed beside her mother and the two of them gazed down at the sleeping baby, and when Esther snuggled up to Harriet as she had been apt to do as a small child and rested her head on her mother's shoulder, Harriet knew a moment of deep thankfulness. Whatever the future held, however this worked out, she and Esther would see it through together. For her daughter and her granddaughter, she would stand up to Theobald, no matter what the cost to herself. But for Esther, her own life would have been miserable over the last years, as he flaunted one mistress after another in her face and belittled her in a hundred different ways. He was a cruel man, as well as an arrogant and spiteful one, and only she – and maybe Rose – knew what she'd had to endure over the years.

She glanced at Rose now, over Esther's head, and Rose's gaze was waiting for her. The two women smiled at each other and there was no condemnation in Rose's face.

There would be plenty from other quarters, though, Harriet thought to herself. Condemnation, gossip, outrage and animosity, all facets of the disgrace that would undoubtedly ensue, once the facts became known. And what people didn't know they would make up, and take great delight in doing so. But things wouldn't be as bad as they would have been before the war; even the most notorious scandals were short-lived in comparison. This would be a nine-day wonder at best.

Esther stirred at the side of her, raising her head to say, 'And he – Theobald – he never suspected anything? Not even a bit?'

It wasn't lost on Harriet that Esther already didn't refer to him as her father. 'No, not for a moment. You look similar to his mother – that's the thing. The same dark hair and eyes. She was a handsome woman, and he's always taken a perverse delight in pointing out that there's nothing of me in you.' It was one of the many ways in which Theobald had attempted to wound her.

'Oh, Mama.' Esther stroked her mother's thin veined hand. 'I would like nothing more than to be like you: you're the sweetest, kindest person I've ever known.' And that was true, but it made it all the harder, and hurt even more, that her mother had kept the truth from her for so long, even though she understood what had driven her to behave so. Her mama, her darling mama, was no relation to her at all. She couldn't believe it. She needed to be on her own and think. Kissing her mother's brow, she said softly, 'Go to sleep, and don't worry.'

Harriet's eyes had filled with tears again and they hugged before Esther left the room. The landing was dark and the house was silent, but once in her room there was a glow from the dying fire, and the white world outside the windows. The baby objected to being put down until Esther had put her to the breast again, where she guzzled happily for a few minutes before falling asleep. Once she was in her crib, Esther stood looking down at her for some moments, filled with a love so extreme it was almost frightening. Harriet had told her that it had been Ruth who had chosen her second name, and the reason for it, and now she murmured, 'My Joy.' She and Monty had decided on Christopher for a boy and Adele for a girl, but now she knew that her daughter's name was meant to be Joy.

Monty . . . She closed her eyes for a moment, unable to believe he had walked away from her when she had needed him most. But he would be back, she told herself passionately, and once he held his daughter everything would be all right. It was the shock, as Rose had said. But he would come back and take her in his arms, and together they'd face what needed to be faced.

Monty came back to the house the following afternoon, and his parents came with him. The events of the previous night – and not least Esther's long labour and the birth itself – had caught up with her, and she had slept on and off all day, rousing merely to feed and change the baby when little Joy demanded it. At over eight pounds, she was not a small baby and seemed to have settled naturally into being fed every four hours, working so vigorously at the breast to sate herself with the thin milky secretion that precedes true mother's milk that Esther's nipples were already more than a little sore. But she didn't mind; the bond between mother and child was already so strong that she tended to wake a few seconds before the baby began to grizzle.

Theobald met Monty and his parents in the drawing room, and what was said between them, Esther and Harriet did not know. Harriet could guess, though; when Theobald brought the three of them to her quarters their faces were grim, and Clarissa's pale-blue eyes were like chips of ice. It was she who spoke first, after ordering Rose from the room. Her thin chin wobbling with outrage as she glared at Harriet, propped against a pile of pillows in the bed, she ground out, 'Have you any idea what you've done?'

Harriet had always known how Clarissa viewed the marriage of Monty and Esther, and the reasons for her reluctance to the match; she did not consider them acceptable in-laws or, to be more precise, Theobald an acceptable member of her family. Harriet's own parents had made little attempt to hide their contempt for Theobald's lack of breeding, but as it had suited them to have their spinster daughter taken off their hands, they'd suffered him with aristocratic forbearance. Clarissa had done the same, but her barely concealed distaste had intimidated and often embarrassed Harriet in the past. Now that feeling was gone.

Harriet looked at the woman she'd never liked and saw her clearly for what she was, but then, as her gaze moved to Monty's young face and she saw the pain it contained, she moderated her reply. 'I'm sorry you feel that way, Clarissa. I was hoping you would try to understand, even if you couldn't forgive.'

'Understand?' Clarissa was beside herself. 'Oh, I "understand" perfectly. You encouraged the match, in order to get your mongrel married off into a noble family—'

'*Mother*.'

Clarissa swung round on Monty as he spoke, her face venomous. 'What else can you call her? Your supposedly wonderful wife? For goodness' sake, face the facts, Montgomery.'

'I don't want you talking about Esther in that way. This is not her fault.'

'Her fault or not, the situation is insupportable. You at least see that, don't you?'

When Monty didn't answer, merely staring at her miserably, Clarissa made a sound in her throat that could have meant anything, and again turned to Harriet. 'A divorce must be arranged, quickly and quietly. And if any news about the child gets out, Esther will say she had an affair with one of these American people, which resulted in a baby. Do you understand?'

Harriet's heart dropped like a stone. Staring at Monty, she said, 'Is that what you want?'

'Of course it is not what he wants; it's not what any of us would choose, but it is the lesser of two evils, and Monty sees that,' said Clarissa tightly.

Harriet glanced at Theobald, but his face could have been set in stone. And Hubert, as usual, was saying nothing and was doing as he was told. Appealing directly to Monty again, she said, 'But you love Esther, and she loves you, and the baby is yours – your *daughter*, Monty. Surely you are not going to abandon them both because of this? I cannot believe it of you.'

'You talk of not being able to believe it.' Clarissa was almost choking in her rage. 'You tricked my son, you tricked all of us; but I, for one, am not at all sure that Esther didn't know the full story.'

'Of course she didn't, Mother,' Monty protested. 'I've told you: Esther had no idea.'

'*You've* told me.' Clarissa's voice dripped scorn. 'And you expect me to put any store by your judgement after this?'

Harriet's voice shook, in spite of all her efforts to control it, as she said, 'Esther has always believed Theobald and I are her natural parents, Clarissa. Always.'

'But you are not, and that is the end of the matter. I will not have our bloodline diluted by this . . . this—'

'*Don't say another word.*'

No one had noticed Esther appearing in the doorway of the room, but now, as they stared at her white face and blazing eyes, it was clear she had overheard enough of the conversation to gather what was being said.

Harriet made a strangled sound in her throat, her hand instinctively reaching out, but Esther's gaze had moved to her husband, and it was to Monty that she said, 'You are in agreement with your mother? You want me and our child out of your life?'

'Esther . . . ' His voice trailed away.

'I see. Perhaps I should have known, after last night.'

'Esther, please don't look like that.' Monty's voice cracked. 'I do love you, that hasn't changed, but . . . '

'You don't want our daughter.'

'Perhaps if we arranged for the baby to be taken care of somewhere, in a different part of the country?' Monty was speaking wildly, his gaze flashing from one to another. 'We could say it was stillborn – something like that – and we could carry on together. No one would have to know.'

Again Esther interrupted him. 'And what of any future children?' she said with expressionless calm.

'There are ways to prevent that happening. You could have an operation, so we'd be sure there'd be no mistakes.'

'Please leave, Monty, and take your parents with you.'

'Esther . . . '

She faced him proudly, her head up and her eyes dark pools of pain in the chalk-white of her face. 'I don't want to see you again, ever.'

'You don't mean that.' And then, as Clarissa went to take his elbow, Monty shook his mother off, saying again, 'Esther, you don't mean that. I know you don't. We could adopt. You could still have a family, like we'd planned.'

'I don't think I have ever meant anything more in my life. And let me make myself plain. I don't want anything from you, Monty. Not a penny piece, all right? From this moment it is as though my daughter and I have died, because that is the way I will think of you from now on.' Rose had come up behind Esther as she had been speaking, the baby in her arms, and now Esther said, 'Mr Grant does not want to see the baby, Rose. I was mistaken. Take her back to my room.'

'Esther, wait.'

Ignoring Monty's agonized voice, Esther swept round and, pushing Rose ahead of her, shut the door behind them. For a moment all was quiet, and then Clarissa said tightly, 'It is for the best, Montgomery.'

'*For whom?*'

'Don't speak to me in that tone. I am not responsible for what has taken place over the last twenty-four hours.'

'She is your grandchild, Clarissa,' said Harriet, her voice low but penetrating, and then she shrank back against the pillows when it appeared that the other woman was about to spring on her, so great was her rage.

'If you are wise, you will not repeat that.' Clarissa breathed deeply, then continued, 'Hubert and I are not without influence, remember that.' Turning to her son and husband, she said coldly, 'There is nothing more that can be accomplished here today, so I suggest we take our leave.'

'Monty?' Harriet tried one last time. 'You will regret it, if you let Esther and the baby go. It's not too late. If you go to her now, you can make it right.'

He stared across the room at her, indecision clear in his face, and then, as his mother said sharply, 'Montgomery, did you hear me? We're leaving,' his eyes dropped, his shoulders slumped and he followed his parents out of the room.

Harriet sank back against the pillows once she was alone, the pain in her chest gnawing at her, as it was wont to do when she became upset or anxious. Guilt and remorse were weighing heavy, but she still couldn't believe that Monty wouldn't go to Esther. He loved her – she knew he loved her. This couldn't be the end. He would stand up to Clarissa; he had to.

When the door was thrust open some moments later, she thought it would be Monty come to say he had changed his mind, but it was Theobald who walked in, quietly locking the door behind him. He hadn't said a word the whole time Clarissa and the others had been in the room, and she hadn't seen him since the evening before, until he had brought them to see her. Now he stared at her, his heavy-jowled face mottled with the temper he was controlling, and still he didn't speak. It was Harriet who said, 'Have they gone? Has Monty gone?'

He didn't answer this. What he did say, and very softly, was, 'I could kill you for what you've done. They could ruin me, the Grants. Do you know that? They might not have much in the way of wealth, apart from that decaying estate of theirs, but who they know is invaluable to me. And now you've ruined everything. They'll never allow Monty to link his name with mine.'

She didn't plead with him or try to excuse her actions, for she could tell by his face it would be useless.

'Monty had already agreed to come in with me, after the war, and with him at my side all kinds of doors would open, but now you've made enemies of them.'

'Is that all that concerns you? What the Grants think?'

'Don't take that tack. Not after what you've done.' He moved closer, his eyes like two bullets as he ground his teeth. 'Useless, you've been, from day one. Dropping my sons before time one after another – nothing could thrive in that scrawny body of yours. Do you know what they'd do to a mare that couldn't breed? Shoot it, because it'd be no good to God or man. All I wanted was one son to bear my name, damn you.'

She was frightened now. There was murder in his maddened gaze. 'I knew how much you wanted a child, that's why I did what I did. We both knew there could be no more babies.'

'So it was all for me? A dutiful, loving wife giving her husband what he wanted?' He gave a bark of a laugh. 'Except that you've never been loving, have you, Harriet? In bed or out of it. Oh, I've known you've always despised me at heart, like your dear parents and the rest of them, but no one else was going to offer you marriage, were they? Not looking like you do. A dried-up stick at twenty-odd – that's what you were. I should have known, damn it. I should have seen what was in front of my eyes. A dockside whore as a wife would've been better than you.'

He had reached the bed, and as her hand fluttered to her chest, he stared down at her, seeing her fear. 'You've made a monkey out of me, presenting that half-breed bastard as mine, and there's not a man worth his salt who would blame me for what I'm about to do.'

Before she realized his intent, he had whipped the stack of pillows supporting her thin frame to one side so that she thudded flat on the bed, and as she opened her mouth to scream, he pressed one of the pillows over her face. She barely struggled, her worn-out heart seizing up almost immediately, but he kept it in place for some minutes, more for the satisfaction it gave him than for anything else.

After a while he removed the pillow and looked down at her. She looked peaceful, serene even, and he felt a moment's anger that she hadn't suffered; but then, he reasoned to himself, it was probably for the best. This way no one would assume anything other than that she had passed away in her sleep.

Methodically he arranged the pillows as they had been when he came into the room, and settled Harriet against them, smoothing her hair and placing her hands together on top of the counterpane. Then he walked across the room, unlocked the door and left the room without a backward glance.

PART THREE

Caleb

1944

Chapter Nine

In the fourteen months that had passed since Joy's birth, Esther had not once regretted returning to Yew Tree Farm the day after Harriet had been found dead in her bed. She would have liked to have stayed for the funeral, but in the circumstances that was impossible, as Theobald had made abundantly clear. She'd left the estate with Joy in her arms and in just the clothes she stood up in, and with Theobald's curses ringing in her ears.

She had arrived in Yorkshire not knowing if Farmer Holden and his wife would take her in, but there had been nowhere else to go and – heartsore, exhausted and at the end of herself – she had returned like a damaged fledgling to the nest where it had been safe. And there she had told her story to the farm's occupants, sitting in the kitchen while a blizzard raged fiercely outside and the wind howled and moaned. But inside there had been warmth and kindness and acceptance, from the five women at least. Farmer Holden had been a little stiff and taciturn, but his wife had clucked around Esther and the baby like a mother hen, and Priscilla, Beryl, Vera and Lydia – although shocked and amazed at the turn of events – had rallied round and, as one, supported their friend in her hour of need.

Inevitably there had been gossip among the folk in the nearby village, once they had seen Joy, but Esther refused to hide her baby away as though she was ashamed of her. She knew she had done nothing wrong. Foreign servicemen from all over the Empire might have arrived in the British Isles, but she had *not* been unfaithful to her husband and she wasn't going to act as though she had been. The people who mattered to her knew the truth; the others could – as Priscilla put it – take a running jump. But . . . it still hurt, as she had confided to her friend.

'Don't you dare let anyone make you feel bad,' Priscilla had said fiercely, her heart going out to Esther; she knew she had been so looking forward to the birth of her child and was deeply in love with her husband. 'None of this is of your doing, darling. You remember that. And Monty might come to his senses, when he has had time to think things through.'

Even as Priscilla said it, part of her was thinking that Monty wasn't good enough for Esther. If he couldn't support her now, when she needed him most, how did that bode for the future? Esther was still the same Esther, and Joy was the sweetest baby imaginable. Didn't he realize that all this had been as much a shock for Esther as for him? Not only that, but Esther had lost the woman she had always thought of as her mother, and was coping with that grief too. And he had simply walked away.

As Priscilla hugged her friend, she wished she could have ten minutes alone with Monty – preferably with a sledgehammer in her hands. And next in line would be his hateful mother.

'If you could have seen Monty's face when he looked at the baby,' Esther whispered brokenly. 'I don't understand it, Cilla. He knows she is his, and yet he let his mother dictate to him like that. He . . . he was ashamed of her, and me.'

Priscilla didn't understand it, either, but then she had never understood racial discrimination. She'd had a fight with her own father about it, before she had left to join the Land Army. They'd been having dinner and she had made a comment about Hitler's cruelty towards the Jews. Her father hadn't exactly condoned Hitler's prejudice, but he'd made a remark about there being two sides to every situation. During his time in India, he'd said, a daughter of one of their close friends had actually become 'close' to a young high-ranking Indian who was a Hindu. Of course her parents had been horrified when they had discovered the affair, and had her shipped off to her grandparents in England post-haste.

'Why horrified?' she'd asked her father.

'Because he was an Indian – a native,' her father had replied, as though she was dense. 'And of a different religion too. Same with the Jews. They should all be living in Israel.'

'What does the colour of his skin or his religion matter, if they loved each other?' she'd replied, starting an argument that had ended up rocking the house. Her father had ranted that if these were the sorts of ideas she had picked up at her private school, and at the finishing school in Switzerland that he had sent her to at great expense, then he regretted every penny; and she had fired back that he was no better than a Nazi. Worse, in fact, because at least the Nazis blatantly declared what they were. Of course she had always suspected how her parents felt, but it had never come out into the open before, possibly because she saw so little of them. A nanny and then boarding schools had seen to that.

Now, remembering all that, she said quietly, 'Esther, I don't understand how America can send their black GIs to fight alongside their white countrymen and yet deny they're equal, or how the colour of their skin makes some people think they are better than other human beings, but it happens. I confess I'd never really thought about such things before the war, so perhaps – if nothing else – it's good that it has stirred such issues up. Especially among flibbertigibbets like me. Maybe, after the war, the world's going to be more of a melting pot, because one thing is sure: it won't go back to how it was. In all sorts of ways.'

Esther had nodded. 'Maybe,' she said, with a little catch in her voice, adding, 'I miss my mother, and Rose. I'm not even sure what Rose thinks about everything. She's very set in her ways.'

And then, two weeks after Esther had arrived back in Yorkshire, Mrs Holden answered a knocking on the farmhouse door one afternoon, to find Rose standing on the doorstep. She'd come to find Miss Esther and the baby, Rose told the farmer's wife. Her late mistress had been generous to her over the years, and she had a nest egg put by that would support the three of them for a while. She had stayed just for the mistress's funeral, but then she had told Mr Wynford what she thought of him and had left, so she wouldn't be getting a reference from him. But that didn't matter, not as long as she and Miss Esther and the little one were together. Wicked, it was, how Miss Esther had been treated; she hadn't been able to sleep since it had happened. So saying, Rose had burst into tears, appearing so bereft that Mrs Holden had whisked her inside and made a pot of tea, over which the two women had chatted for some time.

The upshot of this was that Rose moved into the already crammed labourer's cottage with the girls and Joy, sleeping in the front room on a pallet bed that Mr Holden put in a corner, as the two bedrooms – one holding three single beds without an inch between them, where Lydia, Vera and Beryl slept; and the other, two single beds for Esther and Priscilla, along with Joy's cot – were chock-a-block already. It was Mrs Holden who had made it happen, declaring to her dubious husband that Rose's appearance was the best thing that could have happened. It meant Joy would have a nursemaid during the day when Esther was working, and Rose could lend a hand when required in the house and dairy; and heaven knew she needed help, Mrs Holden had finished darkly. Men had no idea what was involved in cooking and cleaning and washing, besides seeing to the dairy and the swill for the pigs and collecting eggs from the hens.

The farmer had been wise enough not to protest too hard, although he hadn't relished having yet another female about the place. A man's man, he'd known where he stood with his male workers before the war. Women were a different species. Not that he had any complaints about the Land Girls; he had to admit they worked like the dickens and tackled anything. They'd even taken the muck-spreading in their stride. The first time he'd told the girls to take the big, steaming heap of manure from a corner of the stable yard out to the fields by horse and cart and spread it on the land, he'd expected some reluctance, but they'd obeyed without protest and worked for hours on end. He knew from experience that it brought on searing backache and raw, aching muscles, but you wouldn't have known it, except that they were quieter than usual during the evening meal. No, he had no complaint about their work; he just wanted to get back to normal. That was all. Although what normal would be after this damned war was anyone's guess.

Nancy Holden had known exactly what her husband was thinking when she told him she wanted Rose to stay. He was a transparent individual at the best of times. But from the first moment she'd seen Rose standing on the doorstep, she had warmed to her. They were about the same age, which was nice, and she felt they could be friends.

For her part, Rose was delighted. She'd be looking after little Joy, which couldn't suit her better; and giving a hand to the farmer's wife, in return for bed and board, meant that her nest egg stayed intact. After an emotional reunion with Esther when they had both cried, Rose settled into life at the farm like a duck to water.

It had been balm to Esther's sore heart when Rose sought her out, and she had told herself that, with Rose understanding and supporting her, nothing else mattered.

But – and Esther would rather have walked on hot coals than admit this to a living soul – it hurt when people misjudged her and took satisfaction in making their feelings known. Because it was assumed she had slept with a black GI and had been 'caught out' in adultery, a certain type of man thought Esther was easy prey, and their female counterparts took pleasure in slighting her. It didn't help that her speech betrayed her as upper-class, either. She'd actually had one indignant Yorkshire matron accost her in the village shop and declare that with her 'advantages' she ought to know better, and set an example to those girls less fortunate than herself.

With British men feeling less than delirious about the GIs in their midst, along with the cartons of Lucky Strike and Camel cigarettes, nylon stockings, scented soap, chocolate and other luxuries that the American servicemen distributed to the local women with their natural and friendly charm, women who succumbed to the GIs were bitterly resented in some quarters.

American slang had swept the nation too, and even children – who'd learned of comic-book heroes such as Superman with his X-ray vision, and supercop Dick Tracy with his two-way wrist TV – were caught up in the bad feeling generated by the adults. Fathers and older brothers took umbrage at younger family members, who'd previously thrilled to the heroics of Arsenal or Tottenham footballers, renouncing their allegiance to all things British and gawping at the statistics of the B-17 Flying Fortress, with its bomb-sight so accurate that, it was claimed, it could drop a bomb on the Germans into a pickle-barrel from 20,000 feet; or saying to all and sundry that the American troop carriers – huge four-engined monoplanes – made British biplanes look like rubbish from the Science Museum.

Mostly, Esther maintained an aloof front against the spitefulness and criticism, but in the early days of it all, when the pain of Monty's rejection had been unbearable, she'd often cried herself to sleep. And she was a lioness where Joy was concerned, her overwhelming love for her beautiful healthy baby bringing out a protectiveness that was as fierce as it was passionate. And Joy *was* beautiful, and grew more so with every month that passed. The baby's eyes turned an amazing jade-green some weeks after her birth, and her brown curls had a golden tint to them. This, combined with her coffee-coloured skin and ready smile, made her enchanting. The mix of races in her genes had combined to produce a loveliness that was as unusual as it was striking, and even Farmer Holden had become Joy's devoted slave. On the days when it was warm enough to wheel her pram into the fields, so that Esther could have Joy with her while she worked, Esther would look at her child and marvel at how something so perfect could have come from her body.

And now it was the summer of 1944. In the last fourteen months Esther had relinquished the hopes and dreams she'd woven around Monty, mostly without even realizing it, and with their passing had come a healing of sorts, although she was still full of emotions that made sleep difficult some nights. She loved and missed Harriet; unashamedly loathed Theobald; and hated Clarissa. Her feelings weren't so clear-cut regarding Monty. Sometimes she felt she hated him, at other times she felt that a small semblance of love remained; but more often of late she felt nothing at all. It was as though he was dead to her, as she had maintained he would be that last day, when he and his parents had come to the house. From the way Clarissa had talked then, Esther had expected divorce papers to come her way at some point over the last few months, but there had been nothing.

At first, in her grief and rage, Esther had wanted to end the marriage immediately and cut all ties with the past. Now she felt that a piece of paper didn't really matter, one way or the other. She knew she would never marry again, or get close enough to a man that he could hurt her, as Monty had hurt her. How could the colour of their baby's skin, or the fact that her own father must have been black, matter so much to Monty? But it had. And she soon came to realize that Monty wasn't alone in his prejudice. Whenever she left the farm with Joy there were subtle reminders of it, but it had the effect of rousing her fighting spirit and putting iron in her backbone. She wasn't ashamed of who she was, she told herself many nights as she looked into the old spotted mirror in the cottage, and she wouldn't let anyone else make her so. As Priscilla said, it was ignorance and fear of the pack mentality at something (or someone) different that bred intolerance and discrimination – the parents of cruelty and hatred.

Dear Priscilla. Esther glanced at her friend, who had just returned from the village with the daily newspaper. For days everyone had been rejoicing because the Red Army had swept the Germans out of the Crimea, and Allied forces had broken the enemy hold in Italy, and Rome had been liberated. Apparently a short, low-key announcement from General Eisenhower's HQ had followed, telling the world that the long-awaited invasion of Europe by the Allies had begun. Now it appeared that RAF bombers had pounded the German batteries along the French coast two nights ago, and at daybreak they had been joined by the US Eighth Air Force, along with naval forces, in the land and air offensive.

'They're saying the war could be over by Christmas,' Priscilla informed everyone sitting around the farmhouse's huge kitchen table, where they were eating their evening meal.

'Do they indeed,' said Farmer Holden morosely. 'And of course "they" are always right, aren't they?'

The women looked at each other. The farmer had been like a bear with a sore head for a while, mainly due to the number of soldiers and their equipment moving southwards for the build-up to the D-Day landings that were now taking place. It would have taken a brave individual to point out to him that it was southern England that had borne the brunt of the move. The country roads in that part of the country had become dedicated convoy routes, the local woods crawling with soldiers who moved silently under the cover of trees like swarms of jungle ants. But the farmer had lost a portion of his land to the army the year before, and hadn't forgiven the powers that be. New airfields, troop camps and munitions factories were deliberately being placed in rural areas, to avoid the towns and cities that were more likely to be a target of the Luftwaffe, but Farmer Holden refused to see the sense of this.

Esther stifled a sigh. They had been working a twelve-hour day in the fields and she was exhausted; the long June days and short nights were a mixed blessing. On fine days it was good to be out in the sunshine after the harsh winter, but on chilly or rainy days, when she couldn't have Joy with her and Rose took care of the baby while she worked, she hardly saw her daughter. She trusted Rose with her precious baby, and knew that Joy was happy with Rose and the farmer's wife, but as the little girl was often tucked up in bed and fast asleep by the time she came in from the fields, there could be days on end when they were parted.

Overall, though, Esther knew she was lucky at the way things had worked out. She felt she would never be able to repay the kindness shown to her by these simple, good folk, and she would be forever grateful to the farmer and his wife for taking her in without demur, when she had arrived back at the farm like little orphan Annie; and then for welcoming Rose later too.

She finished Mrs Holden's delicious steak-and-kidney pie quickly. It was her turn to settle the calves down for the night in the calf-pens. It was her favourite job. The farmer was building up his dairy herd, and four days after they were born – when the cow's yellow colostrum turned into ordinary saleable milk – the calves were removed from their mothers, which went back into the herd for normal milking in the parlour. The very young, small calves were transferred to the calf-house, an airy barn in one corner of the farmyard, in which individual pens were made for them from straw bales, giving them a snug home of their own in which to recover from the shock of being separated from their mothers.

Esther had found the sight of the newborn calves hidden away in their pens distressing when she had first come to the farm, but had felt better about the process when Mrs Holden had taken the time to explain that in the wild it was natural for the calves to 'lie up', hidden in undergrowth or long grass, while the cows returned to the herd to graze, visiting at intervals to suckle their babies. In the calf-house they were suckled by a human-held bottle, but never seemed to mind the process, guzzling away with their doe-eyes closing in ecstasy every so often. The next stage was teaching them to drink their milk from a bucket, and this was Esther's job that night. She had learned the hard way that the calves were no respecters of decorum, and it needed a firm hand to hold the bucket when they nuzzled their heads into the warm frothy milk.

All too soon, as they grew a little older, the calves would be put into larger pens to mingle in groups of the same age, and to learn to accept hay and concentrates instead of milk. This was the start of their very own little herd and they'd form bonds within the group for the rest of their lives, even when they all became part of the larger dairy herd. Esther wasn't alone in feeling sad when the calves became more independent; the cosy times in the old barn, with the calves' milky breath and warm little bodies snuggled close, were magical; and magical moments didn't come too often amid the hard physical work and exhausting routine.

They weren't supposed to have favourites among the calves, or to become attached to any of the farm animals, come to that. Farmer Holden had been very specific about that, when they had come to the farm as Land Girls, saying it was part of the toughening-up process that was necessary for them to work as they were expected to. But as Esther entered the barn that night she made straight for one particular pen, which housed a dear little calf she had secretly named Bambi, because of her large, seemingly liquid eyes. All the calves were endearingly sweet, but Bambi had almost died at birth and needed extra care and had become a firm favourite with all the girls. Once she was sitting in the pen and Bambi was slurping away, she thought about the news Priscilla had read out that evening. The Normandy operation had been heralded a success so far, and Winston Churchill had revealed that Allied forces had penetrated several miles inland, the resistance of the enemy batteries being greatly weakened by the bombing from war planes and ships. Was Monty in the carnage that must be happening – however the politicians dressed it up?

Esther bit her lip, closing her eyes for a moment. She normally kept all such thoughts under lock and key, but tonight she was particularly tired, the barn was warm and quiet, and the sight of Bambi guzzling her milk out of the bucket on her small knock-kneed legs was poignant.

Would she care very much if she received news that Monty had been killed or injured? It was a question she had asked herself more than once, and she didn't know the answer. He had written to her twice, soon after she had returned to the farm following Joy's birth, obviously assuming that she might seek solace there. She'd gazed at his distinctive black scrawl on the envelopes, her stomach doing cartwheels, and both times had returned the letters unopened, writing 'Gone Away' in the left-hand corner. Whether he'd believed she was elsewhere, she didn't know. Certainly he hadn't attempted to come to the farm to find out, and as the days and weeks and months had gone by, she had told herself she didn't care. He had made his choice, and that was that.

Nevertheless, at odd moments when her guard was down, she wondered about Monty; whether he was dead or alive or injured. She'd accepted that she was probably no longer officially his next of kin. Clarissa would no doubt have seen to that and, with his permission, told the authorities it was his parents who must be informed, if the worst happened. There was no way of knowing if she was right in her assumption, not without making enquiries herself, which she was loath to do.

Once Bambi was settled for the night, Esther moved on to the remaining calves, and she was just leaving the barn when Priscilla came bounding across the yard. 'Come on. I thought you had fallen asleep in there. You haven't forgotten the dance, have you? We're all ready, and there's some hot water for you, and a bar of my lovely oil-of-roses soap to wash away the smell of the farmyard.'

Esther groaned inwardly. The other girls – and especially Priscilla – seemed to have decided that it was time she was 'taken out of herself', as they put it; and the only way, according to them, was to dip her toe in the limited social scene of the village, courtesy of the local hop. When she had declared it was the last thing she felt like doing, she'd met united protest. Even Rose had added her two penn'orth.

'Really, Est,' Vera had drawled, 'you can't carry on being a hermit forever.'

'I agree,' Lydia had put in. 'Do you think Monty is starving himself of female company? He'll be at it like a rabbit.'

'And really, when all's said and done, the village dance isn't exactly a den of iniquity, now is it?' Beryl had said earnestly. 'It's perfectly respectable, Esther.'

'More's the pity,' Priscilla had grinned, her face white with scented night-cream, a gift from the GIs. They had all been in the sitting room of the cottage in their pyjamas, sipping the hot milky cocoa that Mrs Holden always brought over in a big jug at bedtime. 'I'm just *dying* for a smidgen of iniquity now and again, darling. A little sinfulness is so delicious.'

'You're sinful enough for the rest of them put together,' Rose had said thinly. She didn't altogether approve of Priscilla.

'But bad girls have all the fun, sweetie,' Priscilla had returned, only half-joking, 'and who knows what the future will bring? This wretched war might go on for years yet, and where will all the young men be at the end of it? Where will *we* be? Those poor people at Midsummer's Farm didn't expect to have a couple of Hitler's bombs land on them, did they? And that was only a few miles away, as the crow flies. Nothing is certain now, except the moment in which you live, and I don't intend to waste my moments. No one should, and that includes you, Esther.'

Priscilla had a point, they'd all acceded, and Esther had found herself agreeing to accompany the others to the very next dance. Which was tonight. Weakly she said, 'I'd forgotten the dance was tonight, and I'm shattered, Cilla. All I want is my bed. I'll come next time, I promise.'

'No doing, sweetie. Your promises regarding this particular enterprise are like Mrs Holden's pie-crusts – made to be broken. Rose is listening out for Joy, not that your angel child ever stirs anyway. And you are coming out with us, to have some fun. The hours we work, we deserve it. Admittedly the old village hall isn't exactly Covent Garden Opera House' – this had been converted into a ballroom, to satisfy the desire of London's civilian war-workers and the men and girls on leave from the forces to dance the night away, much to Priscilla's envy – 'but we'll make the best of what we have, in true British spirit. There's a band tonight too, so hopefully that'll mean a good turnout.'

It would also mean a heightened possibility of bickering between the GIs and local lads, along with the injured British soldiers, who were recovering from their war wounds in an army convalescent home just outside the village. It had been a grand house before the war, but the owner, a retired colonel, had been happy to 'do his bit' for King and country.

Esther wrinkled her nose at her friend. 'I don't know.'

'Well, I do. And tonight I'm not taking "No" for an answer, as the vicar said to the chorus girl.'

Esther had to laugh. Priscilla was full of outrageous quips and was totally irreverent. She'd thought it a great compliment when one of her GIs had called her a 'sassy broad' and had gone round for days repeating it to anyone who'd listen.

'Oh, come on, Est,' Priscilla said with beguiling charm. 'It's such a beautiful evening. Don't waste it going to bed early. We won't have long there as it is – it's already nearly eight o'clock – but at least we can have a dance and a couple of glasses of Mr Sheldon's home-made wine.'

Mr Sheldon was the local butcher, but his passion was his wine-making, as his constantly flushed face and bright red nose testified to. He always provided a good number of bottles for the monthly village dance, the proceeds of which went to the church-roof restoration fund; and be it rhubarb, elderflower, cherry or one of the other varieties that Mr Sheldon had stocked from floor to ceiling in his cellar, they all had a kick like a mule. Cider and home-made beer were also sold, but not spirits – by order of the WI, which hosted the events and maintained that strong liquor could cause 'problems', with so many young people gathered together. All the girls agreed that a couple of glasses of Mr Sheldon's wine were more lethal by far than a bottle of gin!

'Come and wash. The others are waiting.' Priscilla took the decision out of Esther's hands, pulling her across the yard and then standing over her while she got ready. Priscilla looked at her friend fondly, once she was dressed. Esther was lovely, inside and out, she thought, and she was determined not to let her hide herself away forever. She was too young to be a hermit.

Once the girls were walking into the village, Esther had to admit it was good to be out on such a mellow summer's evening, dressed up in her glad rags for once. She tended to wear her brown breeches and cotton blouses from morning till night, and it never seemed worth changing before she washed and fell into bed after each exhausting day. Tonight, though, she felt young and almost carefree as she listened to the others chatter and rib each other, all of them giggling at Priscilla's awful jokes.

The essence of summer saturated the leaf-bound lane they were walking down. Spring-sown crops grew in the fields on either side of the lane, ears of barley and corn thrusting their various shades of lime-green upon a lush landscape, along with the sweet perfume of honeysuckle and nettle flowers, and the creamy-white blooms of dogwood and elder. Esther found herself breathing it all in in great gulps, as though she didn't work out in the open every day. But somehow it was different tonight.

She glanced at Priscilla walking beside her. The rule 'Make Do and Mend' had been the order of the day since the war began, and clothing had been rationed since the summer of 1941 on a points system: in principle, it allowed people to buy one complete new outfit a year. Much to many girls' dismay, a wartime 'Utility Look' was the main emphasis, with sensible, flat-heeled shoes and square-shouldered jackets imitating the cut of uniforms. This all seemed to have passed Priscilla by. She had arrived at the farm with two suitcases full of clothes – all beautiful creations by Paris designers, the international centre of haute couture. And, as the war had progressed, she had declared that she saw no reason to become what she termed 'frumpy'. Consequently she generously shared her original clothes with the other girls, and they had lovely evenings cutting and altering them to fit in with the current mode, but relishing the wonderful material and flamboyant colours that set them apart from wartime austerity.

With women's magazines packed with tips on how to turn old lace curtains into a 'dashing little bolero' and the like, the girls weren't short of ideas, and when Beryl returned from her one week's annual leave with a parcel of parachute silk that her aunty had given her, they made the most of the unexpected bonus.

Priscilla, in particular, had the knack of wearing anything and making it look stylish. Whether this was a result of her year at an expensive Swiss finishing school just before war was declared, the others didn't know, but they had many hilarious evenings with Priscilla showing them how to walk so that their hips swung and their backs were straight, their chins up as they took turns sashaying up and down the small cottage sitting room. Times that Esther had desperately needed.

Where would she have been, and what would she have done, without Priscilla and the others standing by her, when Monty cast her off so arbitrarily? Esther asked herself, slipping her arm through that of her friend as they walked on. If it had been peacetime and she hadn't had the bolthole of Yew Tree Farm, she would have gone mad with the torture of her thoughts in those first few weeks.

But – she took a deep breath – she *had* had her friends, and dear Rose too; and most of all she'd had Joy, her wonderful, darling, precious Joy, and she was worth every tear and dark time she'd been through. Esther had never expected motherhood to be such a passionate, all-consuming thing. She had loved her daughter from the first moment she had looked into her dear little face, and it made any other kind of love – even the feeling she'd had for Monty – pale into insignificance. So perhaps that meant she had never loved him as she thought she had? She didn't know, but it didn't matter anyway. She had begun a new life, and the past was ashes.

As they drew nearer to the village, her stomach began to flutter with apprehension, despite telling herself that she was being silly. If she was being truthful, though, she knew it wasn't because of tiredness or any of the other excuses she made regularly to Priscilla, in an attempt to avoid accompanying the others to the dances. She'd seen how the self-righteous matrons manning the food and drink tables looked at her, on the couple of occasions she'd weakened and gone with them, along with some of the local girls and lads. She'd even overheard one of the white GIs muttering something about 'the one who did the dirty on her pilot', when he'd nudged his cronies as she'd walked by.

It had upset her, she admitted reluctantly, in spite of telling herself that she didn't have to justify anything to anyone. The folk who mattered to her knew the truth, and if the rest of the world believed she'd had an affair with a black GI whilst her husband was away fighting, then there was little she could do about it. And, surprisingly, it was the white GIs who seemed most upset, which she found difficult to understand. They were fighting with their black countrymen against a common enemy, and yet most of them were fierce about keeping the black GIs 'in their place', as they put it. It was clear they took it as a personal insult when local women danced and socialized with the black GIs, and Priscilla had been taken to task more than once because of it. Her friend had told her that there were fights, both within the GIs' camp and outside, about the issue of black GIs fraternizing with white women.

For the first time in her sheltered life, Esther had been forced to recognize that life was full of cruel contradictions. Since she had become aware of her beginnings, she had taken an interest in the history of America – hitherto, merely another country across the ocean. And the more she had delved, the more things had puzzled her.

Men, women and children from African countries had been snatched from their homes and taken as slaves to America, under appalling conditions; in some cases being treated worse than their owners treated their animals. And yet it was the white GIs – if they were representative of their country as a whole – who were eaten up with hatred and resentment. And of course Britain had her own record of inhumanity to man. Why had she never thought about such things before?

Because it had not directly impinged on *her*, Esther Wynford: daughter of wealthy parents, with a privileged and comfortable lifestyle to match. And, but for the wake-up call that Joy's birth had brought about, she would still be living with her eyes closed to a period of the past that was shameful. And yet her mother had braved her family's wrath, because she had loved her Michael; maybe she had hoped her family would accept him, because they cared about her and her happiness? Or perhaps she had loved him in such a way that nothing else mattered except that they were together? She didn't know. Esther sighed softly. There was so much she didn't know, and at times she ached with wondering.

'Stop daydreaming.' They had reached the village hall and Priscilla turned to Esther, smoothing a stray curl from her friend's forehead in much the same way a fussy mother might, before a child went to a party. 'You're going to enjoy yourself tonight, sweetie. Okay?' As the others went inside, Priscilla added softly, 'Show the world you don't care what they think. They're nothing, these narrow-minded yokels, and the white GIs are even worse. They scorn any colour but their own.'

Esther knew Priscilla was trying to be encouraging and she appreciated her friend's loyalty, but she felt intimidated about entering the hall and was angry with herself for feeling that way. She *hadn't* been unfaithful to Monty; but even if she had, it was no one's business but her own. But she knew she was further condemned in most folk's eyes because her baby was mixed-race, and that was hateful. 'I'm not ashamed of who I am, Cilla, and certainly not of Joy, but who do people think they are, to sit as judge and jury? And why do some white folk think they are superior just because of the colour of their skin? I want to punch them – that's how I feel half the time. I'm me, that's all. And Joy is who she is. Why isn't that enough for other people?'

Priscilla took her hand. 'It is enough, sweetie.'

'Not for a good portion of people inside this hall.'

'Then a good portion of people inside this hall are wrong – it's as simple as that.'

The two girls stared at each other for a moment or two, and then Esther gave a reluctant smile. It wasn't simple at all, they both knew that, but either she buckled under the weight of animosity and criticism, or she took the world by the throat and fought back. She might not know who her parents were – oh, she had two names and a little information about the girl who had given birth to her, and she knew her father must have been black, but what was that in the overall scheme of things? Hardly anything. She didn't know what they were like, as flesh-and-blood people; their natures and personalities; even what they looked like, or whether they were still alive. But she had to live with that. She had Joy. Together they would create their own life.

'So, we're going in. Right?' Priscilla grinned at her.

'Right.' And together they walked into the music and clamour of the village-hall dance.

Chapter Ten

Caleb McGuigan had no wish to be where he was, sitting like an old flame at a wedding, as he put it to himself. Why the blazes he'd allowed Kenny to persuade him to come along to this damned dance he didn't know; he must have been mad. He glanced at his pal, who was sitting at the side of him supping at his glass of beer, and then at the others from the convalescent home gathered around the table. What a motley crew; they'd have a job to put one good body together from the lot of us, he thought with dark humour. There was poor old Kenny, his hands and face burned so badly even his dear old mam wouldn't recognize him; and Wilf and Art, both missing an arm, and Art with a ton of shrapnel still lodged in his chest; Harold minus an ear and an eye, and half his face; and himself . . . He glanced down at the empty trouser leg where his left leg used to be. And him at a dance. A dance!

Kenny had said that at least it got them out of reach of Matron Griffiths for a while, but he'd rather have sat in the grounds of the home with a glass of the lukewarm ginger beer that didn't have a drop of alcohol in it, but which was all the doctors allowed. He hated being a recipient of veiled, pitying glances or, in Kenny's and Harold's cases, shock and even horror, from those who were no good at hiding their feelings. At least Matron Griffiths and her nurses – bossy and tyrannical as they could be at times – treated them like ordinary men, not some poor excuse for such.

'We'll be for it, when we get back,' said Kenny with a great deal of satisfaction. They hadn't asked permission to come to the dance, knowing it would be refused, in a couple of their cases. The five of them shared a dormitory in what had been one of the ten bedrooms of the house, and had decided weeks ago that it was all for one and one for all – hence their absconding from the grounds of the home when they were supposed to be taking the evening air. As Kenny (the instigator of the escapade and the bane of Matron Griffiths's life) had said, the evening air smelled so much better when the fumes of beer accompanied it. None of them had argued. If Kenny fancied a beer, then they were up for it; he'd recently undergone several operations to graft a new nose onto what was left of his face, and his hands were a work-in-progress too, but none of them had ever heard him complain. Caleb knew each of the lads would have crawled on their hands and knees to the village hall, if necessary, to get Kenny his pint.

'Aye, well, just say "Yes, Matron" and "No, Matron"

for once,' Caleb warned drily. 'She'll be spitting bricks as it is, without you getting her going.'

'Believe me, the last thing I want to do is to get Matron going,' returned Kenny with a lascivious leer. 'Now if it was that little Welsh nurse, the one with the come-to-bed eyes and wiggle, that'd be a different kettle of fish.'

'In your dreams, matey,' said Art. 'She's engaged to a major, no less, and rumour has it he's built like a brick outhouse. You wouldn't want to tangle with him.'

'She'd be worth it. Have you seen the way she moves her hips? She knows a thing or two.'

'And one of them is how to keep randy so-an'-sos like you at arm's length . . . '

Caleb swigged at his glass of beer, his mind only half on the banter. Two girls had just walked in the door. One of them he'd seen before, a tall, blonde piece who came regularly with some other girls; but the second was new to him. He expelled his breath in a silent whistle. She was something else too: a looker, if ever he saw one. He found he couldn't take his eyes off her.

He realized his face must have given him away when Harold leaned his way and murmured, 'Your tongue's hanging out, lad, but you can forget about that one. Rumour has it she was married to a pilot, but when they had a happy event, it turned out not to be quite so happy, if you get my meaning.'

Caleb's wrinkled brow was the answer.

'The baby wasn't his. She'd been messing about with one of the black GIs.'

Caleb stared at his friend. He had been born deep in the heart of Sunderland's Monkwearmouth near the docks, and one of the things that had made him want to get out of the grids of terraced streets and back alleys was the knowledge that you couldn't blow your nose without the whole neighbourhood knowing about it. Everyone knew everyone else's business, and what they didn't know, they would make up – always to the detriment of the unfortunate target of gossip. The streets were like one big family, but a dysfunctional family. One that could be as cruel as it could be kind; as unforgiving with its own as with any stranger who attempted to penetrate the unspoken codes and morals. He'd hated the narrow-mindedness, the poverty, the dirt and the blind acceptance of most people that they couldn't change their lot. When he had joined the army a couple of years before war had been declared, his girlfriend of the time had called him an upstart, when he'd made the mistake of telling her why. And maybe he *was* an upstart. One thing was for sure: he'd discovered that, regardless of geography, people were the same the whole world over. And gossip spread quicker in this village than a dose of salts.

Quietly he said, 'When you say rumour?'

'Well, she's got a kid that's not white. Everyone knows that.'

'I didn't.'

Harold could have said that might be because Caleb

rarely left the grounds of the home and was probably one of the most unsociable so-an'-sos he'd ever come across, but he didn't. He was a pal, and everyone got through what the war had thrown at them in their own way. Instead, he took a swig of his beer, before shrugging. 'It's common knowledge – take my word for it. Don't see, myself, what the women see in these GIs.'

'You mean besides the stockings and cigarettes and other luxuries, and the fact they get paid four times as much as us?'

Harold grinned. 'Yeah, besides that.'

Caleb smiled briefly, before his eyes returned to the slim figure across the room. Even with two legs, he would never have had the nerve to approach someone like her. But now . . . He reached for his glass. What would she want – what would any girl want? – with a cripple, and one who still had a couple of operations in store, according to Dr Walton, the last time he'd seen him: 'We need to poke about for more of that shrapnel in your left side, old man, but not till you're stronger. It'll wait.'

The doctor's words came back to him, and for a moment Caleb could see the stocky little man who resembled nothing so much as a goblin, with his extra-large ears and short legs. But he was a great surgeon; more than that, he had the human touch with his patients, which was as good as a shot of morphia on occasion. Caleb knew Dr Walton had fought to save his other leg and, but for the doctor's expertise and to some extent his stubbornness, he'd be minus both of them; but he still

found the loss unbearable on the bad days. Which –
when he looked at Kenny and Harold – he felt ashamed
about. Kenny's girlfriend had fainted clean away when
she had come to see him, and two weeks later he'd
received a 'Dear John' letter. His friend hadn't mentioned
her from that day on, although they'd been planning to
get married in the autumn.

The band was striking up another tune, and inevitably
it was mostly GIs who took to the floor with their female
partners, jitterbugging around the wooden floor of the
hall with such enthusiasm that it vibrated under their feet.
After an hour of looking at the laughing Americans in
their snazzy uniforms enjoying themselves, Caleb knew he
couldn't stand a minute more, without doing something
he'd regret. Muttering that he needed some air, he hauled
himself up on his crutches and shambled out of the
hall, nearly going headlong when one of the crutches slid
under a chair leg and propelled him forward in an undig-
nified scramble. Swearing profusely under his breath, he
reached the door and stepped thankfully outside, away
from the noise and underlying smell of the GIs' aftershave
and their girlfriends' perfume, courtesy of Mother America. He stood for a moment on the top step of the village
hall, and then manoeuvred himself down the half-dozen
wooden slats and onto the surrounding grass.

He suddenly felt desperately tired, with an exhaustion
similar to the one he'd experienced the first few weeks
after being injured, when his life had hung in the balance
for a while. He'd sobbed during the long hours of the

night, once the danger was past, wishing he had slipped away into oblivion. Exactly what his tears had been for, he hadn't known himself. Perhaps for the death of his companions, who had ended up as body parts scattered around him, after the shell had scored a direct hit on their trench; or from self-pity; or even because he was now isolated, cut off from everything he knew. It was only when Dr Walton had happened along one night and had sat and chatted to Caleb for a bit that he had begun to feel more himself.

His tears were a natural reaction to the strain of years of fighting, the doctor had explained, along with the violent shock to his system after sustaining such extensive injuries. It happened in the majority of cases, although – the good doctor had smiled ruefully – men being men, and ever conscious of the British stiff upper lip, it wasn't talked about.

He didn't know if Dr Walton had been speaking the truth or merely being kind, but it had helped, both at the time and in the repetitious setbacks that had accompanied his recovery. If nothing else, he wasn't going doolally, like some of the poor devils he'd seen. The fear of going down that road – of losing his mind – had been as bad as what had actually happened to him.

The warm June sun had sunk below the horizon, and dusk had settled since they had been in the hall. Now, as he stood in the lengthening shadows, the frail, dark forms of bats swooped over his head in the half-light, searching for insects. Despite knowing that the creatures' reputation for getting tangled in hair was a fallacy, Caleb found himself ducking as one came particularly close, and the next moment he had sprawled full-length on the ground, as his crutches slipped away from him.

Cursing himself, and Hitler and the Luftwaffe pilot who had dropped the bomb that had nearly done for him, Caleb didn't notice the dark figure emerging from behind a nearby oak tree, until a tentative voice said, 'Are you all right?'

He peered up into the beautiful young face of the girl he had been staring at most of the evening and, conscious that his language had been ripe, to say the least, he groaned inwardly. His next thought was how he must look, spread out like a beached whale at her feet. 'I'm fine,' he muttered inanely.

His humiliation and embarrassment increased when she retrieved his crutches, saying, 'Let me help you up.'

'I said I'm fine.' It was curt and he knew it, but he wanted nothing more than for her to disappear. Pulling himself into a sitting position, he added, 'I'm sorry, but I am all right, really. I wanted some time by myself, that's all.'

She didn't take the hint. Instead she plumped herself down on the grass beside him. 'I know what you mean,' she said softly. 'It's too stuffy in there, isn't it? Suffocating.'

Had she noticed him watching her? Worse, did she think he had followed her out here hoping to strike up a conversation? Did she feel sorry for him? His thoughts tied his tongue and made colour flood his neck and face.

'I'm Esther,' she said quietly after a few moments.

'Caleb. Caleb McGuigan.'

'You're one of the men from the big house outside the village, aren't you?'

'You can call it what it is: a dumping ground for the crippled flotsam and jetsam the war spits out.' He hadn't meant to say it, especially not in the tone of voice he'd used. He hadn't even been aware he thought of the home in that way.

She was still for a moment. Then, instead of words of encouragement or fatuous praise regarding bravery, or any of the other platitudes that were regularly meted out, she said quietly, 'If that is how you think of yourself and your friends, I'm sorry.'

He shifted uncomfortably, aware that he was being a pillock, as his pals would have put it. But, painfully conscious of his empty trouser leg, the McGuigan mulishness kicked in. 'What other way is there to think?'

'That, but for you and your friends and the rest of our boys, our country would now be occupied by a murderous madman.'

Well, that had put him in his place, hadn't it? Mortified to the depths of his being, Caleb cleared his throat. 'You're right, and I apologize. I'm not normally such bad company.'

'No need to apologize.' Her voice was a cut above and without an accent, so it surprised him when she said,

'You must be from the north, like me. I used to live near Chester-le-Street. Do you know it?'

'Aye, I know it. Me an' some pals used to go for bike rides that way on a Sunday afternoon. I remember the viaduct at the north end of the town. Massive great thing, with eleven arches. I'm from Sunderland, the north side of the river.'

'My mother and I used to shop in Sunderland's town centre sometimes. We'd normally finish up having a cream tea at Binns.'

'Not any more, you won't. It's a burnt-out shell.'

'Really? I didn't know.'

'Aye, the town's been hit hard. The Winter Gardens copped it, along with plenty of factories and shipyards, and some streets have been all but flattened. Near the docks, you see.' It struck Caleb that, for the first time since he had been injured, he was having a normal conversation with a female other than the nurses. Sitting as they were in the shadowed night, it didn't seem difficult, and suddenly he wanted it to go on. 'Have you been back home recently?' Even as he said it, he remembered what Harold had intimated and realized it might be a touchy subject.

When she did not answer immediately, he purposely didn't look at her, his fingers idly plucking at the grass as he mentally kicked himself. Then she said, 'No, not recently', and he breathed again. It was a few moments before the silence was broken once more, and it was Esther who murmured, 'On a night like this you can almost forget there's a war going on. Do you think the men who start wars – like Hitler and the rest of them – ever sit quietly on a warm summer's evening listening to the birds at twilight, and drinking in the scent of flowers as the stars come out?'

He stole a glance at the lovely profile. The sadness in her voice was reflected in her face. 'Do you?' he asked softly.

She shook her head. 'No, I don't.'

'Nor do I. My mother always says if the world was made up only of women, there would be no wars, because mothers think differently. It's men's egos that's the trouble, she says.'

'She's right.'

'Up to a point. As I said to her, if the world consisted only of women, there'd be no mothers anyway, unless by divine intervention.'

His attempt to lighten the atmosphere was rewarded by a soft giggle. 'There speaks the practical male. But I know what your mother means.'

'Aye, so do I, but I'd never let on.'

'You love her very much, don't you.' It was a statement, not a question.

'Aye, course I do. She's my mam. I dare say you feel the same way about yours.'

'Yes, I did.'

'Oh, I'm sorry, is she . . . ?'

'She died just after my daughter was born. You know

I have a daughter?' And then, before he could reply, 'But of course you do – everyone does.'

For the first time he sensed bitterness. Mildly he said, 'Don't tell me you let gossip bother you; not if you're from the north. It's in our blood, isn't it?'

Esther laughed in spite of herself. He was nice. The faint scent of freshly mown grass drifted on the warm night breeze, tinged with the sharper smell of wood-smoke. After a minute or two of sitting in a silence that, strangely, was not uncomfortable, she murmured, 'Some-one's had a bonfire.' And then, before he could speak, she added, 'It's not true. What they say about me.' She didn't know why she'd said it; she'd had no intention of doing so, but suddenly the words had come out of her mouth.

His voice was studiedly expressionless. 'Gossip's rarely true, I've found.'

'In my case, I suppose I can see why people would jump to the wrong conclusion.'

'Listen, you don't have to explain anything to me, or anyone else if it comes to it. Your life is your own affair.'

'I know – that's what I've been telling myself since Joy was born. Sometimes it helps and sometimes it doesn't.'

Her tone conveyed a deep pain, and Caleb didn't know what to say to help her. Carefully he felt his way. 'If you want to talk about it, that's fine. It will go no further. If you don't want to, that's fine too. It's up to you.'

Esther closed her eyes and swallowed. Why it should matter that this stranger knew the truth was beyond her, but it did matter. Perhaps it was because he *was* a stranger? Or maybe it was time she told someone, other than those at the farm, the truth? A kind of test, to gauge people's reactions? Which was silly, because ten to one she wouldn't like the outcome. She didn't want to become cynical, but she had found she didn't like the human race much at all these days.

The band had struck up 'Boogie Woogie Bugle Boy' inside the hall and, along with the music, there were shouts and whoops of laughter. Clearly the dance was going with a bang. And yet, out here in the quiet darkness, it was like a little oasis. She felt she could trust this big, quiet man sitting beside her, but common sense told her that she didn't know him from Adam. Nevertheless . . .

Softly – so softly Caleb had to lower his head to hear her – Esther murmured, 'My daughter *is* my husband's child. I've never been with anyone else but Monty, so when she was born and it was obvious she was mixed-race, it . . . it was a shock. For everyone. It was then that my mother told us the truth.'

Caleb didn't have a clue what she meant. 'The truth?'

'About the circumstances of my own birth. It was like this . . . '

As he listened to the unfolding story – a story that was amazing, even fantastic, but which he didn't doubt was true – Caleb knew he was falling in love with her. Before this night he hadn't believed in the sort of love the poets and la-di-da intellectuals wrote about. Lust he understood, and he'd had his share of sexual encounters since the time he'd taken Mary-Ann Sprackett behind the bike sheds when they were both fourteen, and emerged half an hour later with a big grin on his face. He'd been tall and broad-shouldered even then, and he'd found as he got older that women liked him. He'd be the first to admit he was no oil painting, and he certainly didn't have the gift of the gab like some of his pals, but he'd never had a problem securing the woman of his choice. And there'd been several during his twenty-five years of life. But this one was different.

He said nothing for a moment or two when she finished speaking. Then he spoke as softly as she had done. 'Your husband must be the biggest fool since Adam, but then you know that, right?'

She hadn't known what to expect. Having prepared herself for the worst, relief brought tears pricking at the back of her eyes. Grateful for the darkness, she said weakly, 'I think his mother influenced him.'

'Then he's a weak fool, to boot.'

'Perhaps, but I've come to understand that for some people it matters. Colour, I mean.'

He wanted to deny it, to tell her she was imagining things. But he'd never been much of a liar, and she was right. For some folk it did matter. He remembered when one of the lassies in his street had started walking out with a lad from the Arab quarter in the East End, and the furore it had caused. Her da and brothers had waylaid the individual and knocked ten bells out of him; the lad had nearly died and was in the infirmary for weeks. The upshot of their interfering was that the lass had married the lad as soon as he was out; but when she had come to visit her mam a few weeks later, the neighbours had thrown dog-muck at her and told her to keep away. That had been over fifteen years ago, when he was nowt but a nipper, but he'd never forgotten the barbarity of the way hitherto ordinary folk had rounded on the girl. He'd gone to his mam and told her what had happened and he'd received his second shock that day, because in his mind she had sided with the neighbours, when she'd said it was understandable. When he'd protested, she'd sat him down and told him it was best for like to keep to like. No good came of mixed blood, she'd said; it only caused division and heartache for all concerned. He had disagreed with her then, and he disagreed with her still.

Quietly he said, 'Aye, it does. And religion is another big divide. The gangs of boys in the streets where I grew up were either Catholics or Protestants, and they'd batter you into next weekend if you were on the wrong side. Took great enjoyment out of it an' all.'

'Which were you? Catholic or Protestant?'

'Me? Neither. My parents went to the Baptist Chapel two streets away; still do.'

'So you were all right then?'

'Not really. Us Baptist bairns used to get bashed by both lots.' He grinned at her and she smiled back. 'One of my sisters married a Catholic lad, though. I was only knee-high to a grasshopper at the time, but I remember the carry-on it caused in his family. My mam wasn't too pleased, either, but she didn't interfere, beyond insisting Prudence didn't convert.'

'Are they happy: your sister and her husband?'

'They were. He got killed at Dunkirk. You'd have thought that would have brought his family round, but they won't even come to see Prudence – and her with three little ones. Nowt so queer as folk, as my mam says.'

'And cruel.'

Caleb shot her a glance. 'Aye, that an' all.' He paused. 'But to my mind, that's part of what this war is all about, isn't it? Fighting against cruelty and bigotry? Those poor blighters in Nazi Germany – the Jews an' the rest of them who aren't part of Hitler's "chosen" race – they're the ones who have had it worse.'

'Do you believe this invasion by the Allies is the beginning of the end of the war, like the papers are saying?' Esther asked. She wanted the war to end, of course she did, but it was hard to imagine what life would be like when it did. She had no home, no husband, no family. But she did have Joy, and dear Rose. And her friends.

Caleb shrugged. 'We'll win – the writing's on the wall now – but there's nothing so dangerous as a cornered beast, and Hitler will stop at nothing.' Realizing his words weren't exactly uplifting, he added, 'What was it that Churchill said a couple of years ago, after El Alamein? "This is not the end. It's not even the beginning of the end. But it is perhaps the end of the beginning." Well, I reckon this latest is the beginning of the end that we've all been waiting for.'

There followed a stillness during which they both became lost in their thoughts in the warm darkness. Somewhere close by a blackbird called shrilly, after being disturbed by something or other, and the muted sounds of jollity from the village hall barely impinged on the night. Caleb had the feeling that he could sit here all night. In fact, if he was to die at this very moment, it would be a good end.

When the door to the hall opened and someone called her name, Esther sighed, and he felt that she objected to the intrusion as much as he did. Rousing herself, she called, 'I'm here, Cilla, and I'm fine. I'll come in, in a minute.'

This was followed by the blonde girl he'd seen with Esther earlier bounding down the steps of the hall, saying, 'What on earth are you doing, sitting out here by yourself?' Then she stopped abruptly on catching sight of Caleb. 'Oh, you're not by yourself. Sorry. Didn't know.'

'I said I'll come in a minute.' But Esther was already standing up.

Caleb made no effort to stand himself; it would take a bit of manoeuvring, and he had no intention of floundering around in front of her.

Whether she understood this, he didn't know, but thankfully she made no offer to help him up, merely saying, 'It's been nice talking to you, Caleb.'

He smiled up at her. 'Likewise. Perhaps we can do it again sometime.'

'I'd like that.'

They regarded each other for a moment and her face was unsmiling, but her eyes were soft.

He didn't turn and watch her as she joined her friend and they went back into the dance, but, once the night was quiet and still again, he let out his breath in a deep sigh. Now that she had gone, he wondered at his nerve in speaking to her in the way he had. She was out of his league, big-time.

But she'd seemed to like him, another part of his mind suggested, before he countered it with: *Don't be so daft, man*. Esther would act that way with anyone. She was kind, courteous. No doubt she felt sorry for him too; pity would force her not to rush to get away, in case it hurt his feelings. He ground his teeth for a moment. Oh, to hell with it.

Shaking his head at himself, Caleb struggled to his feet with the aid of his crutches and stood for a moment, his face set. *No barmy ideas, lad*, he told himself grimly. By her own admission, she was a married woman with a bairn; and if her husband had any sense at all, he'd make things right, but even if he didn't, a woman like that wouldn't look the side he was on. Except as a friend, if he was lucky.

He decided not to go back into the hall, but made his way to the low stone wall surrounding the grounds and sat down to wait for his friends. He shouldn't have come tonight, he'd known it was a daft idea; but he also knew he would come again.

Chapter Eleven

Theobald Wynford sat on the edge of the black satin sheets, pulling on his clothes, and when a soft hand caressed his naked back he jerked away. It was then that a voice said, 'It doesn't matter. It happens to everyone at some time or other. Don't take it to heart. Do you want to try again?'

'No, I damned well don't.' He reached for his shirt.

'I still want my money.' The voice was hard now, abrasive. 'It's not my fault. I did everything you wanted me to. It's down to you that you couldn't perform.'

Theobald swung round, his fist clenched. The middle-aged woman with the painted face scrambled back against the stack of pillows as she said, 'Any of that, Mister, and I'll scream to high heaven, and Dickie'll come running. He'll rearrange your face soon as it look at it, so I'm warning you.'

Slowly he lowered his fist. He had seen the said Dickie, and the man was built like a gorilla, with arms on him to match. Standing up, he pulled on the rest of his clothes and then tossed some money on the rumpled covers. 'To hell with you.'

'Aye, you an' all.' The prostitute's lined face grinned at him as though their farewell had been harmonious. Her voice was congenial too as she said, 'Come back for another try, dearie, when you want. I don't bear no grudges.'

Theobald didn't bother to reply. He couldn't wait to get outside the brothel, away from the smell of cheap perfume and sweat and stale alcohol.

Once in the street outside the establishment, which was situated a stone's throw from the old Chester-le-Street graveyard, he took a moment to compose himself. He'd been mad to go there, he told himself, but he'd been three sheets to the wind and not thinking straight. It was the first time he hadn't been able to get it up, but he'd never been to that brothel before – it wasn't his usual haunt. The place had been grubby and that had put him off, and as soon as he had gone in, he'd begun to wonder who might have noticed him entering its doors. Had that been the problem, or the old hag he'd got landed with, damn her? She'd been fifty if she was a day, and it was young flesh that stirred his juices these days. The younger, the better.

Swearing softly, he made his way down the street to the public house where his horse was tethered in the inn's yard. He was untying the animal when the publican appeared at the back door of the premises. 'Oh, it's you. That's all right then. Took yourself off for a stroll, did you?' Theobald stared at the man in the deepening twilight, and such was his gaze that the publican turned away muttering, 'I was only checking the horse wasn't being nabbed.'

Theobald knew why the publican had come into the yard, and it had nothing to do with the horse's welfare. The man had been trying to be clever and let him know that he knew where he'd been.

Cursing the publican and the rest of the world, Theobald hauled himself into the saddle and rode out of the yard. He'd first entered the inn just before lunch, and had drunk his way through a bottle of whisky and two bottles of wine during the afternoon. Then, his loins burning, he'd left the inn and walked unsteadily to the establishment on the corner, which had a red lamp burning in the window. Strangely, he felt stone-cold sober now, and angry. How dare that scum look at him in the way he had? But it was a warning to be more careful. Perhaps he ought to think about having the girls brought discreetly to the house?

Shortly after Harriet's death, his mistress at the time had had the idea that Theobald should make an honest woman of her, now his wife was no more. He'd refused, for the mere idea had been preposterous. Cissy was good for one thing only, and she did that extremely well. But within the month Cissy had taken herself off and married a shopkeeper – a man Theobald suspected she'd had on the go at the same time as him. He hadn't been too concerned. A mistress expected a degree of consideration, and he'd found that increasingly irritating. And so had begun a new era. He'd been able to indulge his predilection for younger flesh and the more depraved acts that common whores allowed, if the price was right. And he always made sure it was.

The August night was a hot one, a warm breeze rustling the ripening ears of corn in the fields on either side of the road, but Theobald was wrapped up in his thoughts and oblivious to the lovely evening.

A couple of days ago French tanks had led the Allies into Paris and, after four years of brutal Nazi occupation, the swastika was no longer flying from the Eiffel Tower. This had made little impact on Theobald, beyond how it would affect his business interests. He'd prospered during the war and had fingers in various black-market pies; he wouldn't like to see them fall by the wayside if the war ended. Selfish to the core, he was concerned by something only if it touched him on a personal level – like his plans for Monty to join him, as his son-in-law, in the Wynford businesses. Nevertheless, he hadn't completely given up on that.

He clicked the horse into a canter, his mind chewing on the problem of Monty, as it was often apt to. The Grant name carried weight; furthermore it opened doors to influential and powerful sections of society, and that wasn't to be sneezed at. He had kept the lines of communication with his son-in-law open, as far as it was within his power to do so, and thus far he had heard nothing about a divorce between Monty and Esther.

The horse was now trotting up the drive towards the house, and Theobald rode the animal around the building to the stable block, where he saw to it himself. The stable boy had long since joined up. All the younger members of Theobald's employ had either been conscripted or had joined up of their own volition; or, in the case of the housemaids and one of the kitchen maids, had hightailed it off to work in a munitions factory in Newcastle, where they could earn the sort of money they had only dreamed of before the war. The house was run by a skeleton crew these days, consisting of the older members of staff: Mrs Norton and the butler, Osborne; Fanny Kennedy, the cook; and Fanny's twin sister, who had lost her husband in the first week of the war and had joined the household as general dogsbody. Under Neil Harley's expert management, the farm was still fully productive, and the number of outside workers remained pretty much what it had always been, thanks to a party of Italian POWs who were marched to the farm each morning by two soldiers from the nearby camp. Most of them were from farming stock themselves and did their work with a mixture of enthusiasm and happy-go-lucky carelessness, distinctive in their dark-blue overalls with large green patches sewn onto them.

Theobald had been furious to find the Italians making little woven baskets and wooden toys for the local children and young women, when he had made a visit to the fields unannounced one day. And even Neil Harley's explanation that the men were doing this in their lunch hour didn't appease him. He would have worked them to death, if he could. Fortunately Neil appreciated the relaxed atmosphere the Italians brought with them, and the fact that they were an important part of the agricultural labour force, so he merely paid lip-service to Theobald's ranting. If the POWs wanted to make toy tractors and trains out of ration cans and wood for the odd half-hour before they started work again, it was all right by him.

Neil was fully aware that German prisoners tended to be more productive and efficient than the Italians, and kept themselves to themselves and had little to do with the locals, but he'd lost two brothers since the war had begun, and the thought of Germans on the farm made his hackles rise. And so he continued to defy Theobald's orders to make the Italians' lives miserable, and the farm ticked along happily.

Theobald wasn't thinking about his farm manager, and what he considered the man's ridiculous weakness with the POWs, as he entered the house by way of a side door from the gardens. He refused to use the kitchen door – the more direct route from the stables – considering it beneath him. He was still smarting from his ignominious failure with the prostitute, and if he'd had a dog, he would have taken great pleasure from venting his anger and giving it a good kicking. As it was, he stormed across the hall towards his study door, yelling for Osborne.

He had the door knob in his hand when Osborne came hurrying from the direction of the kitchen, saying, 'Mr Wynford-Grant is here, sir. I've just asked Cook to prepare him a light repast.' Osborne was always very careful to use the double-barrelled surname, knowing it pleased his master.

Theobald swung round, visibly taken aback. Since the birth of the child he had written to Monty twice, expressing his outrage at Harriet's deceitfulness, his understanding of his son-in-law's actions and his desire that Monty would still consider him a friend and ally. He had even hinted that Monty's place in his business was as secure as ever, once the war was over, should he choose to avail himself of the offer. He had received two short replies back, which had been non-committal. 'Where is he?'

'In the drawing room, sir. I thought it best to suggest he wait until you return, but he's been here over two hours now and—'

Theobald cut off his butler's words with a wave of his hand. 'Bring me some coffee. Strong. Black. And something to eat too.' He was already walking across the hall.

When he thrust open the door of the drawing room, his son-in-law rose to his feet. He had been sitting on a couch in front of the huge fireplace, which, even though the August day had been a hot one, had a wood fire burning in the elaborate iron basket.

Theobald stared at the young man who had left his house all those months ago, in the company of his furious mother. On that occasion Clarissa's last words had been regarding the divorce, and they had been in the nature of a threat: the divorce would proceed exactly as she determined, she'd warned; and Theobald would see to it that Esther did as she was told. A few well-chosen words in the right quarter and Theobald could find himself in the position of a pariah socially, and she didn't need to tell him the result that would have on his business interests, did she? No, she thought not. And so Monty's solicitor would be in touch. But he never had been.

'Hello, Theobald.' Monty forced a smile as he looked at the man he had never liked. And, as he saw his father-in-law's eyes move to his bandaged hands, he said quietly, 'Burns.'

'I'm sorry. Bad?'

Monty thought of the eleven operations that the third-degree burns had necessitated to date; the skin grafts taken from the inside of his thighs; the days and nights of what amounted to fiendish torture, when the stinking pulps of rotten flesh and oozing pus had made every minute seem like an hour. He shrugged. 'Not compared to some.' Which was true. He hadn't had his hands amputated at the wrists, like a couple of the pilots he'd been with in hospital; and his face was unmarked. It had only been in the last few weeks that he could think like this, though, when the pain and misery had become bearable, and the beautiful surroundings of the cottage hospital in the soft Sussex countryside where he'd been sent for treatment had begun to heal his senses.

Theobald tried not to stare. Monty looked ten, twenty years older than he had when he had seen him last. The young, dashing lad was gone for good, and in his place stood a handsome man, but a man with deep lines carved around his mouth. Again he said, 'I'm sorry. The war's over for you then?'

Monty nodded. 'You heard about my parents?'

'Your parents?'

'Last week. One of those damned doodlebugs. Direct hit on the London house. I'd told them to steer clear of the capital, but because they'd got the use of one of those new, purpose-built deep shelters – the ones for ticket-holders only – Mother wouldn't listen. And of course Father went where she led. They never even got out of the house, let alone to the shelter.'

Theobald had read that the second mass wartime exodus of children from London had been under way for some weeks, as the Germans intensified their buzz-bomb attacks on the south-east, but they hadn't seen much evidence of doodlebugs to date in the north. Churchill had declared, 'London will never be conquered and will never fall' at the start of the launch of the flying bombs, but people were beginning to wonder how much the beleaguered capital could take. For the third time in as many minutes, he said, 'I'm sorry, I didn't know.' Personally, he considered Clarissa and Hubert Grant's demise no loss; in fact, their deaths might well work to his advantage. Keeping any trace of his thoughts from showing, he gestured to the couch. 'Sit down, lad. I'm glad you waited to see me. Can you stay the night?'

As he spoke, Osborne knocked and then opened the door. Mrs Norton and Cook's sister brought in two trays, one holding a coffee pot and cups and saucers, along with cream, sugar and a decanter of brandy, and the other piled high with sandwiches, pastries and cakes.

Monty looked at the tray of food. Clearly rationing hadn't bitten in this household, but then that was Theobald all over. If there was a way to get what he wanted, he'd find it. For a moment he was tempted to get up and walk straight out, but caution prevailed. He needed Theobald more than Theobald needed him – that was the crux of the matter; and if Esther's father had meant what he'd intimated in his letters, then he needed to keep things sweet. 'Yes, I can stay over, if it won't inconvenience you?' he said, accepting the plate Theobald passed him, as the servants walked out of the room after being dismissed. 'I don't want to intrude.'

'You're family, as far as I am concerned, Monty. You know that.'

The elephant in the room was too big to ignore any longer. 'How are Esther and . . . and the child?' Monty asked quietly.

'You know as much as me. She's been dead to me from the moment I found out the truth, lad. She and her brat.'

Inwardly Monty winced. 'You must know where she's living?'

'Like I said, she's dead to me.'

'I wrote to her after . . . ' Monty swallowed hard. 'After the baby was born. At the farm. But the letters came back marked "Gone Away".'

'There you are then. She'd skedaddled somewhere or other.'

'Or she didn't want anything to do with me.'

'By rights, the boot should have been on the other foot, Monty. She did the dirty on you, remember?'

'But it wasn't Esther's fault, was it? I mean, it was . . . it was your wife who was to blame for everything. Esther was the innocent party. Harriet said so herself.'

Theobald had stuffed a ham sandwich in his mouth, and now he chewed and swallowed before he said, 'Them two were as thick as thieves, lad, and if the Archangel Gabriel himself came down and told me Esther didn't know about her beginnings, I wouldn't believe him. She knew all right, and that mealy-mouthed nanny was in on it an' all. Upped and left she did, once the funeral was over. Knew she'd been found out – that was the thing – but tried to dress it up as though it was my fault. I ask you. But I'd got her measure, sure enough.'

'Rose left?' Esther had thought the world of the woman. 'Where did she go? To find Esther?'

'I don't know, and I don't care.' Theobald had had enough of discussing the past. It was the future he was interested in. 'Look, Monty, I think a bit of you – always have done. You know how I'm placed; when I thought you and Esther were going to make a go of it, I didn't pull my punches, did I? Harriet took me for a fool, and Esther did the same to you, but I don't see why we should fall out. What's done is done; but, if nothing else, it's been the means of joining our two names. Am I right?'

It was why he had come – to hear this – but now Monty wanted to shout at the swarthy little man in front of him that he wanted none of it. Instead he asked Theobald to go on.

'I need someone I can trust to be my right-hand man, and I'd like it to be you. Simple as that.'

His days of flying aeroplanes were over; Monty knew the air force would either invalid him out or give him a limited-capacity job, fit only for ground duties in the United Kingdom. It had been a shock when he'd learned the extent of his parents' debts after the funeral, even though he had known for years that things were dire. His parents had been the epitome of a lost and dying age; aristocrats wasting away in the grand mausoleum of the ancestral home, which was decaying around them. When he sold everything, there would be nothing left for him, and the London town house was just a pile of rubble. He was suddenly church-mouse poor, and it terrified him. What was the use of being able to trace your ancestors back hundreds of years and having an old and illustrious name, when you didn't have a penny to that name? If Esther had been beside him, it would have been different. He could have faced anything then. How could he have allowed his mother to browbeat him into leaving her? He'd had several women over the last year or so – he'd found the girls were falling over themselves to bed pilots; even nice girls, who before the war would have been asking for a ring on their finger before they went the whole hog. But everything, and everyone, had changed. However, none of the women he had been with could hold a candle to Esther, in bed or out of it. Always, though, when he had been tempted to search her out, the image of the child had stopped him. If she had looked like Esther, it would have been different.

'Look, Monty.' Theobald had paused and seemed to be weighing what he was about to say. 'I don't know quite how to put this, but do I take it you and Esther are still legally married? What I mean is: I haven't heard anything about a divorce, and the last time we met, your mother seemed to suggest that any papers would come here, for me to forward on. Not that I could have done, of course, because like I said, I don't know where—'

'I've done nothing to date.' Monty cut short his father-in-law, his voice terse. It had been a bone of contention with his mother that he was dragging his heels, as she'd put it, but the thought of explaining the whole sorry mess to a solicitor had been beyond him, in the early days. He'd used the excuse of the war to keep his mother at bay, promising her he would see to things in due course, but then he had been shot down and she had refrained from nagging him after that.

His heart began to pound as he remembered the impact of the first bang; crazy, but he couldn't believe he had been hit. He had dodged so many near-misses that his fellow airmen had started to call him 'Miss-'em Monty', and he'd dared to believe he would get through the war without a scratch. Two more bangs had followed in quick succession, and as if by magic a frightening hole had suddenly appeared in his starboard wing. Unbelief had changed to terror in the next instant, when the gas tank behind the engine blew up and the cockpit became engulfed in flames.

He had heard that your whole life passed before you, when death was imminent, but it hadn't been like that with him. Screaming, he'd thrown his head back to keep it away from the searing heat, as his burning right hand had groped for the release pin securing the restraining Sutton harness. That was all he had thought of: to get out of what had become his coffin.

And then suddenly he had done it, and he was out into the wonderfully cool sky, tumbling downwards as blissful fresh air flowed across his face. His training kicked in and he followed the instructions his brain was giving him – the lump of red meat at the end of his right arm searching for the chromium ring on the ripcord. Through the agony his mutilated, raw fingers grasped the life-giving ring and pulled, and with a jerk the silken canopy billowed out above him, mercifully undamaged by the flames. He had never seen anything quite so beautiful as that shining material.

He came back to the present, to his father-in-law saying, 'Don't get me wrong, Monty, but it might be better to leave things as they are, for the time being. If you're up for coming in with me, that is. Being related through marriage oils the wheels businesswise, you know?'

Oh, he knew all right. Monty looked into Theobald's flabby red face, one part of his mind thinking: he's drinking too much and it shows; and the other part processing the fact that it was only really the Grant name that Theobald was interested in. Had the man ever genuinely cared for someone in his whole life? He doubted it. He was a truly obnoxious individual.

'Well?' Theobald tried and failed to keep the note of irritation out of his voice. 'What do you say about taking up a position within the business? There's plenty who'd jump at it, you know, especially with the way things are going to be once the war's over. If folk think they've had it tough the last few years, it'll get worse before it gets better. It was the same after the Great War.'

He would be selling his soul, if he took up Theobald's offer; Monty had known that before he came, but he wasn't a strong-willed individual, like his mother had been. He took after his father – he knew that now. And the thought of being poor terrified him. His mother might have turned up her nose at 'new money' and commercialism, but it was the future. To ignore that was virtual suicide. And Theobald had his thumb in so many pies that even if a couple of them turned bad, it wouldn't matter. He looked down at his hands; he would never fly again, but bent and scarred as they were, they'd serve him in civilian life. But that was the rub. He didn't have the faintest idea what he wanted to do or how to get started. He'd never really had to think about things like that.

Monty took a deep breath. 'If you think I can be of any use, I'd be pleased to join you, Theobald. But I've another operation ahead of me before that would be possible, and a full medical examination before they discharge me.'

'Understood, understood.' Theobald smiled, patting his protruding stomach as he said, 'Try one of these sandwiches, lad. Our own ham and, if I say it myself, there's none better. Harley might be too soft with the POWs, but he's a damned good manager in every other respect. Not that I'd ever tell him that, of course. He'd get the idea he might be due a rise, and you don't lead with your chin, do you. His class will take advantage of any sign of softness, take it from me.' Stuffing a sandwich into his mouth, he chewed and swallowed. 'So you're happy to leave things be, regarding Esther, for the time being?'

Just hearing her name brought a pain equal to the agony Monty had endured from the burns. If only she had been reasonable, and agreed to the child being taken away and cared for somewhere, they could still be together. And they could have adopted children – he'd have had no problem with that. If she'd loved him as much as she said she did, she wouldn't have put the child before him, Monty thought bitterly, something he had told himself many times in the past. At no point in these reflections did he think of the child as his. She was Esther's – evidence of a secret that needed to be hidden at all costs. Indeed, over the last months the tiny bundle in Esther's arms that he had glimpsed briefly, the alien creature with the dark skin and black hair that bore no likeness whatsoever to him, had taken on the image of a monstrosity, in his imagination.

Realizing that his father-in-law was waiting for an answer, Monty nodded.

'That's settled then.' Theobald settled himself more comfortably in his chair after pouring them both a generous glass of brandy. 'Let's drink to the future, lad? What do you say?'

Monty smiled sickly. His old nanny had had a saying that fitted this occasion perfectly. When he had misbehaved or been less than the perfect little boy she insisted on, she'd warn him grimly that if he wasn't careful, he would be riding a handcart to hell. Her words suddenly seemed prophetic.

Chapter Twelve

Esther sat between Priscilla and Rose in the village parish church, listening to the vicar extolling the virtues of God's harvest, as shafts of sunlight cascaded in through the stained-glass window behind him. '"Thou crownest the year with Thy goodness; and Thy clouds drop fatness,"' he intoned, reading from the huge Bible in front of him. '"They shall drop upon the dwellings of the wilderness; and the little hills shall rejoice on every side. Thy folds shall be full of sheep; and the valleys also shall stand so thick with corn, that they shall laugh and sing."'

Priscilla nudged her, whispering, 'Makes it sound so easy, doesn't he? I bet he's never worked from sunrise to sunset in the fields, with Farmer Holden as his taskmaster.'

Esther smiled but didn't comment, aware of the farmer and his wife in the next pew. Adjusting Joy – who'd fallen asleep as soon as the vicar had begun speaking – into a more comfortable position on her lap, she let her mind wander. She had enjoyed the harvest this year, possibly because everyone was saying the war was nearly over, and it would be her last autumn at Yew Tree Farm. But it wasn't just that. There was something wonderfully reassuring and satisfying about working on the land. Under the summer sun she had watched the corn change from lemon-green to bronze and the barley bleach grey, and the fields of oats shine yellow, chequering the farm's landscape in a patchwork of subtle tint and hue. And the poppies . . . She smiled to herself. How she had loved the poppies this year, their silky heads scarlet as they had blazed amid the corn. The scent of the trees on the still air, the sweet warming winds that had bent the tall grain like the roll of the sea or the sigh of a distant tide – it had all seemed infinitely precious somehow.

She glanced to her left where, two rows in front on the other side of the aisle, a number of patients and staff from the convalescent home were sitting. Caleb was there. Her heart jumped and then thudded, before settling into its normal rhythm. They had met a few times since that night at the village dance, although never by pre-arrangement. But she had taken to attending the monthly hop with Priscilla, and the occasional whist drive and other fund-raising activities that the WI tended to put on, and which the men from the convalescent home were encouraged to go along to, if they were fit enough. Part of their reha-bilitation, Caleb had told her wryly: getting back into civilized society, and so on.

She didn't let herself acknowledge that her change of heart, about accompanying the other girls to such events, was anything to do with Caleb, but on the odd occasion that he hadn't been present, the day had seemed a little less bright. She liked his friendship, that was all, she told herself now. He was pleasant and easy to talk to, and kind. Very kind. One hot Sunday afternoon in August she had taken Joy to the village fete with the others, and Caleb had been there with a group of his pals. He had come over as soon as he had seen her and then made a great fuss of Joy, who had immediately taken to him. After buying them all cups of tea and a plate of cakes, Caleb had sat with little Joy on his knee, while Esther had wandered around looking at the stalls. It had been a nice afternoon.

But now it was the last week of September, and the Harvest Festival service signified the official end of summer. Over the last three or four weeks a chilliness had stabbed the air first thing in the morning and mists had lingered in the valley, rolling across the newly ploughed earth that had broken the harvest stubble in the fields. The swallows were getting ready to migrate, screaming their last cries over the farm as they fed, to prepare themselves for their long flight.

Again Esther's gaze fixed on the back of Caleb's head. Everything was going to change soon, if the newspapers could be believed. It was reported all the time now that Britain was winning the war, even though the enemy's new and terrible weapon, the silent V-2 rockets, were bringing terror and misery to London. But German troops were on the run throughout Europe, and the Allies had broken through the main German defence of the Sieg-fried Line and liberated the town of Nancy, the key bastion of eastern France. The papers had been ecstatic about that, saying it was a landmark in the end of the war, because Hitler had decreed that Nancy had to be held at all costs. In the last week throughout most of the country the street lights had come on again, after five years of darkness, and railway stations were being lit again. Passengers on trains, buses and trams could sit and read during their journey, and only certain coastal areas remained in darkness. Things were looking up, as Nancy Holden had declared that very morning at breakfast, only to be told by her husband that it didn't pay to count your chickens before they were hatched.

Again Priscilla nudged her, this time to murmur, 'Look at Peter Crosse, sitting there as though butter wouldn't melt in his mouth. When he asked me out and I said no, his language would have made a sailor blush.'

Esther followed Priscilla's gaze. Peter was the son of the farmer whose farm was on the opposite side of the village from the Holdens', and something of a Jack-the-lad, by all accounts. Having been over twenty-one at the beginning of the war, he had made full use of the exemp-tion from conscription that had applied to farm workers, who were in a reserved occupation. His elderly, doting parents had aided and abetted their only child, declaring that Peter ran the farm, now they were getting on in years. Everyone who knew the family was aware this was stretching the truth, but as Peter Crosse was six-foot-four and handy with his fists, nothing was said. To his face, at least.

The three Land Girls who'd been assigned to the Crosse farm didn't like him at all. One of them had confided to Priscilla earlier in the year that she'd had to slap Peter's face on a couple of occasions, when he'd tried to take liberties. 'Struts about the farm as though he's the cat's whiskers,' the girl had complained bitterly, 'giving his orders and playing God Almighty. And he's got a real chip on his shoulder about the GIs. Calls them every name under the sun. I thought he was going to hit me last week, when he was sounding off about them and I said we wouldn't be winning the war if they hadn't come on board. I wouldn't mind so much, if only he'd been prepared to do his bit.'

Remembering this now, Esther whispered, 'Be careful of him, Cilla. Don't forget what Joyce said to you. He could be a nasty bit of work, if he's crossed.'

Priscilla's chin lifted and her eyes narrowed. 'Nasty or not, there's no way I'd be intimidated into having a date with him.'

'I wasn't suggesting you would. Just be wary, that's all.'

When one of the pious matrons from the village turned round and glared at them for talking during the vicar's sermon, the girls tried to stifle their giggles. It was the same every Sunday. This particular lady, who had a tongue on her like a rapier for the rest of the week, seemed to have made it her life's mission to keep the congregation under control while the vicar was giving his address. Priscilla had made them choke over their cocoa a few weeks ago, when she had solemnly declared that she was sure the lady in question was dying of unrequited love. 'She acts like a simpering schoolgirl if the vicar talks to her,' Priscilla had insisted. 'Haven't you noticed? All goo-goo eyes and fluttering lashes.'

The others hadn't noticed, but since Priscilla had pointed it out, they'd seen it was true. As the vicar was as lean and tall as a beanpole and his admirer was a small, fat barrel of a woman, it had made it all the funnier somehow, and Esther spent the rest of the service not daring to glance at Priscilla.

They emerged from the church into warm, mellow sunshine and, as one, the congregation made their way to the village hall where the harvest feast awaited them. Long trestle tables groaned with food that defied the idea of rationing – for this one day it was as though the war restrictions were just a bad dream. In spite of the heavy penalties that could be meted out by the law for ignoring the restraints of rationing, in the village the local constable turned a blind eye to events such as this one, largely because his wife and daughters would have given him grief if he didn't. A fair amount of 'helping out' went on at the best of times anyway – neighbours exchanging meat, dairy produce or fresh vegetables for canned foods, coffee, spirits or perhaps some extra petrol. It was customary for a large shoulder of pork wrapped in brown paper to be left on the village bobby's doorstep every so often, along with butter or eggs or cheese. It was never talked about, it just happened. Nobody looked on the 'arrangements' that went on as profiteering; it was merely the age-old tradition of bartering that country folk had always indulged in, and farmers were particularly well placed in this respect. Only the week before, a cow had mysteriously injured itself and had had to be slaughtered, and a fox had apparently caused a loss of poultry. Equally mysteriously, exactly the same thing had happened the previous year, as the Harvest Festival celebrations approached.

Bruce Stefford, the village poacher, had managed to do very nicely out of the war, Esther had overheard Farmer Holden complaining to his wife one night. One and eightpence was the price the trapper charged for a decent-sized rabbit, and if the skin was duly returned, Bruce paid twopence back. Apparently someone came round the villages in a van each month and gave threepence each for rabbit skins, and Bruce had been boasting in the pub that he generally had a few dozen to sell on. But in spite of Farmer Holden's annoyance – due mainly to the fact that some of the poaching took place on his land – Esther knew he wouldn't have dreamed of complaining to the authorities. Such was village life, and that was the end of the matter.

The two elderly spinster sisters who lived in a neat little thatched cottage at the end of the village high street, and who were stalwarts of the WI, always had a jar of honey or jam for the right price; a certain widow with seven children could be relied on for small bunches of snowdrops or primroses or lavender, and bags of field mushrooms and other seasonal niceties; and old Mr Buffry, who kept a smallholding and looked very respectable, had a pal who worked at the docks in Scarborough – bags of tea or sugar, or perhaps tinned biscuits or canned food, found their way to the smallholding at regular intervals, and then on to certain neighbours. It was the natural order of things, and village folk weren't about to be told otherwise, not even by Churchill himself, war or no war.

The atmosphere in the hall was merry as everyone tucked into the handsome spread. Farmer Holden and his wife had joined a couple of friends of their own age, and Beryl was sitting with her boyfriend – a local lad who had been invalided out of the army the year before – and his family, so this left Esther and the other three girls and Rose together.

As always, Esther was conscious of the staring and whispers that came her way from certain folk, as she sat with Joy on her knee. Mostly she managed to ignore such rudeness these days. For the moment, Joy was oblivious to the fact that she was a different colour from the other children, but Esther knew that wouldn't always remain so. She and Rose had discussed this on several occasions, when the other girls had gone to bed and she had lingered to have a heart-to-heart with the woman she considered a second mother, and Rose had wisely told her that she had to learn which battles to fight and which to ignore.

'You'll never change human nature, Miss Esther,' Rose said one evening when the pair of them had sat gazing into the dying flames of the fire in the small grate in the sitting room of the cottage. 'There'll always be those who are quick to point the finger and take pleasure from imagining they're better than you, for all sorts of reasons. Where I grew up there was even a pecking order in the street, depending on if you lived in the top end or the bottom end. Mind you, no family I can remember had a whole house to themselves; it was either the top part or the bottom part, or just a room in some cases, but it didn't stop the folk at the top end looking down on the poor beggars at the bottom. These were the families who had nothing and were one step away from the workhouse, and I suppose them at the top and the middle took comfort in the fact that, however poor they were, they weren't as bad as them at the lower end. The bottom end was close to the slaughterhouse and it stank, day and night, and the plaster on the walls was alive with bugs that dropped onto you at night. You could smell the bugs, even just passing the front doors when they were open. But it was more the fact that the people at the bottom end had a different look about them that I remember – a hopeless look.'

'Which end did you live?' Esther had asked, fascinated.

'The top end, such as it was. We had our own yard with a tap in it, and my mother didn't have to fetch water from a central tap in the back lane. That carried some clout, I can tell you. I remember I liked playing with one of the lassies from the bottom end, and I went into her house one day and her mother gave us both something to eat. When I told my mother, she went fair barmy. She stripped me as naked as the day I was born and boiled my clothes for an hour in the wash house, and then she combed out my hair with a steel comb, in case I'd caught nits. She was none too gentle about it, either, just to let me know not to do it again. My scalp hurt for weeks. If she could have washed out my insides, she would have. But she was a good mother in her own way, although not at all well for most of her life. Small she was, like me, and yet every year my father gave her a baby. Dreadful really.'

However hard it might be for her and Joy in the future, it would never be as bad as that, Esther thought thankfully. Although what she was going to do after the war, she didn't yet know. Whatever it was, she and Joy would get through, although she dreaded the inevitable questions that Joy was sure to ask about her father and why he wasn't around. What could she say? He didn't want you because your skin is a different colour from his? Of course she couldn't. Her little girl was the most beautiful, precious and amazing person in the whole world.

Esther glanced down at Joy now, stroking the soft, burnished curls and smiling as her daughter's big green eyes looked up into hers. Not for the first time Esther felt a trace of wonder that she was the mother of such an exquisite little person. Monty didn't deserve any part of her, she thought grimly, and she would fight tooth and nail to prevent him having anything to do with Joy, should that possibility ever arise, which, thankfully, was unlikely. And like a flash of lightning, suddenly and without any lead-up, she realized that any lingering feelings she might have harboured for Monty were truly dead. Even the hate that had fought with love in the first terrible weeks after she had returned to the farm, following Joy's birth, was gone. She faintly despised him, that was all; and with the knowledge came relief.

They ate their fill, and as someone with an accordion struck up a tune on the lawn outside the hall, Farmer Holden and his wife appeared at their table. 'We're making a move,' he said stolidly, 'but you can stay for another hour if you like.' It was a concession and the girls recognized it as such, Rose standing and saying to Nancy Holden, 'I'll come back with you and help you in the dairy, if these want to stay on for a bit.'

But for the fact that she could see Caleb making his way over to them, Esther would probably have gone back to the farm with the other three. There was always work to do and never enough hours in the day, added to which she'd had enough for one day of the villagers and their pointed glances and whispers. As it was, she let the farmer and his wife and Rose go and smiled at Caleb as he joined them, with a couple of his friends at his heels, one of whom was Kenny. As a group they moved out into the sunshine to find some of the young people dancing to 'Chattanooga Choo Choo' while others looked on, and several little children – glad to be out in the fresh air after the lack of space in the hall – dashing about screaming in a game of tag.

Caleb gazed about him, one part of his mind finding it hard to believe that there was a war going on at all. The hell of blitzed towns and cities, the horror and misery of death and destruction had barely touched this quiet little part of England, which was still a green and pleasant land. The war seemed transient and shadowy, and nature the abiding reality.

Then he shook himself mentally. He was going soft, he thought wryly. There was a war all right; he only had to look at Kenny and the others to see proof of it. But he felt he had got back on track in this quiet little backwater of England where the old traditions still held fast, and he was grateful for that. For that, and for Esther. Especially Esther.

Such thoughts were dangerous and he checked himself quickly. Esther wasn't his to be grateful for. He must not forget that. She was a married woman. Furthermore she thought of him as a friend, and only as a friend, and why wouldn't she? He was a cripple. Dress it up however you liked, but that's what he was. The first time he'd seen his stump he had felt sick, and it hadn't helped that the constant pins and needles in the toes that were no longer there had driven him mad. It seemed crazy that the brain could know the foot wasn't there, but the nerves ignored it. And the physiotherapy had tested his resolve to take his injury in his stride – he allowed himself a grim smile at the dark pun. Along with one or two of the doctors, whose bedside manners had left a lot to be desired.

According to one of the home's doctors, the long-deceased war hero, Admiral Lord Nelson, after losing his right arm in the Battle of Santa Cruz de Tenerife, had continued to feel the fingers of this arm, and had believed this provided direct proof of the existence of the soul, since part of his body had continued to be felt even after its physical destruction. The good doctor had clearly meant this as encouragement, and had seemed taken aback when Caleb had replied curtly that he'd never held with the idea of clouds having silver linings. The phantom sensations, which had even included painful cramps in the early days, had often caused him to swear like a trooper, especially when he had been jerked awake in the middle of the night by involuntary movements in a limb that wasn't there.

Touching Esther's arm, Caleb said quietly now, 'Can we talk alone for a moment?'

Esther looked at him in surprise. 'Of course.'

The others had walked over to sit on the lawn in the shade of a large hawthorn tree and were talking amongst themselves, so Caleb led her over to the small wall surrounding the grounds of the village hall and they both sat on the sun-warmed stone, Joy settling at their feet and immediately becoming engrossed in picking the daisies that starred the grass.

Without any preamble Caleb said, 'They're sending me to Roehampton tomorrow, to the Queen Mary's Hospital. It seems they're the best for fitting prosthetic limbs.'

She stared at him. 'For how long?'

He shrugged. 'I understand, after the leg's made to my requirements and fitted, I'll need to learn how to use it. There's a period of physical exercise and rehabilitation involved, and there's still the op to remove the shrapnel in my side. Whether that'll be done before or after, my doctor here doesn't seem sure, or even whether I'll come back. The thing is' – he hesitated for a moment – 'I wondered if you'd like to keep in touch? To write? Of course I understand if—'

'Of course I would.' She didn't have to think about it. '*Of course.*'

Caleb's heart leapt. It had taken all his courage to ask, and he hadn't been sure if she would brush him off or agree just to be kind, which was even worse, but she had spoken as if she really meant it. Considering what he was feeling, his reply of 'Good' sounded lame, even to his own ears. He reached in his jacket pocket and handed her a piece of paper. 'That's the address.'

For a moment their fingers touched and Caleb felt the impact in every nerve of his body, as he had on other occasions when the slightest contact had sent his pulse racing. It was ridiculous, he told himself for the umpteenth time, as he felt his face flushing, and it wasn't as if he hadn't had a woman before. He was no pimply schoolboy, wet behind the ears, but Esther affected him like no other woman ever had, and there wasn't a damned thing he could do about it. Reaching down to the child at their feet, he ruffled Joy's curls, saying, 'I shall miss her. She's growing up so fast.'

'Yes, yes, she is.' Esther didn't know what else to say. She was shocked at how devastated she felt that Caleb was leaving. He was just a friend after all, and he had never once indicated by word or deed that he thought of her as anything else but that. She had to pull herself together. And at the back of her mind she knew that she would run a mile if he *had* indicated that he thought of her in a romantic fashion. She didn't want that, not from any man – ever. She would never let herself be hurt again, and the only way to protect herself and Joy was for the two of them to be their own little unit together. So why had she felt so . . . strange? It didn't make sense. *She* didn't make sense. And it was unnerving.

Her thoughts made her voice a little wooden as she said, 'What time do you leave tomorrow?'

'Early morning, I think. There's a couple of us.' He glanced across at the group under the hawthorn tree as a gust of laughter wafted towards them. Kenny playing the fool, no doubt. Quietly he murmured, 'Do me a favour, would you? If you see Kenny at any dos like this, have a chat with him. He might seem the life and soul of the party, but it's a mask he's hiding behind, half the time. His girl did the dirty on him and it hit him hard, although he'd never admit it. And some folk don't bother to hide what they feel when they see him for the first time – you know what people can be like.'

'Oh yes, I know all right.'

'Hey, I'm sorry, I didn't mean . . . '

'I know.' She smiled at him more naturally, his chagrin restoring her equilibrium. Caleb was just Caleb, her friend, and she was getting in a dither about nothing. Softly she said, 'I'll look out for Kenny, and I'll tell the others to as well; they'll be glad to do it. We all like him, he's a nice man.'

Equally softly Caleb murmured, 'Thank you, lass. I appreciate it.'

Peter Crosse stood leaning against the wall of the village hall. To an onlooker it would seem that he was idly sipping from his glass of beer, his eyes half-closed against the sun. In reality he had been watching Priscilla and the group under the hawthorn tree since he had exited the hall. In recent months he'd found that Priscilla had become a thorn in his flesh, and one he couldn't rid himself of. Tall and good-looking, he had always been used to a certain amount of success among the village girls; he clicked his fingers and mostly they tended to come running. The fact that he was the only son of a successful farmer didn't do him any harm in the attraction stakes, either. But come the war, he'd found the Land Girls were a different proposition. The ones on his father's farm had made it clear they didn't appreciate his roaming hands or attempts to seduce them in the hay loft and, after their complaints, his father had warned him in no uncertain terms to leave them alone.

He ground his teeth for a moment. The memory still rankled.

On the one hand, they all thought themselves a cut above, he told himself morosely; and on the other, they went with anyone. Anyone but him. That blonde piece had made no secret of seeing one of the black GIs some months back, before she moved on to someone else. Morals of an alley cat, she had. Her friend an' all, but she'd got caught out, hadn't she?

His gaze moved to Esther and Caleb for a moment, and his lip lifted in a sneer as it rested on the child playing at their feet. Rumour had it that her husband had told her to sling her hook and take her by-blow with her, and he didn't blame him. She'd been lucky to get off so lightly.

More laughter from the group under the tree brought his attention back to Priscilla. His eyes narrowed. She needed teaching a lesson, that one. Refusing him, and yet giving it to half the American air force. Damned Yankees.

One of the village girls that he had been seeing on and off for some time sidled past him, giving him the eye, but he didn't respond and she walked off with something of a flounce to her step. A slight smile touched his lips momentarily. For a second he was tempted to follow her and take advantage of the blatant invitation in the swing of her hips. Nora was only fifteen and she'd been a virgin when he'd first had her, but gratifying as that had been, she bored him. Now the blonde, Priscilla – that was a real woman. He bet she knew plenty to keep a man panting for more.

One of his childhood pals who had been wounded and shipped home after the D-Day landings in Normandy joined him, following his gaze. 'I heard you asked that one out and she gave you the cold shoulder. I'd give up, mate. She likes blokes in uniform, by the look of it.'

There had been an edge to his friend's voice that Peter didn't miss. He was well aware that his staying at home rather than joining up hadn't gone down well in some quarters. But, like his mother said, was it worth getting your head blown off, to be one of the boys? He didn't even have to think about that one. Without looking at the man at the side of him, he said evenly, 'How's the arm, Greg?'

'So-so. Getting there.'

Aye, it might be, but according to his mother, who had been chatting with Greg's mother, Greg's mangled arm was the least of his problems. His lower stomach had taken some of the blast and, according to the doctors, he'd never function properly as a man again. Greg's mother had sworn his own mother to secrecy, but knowing that Greg had been one of his pals, she had told Peter, to prepare him in case Greg ever wanted to talk about it in the future.

'Good.' Peter still didn't glance at him. 'Won't be long before you're chatting up the lassies again then. Nothing like getting your leg over to boost the old system, is there? It's what makes life worth living.'

For a moment there was silence. Then Greg's voice came, raw and husky, 'Aye, too true, man.'

'There's more than one gagging for it round here, I tell you. Must be the country air, eh?' Peter nudged him, smiling. 'Now you're back for good, you can start thinking about a wife and family in the future. Must be a relief to know your days at the front are over, and you made it.'

This time the pause was longer. 'Aye, it is.'

'Any girl in particular you've got your eye on?'

'No, not really. Look, I've got to go.'

'All right, mate.' Peter watched him walk away and let Greg get a good few paces before he called out, 'Any time you fancy going out in a foursome, I know two lassies who'd be up for it. You just let me know. Okay, mate?'

Greg didn't turn round or reply, merely raising a hand in acknowledgement as he walked on, his head bowed.

Peter let out his breath in a satisfied sigh. That'd teach him. His gaze returned to Priscilla again, and his mouth tightened. Greg's words had rankled. She'd rather sit with that bunch of cripples from the home than give him the time of day. And he'd asked her properly too, suggesting a drink and a meal. *Uppity mare!* But he'd settle the score, if it was the last thing he did.

It was only a minute or two later that he noticed Priscilla stand up and say something to the others, before walking across to the two sitting on the wall. Within a few moments she was making her way out of the grounds of the hall and onto the lane outside, where she proceeded to walk in the direction of the Holden farm. And she was alone.

Casually he put down his glass and sauntered across the grass, his hands in his pockets. Excitement was quickening his breath and causing a stirring in his stomach. They always went about in twos and threes, these girls, as though they were joined at the hip. He wouldn't get another chance like this one.

Once out in the dusty, sunlit lane he walked a little faster.

Priscilla had been a martyr to blinding headaches for years. They usually affected only one side of her head and were accompanied by nausea and visual disturbances, and when she had felt this one beginning, she'd known she only had a limited time to get back to the farm and lie down in the quiet of her room before she became incapacitated. Twenty-four hours and she would be as right as rain, but just at the moment the only thing on her mind was to get somewhere peaceful and dark and let the agony pass.

She hadn't let on to the others that she'd got one of her headaches coming, knowing that they would insist on accompanying her home, and she didn't want to spoil the other girls' enjoyment of the afternoon. Heaven knew they didn't get much free time. And so she'd said she wanted to check on the new foal that had been born that week, and which she'd helped bring into the world. It had been a thrilling experience and one she would remember all her life, she thought now, trying to picture the cute little baby and to ignore the throbbing in her head. But it was no good. Every shaft of sunlight was like an arrow through her eyes into the back of her brain.

She was oblivious to Peter's rapid approach behind her, right until the moment he touched her on the shoulder and nearly made her jump out of her skin. She spun round, wincing as the movement brought the nausea close to the surface.

'In a hurry, aren't you?' He stood still, his hands at his sides and a slight smile curling his mouth. 'Where's the fire, or is it just us yokels you want to get away from?'

In spite of her pain, Priscilla's voice was at its most upper-class as she said tightly, 'I have a headache, that's all.'

'A headache? I've heard women like you get headaches. Working-class lassies can't afford the luxury of them.'

'Don't be ridiculous.'

'Ridiculous, am I? But then, that's how you *would* see a country bumpkin like me. But for the war, those hands of yours would still be lily-white and soft as silk, wouldn't they? And when the war's over, you'll no doubt make your fine friends laugh at the tales you tell of life with the peasants. I've got your measure, sure enough.'

Priscilla felt a curl of fear tighten her breath, but no

trace of it came through in her voice as she said, 'Don't blame me for your inferiority complex, Peter Crosse.'

He didn't have the faintest idea what an inferiority complex was, but the term 'inferior' stuck in his craw. 'Oh, you know me name then? That's something, I suppose.'

'I've had enough of this.'

When she made to swing round, he moved swiftly, positioning himself in front of her, his legs apart.

'Get out of my way.' Her voice was trembling now.

'And what if I don't want to?' His voice dropping almost to a whisper, he said, 'I asked you out proper, didn't I? Now didn't I? But I wasn't good enough for you. You like a uniform, don't you? I know, I know. And then any-one will do. Black, white – you're not fussy. You've got a name for yourself in these parts, you an' that friend of yours.'

'Then why did you ask me out?'

'Cos I didn't see why I shouldn't have a bit of what's on offer, if you want the truth.'

Through the piercing headache and the lights that were now blinding her vision, Priscilla knew what was going to happen. A power bred of desperation made her suddenly thrust out her hands and push him so hard that, taken by surprise, he stumbled backwards and fell over. Turning, she ran down the lane, but hampered as she was by her physical condition, she'd only gone a short distance when she heard him right behind her. It was then that she screamed, a high-pitched animal sound of terror, but as he threw himself on her and she fell hard to the ground, the breath was knocked out of her body.

Dazed, she felt Peter pull her into the grass verge and down a small slope, to what in winter was a boggy channel, but in the summer months had dried out into a mass of tall ferns and wild plants. He had one hand clamped over her mouth to prevent her screaming again, but, even half-fainting as she was, she fought him. She felt her dress being yanked up over her thighs, and then his hand was groping at her knickers and his fingers were probing at her bare flesh . . .

Kenny didn't know what it was that had alerted him to Peter Crosse leaving the harvest celebrations so soon after Priscilla. Perhaps there had been a furtiveness to the other man's demeanour, or maybe it was simply that he knew the farmer's son had his eye on her, although Priscilla had made it clear she wasn't interested. Something had made him uneasy anyway, and although he had felt slightly absurd, he had found himself following the broad-shouldered figure of the other fellow, but at a distance.

He had lost sight of Peter in a curve in the lane when he heard the scream, a scream that curdled his blood. And then he was running, his boots sending dust and tiny stones scattering into the warm, still air.

Peter was so intent on what he was trying to do that he wasn't aware of Kenny until a roar like a charging bull elephant caused his head to swing round. And then Kenny was on top of him, the force of his body knocking

Peter sideways, off Priscilla and head-first into a tangle of vicious brambles at the side of the ditch.

Priscilla raised herself to her knees, and in the brief respite as Peter swore and pulled himself free, Kenny managed to haul her as best he could with his crippled hands away from the small gully and up onto the lane, saying urgently, 'Get away from here,' as she gasped and spluttered incoherently.

And then Peter was on him, growling curses, and the two men were having a fight that was terribly ill-matched. Not only was Peter taller and heavier than Kenny, but Kenny's maimed hands – with skin that was still tissue-thin – put him at a hopeless disadvantage. A knockout blow sent Kenny to the ground, and as his head rang, he felt the other man's hands around his neck as Peter sat astride him.

With blood leaking from his crippled hands, he grappled at the hands locked in a stranglehold at his throat, but his clawing fingers didn't have the power to make any impression. He thought how strange it was that he was going to meet his end like this, on a quiet lane in England, after surviving the horrors of the last years, when a thwack above him released the iron vice on his windpipe and brought him back from the edge of unconsciousness. And then Priscilla was cradling his head in her lap, screaming and crying, and he heard muffled shouts somewhere in the distance.

Kenny just managed to turn his head and see Peter Crosse spreadeagled beside him, knocked out by the massive lump of wood that Priscilla had wielded like a club, before he relaxed into the blackness that was rushing to meet him.

PART FOUR

The End of the End

1945

Chapter Thirteen

Eliza McGuigan stared at her son, and Caleb stared back at her. The two of them were sitting in the kitchen enjoying a last cup of tea before they turned in for the night, after Eliza had listened to *Evening Prayers* on the wireless. She always listened to *Evening Prayers* because Caleb's father, Stanley, was in the artillery somewhere in Germany, and she felt it was a way of staying in touch with him. She liked to imagine him, wherever he was, listening too and thinking about her. Not that she knew for sure whether it was broadcast in Germany, but she didn't want to know. She preferred to think it was, and feel comforted. Now she said weakly, 'Did I just hear what I thought I heard?'

Caleb nodded, his cup halfway to his mouth, as it had been during the announcement. A few seconds before, just as *Evening Prayers* had been due to start, the familiar voice of Stuart Hibberd on the BBC's Home Service had said, 'Here is a newsflash. The German radio has just announced that Hitler is dead. I repeat, the German radio has just announced that Hitler is dead.'

There had been no further comment; no speculation as to whether the report was correct or a figment of wishful thinking, and no change to the normal schedule of programmes. *Evening Prayers* was already beginning.

'They wouldn't say something like that if it wasn't true, would they?' Eliza asked shakily.

'It's the BBC.' It was answer enough.

'So you think he's really dead? That it's over?'

Caleb nodded. 'This time it really is the end of the end.' There had been so many false expectations, but as the new year had come into being, the colossal investment and sacrifice of D-Day had started to pay dividends. Thousands of fighting ships, assault craft, merchant vessels, aircraft and more than three and a half million men had been flung into Europe, and as the sixth year of the war had begun, victory had seemed within sight. For the next three months epoch-making events had followed one another in breathless succession.

Remembering these, Caleb said now, 'It was on the cards, Mam, from the time the Allies crossed the east bank of the Rhine and Montgomery penetrated into the Ruhr. Mussolini's gone and the German forces are surrendering unconditionally. Aye, it's over.'

'Oh, lad, lad.' Eliza burst into tears. 'I want to believe it, but I'm scared to.'

'It's all right, Mam. It's all right.' Even as he spoke, Caleb asked himself how it could possibly be all right:

for them, for Britain; even for the ordinary people in Germany, who had been fed a tissue of lies by a madman who had caused such unbelievable sorrow. Countries had been all but destroyed, and for what? For what?

His mother must have read in his face something of what he was thinking, because she took his hands, saying through her tears, 'It's the future we've got to think of now, lad.'

He couldn't answer her as he would have liked to. His mother was a good woman and he loved her, but the terrible discoveries that had been made by the Allied troops advancing into Germany were beyond her comprehension. Everyone knew that Belsen, Buchenwald, Nordhausen and other concentration camps existed, but few could imagine what had gone on within those places. And the truth, as the newsreel cinemas were portraying, was unimaginable. Caleb had chosen to go and watch those newsreels because he had needed to know the stark, unvarnished truth. His mother had not. And he understood. Still, it coloured his hope for the future – any future – in a world where such things could take place. He wouldn't insult the animal kingdom by calling the perpetrators of such unspeakable crimes 'animals'. They were monsters, fiends, demons. But ones who walked on two legs and were made in the image of their Creator. How was that possible? Such thoughts kept him awake most nights and haunted his days, until he thought he would go mad. He had read the reports from the BBC correspondent, Richard Dimbleby, who had been the first reporter into Belsen, the world of nightmares. And they had given him nightmares, sure enough. The ghastly bestiality was unthinkable to the human mind, and yet it had happened.

'Caleb?' His mother shook his hands gently. 'Do you hear me? You have to think of the future now.'

'I know, Mam. I know.' He extricated his hands from hers and finished his tea. If any good at all could come out of those concentration camps, it was that their existence alone justified the war. No one could have any doubt – after Belsen and Dachau and Buchenwald and Ravensbrück, and all the other terrible names that were going to be engraved in the history of infamy – that the sacrifices that had been made to stop the Nazis were worth it.

He glanced down at his legs. To all intents and purposes he looked whole and, since he'd had the prosthesis, his outlook on life had changed at a personal level. True, the stump was sore at times, and he had the occasional stubborn ulcer on it, which he had to bathe in neat methylated spirit, the most effective and cheapest way to avoid infection; but he'd come to terms with that. He could walk tall again, and felt like a man rather than a cripple. He'd said the same to Esther in one of his letters, and she had written back that he had always been a man, as far as she was concerned. His heart had jumped at that, and then he'd read on and she had added, 'Same as Kenny and Harold and the others.'

He glanced at his mother, who was now sitting with

her eyes shut listening to *Evening Prayers*. He had told her about Esther and her circumstances – all of it, except the way he felt about her. But he dared bet his mother had cottoned on anyway; she was a canny old bird, his mam.

He waited until the programme had finished and his mother had switched off the wireless and dampened down the fire in the range with slack and wet tea leaves, before he said casually, 'I was thinking I might suggest to Esther that she looks for somewhere round here, once she leaves the farm. It's familiar territory to her, being from Chester-le-Street, and with her being on her own with the bairn, a friendly face or two is no bad thing.'

His mother stopped what she was doing and turned to face him, wiping her hands on her apron. 'I thought she'd got this servant of hers – Rose – with her?'

'Aye, she has, but Rose isn't really a servant any more.'

'So she's not on her own then.'

He shrugged.

Quietly Eliza said, 'Be careful, lad.'

'Careful?'

'Aye, careful.'

Caleb raised his eyebrows. 'Meaning?'

'Look, lad, I don't want to state the obvious.'

Caleb's eyes narrowed. 'Humour me.'

His mother sighed. 'She's not of our class, lad. You know that. Furthermore, she's a married woman with a bairn – a bairn that's . . . well . . . '

'You can say it, Mam. A bairn that's black, or at least

227

a different colour. And that's the real problem here, as far as you're concerned, isn't it? Admit it.'

'Don't take that tone with me, Caleb. It is part of it, aye, but not all, so don't put words in me mouth. You might not believe it, but I'm thinking of the lass and the bairn here, an' all. She's one of the gentry, and you said yourself she talks different. Add to that the bairn, and how do you think folk round here are going to see her?'

Caleb's voice was clipped and hard when he said, 'I don't know, Mam, but as you seem to have all the answers, you tell me. How are folk going to see her?'

'Like a creature from a different planet, and you know it at heart. I'm not saying it's right, but it's the way it is, and human nature will never change. Until the war, when the GIs came over, no one round these parts had even seen a black man, unless you count the Arabs in the East End or the occasional glimpse of a black sailor down at the docks. But not in these streets, not living as one of us. And if a lass went with an Arab, then she was as good as dead to her family. She would have to live among them, in their quarter. Now you know that, Caleb, so don't shake your head like that.'

'I know it, but it's wrong, don't you see? Damn it! Mam, what have we fought a war for, if not to do away with such thinking? And I don't care what you say. Times are changing. The black GIs *did* come, and things have been shook up.'

'Maybe in London and the big cities, but here?' Eliza glared at the son she loved with all her heart and was inordinately proud of. 'You say Esther looks white, so there'll be only one conclusion, as far as the women round here are concerned. They'll dub her a loose piece, one who enjoyed her war to the full and got caught out. The number of men she's had would double every time they gossiped on their doorsteps, lad, and when she opened her mouth, it would make things ten times worse. Her with all her privileges to sink so low, they'd say – she's a bad lot. Pity the man who gets mixed up with her.'

'I don't care what they would say,' he said grimly.

Eliza stared at him as she prayed silently. *No, God, no, not this.* Not on top of everything else in the last six years: her lad getting injured, and Stanley still away out there somewhere, and Prudence's husband dead. She'd gone through enough. She didn't want her Caleb to become an object of derision, for having been snared by a lass they'd label no better than a dockside whore. Her face working, she murmured, 'If you take up with her, you'll be the talk of the streets, a laughing stock. They . . . they'll show no mercy.'

Her distress, which he knew was motivated by love for him, melted Caleb's anger. Reaching out, he drew her into his arms, speaking above her grey head as he whispered, 'Don't cry, Mam. Please. And I'm not taking up with her – not like that. She . . . she doesn't see me in that way. All this with her husband has put her off men for life. We're friends, that's all, but I'd never forgive myself if I wasn't there for her. She . . . she needs me.'

Far from comforting Eliza, Caleb's words only

increased her anxiety. This lass had brought out his protective side, and what man doesn't want to slay the dragons and rescue the beautiful young maiden? Esther had played him like a violin, that much was obvious, whether or not her story was true. And, by her own admission, she was still married to this pilot bloke, a man of her own class. If the child *was* her husband's and her tale was true, then she was half-black, however she looked on the outside. And – Eliza's breath caught in her chest in a hard lump – she didn't know how she felt about that. She had never thought of herself as prejudiced, but now, faced with this . . . And if Esther's story was fabricated to get Caleb's sympathy, and she really had been messing around with a black GI while her husband was away fighting, then she was a bad lot. Either way, she didn't want this lass for her lad. It might be true that Esther wasn't interested in him in a romantic way, although she doubted it, but Caleb certainly wanted her. A blind man could see it. And, with a bairn to take care of, she could well see him as a handy meal ticket.

Above her head Caleb's voice rumbled on. 'Anyway, she might not want to come and live in these parts – a lass like her. We've never really talked about when the war is over, and I haven't seen her in months, don't forget. You can only say so much in letters. For all I know, she might have other plans. But . . . but I need to find out. That's all, Mam. All right?'

'I can't stop you.'

'No, Mam, you can't.' They were facing each other

again, Eliza having pulled away from him. 'And I understand your concerns, I do – whatever you think to the contrary – but my course is set on this. I'd like it to be with your support, but if not, it won't make any difference to what I do.'

'That's told me then.' Eliza turned and walked out of the room without another word, still visibly upset.

Caleb swore softly, running his hand through his hair once he was alone, the news about Hitler forgotten. He hadn't seen Esther since the day he had left for Roehampton. He had stayed there for some weeks, before being transferred to Sunderland Infirmary, where he'd had the operation to remove the final pieces of shrapnel from his body. He'd requested that this be done in the original hospital in Yorkshire and had been told this was not possible. Once he left Sunderland Infirmary, a doctor had informed him, he could go straight home, so that was good news, wasn't it? And in the meantime arrangements were under way for his official discharge from the army. It wouldn't be long and he could start making a new life for himself.

He had thanked the doctor, knowing he meant well, but a new life without Esther in it was merely an existence. And he was frightened – terrified – that with so many miles between them, they would lose touch. It happened to so many folk, for wartime friendships were transient things. And so he had written his letters and waited impatiently for hers, fretting and worrying and snapping at his poor mother, who was patience herself, putting

Caleb's ill temper down to his physical trauma. And throughout all this he'd had to endure hearing from Kenny how well his romance with Priscilla was progressing. Not that he begrudged his friend a bit of happiness, he told himself now; and Kenny had certainly proved his mettle that day, when he'd fought that big oaf of a farmer's son. But Caleb just wished his own love life was that uncomplicated.

Love life. He gave a 'Huh' of a laugh in the back of his throat. He wished.

Slumping down at the table again, he gazed morosely at the teacups, before straightening his shoulders. Enough! What the hell was the matter with him? The only way he would have Esther in his life in any capacity was if he made the effort to make it so, and he would write to her tonight. If she wrote back and said she had already made plans that didn't include him, that would be his answer. Better he knew, one way or the other.

He wrote the letter in five minutes, determined not to agonize over it or change anything. Sealing the envelope, he stuck a stamp on the right-hand corner and then pulled on his cap and jacket, before opening the scullery door that led into the yard.

It was a cold night, in spite of the calendar stating that it was the first of May, with a touch of frost glinting on the flagstones and covering the top of the five-foot brick wall that separated their back yard from the ones on either side. Opening the small iron gate, Caleb walked along the cobbled lane, taking care not to slip. In spite of the last blackout restrictions having been lifted nearly two weeks ago, most of the terraced houses were in darkness, their occupants tucked up in bed.

Once in the street beyond the back lane, he made his way briskly to the red postbox on the corner. On reaching it, he paused for a moment as he held the envelope in front of the gaping mouth. Looking up into the vast expanse of black sky alive with twinkling stars, he said out loud, 'Be with me in this.' And then he let the letter that carried all his hopes and dreams for the future fall into the box.

Chapter Fourteen

'Will you please stop worrying, Esther. Of course Caleb will be pleased to see us. Why on earth wouldn't he be?' Priscilla ground the gears of the old farm truck that she'd persuaded Farmer Holden to lend them, after she'd used her charm to obtain some petrol from one of her old flames at the American camp. Kenny, who was sitting beside her and between the two women, winced at the noise, but with his hands still a work in progress he couldn't drive the truck himself.

Turning her head, Priscilla nudged him with her elbow. 'Isn't that right, darling? Won't Caleb be tickled pink, us surprising him like this? We couldn't let him celebrate the end of the war by himself.'

'He won't be by himself,' Esther said quietly, cradling Joy to her, who had fallen asleep a few minutes before. 'He'll be celebrating with his family and friends, like everyone else.'

'So?' Priscilla tried to avoid a large pothole in the road they were travelling on, failed and the occupants of the truck rose a few inches in the air before settling back on the battered old seat. 'We're bringing enough for everyone.' The canvas bags in the back of the truck were bulging with food that the kindly Mrs Holden had packed up for them, including a whole cooked ham, and Priscilla's GI had slipped her a couple of bottles of whisky along with the petrol. 'We simply couldn't let VE Day go by without seeing Caleb, sweetie.'

Since the collapse of the Reich and the ceasefire in the west, everyone had felt the war in Europe had to be over, but although the surrender of the German forces on Lüneburg Heath on 4 May had prompted huge headlines in the newspapers on 5 May, no announcement about VE Day had been forthcoming from the government, and the celebrations in Britain had been muted. Everyone was pleased that the Germans had given in to Monty, of course, but no one really knew what was happening on the eastern front with the Russians. All the papers were full of what was being arranged for VE Day – parades, parties, the pubs staying open all hours, and what-have-you – but what everyone wanted to know was *when* it was going to be, and no one in authority was saying anything. Neighbours were pooling their coupons, their egg, flour and butter rations and the rest for street parties, but the delay had taken the edge off the euphoria, and everyone was complaining that it was a strange way to end a war.

Then yesterday, on 7 May, a terse little broadcast from the Board of Trade declaring, 'Until the end of May you may buy cotton bunting without coupons, as long as it is red, white or blue, and does not cost more than one shilling and threepence per square yard' sent everyone's hopes soaring that an announcement was imminent. As Mrs Holden had said, the writing was on the wall, because the Board of Trade wouldn't give anything away unless it had to. And sure enough that evening, when the BBC interrupted a piano recital, it was to read out a bald statement from the Ministry of Information. The nation had thought heroic prose would be appropriate for the occasion, but that had clearly been eschewed by the Civil Service, and instead, in stilted language, a wooden voice proclaimed, 'It is understood that, in accordance with arrangements between the three great powers, an official announcement will be broadcast by the Prime Minister at three o'clock tomorrow, Tuesday afternoon, 8 May. In view of this fact, tomorrow, Tuesday, will be treated as Victory in Europe Day, and will be regarded as a holiday. The day following, Wednesday May 9, will also be a holiday. His Majesty the King will broadcast to the people of the British Empire and Commonwealth, tomorrow, Tuesday, at 9 p.m.'

Remembering this now, Esther recalled how Farmer Holden had reacted when he'd heard the news. Whereas his wife had been beside herself with joy that it was officially over, the farmer had glared at them all around the dinner table and said, 'Well, I'm sick and tired and browned off with the government, I am. The way they've behaved – why, it's blooming insulting to the British people. Stood up to all what we've stood up to, and then they're afraid to tell us it was peace, just as if we was a lot of kids. It's like they don't trust us to behave ourselves. Well, they can keep their VE Day and shove it up their—' He had stopped abruptly, aware of little Joy staring at him, thumb in mouth. 'Stick it where the sun don't shine,' he had finished grumpily.

Mrs Holden had looked round the table at the others, her eyes bright with suppressed laughter, and then they had all burst out laughing, until even the farmer had given a reluctant smile. And he couldn't have been feeling as put out as he had tried to suggest, because when Priscilla had put forward her plan to go and see Caleb the following day, he had granted them both the day off, once the other three girls had promised they would still be around and would only go into the village once the essential farm work was done. Work rarely stopped on a farm, VE Day or no VE Day.

And so, with Rose saying she should go, and with Vera, Lydia and Beryl encouraging the idea, Esther had found herself reluctantly agreeing to accompany Priscilla and Kenny. She hadn't replied to Caleb's last letter, suggesting that she might like to find somewhere to live in Monkwearmouth, for a number of reasons. For one, Mrs Holden had told her and Rose that they could stay on in the cottage when the other girls left and continue to work at the farm indefinitely, and she knew that was what Rose wanted. Rose and the farmer's wife had become close, being roughly the same age, and whether working together in the dairy or doing the baking and cleaning and washing, the two women chattered away nineteen to the dozen and enjoyed each other's company. Both fairly worshipped the ground Joy walked on and were the devoted grannies she would never have, family-wise. But while part of Esther was tempted to hide away from the world at the farm, another part of her knew that once the other girls had gone, her life would be terribly constricted. She would have Joy and Rose, of course, but without Priscilla and the other three, and the camaraderie and laughter that had kept her going in the worst times, her life would consist of hard work and little else. She had had her twenty-first birthday in November the year before, so she was still young. She didn't want to be buried alive. And the villagers were so narrow-minded and judgemental; how would Joy fare at the village school, once she was old enough? Children could be crueller than their parents.

Then again, if she did leave the farm, what work could she do? And she knew Rose would feel that she had to leave with her, even though her old nanny was so happy and settled. Moving to the town and starting from scratch would be hard, whereas she knew where she was at Yew Tree Farm, and so did Joy.

But – Esther's heart lurched and then thumped hard – the farm was so far away from Caleb and it would be inevitable that they would lose touch, and she'd had to face the fact that she didn't want that. But neither did she want more than friendship, did she? She bit her lip, worrying it like a dog with a bone. The truth of the matter was that she didn't know *what* she wanted about anything. Her mind just went round and round in circles.

'Isn't it a simply glorious day?' Priscilla trilled happily, one hand reaching out momentarily from the wheel to squeeze Kenny's arm as they exchanged a smile. Her comment had nothing to do with the weather, which hadn't risen to the momentous occasion, but everything to do with being with the man she loved. Esther had to smile at them; they were so crazily in love. And she understood exactly what Priscilla meant. Direct opposites – Priscilla being a somewhat dizzy, bubbly and unbridled debutante, and Kenny every inch a stolid working-class man, with more rough edges than a chainsaw – but somehow their union was going from strength to strength. Priscilla had confessed to Esther that she'd never been in love before, but now she couldn't imagine life without her Bear, as she affectionately called Kenny; and for his part, Kenny's love for Priscilla shone out of his poor disfigured face in a way that brought a lump to the throat.

'It is a lovely day,' Esther agreed softly – as every day was, for the couple beside her. And she was glad for them.

The farm was situated on the edge of the Yorkshire Dales between Richmond and Darlington, the small village close to the farm being one of many dotted about the landscape, but they had long since left the area and now, an hour later, were approaching countryside that was familiar to Esther. The country road Priscilla had taken wound round the outskirts of Chester-le-Street and, ridiculously, Esther felt physically sick until they had passed the town and were approaching Washington.

The day had dawned wet and thundery, but by the time they had left the farm and picked Kenny up, a weak and watery sun kept popping out to show its face now and again from behind the clouds. The thing that had struck the three in the truck most of all was the uncanny silence as they'd travelled through hamlets and villages. They hadn't expected to see much traffic, as motorists were only allowed two and a half gallons of petrol per month (and then only folk like special constables and wardens, and so on), and of course there were no aircraft, as there had been constantly for the last years, but it was the absence of pedestrians in the towns and villages that was strange. And then, as they reached the outskirts of Sunderland, it was Kenny who came up with the reason. 'They're all indoors preparing for the celebration teas this afternoon,' he said suddenly. 'Of course they are.' Looking up into the sky, which was beginning to cloud over again, he sighed and murmured as much to himself as to Esther and Priscilla, 'That earlier rain was like the heavens weeping for the dead, before rejoicing.' And almost as though this was the signal for release, the next road they turned into was full of folk putting up bunting and flags and streamers.

They had left the farm after helping with the milking and other jobs and then spending time getting washed and changed, so it was eleven o'clock when the old truck trundled into the warren of streets north of the River Wear. The devastation suffered by the streets, shipyards, factories and Wearside families from the Luftwaffe attacks was apparent everywhere, but as Wearside and Tyneside were a hub of shipyards and steelworks, along with the docks and other industry, everyone had known that was going to be the case. Not that it made the reality any easier to bear. Unfortunately Sunderland lay in the flight path that the Luftwaffe had used for raids on the Clydeside area too, so along with suffering independent attacks, it was where the Luftwaffe had often dropped the last of their bombs at the edge of the coast, before heading home to Germany.

As they made their way to Bright Street, where Caleb lived, the three of them stared aghast at the craters and shells of buildings and general destruction. Caleb had written to Esther that large areas of the town had been flattened, but now she was seeing it for herself, she was overwhelmed by the enormity of what ordinary people had gone through. Not for the first time in the last twenty-four hours, she offered up a silent prayer of thanks that the horror was really over at last.

As Priscilla pulled up outside Caleb's house, Joy stirred and opened sleepy eyes. 'We're here, darling,' Esther whispered, her stomach a mass of butterflies. She was nervous. Not just of arriving unannounced like this, or of meeting Caleb's family, but of seeing him again. Letters were one thing; someone in the flesh was completely different. He hadn't mentioned any girls in his correspondence, but that didn't necessarily mean he wasn't seeing someone. What if she was here, with him?

And then she admonished herself sharply. What if he did have a girlfriend? He was a free agent, wasn't he? They were friends, that was all; and he had never indicated anything else. Nevertheless she bitterly regretted falling in with Priscilla's plan as they climbed out of the truck into the terraced street. There were a number of men in shirtsleeves carrying trestle tables that they had clearly borrowed from a church hall or somewhere coming towards them, and bunting was criss-crossed across the street, along with Union Jack flags dangling from bedroom windows. Preparations for the street party were under way.

Feeling sick with nerves, she positioned herself behind Kenny, as Priscilla knocked on the front door of the house, aware of the stares from one or two of the neighbours, who had clearly heard the old truck's rasping engine and had come to their doors to see what was what. One of the men carrying the tables called to them, saying, 'You can't leave that here for long. Take it round the back lane and park it there, if you're going to be here any length of time; we need the room for the tables and chairs and what-have-you.'

Priscilla nodded, calling back brightly, 'Righty-ho, will do,' in her cut-glass accent, causing the man to stop dead in his tracks, his face a picture, so that the fellow carrying the other end of the table dropped it on his foot.

Amid cursing and muttering from the man in question,

the front door opened to reveal a small, stout woman, whom Esther knew instantly was Caleb's mother. The woman's hair was grey and thick, her eyes brown and round, but it was in the shape of her face and the fullness of her wide mouth that the likeness to Caleb was most obvious. She stared at them, and Esther had to admire her when the woman's gaze took in Kenny without flinching. Although Kenny's last two operations had given him a passable nose, most people couldn't hide their shock when they first saw his injuries. It was different when the brown eyes rested on Joy, still half-asleep in her arms. Then Caleb's mother's gaze narrowed and her mouth straightened. 'Can I help you?' she said stiffly, directly to Priscilla.

It was Kenny who answered. 'We're here to see Caleb, if that's possible? I was with him in hospital in Yorkshire. Kenny's the name.'

It was clear to Esther that Caleb's mother pulled herself together with some effort, but her voice was warmer as she said to Kenny, 'Oh aye, lad. He's often spoken of you. Come in. He's in the kitchen. Go on through and surprise him.'

As she stood aside for them to pass into the house she raised a smile of sorts for Priscilla; Esther she looked straight through. Kenny had paused in the hall and now, after shutting the front door, Caleb's mother bustled past them, saying, 'I said go through, lad. Don't stand on ceremony,' and they all followed her into the kitchen.

It was a small room, but clean and tidy. A scrubbed

table with chairs beneath it, a chiffonier holding crockery and dishes, and two comfortable armchairs set at an angle to the black-leaded range, plus a long wooden settle with thick flock cushions were crammed into the limited space, barely leaving enough room to edge round them. But Esther didn't notice any of this. Her eyes were on the tall, dark-haired man who had clearly been sitting at the kitchen table having a cup of tea and reading the paper. For a long moment their eyes held and they were both oblivious of the others, and then the two men were laughing and shaking hands, Caleb's mother was urging them all to sit down and it was general mayhem for a minute or two.

Well, it had to happen one day, didn't it? And she'd pre-pared herself for when it did. She just hadn't expected it to be today, of all days. As she went about mashing the tea, Eliza's head was spinning, although she gave no in-dication of this with her calm, controlled movements and lack of expression. And she could see what had captured her Caleb, for the girl was a beauty – the bairn an' all, in her own way – no doubt about that.

Walking across to the chiffonier, her eyes went to the rose-patterned tea service that had been a wedding pres-ent and which was only brought out on high days and holidays, or when the vicar paid a visit. Eliza was proud of her tea service and, after she had heard Priscilla talk, had decided to use it. Now her hand paused and instead reached for the everyday mugs that the family used.

They'd have to take her as they found her, she told herself grimly. She wasn't about to try and impress anyone.

The milk was already on the table and, bringing the big brown teapot and mugs to the table, she said evenly, 'There's no sugar, I'm afraid. What we had has been used for the cakes for this afternoon's tea, and sweets for the bairns.'

'Oh, that reminds me.' Priscilla jumped up like a jack-in-the-box. 'We brought some bits from the farm, Mrs McGuigan. I do so hope you don't mind all of us descending on you like this, but we so wanted to see Caleb on this special day, didn't we, darling?' she added to Kenny, before continuing in the same breath, 'But if you think your neighbours might object to us sharing the celebrations, then of course we won't intrude.'

Flustered as much by Priscilla's voice – which she termed la-di-da – as by the way the girl had come straight to the point, Eliza said stutteringly, 'N-n-no, of . . . of course not.'

'Oh, lovely! I'll bring the bags in then, shall I? There's one of Mrs Holden's fruitcakes, which are absolutely divine, and a ham-and-egg pie and all sorts of goodies. She *adores* cooking, Mrs Holden and, being a farmer's wife, the rationing hasn't really affected her at all. Whoops! I shouldn't really say that, should I, but it's the truth.' Priscilla gave a peal of laughter, taking Eliza's arm as if she was an old friend. 'Come and see what we've got. There's a ham we can cut up, once they start putting the food out too, and . . . '

As Priscilla disappeared with Eliza, Caleb grinned at the other two. 'My mother doesn't know what's hit her, with Cilla,' he said wryly. 'She's never come across anyone like her before.'

'Who has?' Kenny responded, a wealth of love and pride in his voice.

Esther merely smiled. At this moment she had never envied Priscilla's easy way and total lack of shyness more. For herself, she felt as tongue-tied with Caleb as she did with his mother, who she was sure did not approve of her son's friendship with a married woman with a mixed-race daughter. As though he had picked up on her thoughts, Caleb said softly to Joy, who was sitting on Esther's lap sucking her thumb, 'How's my big girl then? My, you've grown.'

Joy stared at him without replying and Esther said hastily, 'She's going through a shy stage. She's the same with everybody. Just ignore her for a bit, and she'll settle down.' Joy had had her second birthday in the middle of April, and almost from that very day had decided all men were suspect. Priscilla had remarked that Joy showed great wisdom for one so young.

'She's beautiful,' Caleb said quietly.

Esther smiled a more natural smile. She had put Joy in her best dress – a pretty, pale-yellow smocked frock with matching pants, which Rose had made her for her birthday on Mrs Holden's little sewing machine – and brushed her burnished curls until they hung in shining ringlets framing her heart-shaped face with its huge green eyes, and to her Joy looked enchanting. 'Thank you.' Clearing her throat, she added, 'I hope we haven't put your mother out, coming like this. We should have let you know.'

'Don't be daft.'

He had spoken too quickly, and they both knew it. Kenny spoke into the embarrassing pause that followed, making some comment about the forthcoming speech from Winston Churchill, scheduled to be broadcast at three that afternoon, after which the festivities would begin in earnest, and as the two men continued the conversation, Esther hugged Joy to her again. Caleb's mother's disapproval had made up her mind about one thing: she wouldn't take him up on his offer to help her find somewhere in the immediate district to live. In fact, it was probably better if she cut all contact with him. She didn't want to come between him and his family. His mother didn't like her and that was fair enough, she told herself silently, swallowing against the lump in her throat. But if Eliza was openly hostile, or unkind in any way to her daughter, then she would take her to task, Caleb or no Caleb.

Outside in the street Priscilla had opened the door of the truck, but hadn't immediately reached for the bags wedged at the back of the long seat. Instead she said – very quietly for her – 'Can I have a word with you in private, Mrs McGuigan?'

Eliza looked at the fancy toff, as she had termed

Priscilla in her mind. 'Well, there's no one listening, as far as I can tell, lass.'

'It's about Esther.' Priscilla had seen the way Caleb's mother had looked at her friend and, as always, had decided to rush in where angels fear to tread. 'I don't know what Caleb has told you, but whatever he has said, you might be thinking that he has merely been fooled by a pretty face.'

Completely taken aback, Eliza rallied enough to say, 'It wouldn't be the first time a lad has been taken in by the turn of an ankle.'

'I dare say, Mrs McGuigan, but in Esther's case you couldn't be more wrong. She's a good girl and a fine person, and has been treated shamefully, first by the man she thought was her father and then by her husband. Has Caleb told you the circumstances of her birth? About her real father and mother?'

Stiffly now, Eliza said, 'He told me what she told him, aye.'

'Well, every word is true. I've never seen anyone more in love than Esther was with her husband, and she never even looked at another man, let alone kissed one. When he treated her as he did, it broke something in her and it was terrible to see. He even said that if she abandoned Joy – had her brought up in an orphanage somewhere, or given to someone else so that she would never see her again – he would stay with her; but they would have to adopt children, if she wanted more, because of her father being black. But there was no way Esther was going to have Joy put away. Did Caleb tell you that too? And that Esther is proud of her daughter, as she has every reason to be; and neither is she ashamed that her father's skin was a different colour from her mother's. I think that is as it should be, and if more people thought that way, this terrible war and all the millions of deaths would never have happened. What does the colour of a person's skin matter, Mrs McGuigan?'

'It does to some folk round here, lass.'

'And to you, Mrs McGuigan? Does it matter to you? It doesn't to your son, and you ought to be proud of him.'

The quick jerk of Eliza's head and the straightening of her lips told Priscilla that Caleb's mother didn't appreciate being taken to task in this way, but Priscilla didn't care.

'I can tell you that Esther has been hurt so badly I don't know if she will ever trust a man again, and she certainly has no plans to ensnare Caleb, Mrs McGuigan. Now, I also think that Caleb is biting at the bit to be ensnared, but it takes two, and in this case it's far too early for Esther. That is the truth. She isn't trying to trap him, whatever you may think.'

'She certainly has a friend in you.'

'Yes, she has.' Priscilla had been leaning close to Caleb's mother. Now she straightened, reaching for the bags and passing one to Eliza. 'And if you give her a chance, you will see she is a lovely person, and that little Joy is the sweetest child imaginable. And, Mrs McGuigan,' Priscilla's voice lowered still further, 'if you rebuff Esther now, you run the risk of losing your son: here inside, where it matters.' She touched her heart. 'Their relationship might never come to anything – who can say? – but Caleb will always think that you had a hand in spoiling it for him.'

Just as quietly Eliza said, 'You can say all that, and then you can swan off back to your highfalutin friends and la-di-da family and forget us. I have to live round here, and so does Caleb, and I know the way they think. He'll be hanged, drawn and quartered in their gossiping, and it'll break him.'

'If you think that, then you don't know your son very well, Mrs McGuigan.'

Strangely, Eliza did not turn on her, as Priscilla expected, knowing that she had gone a mite too far. Instead Caleb's mother looked at her levelly for a moment, and her voice was flat as she said, 'You think you know him better than me?'

'I think your love as a mother is blinding you to the way he has grown up and matured during the war, and especially after his injuries. He's a strong man, in every sense of the word, Mrs McGuigan, and I think you are a strong woman too. Esther needs friends like you and Caleb.'

Eliza stepped back with a bag in each hand. 'I can't put things like you do – I haven't had your education and I don't know how to express meself – but I do know my neighbours, and they can be as cruel as any of Hitler's lackeys.'

They stared at each other. 'Change is coming, Mrs

McGuigan. The war has seen to that. Nothing will be the same again. And, incidentally, I won't be going back to my old life; not if Kenny asks me to marry him, which I hope with all my heart he will do. My place will be with him and he's a working-class man, just like Caleb. Class and all that – it's rubbish. It's what we do with our lives that counts. The First World War started the change, and this one has stirred things up even more. And I think that's so, so good.'

'And you think your mam an' da will welcome Kenny into the fold? I think not, lass.'

'It doesn't matter, one way or the other. Now is the time to think for ourselves and stand up for what's right. Or what have we been fighting for these last awful years? Don't you *see*, Mrs McGuigan?'

'What I see, lass, is that there is much more to you than you first let on.' Across the bags the two women surveyed each other for a long moment. Then Eliza said, 'Bring them bags in and we'll see what's what. And you'd better drive that big old truck round the back, or they'll be banging on the door asking for it to be moved.'

Priscilla nodded, her voice chirpy again as she trilled, 'Righty-ho, Mrs McGuigan. We don't want to upset the natives, do we?'

Chapter Fifteen

Caleb tried not to stare at his mother. Eliza was sitting with Joy on her lap, enjoying a cup of tea before Winston Churchill was due to speak. The child had her thumb in her mouth and was half-asleep, and every so often Eliza caressed the shining curls of the little girl as she chatted with the others. If someone had told Caleb earlier that day they would be sitting here like this, he would have laughed in their face. But then Joy could melt the hardest heart and, with the guilelessness of children, she'd taken to Eliza and showed it.

Caleb breathed a silent prayer of thanks. His mother's response to the child had knocked him for six. He'd thought, when the little party arrived earlier, that he was going to have to take his mother aside and tell her to behave herself, but instead her initial stiffness with Esther had melted like the morning mist before the sun. And she was behaving towards Joy exactly as she would with any of her grandchildren. He couldn't get over it.

Esther, sandwiched between two of Caleb's sisters,

who'd arrived to share the momentous day with their mother, was thinking along the same lines, and had come to the conclusion she had misjudged Eliza earlier. Nevertheless she was still wary of Caleb's mother and of his sisters too; and when the oldest sister, Prudence, who had worked as a nurse before her marriage and had returned to it when war had broken out, came through the back door in the next moment, Esther watched the woman's eyes widen as they fastened on Joy. Esther gave a silent sigh. She felt horribly awkward and somewhat hemmed in among the company, and her initial misgivings that they were intruding by descending on Caleb's mother like this returned tenfold.

It was clear to everyone that Prudence had been crying, and Esther understood why. Prudence's husband wasn't coming home, like Clara's and Ida's. The euphoria of the day and the mad gaiety pervading the streets must be bittersweet to her. Caleb had told her before that, but for the bairns and her nursing work, which Prudence loved, he would have feared for his sister's state of mind after she had learned of her husband's death.

Caleb introduced the visitors to his sister, and as Clara stood up to make a fresh pot of tea, Prudence sat down in her seat. The children were playing some game of their own with others from neighbouring houses in the lane beyond the back yards, amid much squealing and shouting and screaming, and Prudence said flatly, 'They'll all be as sick as dogs before the day is out, what with the excitement and the party tea, you mark my words. They're going mad out there.'

'It's only one day,' said Ida, reproof in her tone.

Prudence looked as though she was about to say something, but changed her mind, turning instead to Esther as she said quietly, 'It's nice to meet you, lass. Our Caleb has spoken of you often since he's been back.'

Esther didn't know quite what to say to that, but something in Ida's treatment of her sister's obvious grief made her want to reach out to Prudence. Just as quietly, and hoping she wasn't putting her foot in it, she said, 'I'm so sorry about your husband. Caleb said you two had something very special, and today must be difficult for you.'

For a moment Prudence didn't answer and Esther panicked that she shouldn't have mentioned him, but then – like a balloon deflating – the rigidity went out of Prudence's body and she said softly, 'Thank you, lass. I appreciate that. Everyone thinks I should be over it by now, especially as there are plenty of others in the same boat, and Mam and the others change the subject if I try and talk about him. It's the way round here, I suppose. Grin and bear it. And I am; I am bearing it, but I keep thinking what a waste. What a terrible waste. He was such a lovely man, always laughing and joking, and never a bad word about anybody. He worked in the docks and he needn't have gone into the army at all, but no – he had to go and do his bit, as he saw it. And for what? He's never even seen our last bairn, and she'll never know what a grand man her da was.'

'You can tell her.' Esther reached out and squeezed Prudence's hand. 'You can keep his memory alive, and that is only right and proper too. Don't stop talking about him, and don't let anyone make you feel bad for grieving.'

Prudence smiled a watery smile. 'No, I won't. I won't.' She took a deep breath and sat up straighter. 'Your little un' is bonny, isn't she? I don't think I've ever seen such a beautiful little lassie. Our mam is clearly taken with her.'

'I was worried your mother would think we were intruding – descending without warning.'

'Oh, Mam loves a houseful, always has; and you've made Caleb's day. Has he told you he's managed to find himself a job? It's driven him mad, sitting at home all day twiddling his thumbs.'

Esther shook her head. For most of the time they had been here the two men had sat together talking, and she and Priscilla and Caleb's mother had chatted. Or, rather, Priscilla and Caleb's mother, she corrected herself ruefully. Try as she might, she hadn't been able to relax and had used Joy as an excuse not to join in the conversation half the time. Joy had had a long nap on her lap after lunch, but had woken up when Clara and Ida had arrived with their children. Esther felt that, with so many folk crammed in the kitchen, her silence hadn't been so obvious. Not that she was a chatterer anyway; she never had been.

'Aye, he's got himself set on at Thompson's shipyard,' Prudence said with a hint of pride. 'He was a riveter there before he decided to go in the army, but course he can't do that now, not with his leg. The job's dangerous enough for blokes with two legs, let alone one. Anyway, he took himself off to see his old supervisor an' had a chat, an' Mr Brown said he'd see what he could do; an' true to his word, he got back to Caleb to say he'd arranged an interview for him with someone in the offices. He's always had a bit up top, has Caleb. Not like the rest of us.' She grinned and Esther smiled back. 'So the upshot was they offered to train him up as a draughtsman!' This was said with a flourish.

'That's wonderful.' Esther glanced across at Caleb. 'He didn't mention it in any of his letters.' She felt a little hurt.

'Oh, it's only happened in the last few days, lass,' said Prudence hastily, 'and to tell the truth, he feels a bit bashful about it, though I don't know why. He says being an apprentice at the age of twenty-six is nothing to crow about.'

Prudence clearly disagreed, and her pride in her brother was tangible. Esther found she liked this sister more and more. 'Well, I think it's marvellous,' she said warmly, 'and I'll tell him so, when I get the chance. When I first met him he was very down about his leg, and he's rallied round and is clearly going to make something of his life, no matter what.'

Prudence stared at the girl she had heard so much

about from her brother, when he called by some evenings to see her and the bairns. He would share their evening meal and play with the two older children while she put little Emily to bed, and would then help her settle Arnie and Francis. She knew Caleb was trying to do his bit as a stand-in da for the boys, although nothing had been said between the two of them, and she loved him for it. She also knew how much he thought of this beautiful girl with the sad, sad eyes, although clearly Esther was unaware of Caleb's feelings or the fact that it had been she herself who – as she'd put it – had caused him to rally round and make something of his life. Carefully feeling her way, Prudence murmured, 'Everyone needs something – or someone – to live for.' And in case that was too obvious she added, 'With me, it's the bairns. I don't know what I'd have done without them after Dunkirk.'

Esther nodded. 'He lives on in them.' Even as she said it, she felt an overwhelming flood of emotion. She wished Monty had died before their baby was born and she could think that way about him; could have believed that he would love her and their child, no matter what the circumstances.

Eliza interrupted her thoughts, saying loudly, 'Shush, everyone, it's three o'clock,' as she motioned to Clara, who was now sitting closest to the wireless, to turn it up.

Right on cue, the familiar and much-loved voice began: 'Yesterday at 2.41 a.m. at General Eisenhower's headquarters, General Jodl, the representative of the German High Command, and Admiral Doenitz, the designated head of the German state, signed the act of unconditional surrender of all German land, sea and air forces in Europe, to the Allied Expeditionary Force and simultaneously to the Soviet High Command ... Today, this agreement will be ratified and confirmed at Berlin ... Hostilities will end officially at one minute after midnight tonight, Tuesday, 8 May, but in the interests of saving lives, the "Cease Fire" began yesterday to be sounded all along the front.'

At this Eliza, never one to show outward emotion, began to cry unrestrainedly, and Esther quietly got up and took Joy from her lap, before sitting down again next to Prudence.

'I should not forget to mention that our dear Channel Islands, the only part of His Majesty's Dominions that has been in the hands of the German foe, are also to be freed today,' the steady voice went on. 'The Germans are still in places resisting the Russian troops, but should they continue to do so after midnight, they will, of course, deprive themselves of the protection of the laws of war, and will be attacked from all quarters by the Allied troops.'

'Protection of the laws of war?' Kenny burst out passionately. 'What about all our poor devils in their concentration camps? Did they have protection?'

Caleb whispered something gently to his friend and Kenny subsided back in his seat, visibly shaking with the force of his feelings.

'It is not surprising,' went on Churchill, 'that on such

long fronts and in the existing disorder of the enemy, the orders of the German High Command should not, in every case, be obeyed immediately. This does not, in our opinion, with the best military advice at our disposal, constitute any reason for withholding from the nation the facts communicated to us by General Eisenhower of the unconditional surrender already signed at Rheims, nor should it prevent us from celebrating today and tomorrow, Wednesday, as Victory in Europe days. Today, perhaps, we shall think mostly of ourselves. Tomorrow we shall pay a particular tribute to our Russian comrades, whose prowess in the field has been one of the grand contributions to the general victory.'

He paused. 'The German war is therefore at an end.'

The occupants of the kitchen heard the cheers and shouts and clapping from outside the house following the last sentence, but inside, apart from Eliza's quiet sobs, the silence continued. Each of them was aware of the men from this particular family still far away on forcign soil and that, in Eliza and Clara's cases, they hadn't heard from their husbands in weeks.

After a moment or two Churchill's voice came again: 'After years of intense preparation, Germany hurled herself on Poland at the beginning of September, 1939, and, in pursuance of our guarantee to Poland and in agreement with the French Republic, Great Britain, the British Empire and Commonwealth of Nations declared war upon this foul aggression. After gallant France had been struck down, we from this island and from our United

Empire maintained the struggle single-handed for a whole year until we were joined by the military might of the Soviet Union, and later by the overwhelming power and resources of the United States of America. Finally, almost the whole world was combined against the evil-doers, who are now prostrate before us. Our gratitude to all our splendid Allies goes forth from all our hearts in this island and throughout the British Empire.'

'Even if they did leave it a bit late,' the irrepressible Kenny put in caustically, earning a 'Shush!' from Priscilla.

'We may allow ourselves a brief period of rejoicing, but let us not forget for a moment the toils and efforts that lie ahead. Japan, with all her treachery and greed, remains unsubdued. The injustice she has inflicted upon Great Britain, the United States and other countries, and her detestable cruelties, call for justice and retribution. We must now devote all our strength and resources to the completion of our task, both at home and abroad.'

Again a brief pause, then: 'Advance, Britannia! Long live the cause of freedom! God save the King!'

They were all crying now, and as the children bounded in from the yard shouting, 'The war really is over! It's over!', everyone began hugging and laughing amid their tears.

Suddenly Caleb was in front of her, and Esther looked up into his eyes for a split second, before he took her into his arms for the first time in their acquaintance. The hug was brief, from one friend to another, but Esther was vitally aware of the bigness of him, the breadth of his shoulders and the controlled strength in the arms holding her close, as he murmured above her head, 'The final end of the end, Esther. Let's hope the world has learned there's nothing more precious than peace.'

Prudence's little girl came to stand in front of them and tugged at Caleb's trousers. 'Uncle Caleb, what does it mean: the war has ended?' she asked anxiously.

As they parted, Caleb bent down and lifted her up, smiling as he said, 'It means you will see lights at night in the streets, and windows lit up, hinny. And no more sirens – never again.'

'But Arnie and Francis say our da is never coming home again. Is that true?'

She was five years old in three months' time and had never seen her father, being born two months after he had died. And her brothers barely remembered him. With a lump in his throat, Caleb said huskily, 'He would have liked to have come home, Emily, because he loved you and your brothers and your mam very much. That's why he went to fight the baddies, to try and protect you all. But Arnie and Francis are right; he's not coming home because he's in heaven now, where he still continues to protect you and them, and your mam. But your mam misses him very much. Will you remember that and be extra-good for her?'

Emily nodded. 'It's them that's naughty anyway, Uncle Caleb. Arnie and Francis. But I'll tell them that Mam's sad and that they've got to behave themselves.'

'Aye, lass. You do that.'

As they watched her disappear, full of self-importance, to find her brothers, Esther said softly, 'You're very good with children, aren't you?' For such a big man, Caleb was incredibly gentle.

'I like them,' he said simply.

He would make a wonderful father. Where the thought came from she didn't know, but it threw her, and suddenly she was flustered and flushed, covering her confusion by saying, 'Where's Joy toddled off to?'

Caleb smiled, his eyes crinkling. 'There, with my mam again.' He nodded across the room, and sure enough Joy was sitting on Eliza's lap, snuggled close to her.

This was all too much. Feeling as though she was drowning and not knowing why, Esther murmured faintly, 'I need some fresh air – I'm sorry.'

She must have looked as strange as she felt, because Caleb said swiftly, 'Come on, come with me,' which was actually the last thing she wanted. Nevertheless she allowed him to take her arm and lead her through the throng and out into the back yard, where a faint drizzle of rain was misting the air.

Esther took refuge in banalities as she said, 'Oh dear, I hope the rain doesn't spoil things.' She had never been more conscious of Caleb as a man, and it was disturbing.

'You must be joking,' he said softly, worried about the pallor that had drained her face of all colour in the last few moments. 'This is the north, and nothing will be allowed to get in the way of this street party. I took a look in the street a while ago, and the tables reach from one side of the road to the other.' Which wasn't difficult in the narrow terraces. 'Apart from the hillocks of bread and butter, and the bowls of multicoloured jelly, there's almond whirls and fairy cakes and a host of other indigestibles, along with bottles of lemonade and cream soda and raspberry fizz. And, of course, the barrels of beer placed at strategic intervals along the street.'

He was aware that he was babbling somewhat, but somehow the atmosphere was charged.

'Makes a change for the street parties to get an airing for something other than an event empurpled by royalty, don't you think?' He liked that: 'empurpled by royalty'. He'd read it in a newspaper article the day before. 'We had three in three years, ten years ago, what with the Silver Jubilee of King George V and Queen Mary, then the accession of Edward VIII when poor old George turned up his toes, and then after the abdication the present King stepping up to take over the family business.' He grinned at her, pretending not to notice her strained face. 'All the old wives round here were in their element. There's nothing they like more than a good old-fashioned knees-up.'

His easy conversation had calmed the panic that had suddenly hit her out of the blue, and Esther was able to smile back. 'I've never been to a street party,' she said a little wistfully.

'No? Then you will enjoy this one, I can guarantee it. And of course the bairns eat too much and have belly-ache.' His voice dropping, he said softly, 'I heard what you said to Prudence, by the way, and I appreciate it. Ida doesn't mean to be insensitive, but she invariably is; and Pru is still struggling with everything.'

She'd had no idea he'd been able to hear them, and found herself trying to recall what she had said when the conversation had turned to Caleb.

As though he'd read her thoughts, he continued, 'I was going to mention the job next time I wrote, by the way.'

'I'm very pleased for you,' she said a little primly.

'Thanks.' He suppressed a smile. He had the notion that she had been a little put out to learn about the job second-hand from Prudence. 'It's all happened in the last week.'

'Yes, your sister said.'

'Of course, as an apprentice, I won't be earning much for a while, but once that's finished I'll see about moving out and getting my own place.' He kept his voice casual, as though he hadn't been thinking about how to let her know that he didn't intend to stay with his parents long-term.

'Won't your mother miss you?'

'Not once Da's home. Besides, there's always one or the other of my sisters and their brood round here. Anyway, that's in the future.' As voices from inside the house called his name, he said, 'I reckon the party's about to begin. Come on.'

And when he took her hand and led her back into the house, she didn't pull it from his.

*

The afternoon sped by in a melee of children running hither and thither and playing games; food and more food; endless toasts drunk to victory; and laughter. Much laughter – bred of overwhelming relief that, after all the rumours that the war was about to end, it had actually happened. One enterprising matron had organized a Punch-and-Judy show for the children later in the afternoon, once everyone had eaten their fill. This had proved fortuitous as, true to Prudence's prediction, a number of the little ones had eaten too much and were feeling nauseous and needed a break from the mayhem.

The street parties all over the country were due to end with fireworks and bonfires, with effigies of Hitler replacing the traditional Guy Fawkes. This would occur once King George VI had given his address on the wireless at nine o'clock. Esther, along with most of the other women, had been busy taking care of the children during the afternoon; and then, once everyone had eaten their fill, some of the tables and trestles were moved to make more room for games after the Punch-and-Judy show. It was only then that she had another word with Caleb. He joined her as she stood drinking a cup of tea, watching Joy sitting cross-legged in the midst of his sisters' children, all of them entranced at the sight of Mr Punch knocking six bells out of the long-suffering Judy.

She smiled at him. 'She's had a lovely time. It's a shame she's too young to remember it for long.'

'There'll be other good times.'

Esther's smile faded. She hadn't missed some of the

glances that had been sent her way and Joy's. On the farm, she didn't even think about the colour of her daughter's skin, but here, among the sea of white faces, Joy stuck out like a sore thumb. She didn't want life to be difficult for her beloved child, but neither did she want to hide Joy away from the world. She wouldn't be doing her daughter any favours in the long run. Hateful though it was, Joy was going to have to learn how to cope with the inevitable prejudice that would come her way.

Now, as Caleb murmured, 'Have you thought about what I said in my letter – about you coming to live in these parts?' she realized that at some point during the day she had come to a decision, without even knowing it.

She nodded. 'I'd like to, it's just the practicalities that need to be worked through. I'd have to find work and somewhere to live; perhaps even childcare for Joy. Of course it wouldn't happen for some months yet. The war might be over, but the Land Army will carry on doing their bit for some time.'

Caleb managed to keep the elation out of his voice as he said quietly, 'Childcare? Wouldn't Rose look after Joy, if you got a job?'

'She would, but . . . ' She turned to look at him. 'She's so happy on the farm, Caleb. And she and Mrs Holden have become bosom friends. It doesn't seem fair to drag her away from that, and then expect her to stay at home all day by herself with just a little toddler for company. She would do it, of course she would do it, but she'd be lonely.'

'She'd have Joy in the day, and you in the evening.'

'I know, but on the farm she's busy and fulfilled.'

'I can't see Rose staying put, if you and Joy left.'

Esther shrugged. 'We'll see. I could pay her a visit now and again at the weekends perhaps, or she could come and stay for a bit every so often. Anyway, it won't happen for a while. Not until Farmer Holden gets some of his men back – the ones who survived the war, that is. And he's full of doom and gloom about the future, as it is. He keeps going on about the government's 'great betrayal' of 1921, when the state abandoned its policy of support for the farmers, and he's worried they'll do it again. If he's said it once, he's said a hundred times that his labourers' pay before the war was forty-eight shillings a week and now the national minimum is seventy shillings. And it's not as if he and Mrs Holden live in the lap of luxury, to be fair, for the farmhouse is basic, to say the least.'

The more Esther said, the less reassured Caleb was that she would actually leave the farm, but he knew he couldn't articulate this. He didn't want to say or do anything to frighten her off. Feeling he was treading on eggshells, he cleared his throat. 'Things will work out,' he said gruffly. 'And if you did decide to live round here without Rose, I dare say Mam would lend a hand with Joy. She loves little 'uns, as you've probably gathered.' What his mother would actually say if this proposition was put to her, he didn't know; he'd cross that bridge if he came to it.

Again Esther said, 'We'll see,' but in a tone that signified the conversation was at an end. And with that Caleb had to be content.

All the children in the district had been building an enormous bonfire on a bombed site just beyond the end of Caleb's street, and had given the affair due publicity, making their own posters and fixing them to various street lamps. Everyone had been instructed to bring friends along, and the older boys had made their own fireworks and flares. Even the adults had participated in the making of Hitler. One old lady had given a jacket, another a pair of trousers, and so on, until Hitler's rig was assured. A retired dressmaker who lived at the corner of the street, and who had umpteen excited grandchildren, had even given the dressing-up a professional touch, altering the garments until they fitted the effigy to perfection. The local bobby had made the face and had helped the lads fit up some macabre gallows, which the chief fire-watcher and warden had erected, before stringing up Hitler's body.

Union Jacks and bunting were hung from wooden posts in front of the bombed site, and the proceedings had been billed to start at dusk, at ten o'clock. It was clear the bonfire was the highlight of the day for the children. They had several planks supported by bricks, which were intended as seats for the elderly or infirm; and the dressmaker had promised that two strong men could carry out her piano just before the show was due to begin, and she would play for everyone.

Early that morning, when they had set off from York-shire, Esther had imagined they would leave Sunderland at the end of the afternoon, if not before. Now she real-ized that Priscilla and Kenny had no intention of starting for home until they had wrung every last moment of enjoyment out of the day. And she couldn't blame them. A victory at the end of the bloodiest war in history was worth celebrating, after all.

At ten to nine all the members of Caleb's family once again crowded into his mother's kitchen, a hush falling across them as nine o'clock chimed. It was slightly eerie to think that the same reverent silence was abroad across Britain, and much of the Empire.

The somewhat uncertain voice of the King crackled at precisely nine o'clock: 'Today we give thanks to Almighty God for a great deliverance. Speaking from our Empire's oldest capital city, war-battered but never for one moment daunted or dismayed, speaking from London, I ask you to join with me in that act of thanksgiving. Germany, the enemy who drove all Europe into war, has been finally overcome. In the Far East we have yet to deal with the Japanese, a determined and cruel foe. To this we shall turn with the utmost resolve and with all our resources.'

Here Eliza gave a hiccup of a sob. She was terrified that her Stanley would be sent to fight the Japanese.

'But at this hour,' the very human voice continued, 'when the dreadful shadow of war has passed from our hearts and homes in these islands, we may at last make one pause for thanksgiving . . . '

Esther glanced around the assembled faces. Was Monty alive? He was her husband – the father of her daughter – and yet she didn't know. It said it all, somehow.

'Let us think what it was that has upheld us through nearly six years of suffering and peril. The knowledge that everything was at stake: our freedom, our independence, our very existence as a people; but the knowledge also that in defending ourselves we were defending the liberties of the whole world; that our cause was the cause not of this nation only, not of this Empire and Commonwealth only, but of every land where freedom is cherished, and law and liberty go hand in hand.'

The King's words resonated in Esther's heart like a physical blow. Cruelty and injustice: that was what the King was talking about. But it wasn't just Hitler and Goering and Mussolini who were guilty of that crime; it was every man, woman or child who judged another on their position in society, the name of their ancestors, the colour of their skin, their religion or their culture. She had never seen it so clearly before.

'In the darkest hours we knew that the enslaved and isolated peoples of Europe looked to us; their hopes were our hopes; their confidence confirmed our faith. We knew that, if we failed, the last remaining barrier against a worldwide tyranny would have fallen in ruins. But we did not fail. We kept faith with ourselves and with one another; we kept faith and unity with our great allies. That faith, that unity have carried us through to victory.'

Was Monty listening to this somewhere? And if so, would he see the irony of the King's words? Esther thought bitterly. Monty had fought on the side of the true and righteous, according to what she was hearing, and yet he had thrown away what they'd had together, because her father was a different colour to himself. Hitler, in his madness, had waged war even in his own country against the disabled, the Gypsies, the Jews and those Germans with a different-coloured skin. Monty had seen that was wrong and had been prepared to take up arms against it, and yet towards his own wife and child he'd behaved no better than Hitler.

'There is great comfort in the thought that the years of darkness and danger in which the children of our country had grown up are over and, please God, forever.'

The rest of the King's words were lost to Esther; she sat in a dark turmoil of her own. Right and wrong – it really was as simple as that. It wasn't which side you'd fought on in this terrible, bloodthirsty war. It was all to do with your own heart and soul, the bit of you that made you *you*. There were probably ordinary German people, housewives and mothers, fathers and brothers, who had been against Hitler and his Nazis and had paid the ultimate price because of it. And on the other side – the side that supposedly stood for freedom and equality of man – there were men like Monty, who had fought and risked their lives, and yet were capable of turning their back on their own child because she didn't fit into what they perceived as socially acceptable. How could that be? *How on earth could that be?*

'Esther?' She came back to her surroundings as Prudence took her arm. 'Are you all right, lass?'

Amazingly, she was. 'I'm fine.' She forced a smile. 'Absolutely fine.' She could put her head on the pillow at night and sleep with a clear conscience. She had done nothing wrong, and suddenly that was of vital importance. As the GIs would say: she was one of the good guys.

It was a moment of epiphany and she recognized it as such.

A short time later, with Caleb at her side and a sleepy Joy cradled in his arms, she walked with the others to the site of the bonfire, where the chief fire-watcher was already standing, ready to light the fire at the stroke of ten o'clock. The neighbourhood children were beside themselves with excitement, and when one of the older boys who'd been designated with the honour handed the chief fire-watcher a long pole, at the end of which was a rag soaked in paraffin, a sudden quiet descended. Immediately the fire was lit, a long and sustained cheer went up.

The children danced around the bonfire yelling at the top of their voices; flares were let off and fireworks shot up into the sky, and occasionally into the crowd too, causing brief panic. The dressmaker's piano was at the ready at a suitable distance from the flames, and soon the lady in question had begun to play a selection of popular songs: 'Roll Out the Barrel', 'Tipperary', 'Daisy, Daisy', 'The Lambeth Walk', 'Knees Up Mother Brown' and other rousing tunes to stir the people's patriotism, which was tangible.

Grown-ups, young people and children joined hands and danced and sang, their voices ringing out, while other folk stood quietly enjoying the scene, and thanking God they were alive. Once the fire died down, potatoes were cooked in the ashes; and more beer, saved for the end of the day, was brought out and handed around.

'Glad you came?' Caleb smiled down at her, with Joy fast asleep in his arms, and Esther smiled back, nodding. Priscilla and Kenny were wrapped in each other's arms at the edge of the flickering light, but she couldn't pick out Eliza or Prudence or any of the others. It was gone midnight, but no one seemed to want to go home, although some mothers of small children were beginning to try and round up their offspring. Everyone seemed to feel it was a never-to-be-forgotten experience – one that so easily might not have happened, if Hitler had got his way.

'It's been a wonderful day,' she said softly, 'but I can't help thinking that . . . '

'What?' he said as she hesitated.

'That now the future is in front of us, and everything is going to be so different from the last few years.'

'And that's a bad thing?'

'No, no, of course not, but things that have been put on the back burner because of the war will have to be dealt with.'

Since that first night at the village hop, when they had talked in the moonlight and she had told him her story, Caleb had never brought up the subject of her husband. He had thought about him often enough, accepting wryly that he was intensely jealous of a man he had never met. Esther had loved him – perhaps did love him still – and her husband had let her down in the worst way possible, abandoning her and her baby. But women were forgiving creatures, and she had said herself that her husband had been her first and only love. Perhaps he hadn't brought the subject up because he didn't want to risk finding out how she really felt? he asked himself now. And she was right: while the war had been going on and everything had been up in the air, it had been easier to put off the inevitable. He wasn't proud of the fact, but he had often prayed that this Monty would meet his end, courtesy of one of Hitler's bombs.

Now, cautiously feeling his way, he said, 'Was that a general observation, or something more personal?'

'Both, I suppose.'

Caleb was a northern man to the tips of his toes and, in spite of not wanting to frighten her off, nothing on earth could have prevented his next words. It was speak or burst. 'You're thinking of him – your husband – aren't you?'

Again she nodded.

His stomach churning, he said gruffly, 'Have you heard from him? Is that it?'

'No, I haven't heard a thing, so I suppose that means

he is still alive, or someone would have to let me know. And if he is alive, if I'm not a widow' – she flashed him a quick glance, but he kept his face expressionless – 'then divorce proceedings will have to be faced.'

'Perhaps he doesn't want a divorce. He might have changed his mind.' Caleb's lips had become dry and he ran his tongue over them before he could say, 'Have you considered that possibility?'

She didn't reply directly to this. What she did say, and in a tone that brooked no argument, was, '*I* want a divorce, Caleb.'

'You do?' Such emotion flooded through him that he felt faint.

'I don't love Monty any more. In truth, I wonder if I ever knew the real Monty, or whether I fell in love with what I imagined he was. Does that make sense?'

He didn't know, but he wanted to hear the rest of it and so he nodded, his eyes never leaving her sad face.

'I thought it was a forever love, and that nothing but death could part us. That he loved me for exactly who I was: warts and pimples and all.' She gave a weak smile. 'But . . . ' She shrugged. 'He didn't. I've asked myself: if the position was reversed, and when Joy was born it had turned out that Monty was adopted or something and had a black parent, would I have felt differently about him? And I can say from the bottom of my heart that I wouldn't. But perhaps that's just me and I asked too much of him – of anyone in that position.'

'No, you didn't.' His heart was in his voice.

She made a little inarticulate sound, her eyes holding his, and for a moment the scene in front of them faded away and the night was hushed.

But for the sleeping child in his arms, Caleb would have drawn Esther to him, then and there, and declared that she was the most amazing, beautiful, exquisite creature in all the world, and that nothing in heaven or hell could have stopped him from being at her side, if he'd been Monty. As it was, his voice shaking slightly, he said again, 'You didn't, Esther. The fault is his. Only his.'

The expectant hush continued for a moment more, before Esther could bring herself to murmur, 'Thank you.' She felt as though she was on the brink of a chasm; a chasm that had opened so suddenly it had taken her breath away. Why couldn't Monty have been made of the same stuff as Caleb? Caleb would never have walked away and left his wife and child to fend for themselves, whatever the circumstances. There wasn't a shadow of turning in Caleb's big, strong frame. How was it some women ended up with men like Caleb, whereas she . . . ?

Something in her mind checked the mistake of continuing down that path – a path that could only bring further heartache. Caleb was a kind, good man, and she knew he cared about her as a friend, but he had never said one word indicating that he wished their relationship was something more. She must remember that. And why would he? When Caleb got romantically involved, it would doubtless be with a girl untainted by the past, some eager, bright young thing with no skeletons in the cupboard, who could offer him all of herself, with no reservations. And he deserved that, he really did.

Suddenly Esther felt as old as the hills and weary of life, and the corners of her mouth drooped.

Caleb saw her expression and he could have kicked himself. He had obviously done the one thing he hadn't wanted to do and unnerved her. Had she guessed how he felt and been embarrassed? Thank goodness he was holding Joy and hadn't been able to follow through on the desire to take Esther in his arms and hold her. She would have probably called an end to their tenuous friendship, right then and there. Damn it, he had to be more careful or he would lose her altogether.

He was as relieved as Esther when Priscilla and Kenny came up behind them in the next moment, Kenny slapping Caleb on the back as he said, 'I think it's time we started to make a move for home.' And Priscilla took Esther's arm as she breathed, 'Hasn't it been a truly wonderful day, darling? I'm so happy I could burst.'

'Wonderful,' Esther agreed quietly.

Eventually they found the others in the crowd and said their goodbyes, but only Caleb accompanied them to the truck parked at the end of the back lane, still carrying the sleeping Joy in his arms.

In contrast to Priscilla's exuberant leave-taking of Caleb, when she flung her arms round his neck and deposited a smacking kiss on his cheek, Esther merely smiled and nodded. Caleb's goodbye was equally subdued, and once they were all packed in the truck and it trundled noisily off, leaving Caleb standing looking after them, Esther began to have niggling regrets about mentioning Monty to him. And the more she thought about what she had said, the more she began to panic. Would Caleb think she had told him she didn't love Monty, and wanted a divorce, because she had hoped he would declare that he had feelings for her?

She felt hot all over in spite of the chilly night.

By the time the truck reached the farm after depositing Kenny at the home, she felt like a wet rag. Joy hadn't stirred during the journey, and as Priscilla turned off the ignition and they climbed out of the vehicle, Esther thought longingly of her bed. She needed to sleep. Perhaps she'd feel differently in the morning and see things more clearly, because at the moment it felt like the end of the world. She didn't want to lose Caleb as a friend, or for him to think badly of her. She needed him in her life.

The night was pitch-black, a cloudy sky obscuring the moon and stars, but a light was still burning in the cottage, causing Esther to murmur ruefully, 'Oh dear, it looks like Rose has waited up for us, and I told her not to. She needs her sleep.'

The two farm collies, Gyp and Badger, that slept in one of the hay barns came sniffing at their ankles to make sure all was well, but as Esther and Priscilla walked towards their cottage, the two dogs slunk away into the darkness.

They hadn't reached the cottage when the door opened. Obviously the truck's noisy old engine had alerted Rose to their arrival. But then Esther stopped dead, shocked to the core. She often marvelled afterwards that she hadn't dropped Joy, because all feeling seemed to drain from her limbs as she stared into Monty's handsome face.

He stood there in the doorway, still very much the gentleman and dressed as immaculately as always, and his voice was the same when he said, 'Hello, Esther. I'm sorry to arrive unannounced like this, but I wanted to see you . . .'

Chapter Sixteen

It was fifteen minutes later.

Joy was tucked up in her cot and fast asleep, and Rose had insisted on taking Esther's bed for the night, so that Esther and Monty could have the front room of the tiny cottage to themselves to talk in privacy.

When Esther came down the stairs after settling Joy, she found Monty sitting bolt upright in his chair, his gaze riveted on her face. The first words he spoke to her were about Joy, and nothing he said could have hit her on the raw so completely, which was strange in view of their content.

But it wasn't what he said exactly, more the note of wonderment – and, yes, relief – in his tone when he said softly, 'She is beautiful. Our daughter, she really is quite lovely.'

Esther stared at him. Joy had awoken for a few moments when she'd been carried into the cottage, almost as though the child had sensed her mother's turmoil and distress, and Esther had noticed the widening of Monty's eyes as he'd gazed down into the exquisite face. For a moment she had seen her daughter as Monty was seeing her: the warm, coffee-coloured skin that was such an amazing backdrop for her huge, jade-green eyes with their thick lashes, her delicate features and her golden-brown curls. She had felt both resentment and alarm when she had seen Monty's expression, and now this feeling was increased a hundredfold. Stiffly she walked across the tiny space and sat down opposite him in the old arm-chair in front of the fire, and the stiffness was reflected in her voice when she said, '*My* daughter, Monty. You made it perfectly clear two years ago how you felt about her. And me.'

Monty stared at his wife. When he had arrived at the farm just after lunch he hadn't known if Esther was living there, but he had hoped the farmer might be able to give him an idea of where she had gone, if not.

The first person he had seen as he had climbed out of his car was Rose. She had been coming out of a barn a short distance from the farmhouse, and she had stopped dead, gazing at him with an open mouth and blinking eyes, as though she couldn't believe what she was seeing.

So Esther *was* at the farm, he'd thought, his heart leaping in his chest, before the feeling of apprehension and dread that always accompanied thoughts of the child came into play. But the desire to see Esther had been eating him up for a long time, even before Theobald had begun to insist that he trace her whereabouts; and so he had used his charm on Rose and the farmer's wife and had spent the afternoon in the farmhouse. Admittedly his charm hadn't worked on Beryl, Vera and Lydia when they had come back from an hour or two at the village celebrations, but he hadn't risen to any of their barbed comments and had kept his temper. Eventually, when the three girls had retired for the night, he walked across to the cottage with Rose and sat and waited for Esther there.

He had been very careful to say and do all the right things with Rose; he knew he needed Esther's old nanny on his side, whether or not he decided to take Esther back, as Theobald was insisting. From what Rose had confided, it seemed Esther was devoted to the child, which he saw as the major problem, but he decided to see Esther first before he considered anything further.

And then she had come back; he had seen her face and had known he loved her more than ever, although she was not the young girl he'd left two years ago. She was very much a woman now, and he wanted the woman even more than he'd wanted the girl.

Gathering his thoughts, he said gently, 'I know you're angry with me, and you have every right to be, but looking back, I don't think I was in my right mind when Joy was born. The war, everything I was going through, it takes a toll. And then, just after that, I was shot down' – he held out his hands for her to see them clearly – 'and for months on end I didn't know much.'

There was no way she could find out the truth, he reassured himself silently, either about the fact that the incident had occurred a good time after the child's arrival, or about the women he had had after he had left her.

'Then came all the operations on these.' He nodded at his bent and crippled fingers. 'But at least they got them to a point where I can function relatively normally, drive and look after myself, and so on.' He smiled bravely.

Esther said nothing, keeping her face blank with enormous effort, but behind the calm facade her mind was racing and her heart was thumping so hard it actually hurt.

'I want us to go back to the way it was, Esther. And your father is prepared to meet you—'

'My father is not known to you.'

'I mean Theobald. He—'

'I want nothing to do with him.' She felt she was on solid ground here, at least. When Monty had been talking about his hands, she had imagined what he must have gone through and it was weakening her. She knew, from some of the things that Kenny had said, that Monty would have suffered the torments of the damned. She could see in his face that pain had aged him. 'Let me make one thing absolutely clear, Monty. Theobald Wynford is no relation of mine, and I am thankful for it,' she continued flatly. 'I want no claim on him, and he has none on me.'

Reproachfully he said, 'You don't feel that is a little hard? He was the deceived, Esther. Not the deceiver.'

She didn't deign to answer that. 'Why are you here, Monty?'

'I told you. I want us to be together again.'

'That is impossible.'

'Why? We are still man and wife, and there is the child to consider. Do you want her to grow up without a father?'

'Better that than knowing that her father is ashamed of her. We both know how you feel. You made it abundantly clear two years ago.'

'I've explained about that.' In truth he had had the biggest shock of his life when he had seen the little girl today. She was the most exquisite child he had ever seen, and nothing like the little scrap he remembered on the day of her birth. True, she was still clearly not white, but with his mother gone, that didn't matter so much. People would assume Esther had misbehaved and he had been magnanimous and forgiven her, and as long as he made sure there were no more children, who would ever know any different? But he could deal with that problem in the future. For now he had to convince Esther to come back to him. 'I regretted it immediately and, but for the fact that I was shot down, I would have found you and made things right. You have to believe me, darling.'

Did she? Did she believe him? she asked herself, staring into the undeniably handsome face. If Monty had turned up on the doorstep a little while after Joy had been born, saying what he was saying now, she would have taken him back with open arms, she knew that. She would have been delirious with relief and happiness. But now? It was different. *She* was different.

'You mentioned Theobald. You clearly have some contact with him, then?' she said, aware that she was prevaricating about the main issue and the fact that she didn't trust him. Because she didn't, she thought with a dart of shock. Not at all.

In view of her earlier comments, Monty was aware she might not like his reply, but she had to know the situation. Carefully he said, 'I work for him, Esther. My parents were killed when a bomb dropped on the London house, and it transpired they had huge debts, so there was nothing left after the creditors had been paid and everything was settled. Your father – Theobald,' he corrected swiftly, 'offered me a job, as I was family.'

Her face expressed her amazement. Monty hadn't liked Theobald any more than she had, and after the way her so-called father had treated herself and Joy, she would have thought that would have been enough for Monty to have nothing more to do with him, if he did really still love her. As for the 'family' comment, Theobald did nothing out of the goodness of his heart. Stiffly she said, 'I gather the Grant name still opens doors for him?' She wasn't stupid, and he needn't treat her as though she was.

Monty shifted uncomfortably. 'I suppose so.'

'And you are happy to work for him? Knowing what he is really like – how foul he is?'

'I didn't really have much of a choice.'

'Everyone has a choice, Monty, so don't give me that.'

His face was burning now, the colour suffusing it almost scarlet. 'I've explained why.'

'Yes, you have.' For the first time since he had come into her life she was seeing Monty without rose-coloured glasses. Why had she never noticed the weakness in his mouth, she asked herself, or how much he resembled his father? She had always wondered why Hubert hadn't stood up to Clarissa, but now she saw the flaw that had been in the father was in the son. And if Hubert hadn't been capable of wearing the metaphorical trousers in the relationship, maybe Clarissa had been forced to put them on and assume the role?

'I'm your husband, Esther, and Joy's father.' Monty couldn't believe what was happening. He had thought that, after some initial tears, she would fall on his neck in grateful happiness. He was offering her everything – support, stability, his name and protection – and her future would be secure. Couldn't she see that? And she loved him. He knew she still loved him. She had been crazy about him. 'Don't you want us to be a family?' he said softly. 'As it was meant to be?'

She looked at him for a long moment before saying, with a touch of sadness, 'No, Monty, I don't.'

He felt the colour flooding his face again. 'You don't mean that. I know I hurt you and I'm sorry, but I've told you: it was a combination of the war and shock and—'

'Your mother.' Her chin had risen. 'Don't forget your mother, in your excuses. But she's not to blame, not really.'

He closed his eyes for a second, lowering his head and turning it from side to side, before looking at her again. 'You need time, I understand that. Once you have thought about this, you will see it is the best thing for all of us.'

There was a long pause and, when she made no reply, he said, 'I love you, Esther, and I know you love me.'

She shook her head slowly. 'No, Monty, I don't. My love took a while to die, I admit that, but die it has.'

'I will never believe that. You want to punish me.'

'Strangely, no.' She stood up, twisting her hands together before realizing what she was doing and bringing them to her sides. 'We're different people now, you must see that?'

'I am the same.'

'Then I can only say I didn't know the real you when we got married.'

'I'm not going to give up, Esther. You are my wife and your place is at my side, living the life you were born into, rather than existing in this' – his nose wrinkled – 'this pigsty. It's one thing to do your bit for the war effort, but now . . . '

How could she have thought she loved him? How could she have made such a terrible mistake? 'Please leave, Monty.'

He stood up, rubbing his scarred hand tightly along his jawbone. For a moment she felt a dart of pity, before she told herself not to weaken. His suffering didn't alter who he was.

'I shall come back, Esther.'

'I would prefer you not to. In fact' – she took a deep breath – 'I would like a divorce, Monty, now that the war is over.'

His eyes narrowed and his voice was very soft. 'No.'

Esther blinked. For a moment the look on his face reminded her of Theobald. It was this that made her say, 'Does he know you're here? Theobald? Did you tell him you were coming to see me?' Was he behind Monty's change of heart?

Monty turned from her and walked to the door, opening it and then facing her again. 'He knows. Furthermore, he's prepared to let bygones be bygones.' He didn't add that Theobald's take on the matter was that, if Esther came back into the fold and acted the good wife, it would do the business no harm; and the child could be kept in the background until she was shipped off to a boarding school somewhere in the south.

'How big of him,' said Esther, cuttingly.

'You seem to forget that Harriet did him a great wrong when she deceived him. He was in shock – we all were – when the truth came out. You can't blame him for reacting the way he did.'

'Can't I?'

She stared at him, and it was his eyes that fell away from hers as he muttered, 'I thought you would be more reasonable.'

'I'm sorry to disappoint you.'

Monty took a deep breath. 'I don't want to leave on

bad terms. Please think over what I have said, and most of all that I love you. I have always loved you, and I will always love you. I won't give you a divorce, Esther, not feeling the way I do. I want to be clear about that. I want you back as my wife, and I won't stop until you are at my side, where you belong.' His sheer audacity was breathtaking, and something of what she was feeling must have shown in her face because he murmured, 'I know, I know. I failed you. But I'll make it up to you. Remember how happy we were? The life we'd planned to have together? It can still happen. I'll fight to make it happen.'

When she said nothing, he continued gently, 'Goodbye for now, my darling,' stepping outside and shutting the door behind him.

Esther stood quite still for a moment or two and then walked across the room and shot the bolts at the top and bottom of the door. They were stiff and rusty, rarely having been used, and she caught her finger on one of them. She looked at the spot of blood that had formed, and for a moment she wanted to cry. He had left her heart bleeding two years ago and, in spite of his fancy words, he seemed almost oblivious to how much he had hurt her then. At bottom, he still felt that he was completely justified.

Walking back to her chair, she sank down, her whole body trembling with reaction. She sat there for long minutes, her head in her hands, but after a while she straightened. She was tired, so tired, but one thing was certain in her weary mind. It was over. She would never go back to him and she didn't want Monty within a hundred miles of Joy, although that might prove more difficult, because she believed him when he said he would fight. If the future had seemed an uphill struggle before, suddenly it looked a whole lot worse. But she wouldn't waver. The Bible said that a house divided against itself would fall, and that's what any home with Monty would be: divided and just waiting to fall.

Chapter Seventeen

Theobald's hard, jet-black eyes were fixed on his son-in-law. Monty had just helped himself to ham and eggs from the covered dishes on the sideboard and had sat down at the breakfast table. When he began to eat without speaking, Theobald barked one word: 'Well?'

Monty raised his eyes, swallowing the food in his mouth before he said, 'I presume you're enquiring how I got on yesterday?' The reply was cool, but there was no trace of irritation at his father-in-law's manner in Monty's voice, even though inwardly it irked him.

'Of course, what else? You were damned late back, weren't you? I didn't get to bed till gone three, and you weren't in then.'

'Esther had gone out for the day when I got to the farm, so I had to wait until she returned.'

'So she was there, then? You found her?'

'Yes, I found her and the child.'

'And?' Theobald leaned forward, his body radiating impatience.

Monty shrugged. 'I've made contact.'

'You've made contact?' Theobald's voice had risen. 'What the hell does that mean: you've made contact? Did you spell out the benchmarks when she comes back, because I'll expect her to toe the line.' There wasn't a trace of doubt in his mind that Esther would seize the opportunity to resume her position in the family. 'She'll do as she's told, under my roof.'

'It wasn't like that.' Monty took a sip of his coffee.

'Give me strength – it's like pulling hen's teeth. Are you doing this on purpose, to spoil my breakfast?'

'She told me she wants a divorce. Is that clear enough?'

Theobald sat back in his chair, let out a long, irritable sigh and said, 'All right, let's have it all. Word-for-word.'

And Monty gave it all to him, word-for-word, including his wife's comments about Theobald. When he had finished speaking there was silence for a moment or two. He could see that Theobald was furious, for he had flushed a deep puce, and in spite of his own chagrin and deep disappointment, Monty admitted to feeling a certain satisfaction at his father-in-law's vexation. Since leaving the air force and coming to live at the house, there had been many occasions when he had almost decided to throw in the towel and tell Theobald what he really thought of him; but the fact that he knew he was 'living in clover', as his air-force pals would call it, had stilled his tongue. But really, he asked himself now for the umpteenth time, was it worth it? The more he'd learned about Theobald, the more he'd begun to despise and loathe him

– and himself. He had allowed himself to be bought, he knew that, and any time he didn't jump as high as Theobald told him to, his father-in-law dangled the carrot of the wealth Monty would inherit in the future. When he had objected to a particularly blatant bribe that Theobald was offering a supposedly righteous pillar of the community recently, Monty had been told to shut up or clear out. Of course he had done the former, as Theobald had known he would, and when a similar occasion had occurred a few days later, he had followed orders once again.

But it wasn't just Theobald's dubious business dealings that made him feel dirty, Monty thought now. Within a short while of living at the house, he had been woken one night by shrieking. Startled out of a deep sleep, he'd sat for a minute or two wondering if he had dreamed it, because the night was quiet again, but then a muffled scream had drawn him out of bed and onto the landing. Armed with a poker from the fireplace in his bedroom, he had crept to the stairs that led down to the floor below, where Theobald's suite of rooms was. He had been genuinely concerned that some ne'er-do-well had got into the house and attacked his father-in-law. Quite what had made him hesitate outside the door to Theobald's rooms, he didn't know. Some sixth sense perhaps. As he'd stood there, his ear pressed to the door, he'd distinctly heard Theobald's deep baritone laugh and then a female voice, sounding urgent and distressed, although he couldn't make out the words.

Despite knowing that he should leave well alone and go back to bed – whatever was happening inside, Monty felt satisfied Theobald wasn't in danger – he'd stealthily tried the handle of the door instead. It had opened and he'd pushed it so that he could hear through the crack. The voices had been clearer now. The female was saying, 'You're too rough. Look at her, she's bleedin'. I didn't bring her along for you to do this.'

Someone else was crying in the background, low muffled sobs, and then his father-in-law had growled, 'For crying out loud, don't make such a fuss. Look, I'll give you both double, all right? Now that's fair. Untie her, and we'll get down to the real business.'

Monty had often wished since then that he hadn't opened the door further, so that he could see into the room. The sight that had met his eyes was burned into his mind now. A young girl, no more than eleven or twelve years old, was spreadeagled on Theobald's bed, face-down, with ropes securing her wrists and ankles. Blood was visible from the weals marking the naked white body, and a second girl, just a year or two older, was kneeling beside the bed, pulling at the cords securing the first girl. Theobald, as naked as the day he was born, was watching them, the whip he was holding dangling from one hand.

Monty had stopped breathing. He knew he'd stopped breathing because, when he had to take a breath, it had come in a gasp that had alerted the occupants of the room to his presence. As he had met his father-in-law's eyes, panic had made him bang the door shut and high-tail it back to his quarters. When he'd reached his room he'd sat for some minutes on the edge of the bed, waiting for Theobald to storm in. But he hadn't.

The next morning Monty hadn't known what to expect, but the last thing he'd imagined was Theobald behaving perfectly normally when he came down to break-fast. There was no sign of the girls; presumably they had been packed off to wherever they had come from. And so the two of them had sat and eaten their meal, Theobald seemingly engrossed in his newspaper. But just before he had risen from the table, his father-in-law had put down his paper and said, 'You're welcome to join me for some entertainment, Monty. You don't have to creep about the house spying on me. A young man like you has his needs, I know that.'

'I beg your p-pardon?' He'd hated himself for stuttering.

'Night recreation. Tell me the sort of thing that tickles your fancy, and I'll arrange it. We're both men of the world.'

He had stared at Theobald. Instead of the well-dressed individual in front of him, he'd seen in his mind's eye a swarthy body, liberally covered in hair like an animal. And the obscene erection. Stammering even more, he'd got out, 'I–I didn't mean to p-pry. I heard something – n-noises.'

The gimlet eyes hadn't left his face. 'Aye, well, if you hear anything more, you'll know what it is, won't you, lad? I've made the decision that in future I'm having my entertainment brought to the house. More private, that way.'

He'd swallowed hard. 'Those girls?'

'There's a woman who supplies me,' Theobald said shortly.

When his father-in-law had left the table without further conversation, Monty had sat staring after him for a long time. It was then that he should have packed his bags and left this house, where the very air was contaminated by its owner, he thought now. But he hadn't. He had stayed, and in so doing had shut his ears to sounds in the night, along with many other things that went on.

Theobald surprised him when he spoke now. Instead of the tirade of curses and swearing Monty had expected, his father-in-law said softly, 'She always did have spirit. I used to think she got it from me, as Harriet was a spineless individual, but no matter. And you saw the child, you say? What's she like? Black as the ace of spades?'

For the first time since his daughter had been born, Monty felt a surge of defensiveness on her behalf. Coldly he said, 'Actually, she's lovely. Beautiful in fact, with the greenest eyes I've ever seen and golden-brown curls.'

Theobald's eyes narrowed. 'So she looks white?' That would make things easier all round.

Monty hesitated. 'No, no, she doesn't. Her skin is too dark for that.'

'So the problem remains? Still, it doesn't have to be

broadcast. There are plenty of good boarding schools where the girl would be well treated, and Esther could visit her whenever circumstances allowed. Did you explain that to her?'

'We never got that far. I told you, she has no intention of coming back. She was adamant in that regard.'

'Oh, she'll come back, if I've a mind for her to, lad. Don't you fret about that. Certain of our associates would drop us quicker than a dose of salts, if divorce was mentioned – mainstays of the church, some of 'em. They're up in arms about this modern wave of divorce that the war has caused, as it is, pious lot.'

Monty kept his face blank with some effort. Theobald was a lecher of the worst kind, and most of his business dealings were questionable, to say the least; and yet to those associates that he'd mentioned he acted as though he was as pure as the driven snow. Furthermore Theobald insisted that Monty accompany him each Sunday to the parish church, where his father-in-law sat as though butter wouldn't melt in his mouth, as holy as you like. Since he had got to know Theobald better, Monty had found himself glancing round at people and wondering what they were really like under the outward veneer – something that had never crossed his mind before.

Theobald tugged at his brocade waistcoat, which had been fitted to disguise the enormity of his protruding stomach, and glared at Monty. Esther's husband was a pathetic excuse of a man and as weak as dishwater, and yet, he supposed, that worked to his advantage on a day-to-day basis. 'See to it you tell her what's what, when you go back there. Women are like horses: they need a firm hand, and to know who is in control. Do you understand me?' He paused on the threshold of the room. 'When are you going back to the farm, by the way?'

'I don't know.'

'Well, make it soon. I've got enough on my plate, with the war finished and one or two things up in the air. It won't be long before the Japanese surrender an' all, and everything will go haywire, you mark my words. I keep my ear to the ground; I know what's going on, and people don't want to go back to like it was before the war, with the dole, the means test, unemployment marches, and the like. The business will need to diversify, because I wouldn't be surprised if Labour get in when there's an election.'

Monty stared at his father-in-law. The Labour Party had never had an overall majority in British electoral history, and Churchill was the people's hero. Of course the government of the country would continue to be safe in Tory hands.

'You don't believe me?' Theobald correctly read the expression on Monty's face. 'We'll see, my lad. The common horde might cheer themselves hoarse for Churchill – like yesterday in Whitehall, when he was on the balcony in his famous siren suit and homburg hat – but their loyalty is fickle. They're peasants, and they'll give their allegiance where the wind blows. The only way to deal with the working class is with an iron fist – it's all they understand. The vote! Worst thing they ever did when they gave it to the common man; gave 'em ideas above their station.'

Monty had heard it all before. Just to annoy his father-in-law, he said mildly, 'Women carry as much weight as men in the voting stakes now, don't forget.'

Theobald snorted. 'When did you ever hear a woman say anything worth listening to? Their brains are inferior, everyone knows that, and their grasp of politics is non-existent.'

Monty found he couldn't stand listening to another of Theobald's bigoted rants that morning. He'd had no sleep, arriving back at the house as dawn was breaking and then sitting at his bedroom window for some time before he had a bath and a shave. Seeing Esther in the flesh had made him want her, to the point where he could think of little else, and he had been cursing himself for ever walking away from her. But what else could he have done? he asked himself for the umpteenth time. She'd had a black baby, and he couldn't just ignore what she carried in her genes, damn it. Unlike her, the child would never pass for white, that was for sure. Nevertheless, Joy was outstandingly lovely and that was the important thing for a girl as she grew older. Or it had been, before this war had turned the world on its head. He recognized that, in the absence of fathers and bread-winners, women had dug the land, driven trucks and large vehicles, taken hard and dirty jobs in factories and had held their own in a previously all-male environment.

Consequently they'd become tougher and more independent, and certainly free-thinking in a way that would have been unbelievable a decade ago. Pandora had been let out of her box.

He didn't like it. His jaw clenched. He wished the world could go back thirty, forty years, back to the old ways. His mother might have been an elitist, but she had been right in so many things.

He stood up, brushing past Theobald. 'I need to have a lie-down for an hour, I've got a stinking headache.'

'Aye, well, only an hour then.' Theobald followed his son-in-law out of the room. 'There's work to be done, don't forget. And don't leave it too long before you sort out your wife. Sweet-talk her, charm her, use brute force if necessary – I don't care – but I don't want that harpy causing me problems. She was fair barmy about you, as I recall, so it shouldn't be too difficult to get her back here and behaving herself.'

'That was then; this is now. I told you, she's different.'

'Different, is she?' Theobald's meaty hand clamped itself on Monty's arm, swinging the younger man round to face him. 'Well, maybe she is and maybe she isn't, but you're much the same, as far as I can see, and unless you've lost your touch with the ladies, this should be a walk in the park.' His grip tightened. 'See it clearly, for crying out loud. She's on her own with a brat to feed and clothe, isn't she? So compare that to living in the lap of luxury with the man she loves. Come on, lad, even you can see the gods are with you.'

Stiffly Monty said, 'Esther told me she doesn't love me any more. I told you, she wants a divorce.'

Theobald looked into the handsome aristocratic face. He would have liked nothing more than to smash his fist into it. The muscles of his stomach tensing, he forced himself to take a breath before he said, 'She's having you on, lad. They're all the same. She's making you sweat a bit – her pound of flesh, as it were. But, frankly, I don't care one way or the other. You *make* her love you again, if she's cooled off, all right? Promise her what she wants and get her purring again, because I want her back here where I can keep an eye on her. Is that clear?'

Monty nodded.

When Theobald shook the arm he held, growling, 'I *said*, is that clear?' Monty jerked himself free of his father-in-law, his voice tight as he muttered, 'Yes, yes, it's clear. Damn it, it's clear.'

'Good.' Theobald's voice was more moderate. 'Go and have your lie-down, lad, but don't be too long about it. I expect you to at least try and earn some of that salary I pay you.'

The two men stared at each other, their mutual dislike a tangible entity, and when Monty's gaze dropped and he turned and made for the stairs without another word, Theobald smiled to himself. Monty might have flown his little aeroplanes and had a stab at Jerry, but he had the backbone of a damned jellyfish. But he'd bring Esther's husband up to scratch, or his name wasn't Theobald Wynford.

He glanced around the gracious hall and at the gold-framed portraits on the walls. His father had sweated blood to rise in the world and make good the Wynford name, and he'd carried on in the same vein. His whole life had been devoted to it and he didn't begrudge a moment of it. It was the only thing that mattered. And no one – least of all the little bastard that Harriet had foisted on him – would spoil that achievement for him. He would kill her first; her and her brat. But it wouldn't come to that.

He wiped the tiny beads of perspiration that had formed on his upper lip with a crisp linen handkerchief, stuffing it in the pocket of his jacket. Again taking a calming breath, he let his senses be soothed by his surroundings. He had survived the war, hadn't he? Steered his ship through stormy waters and, by his own shrewd ingenuity and dexterity, it was still afloat. That was where he was one up on the so-called 'upper crust' like Monty's parents. Born with silver spoons in their mouths, they had been willing to choke on them before they would try and change with the times. But he wasn't afraid to do whatever was necessary to safeguard what was his – be it legal or not. And what was the law anyway? Just a set of rules and regulations to ensure that those at the top of the pile kept those at the bottom in their place.

Osborne appeared from the direction of the kitchens, and Theobald barked, 'Get the car brought round. I'm going into town.'

As the butler scurried off, Theobald walked to the

front door and opened it, the warm May air causing him to sniff appreciatively. He had given in to the kudos and social prestige of owning a good motor car years ago, and now he wouldn't be without his comfortable Bentley. He sniffed again, a sense of well-being causing his chest to expand. No one would take away what he had achieved, he thought again. It simply wasn't an option.

Chapter Eighteen

It was the week before Christmas. The occupants of Yew Tree Farm had been snowed in for the last ten days or so, something that occurred fairly regularly in Yorkshire during the winter months each year. No one was concerned, and for Esther it had come as a definite blessing. Since VE Day Monty had turned up on the doorstep several times, even though she had made it perfectly clear over and over again that she had no intention of going back to him. The impassable roads meant that for the first time since May she could relax, rather than being on edge that his car would arrive and he'd leap out with more armfuls of flowers and boxes of chocolates.

Not that Priscilla and the others objected to the chocolates. Esther had refused to sample even one, as a matter of principle, but her friends had had no such compunction, munching their way through the heavenly layers in ecstasy, each time Monty had gone.

'You do know that these chocolates are almost certainly black-market goods?' Esther had said severely, the first time the other girls had fallen on the confectionery after Monty had refused to take it back with him. She suspected Theobald had had a hand in obtaining them. He'd have no scruples in that regard whatsoever.

'I don't care.' Priscilla had rolled her eyes, her mouth full of praline. 'I'm sorry, sweetie, but I really don't. Not that I think you should give in to the rotter. He's not the man for you, darling, and I wish you would agree to setting Gyp and Badger on him. But, failing that, the chocolates are just . . . ' She couldn't find words to express her pleasure.

Smiling in spite of herself, Esther shook her head. 'You are incorrigible.'

'I know it, sweetie, I really do, but the way things are going, a girl has to make hay while the sun shines.' Priscilla grinned at her. 'That's my excuse anyway. I mean, who would have thought there'd be rumours about bread and flour being rationed soon? That didn't happen even in the war.'

Esther nodded. All the papers talked about now was the government's drive to emphasize how serious the food shortage was. Tens of thousands of servicemen were being demobbed each month and were coming home to a different Britain from the one they remembered. The public, which had been willing to make great sacrifices during the war, was now becoming increasingly impatient at being faced in peacetime with an even more austere diet, but all the signs were that things would get even worse in 1946. Everything was topsy-turvy and up in the air.

Everyone at the farm had watched in amazement when in the summer a Labour landslide in the General Election had booted the Tories and Winston Churchill out of power, and Labour and Clement Attlee's 'government for the people' into Downing Street. There had been wild euphoria for a couple of months, with talk of Social Security and a National Health Service exciting everyone, and nationalization of the coal industry and the Bank of England, but then the grim reality had started to creep in.

Monty had been quick to capitalize on the dire forecasts and general discontent. 'Life is going to be a hell of a struggle for everyone,' he'd said earnestly on his last visit to the farm at the end of November. 'And I don't want you and Joy to be caught up in that. I want you to come home, and so does Theobald. Back where you belong.'

'I don't belong there, though, Monty. We both know that. I never did.' Esther had stared him straight in the eye. 'I loved Harriet as a mother, but in actual fact I wasn't related to her or Theobald. My parents are American, and my mother's name was Ruth Flaggerty.'

Monty had ignored that. 'Think of Joy,' he had said persuasively, his voice soft. 'Of the advantages she'll have, as my daughter and Theobald's granddaughter.'

Esther had stopped him short there. It had been the wrong tack to take. Her voice icy, she'd said, 'There's no way on earth I would ever allow Theobald to make any claim on Joy, even if he really wanted to, which I don't believe for a moment he does. I don't know why he is so suddenly as agreeable about the pair of us as you say he is, but I've no doubt at all it will be because it suits him for some reason.'

She could tell from the expression on Monty's face that she had hit the nail on the head, whatever he said to the contrary. It had made her think, and the more she had thought, the more uneasy she had felt.

She had discussed the matter with both Rose and Priscilla, and much as she loved Rose, she knew she wouldn't talk to her about Monty again. Rose had been starry-eyed at Monty turning up at the farm, declaring that Esther's place was at his side. 'He's explained that he was injured, before he could make amends,' Rose had said reproachfully, 'and when all's said and done, he *is* your husband, Miss Esther. You belong in his world – you're a lady. And I wouldn't worry about the master. Mr Monty will deal with him.'

Esther had wanted to say that Theobald was not Rose's master, nor was she convinced that Monty would 'deal with him'. In fact she had the distinct impression Theobald was calling the tune. But she hadn't. She had looked into Rose's lined, devoted face and had known that her old nanny only wanted the best for her, and the best – in Rose's opinion – was a life of ease and comfort in the upper stratum of society.

Priscilla, on the other hand, had mirrored Esther's own suspicions and reservations. 'Darling, I've never met your once-supposed father, nor have I any wish to, but from all you have told me, he's up to something when he says he wants you back in the fold. A leopard doesn't change its spots. And I can't help feeling that if Joy wasn't the utterly breathtaking creature she is, Monty wouldn't be so keen to claim her as his own. I'm a great believer in the notion that when the chips are down, it's one's first response that counts. And neither your Monty nor Theobald rose to the occasion.'

'He's not *my* Monty,' she had answered sharply.

Priscilla had raised her eyebrows. 'In a nutshell, darling. In a nutshell.'

Esther bit hard on her bottom lip. She had been lying in bed for what seemed like hours now, and it must be past one o'clock in the morning, but sleep had never seemed so far away. Her mind was a maelstrom of 'what ifs' and 'maybes' and mostly they centred around Caleb. Which was ridiculous, perfectly ridiculous, because the tone of his letters told her he thought of her as a friend, and nothing more. But in meeting him, she had encountered the sort of man she wanted to spend the rest of her life with. Someone who didn't judge her according to her genealogy; who didn't give two hoots about her pedigree. And Monty cared very much about such niceties. He had two years ago, and he still did, whatever he said to the contrary.

She turned carefully in her bed, not wanting to wake Priscilla on one side of her, or Joy – curled up like a tiny animal and fast asleep in her cot – on the other side. She gazed at her daughter in the dim light, the love she felt for this vulnerable, fragile piece of herself causing her breath to constrict in her chest. She would work her fingers to the bone to provide for her, and no matter what happened in the future she would never ask Monty for help.

Decision made, for good or ill, she told herself. She felt a great sense of peace flowing through her veins and a quietening of her spirit, and with them came courage.

Rose had talked about her belonging in Monty's world, but nothing could be further from the truth. She didn't belong there, but neither did she fit into Caleb's world. She was betwixt and between, as Rose was apt to say; she didn't belong anywhere. But that didn't matter. She had Joy. That was all that was important, and they could create their own special world, just the two of them.

For a moment she experienced a sense of exhilaration in which fear and apprehension about the future were swept away. She would be strong for her precious child and she wouldn't let anyone hurt her, and one day she would tell Joy about her grandparents and the great love they had for each other. A love that had caused them to defy cruel convention and man-made tradition and propriety; she would teach Joy to be proud of her mixed heritage. What had the war been about, if not fighting to establish that each child, each person on earth, was formed in the image of their Creator and was unique and special, be they Jew or Gentile, able-bodied or disabled, black or white? And she and Joy had survived the war.

She hugged herself tightly, shivering slightly under the coarse blankets.

She had been so young when the war had begun, full of enthusiasm and certainty and the energy of youth. She had married and borne her child, but it hadn't been the war that had stolen the simple ordinary joy that a young couple feel together on the birth of their firstborn. Monty had forced the agony of separation, along with Theobald and Clarissa playing their part.

She was a different person now from that romantic, girlish creature who had imagined that Monty was her knight in shining armour. So much so that she barely recognized the ghost of the old Esther, with her privileged upbringing, lovely clothes and somewhat empty head.

She smiled ruefully. But she was strong now. She didn't need Monty or Theobald's wealth; she would manage on her own, without the support of any man. She didn't allow her mind to dwell on what 'any man' meant, and neither would she in the future, she promised herself firmly. That road would merely lead to heartache and disappointment, and she had already had enough of those to last a lifetime.

With the silent pep talk over, she snuggled further under the covers, determinedly shut her eyes and was asleep within minutes.

Esther's resolution was turned on its head within the week. A sudden thaw had freed the locked-in north's roads and country lanes, but in so doing turned them into thick rivers of mud and boggy quagmires. It made ordinary life on the farm just that little bit more difficult, and Esther and the other girls admitted privately to each other that they were glad this would be their last winter as Land Girls. A couple of Farmer Holden's old farm labourers had returned unscathed from the war, one of whom had twin sons of sixteen who wanted to work on the land, and over the last two or three days it had been agreed that the four of them would start work in the New Year. Esther and the others would stay on for a brief transitional period, but would then resume their normal lives – whatever that meant these days, as Vera commented soberly.

Mrs Holden had quietly repeated her offer to Rose and Esther that they could stay on at the farm if they wished, but something had clarified in Esther's mind over the last days. She had taken Rose aside, and the two of them had had a long talk when the other girls were in bed. Esther had begun by saying how much she loved Rose, would always love her and appreciate the unstinting support Rose had been since Joy was born. 'But,' Esther had said gently, holding her old nanny's hands in hers, 'I can't stay at the farm, Rose. It's not right for me and Joy. But' – she'd paused, trying to find the right words to say so that Rose wouldn't be hurt – 'I do think it's right for you. You love it here with Mrs Holden, and she is fond of you. The two of you are more like sisters than anything else, and she's come to rely on you as though you were family. Now you know that's true, don't you?'

Rose had stared at the girl she thought of as her own daughter, although – and here she had had to face something she had been trying to put to the back of her mind for some time – Miss Esther wasn't a girl any more. She was a woman, and one who intended to stand on her own two feet and take charge of her life. And Rose admired that, of course she did, but she couldn't see eye-to-eye with her over the matter of Mr Monty. Now the master was a different kettle of fish – nasty piece of work he was; but Mr Monty was a gentleman born and bred, and no one could have done more to make amends than he had. A shred of hope made her say, 'Do you mean you're going back to Mr Monty?'

'Rose, you know that is never going to happen.'

'Then what? What will you do?'

It was a good question and Esther hoped Rose didn't press for the finer details when she said, 'I shall get a job and rent a couple of rooms for myself and Joy. The one good thing about the war is that, of necessity, more nurseries and crèches have sprung up for working mothers.'

Rose had stared at her askance. 'I'll come with you and look after her, and you know I've got a bit put by. We could rent a nice little house and—'

'And you would be stuck there all day, with just a toddler for company, knowing no one and just waiting for me to come home.' Esther had pressed one of Rose's lined hands to her cheek. Rose was over sixty now and had devoted her life to serving others. Esther had never seen her so happy as in the last years at the farm; it was as though she had been born for farm life. Nancy Holden had already hinted to Esther that, if she decided to leave and Rose chose to stay, she would see to it that Rose joined herself and Farmer Holden in the farmhouse, as one of the family. 'Joy and I will come and see you and Mrs Holden when we can, I promise, and you can come and see me. Sunderland isn't a million miles away, now is it?'

Rose had said nothing for a moment. Then she murmured, 'Are . . . are you going to him?'

Esther didn't prevaricate. She had no secrets from her old nanny, and Rose knew about Caleb's suggestion that she might like to live near him and his family. 'A friend on hand' was the way he had put it. It had unnerved her when she had first read it, but since VE Day a change had taken place in her thinking. She didn't for a moment imagine that Caleb would take on her and someone else's child, especially a child who would invariably be a talking point among his neighbours and friends. He had never, by word or deed, suggested he was feeling that way. But now she knew that she didn't want to lose his friendship and support, at a time when she would need it most.

Quietly she said, 'I've told you before: Caleb is my friend. That's all. But his mother seemed to take to Joy, and it would be good to know folk are at hand if a crisis should happen. So, yes, I'm thinking of looking for somewhere in Monkwearmouth.'

'I see.' Rose's disapproval had been unmistakable.

'Please don't look at me like that, Rose.' Esther took Rose's hand again, squeezing it. 'Please, I need you to understand. You, of all people.'

'Well, I don't.' But Rose had left her hand in Esther's. 'Not when you have a husband who is falling over himself to make things right.'

'Some things can't be made right.'

'Aye, they can, with a bit of give and take on both sides.'

'It's not like that, Rose, and you know it at heart.'

'Mr Monty is Joy's natural father, Miss Esther, that's the thing. And he wants you both back with him. A child should grow up with her parents – both parents, if it is at all possible – and the way I see it, for Joy it *is* possible. It's only you that is preventing it. I'm sorry, but that's what I think.'

Monty said the same thing every time he called at the farm. Esther knew it was emotional blackmail, but it still hit a raw nerve and caused her to question herself now and again. But she always came back to the way Monty had reacted when Joy was born and, even more than that, the way he had spoken the next day, when he had had time to think and consider his words. He'd asked her to send their baby away somewhere, to hide her, in essence; and then he'd stipulated that they would have no more natural children of their own. As Priscilla had put it, a leopard doesn't change its spots. Not over something so fundamental. Rose might indulge in the luxury of burying her head in the sand with regard to Monty, but she could not. Not as Joy's mother.

'Rose, I believe with all my heart that Joy is better off without Monty.'

'Then you are wrong, Miss Esther, and you'll regret it.'

Letting go of Rose's hand, her voice was firm as she said, 'I've made my decision about Monty, Rose, and I shan't change my mind. Monty doesn't love her unconditionally, like a father should.'

'Now you don't know that.'

'Yes, I do.'

'Well, it still isn't right you going to live in them back streets, Miss Esther. You a lady. Your poor mother would turn in her grave.'

'Harriet was a wonderful woman, but she wasn't my mother, Rose. I'll always be grateful to her for the love she poured out on me, but the truth is that I am not related to her by blood at all. You know that as well as I do.'

They had stared at each other, and then Rose had said words that cut her to the quick. 'You've grown hard, Miss Esther.'

And now it was Christmas Eve and in the last twenty-four hours the temperature had dropped sharply again, freezing the ground so that the ridges of mud were as hard as iron and a layer of ice made walking treacherous.

Not that that stopped work on a farm. It was almost midday and although the sun was shining the air was bitterly cold, and every now and again, as though warning of what was in store, a snowflake drifted down.

Esther was walking across the farmyard after collecting some eggs from the poultry house. This was situated in the middle of what Mrs Holden quaintly referred to as the 'hens' meadow' – a small grass field that allowed the birds to range freely. The hens seemed very happy feeding on oats and chat potatoes, with just a small proportion of rationed imported foods, which were allowed at only a quarter of an ounce per bird. Of course the egg yield was low in winter, as egg production depends on the length of daylight, but nevertheless Esther had a nice basketful for the farmer's wife.

She heard the car before she saw it and groaned. Not Monty – not on Christmas Eve. Mr Holden had cut down a small fir tree that morning and they were planning to decorate it after lunch with the ancient collection of baubles, tinsel and bits and pieces that the farmer's wife had had for years. Esther had been looking forward to spending time with Joy and the others. It was the first year her daughter had really understood about Christmas. For weeks now Esther had spent her evenings, once Joy was tucked up in bed, making a beautiful rag doll with an embroidered face and masses of thin strands of yellow rope hair, along with a wardrobe of different outfits that the child could dress the doll in. Priscilla had sorted through her clothes and given her one or two lovely things to cut down for the purpose. As Lydia had remarked, it came to something when a doll was better dressed than the rest of them! And the afternoon had been going to be a precious lead-up to Christmas morning, but if Monty was here, everything was spoilt.

Esther turned, steeling her face to show no emotion, and then almost dropped the precious eggs, as she took in the ancient Morris Minor with a stranger at the wheel and a grinning Caleb sitting in the passenger seat. The car drew up, but only Caleb got out, calling over to her, 'All right if I invite myself to stay for a couple of hours?'

Somehow she managed to retain her composure, although her voice was a little shaky when she said, 'Of course it is, but what on earth are you doing here?'

'This is Bill, a pal from the home who happens to live near me, and when I bumped into him and he said he was going to drive down to see some of the lads who are still stuck there, I asked him if he'd mind if I rode along.' Caleb put a thumb up to his friend, who waved and then disappeared back down the farm track, as Caleb walked to Esther's side with the one-sided hip-swinging gait that gave away his injury. His arms were full of wrapped parcels and, as he reached her, he said, 'Bits for Joy, from me and Mam.'

'From your mother?' Esther tried, and failed, to keep the amazement out of her voice.

'And me,' he qualified.

'Thank you. I . . . I don't know what to say. It's . . . it's very kind of you both.'

'Is she excited?'

'Who?'

'Joy. Is she excited about Father Christmas and all?'

Trying to pull herself together, Esther managed a smile. 'Yes, yes, she is.' Hoping Caleb wouldn't see how flustered she was feeling, she said, 'Come on into the farmhouse and have a hot drink. You must be frozen.'

'A bit.' Truth to tell, he felt he was in the middle of what his mam would term a 'hot flush'. He'd felt his temperature rise the moment he had seen her, and he felt weak with relief now that Esther hadn't given any sign that she wasn't pleased to see him, or considered him turning up like this an intrusion.

When they entered the farmhouse Nancy Holden made Caleb very welcome, after her initial surprise. She knew all about him from Rose, but in this one thing she didn't agree with her friend. If the man had designs on Esther, then she saw nothing wrong with it; and she had no time for the other one, whatever Rose said. Why should Esther take the swine back, after what he'd done? No, in Nancy's book, if a nice man like Caleb was prepared to take on the lass and her bairn, then he was all right. Not that anything like that had been said of course, according to Esther. Apparently they were just friends. But to her mind, a bloke didn't travel all this way with a pile of presents for the bairn if he wasn't soft on the mother.

Priscilla and the others had been working in various places about the farm when Caleb had arrived, but as they all congregated in the farmhouse kitchen for the midday meal, each of the four girls gave him an equally warm welcome. Farmer Holden was surprised when he walked in, but a certain warning look from his wife caused him to be more tactful than usual and, being a man's man, he and Caleb were soon discussing the state of the country, which in the farmer's opinion, was in a worse mess now than during the war. Consequently it was an amiable little group who sat around the scrubbed table eating Mrs Holden's steamed meat roll and roast potatoes in dripping.

Caleb's eyes had widened when he had seen the huge meat roll appear on the table, and he had sniffed the air for all the world like the children in the Bisto advert. Mrs Holden had laughed. 'Hungry, lad?'

'Ravenous, but I didn't expect a meal, Mrs Holden. I've brought some sandwiches with me.'

'Sandwiches!' The farmer's wife snorted her disapproval. 'They're not a meal for a grown man on a day like this. Get some meat roll and tatties down you, and let's hear no more about it. Any friend of Esther's is welcome here, lad.' Nancy purposely didn't glance Rose's way at this juncture, because she knew full well what her friend was thinking.

They all tucked in. Joy had insisted on sitting on Caleb's lap, seemingly having lost any shyness with this nice man, who had given her a big bag of brightly wrapped sweets when he'd arrived. Although Esther had protested on both counts – with the sweets, because they would spoil Joy's meal; and with Joy sitting on Caleb's lap, because it would spoil his – she had been shouted down by everyone. 'It's Christmas Eve, lass,' Mrs Holden had said, regarding the sweets. 'Let the bairn have her treat.' And Caleb had lifted Joy onto his lap, saying, 'If she wants to sit with me, that's grand, isn't it, hinny?' and Joy had dimpled up at him. Esther conceded defeat.

They were in the middle of the meal and were all laughing at some story Priscilla was telling about her altercation with one of the more stubborn cows, when the kitchen door that led out onto the yard opened, letting in a gust of icy air. They turned as one, to see Monty standing in the doorway. 'I knocked, but you were clearly having too much fun to hear me,' he said with a smile that didn't reach his eyes. And his eyes were looking straight at Joy on Caleb's lap.

Chapter Nineteen

It was an hour later – possibly the most uncomfortable hour of Esther's life. She had been so taken aback to see Monty standing there that for a moment her brain had frozen, but Priscilla had risen to the occasion. Her manner light and easy, Priscilla had trilled, 'Let me do the honours. Caleb, this is Monty Grant, and Monty' – she had looked Esther's husband straight in the eye – 'this is Caleb McGuigan, a great friend of ours. We all met when Caleb was billeted a short distance from here, recovering from injuries sustained in action.'

The unspoken warning was clear: you be nice to Caleb, because he's got a darned sight more right than you to be here; and if one of you is leaving, it won't be him.

Esther had watched as Monty had taken visible control of his expression, pulling it into something approaching pleasantness as he had said, 'How do you do? I'm Esther's husband.'

He hadn't thought Monty was her brother. Caleb rose,

with Joy positioned in one arm as he held out a hand to the man who had broken Esther's heart. He didn't smile. 'How do you do.' Part of him was looking on and thinking wryly, 'How civilized.' The other part wanted to kill Monty.

Monty was holding a box in one hand that was wrapped in festive paper, and now he turned his gaze on the child in Caleb's arms as he said, 'Do you want to see what Daddy has got you for Christmas?'

His answer was Joy turning her face away from him and burrowing it into Caleb.

For a moment silence reigned. Esther was furious at Monty's proprietorial attitude, but aware that causing a scene would help no one, she bit her tongue, saying coolly, 'We're just finishing our meal. Would you like a hot drink?' and somehow the acute embarrassment blew over. No one could fail to feel the charged atmosphere, however, and whether it was that which caused Joy to cling to Caleb like a limpet, or simply that she associated him with the happy day in the summer when his mother and Caleb had made such a fuss of her, Esther didn't know. But the child would not be parted from him, even when they all went through to the sitting area to dress the tree.

Caleb was delighted. Not only by Joy's total acceptance of him, but by the way it had got under Monty's skin. That was petty and beneath him, but he didn't care, he thought, as he helped the child to wind strands of tinsel around the sweet-smelling little tree. He had known immediately who it was standing in the doorway, even before anyone had spoken, and perhaps not surprisingly he had disliked Monty on sight. The handsome face under a shock of blond hair, the impeccable and expensive clothes, and the air of ownership regarding Esther and Joy had made him want to punch the man on the nose. And – and here he admitted to a feeling of shame – having seen Monty, he was frightened of Esther's husband. Not of the man himself, never that, but of Esther's feelings towards him. She had loved him once, heart, soul and body; and, looking at the man, Caleb could see that Esther and Monty had fitted together very well. They were of the same class, they had had privileged upbringings with everything that entailed, they spoke in the same way – oh, a hundred things, he thought wretchedly, as he handed Joy a pretty bauble for the tree. And what was he, in comparison? Nothing. He must have been mad to come here today, hoping for . . .

What? he asked himself. What had he been hoping for? He didn't really know. What he did know was that he couldn't have let another month, another week, another day go by without seeing Esther, and Christmas had provided the perfect excuse for his visit. Hell, he didn't know which way was up, and that was the truth of it. As his mam had said only the other day, when he'd sat morosely staring into the fire after his evening meal, he'd end up in the loony bin over Esther.

It didn't take long to decorate the tree, with everyone helping – everyone, that is, but Monty, who sat on the perimeter of the group. Once it had been completed, the farmer made it clear there was work to be done, Christmas Eve or no Christmas Eve, and the rest of the girls, along with the farmer and his wife and Rose, went in various directions. Priscilla made a point of wishing Caleb a merry Christmas and giving him an affectionate peck on the cheek, her leave-taking of Monty being altogether less warm.

Rose, on the other hand, completely ignored Caleb before she left to help Nancy in the dairy, to the point where she was positively rude, causing the farmer's wife – who thoroughly disapproved of Rose's conduct – to make more of a fuss of Caleb that she would normally have done. It was all awkward and uncomfortable, and even Priscilla was glad to get out of the farmhouse and leave Esther alone with the two men and the child.

As the door closed behind them, it was Caleb who broke the silence because he had decided he was blowed if he would allow Monty to intimidate him with his air of superiority; an air that even Caleb, in his irritation, recognized was natural on the other man's part. But that only made it worse. Staring straight at Monty, he said, 'So how are you finding civilian life? Takes a bit of getting back into, doesn't it.'

Monty's gaze was ice-cold, but he allowed none of the anger seething under his cool exterior to come through in his voice as he said, 'Not at all. I work with Esther's father in the family business.'

'He is not my father.' Esther's body was taut, her face set. 'And I've asked you not to refer to him as such.'

'Really, darling, this is not the time or place to discuss such things.'

'I disagree.' Esther had reached boiling point. She knew exactly what Monty was doing, and had done from the moment he had stepped into the house. His attitude, and every word he'd spoken, laid claim to her and Joy and, in so doing, stated that Caleb had no right to be here. 'It just so happens that Caleb's a good friend of mine and we have no secrets. And I am not your darling.'

'I see.'

'I doubt it.' There was the slightest pause before Esther bent down and lifted Joy, who was playing with an empty cardboard box and a strand of tinsel near the tree, into her arms. 'Please leave, Monty. I've asked you time and time again not to come here, and you know I mean it, so this is purely your fault.'

Monty had flushed a deep red. 'How long has it been going on? With him?' He was speaking to Esther but he was looking at Caleb, their eyes locked in mutual hate.

As Caleb took a step towards Monty, his fists clenched, and Esther said, 'Please, Caleb, no,' there was a cheerful toot-toot-toot from the yard outside. For a moment Caleb's gaze remained on Monty, and it was only Esther whispering, 'Caleb, please, it's Christmas Eve; think of Joy. Your . . . your friend's here to pick you up, I think,' that broke the deadlock. She took his arm. 'I'll come with you.'

They left Monty staring after them, but once outside Caleb muttered, 'I should have hit him. Damn it, I should have knocked his smug block off.'

'Not in front of Joy.'

'No . . . ' He shook his head, as though to clear his thoughts, then reached out and ruffled the little girl's curls. 'I'm sorry, I shouldn't have come.'

'Don't say that.'

The odd snowflake or two was still drifting aimlessly in the bitterly cold air, scouts for the rest of the pack in the laden sky and, as one landed on Esther's nose, Joy giggled. 'Fairy, Mummy. Fairy.'

'She insists on calling them that: ice-fairies,' Esther said softly, not knowing what to say to put things right between them. But she didn't want Caleb to leave like this.

He looked at mother and child, both so beautiful that they caused a physical ache in his chest. Turning, he raised an arm to his friend, who was revving the engine of the car. 'He wants to go – I can't keep him waiting.'

'No, of course not.' Summoning all her courage, she said, 'I know it's been awkward for you, with Monty, and I'm sorry about that, but . . . but I'm glad you came, Caleb. It's made Joy's Christmas.' She took a deep breath. 'And mine.'

'Do you mean that?' He felt so downcast that he didn't care if he was going to make a fool of himself. He couldn't carry on like this; his mam was right. He had to know if there was ever going to be any hope for him.

He'd wait for her – a lifetime, if that's what it took – but he had to know that she didn't look on him as just a friend and nothing else, because that wasn't enough. Not having seen Monty, and knowing he was still sniffing about. 'I mean, *really* mean it, Esther?'

Her heart was thudding so hard she was sure he must be able to hear it, as she read what was in his face. He cared about her, in *that* way, she thought wondrously. For a moment a rush of fear and panic – about daring to trust someone again with her love – caught her breath in her throat, but then she continued to hold Caleb's steady gaze. As she searched his rough, rugged features she saw what she needed to see. 'With all my heart,' she whispered with a tremulous smile.

There was no answering smile on his face, but he touched her cheek. 'That's all I wanted to know. I know there are things to sort out' – he glanced back to the farmhouse for a moment – 'but I can wait. I just needed to know that you wanted me to wait.'

Like Caleb, Esther knew this was a time to cast away pride. 'More than anything else in the world, but . . . but you do understand what it would mean? If . . . if we married and there were children? I mean' – she stared at him helplessly – 'you know what I mean.'

For her to talk about the future like this was beyond his wildest expectations. Softly, a smile touching his lips, he said, 'If you're trying to say that, with me as a father, they wouldn't all be as beautiful as Joy, then I can live with that.'

'Caleb.' Her lips trembled and pressed together for a moment before she continued, 'It's important you face it now.'

His face losing its tender smile, he forgot all his promises to himself to take things slowly and, careless of the man in the farmhouse or anyone else who might see them, took Esther in his arms, so that she and Joy were enfolded against him. 'Let's get one thing straight,' he said very quietly, above the silk of her hair as she rested against him. 'You are a beautiful, desirable, incredible woman that any man would be proud to call his own. And you are unique, as we all are. I don't know why you would even consider looking twice at a man like me, but I will love you and Joy – and any little ones we might have – till the day I die, and beyond. When you are free and I can ask you to marry me, I shall tell you this again; but until then, will you hold it in your heart and believe me? That man in there is the biggest fool in history. He had a pearl of great price and he threw it away. Two pearls of great price,' he added softly, reaching for Joy and lifting her out of Esther's arms into his own. He smiled down at the little girl, who beamed back at him. 'I've got to go now, hinny, but you look after your mam for me, all right? She needs a lot of love.'

Still holding Joy, he bent his head and kissed Esther. It was a sweet, fleeting kiss, their first. Tasting the salt of her tears, Caleb murmured, 'One more promise, sweetheart. I will never make you cry again. We'll be as poor as church mice, no doubt, but as far as it is within my power to do so, I will make you happy.'

Placing Joy tenderly in her arms, he stroked Esther's face one last time and then turned and walked to the car. His shoulders were straighter than they had been since the morning he had woken up in a military hospital and learned they had cut off his leg to save his life.

Monty had been watching them the whole time, and now, as Esther continued to stand in the middle of the yard, her gaze following the car winding its way down the farm track, he ground his teeth together in fury. She was shameless, behaving like that, as though she were a single woman and fancy-free. And with *him*, as rough-and-ready a type as he'd ever laid eyes on. He could scarcely believe Esther would sink so low. He saw it all now: this fellow was the reason she wouldn't come back to him. Why had he never thought she might have found someone else?

The answer came as though someone had spoken it out loud. Because, at the bottom of him, he'd never doubted that if he wanted her back she would eventually agree – after a suitable period of punishing him, of course. In returning to him, Esther had everything to gain, besides which he knew how she had loved him when they'd married, and before. She had never made a secret of her feelings, not like some girls would have. It wasn't in Esther to play the coquette and lead a man on.

The sudden memory of how it had been in the early

days caused his shoulders to slump, his body deflating, and in the place of outrage came a wave of loss and despair. He hated his life, he thought bitterly. He hated being at Theobald's beck and call twenty-four hours a day. He couldn't stand the prospect of another winter under his father-in-law's roof, with the long, cold nights seeming to stretch on forever. And Esther, betraying him like this: how could she take her marriage vows so lightly?

It didn't occur to Monty that he had slept with several women after he had walked out on her, and if someone had pointed the fact out to him and had accused him of being a hypocrite, he would have strenuously denied the charge. As far as he was concerned, none of his affairs had meant anything and so they didn't matter; besides which, men behaved that way, with the stress of war. It was acceptable, even expected. But with women it was different.

The door opened and Esther entered the house, but Joy was no longer with her. Esther had taken the child through to the dairy and left her with Rose and the farmer's wife while she said what she had to say to Monty.

Monty got in first. His voice scathing, he bit out, 'I can't believe you've encouraged the attentions of that fellow. He's not of our class, and it does not become you.'

Esther stared at him. At this moment she was seeing him as he really was. The rose-coloured glasses were not only off now, but were smashed into a hundred pieces. She felt no anger or sorrow about the end of their marriage; merely painful regret that Joy had such a man for a father. Her precious baby deserved better. Certainly a father who loved her exactly as she was. Quietly she said, 'On the day that Joy was born, I accused you of being ashamed of her – and of me – and you couldn't deny it. And the next day, when you had had time to consider your actions, you proposed that if I agreed to our baby being taken away and brought up goodness knows where, and if I had an operation to prevent the conception of more children, you would do me the great honour of continuing to be my husband. When you talk of us getting back together again and living as man and wife, does that mean you will acknowledge Joy as your daughter, and that you would welcome further children?'

He stared at her, taken aback at her directness, his Adam's apple moving up and down as he swallowed hard.

'I thought not.' And as he went to speak, she said, 'No, don't say anything, Monty, and certainly don't lie. It didn't need thinking about.'

Neither of them spoke for a moment and then Monty muttered, 'I do love you. I want you to know that. I always will.'

But not enough; not nearly enough. True love was open and unconditional. Gently she said, 'You loved the old Esther, Monty, the one you knew before Joy was born. She doesn't exist now. You could say I have grown up, I suppose, because when I look back now, I realize how young I was.'

'You're young now.'

She would never be young again, and she didn't fool herself that the road ahead was going to be easy, even with Caleb at her side. People were cruel, and she didn't mind that for herself, but she knew she was going to suffer as any mother would when spiteful talk hurt her child. Not only that, but if she and Caleb got married and had children, it would be the same for them too. But the alternative – of hiding away, of having no more children, of letting the bigots and mean-minded win – was not an option.

'Are you going to him?' Monty asked stiffly.

She sighed. 'What does it matter?'

'It matters to me, damn it. I won't give you a divorce, Esther. I told you that before, and I mean it. And I shall insist on seeing Joy whenever I want – I have the right. I am her father, and any court in the land will back me.'

'You're trying to blackmail me?'

'I am saying it would be far better for Joy – and simpler all round – if you agreed to live as my wife again. It's what you're used to, damn it, not this hovel. And I wouldn't impose any demands on you, I promise you that. It would be separate bedrooms until you felt you were ready.'

Was he mad? Or did he think she was stupid? 'Of course you wouldn't,' she said flatly. 'You don't want more children. We've ascertained that.'

'I didn't mean it like that.'

She had told Monty she had changed and she'd meant it, but now it dawned on Esther just how much of a different person she had become, when she thought about what she was going to say next. Looking him straight in the eye, she said very calmly, 'No court would back you, Monty, regarding Joy. In fact you would be laughed *out* of court, because I would swear on oath that she is the result of a liaison with a black GI. I look white; you look white. Who would a judge believe?'

After a tense moment during which their gazes locked, and with the words coming tight from between his lips, he said, 'You wouldn't.'

'Yes, I would. Instead of a quiet divorce that would pass virtually unnoticed, it would attract quite a bit of attention, don't you think? And scandal. Scandal, Monty: the very thing the Grant name doesn't want.' In spite of her determination to remain calm and composed, an edge of bitterness accompanied the last words.

'You would lie under oath? Commit perjury?'

'For Joy's happiness? Without even thinking about it.'

'She would be happy if you came back to me. She'd be able to have anything she wanted – money no object.'

'Money doesn't buy happiness, Monty.'

'You won't be saying that when you're living in squalor with that fellow,' he barked back.

'Don't shout at me. I won't stand for it.'

Monty, his jawbone working hard under the skin, breathed in deeply. 'Theobald won't let you do this – I mean it. You were raised as his daughter and bore his name. He doesn't want a divorce in the family.'

'*Theobald?*' In spite of all her good intentions, it was the final straw. 'Do you think I care what he wants? He is as good as dead to me, and you can tell him that. And you can tell him something else too: if he tries anything – anything at all – I promise you I'll make good on my threat to disown you as Joy's father. And publicly; very publicly. You tell him that, word-for-word. His precious name will be dragged through the mud.'

'You're making a big mistake.'

'No, Monty. I made my mistake three and a half years ago when I married you. And one last thing you can tell Theobald: I shall be filing for divorce in the New Year.'

He glared at her, burning with anger and humiliation, and if he could have struck her dead at that moment, he would have done so. Instead he swung round, reaching for the parcel he had brought for Joy, which lay still wrapped under the Christmas tree. Tearing it open, he took the fancy doll with the smiling porcelain face from its box and, with one vicious blow, dashed it against the worn old flagstones. 'If you want her to have nothing from me, that's exactly what she'll get – nothing.'

Again they were staring at each other, Esther's face drained of colour, and Monty's as red as a beetroot. She was trembling, but her voice was steady as she said, 'Please leave, Monty, and don't come back again.'

For a moment she thought he was going to hit her, but then he pushed past her, almost knocking her over, and left, slamming the door behind him. She didn't move; even when she heard his car start up and the sound of it disappearing down the lane, she couldn't persuade her frozen limbs into action. It was only when she looked down at the remains of the doll at her feet, at the little smashed face and limp arms and legs, that she sank to the floor, gathering it to her and swaying back and forth as the tears came.

PART FIVE

All Things Work Together for Good

1946

Chapter Twenty

'Well, here you are then, lass.' Eliza McGuigan tried to hide her dismay as she glanced round the room in which she was standing. Outside the March day was bitterly cold and the raw north-east wind cut like a knife, the snow packed hard on the ground, with a fresh fall added to it nearly every day. Inside the small room at least it was warm, Caleb's mother told herself, but then it doesn't take much to heat a rabbit hutch, and that's what this place was.

Esther knew exactly what Eliza was thinking, but as she had told Caleb the night before, she couldn't afford to be choosy. She had saved some of her wages for the last couple of years, in anticipation of this time, so she had a small nest egg to tide her over while she looked for work and found a nursery place for Joy during the day. But every penny had to stretch to two, and this room in a terraced house three streets from Bright Street had been cheap. It had been easy to see why. It was one of two bedrooms in the two-up, two-down building; the other upstairs room being occupied by an elderly married couple, and the front room and kitchen downstairs being the domain of a family of eight. The tap in the yard provided water for the household, and the wash house with its ancient boiler and the brick-built privy more or less filled the remaining space outside.

When the wife of the downstairs family – her landlady – had shown her the room the week before, she had been apologetic about the state of it. 'I know it's a mess, lass,' she'd said as she'd opened the door from the landing, 'but with six bairns and a full-time job, I've not had time to do anything to it since Mr Mason left. Gone back south he has, and good riddance. Filthy swine, if ever I saw one. Eighty years old, he was, and always saying he couldn't do this and couldn't do that, but he'd nip off to the pub quick enough. His sister's said he could go and live with her, now her husband's passed on – apparently the husband couldn't stand Mr Mason, and I'm not surprised – but I doubt she knows what she's taking on. Still, that's not my concern. Anyway, that's why I'm not asking much for it, cos I know you'll have to spruce it up a bit, and I doubt you'll be able to use the bed. Not particular in his habits, Mr Mason.'

That was the understatement of the year. As Esther looked at Caleb's mother's face, she wondered what Eliza would have said if she'd seen the room before she and Caleb got to work on it. Esther had moved from Yorkshire the week before and had stayed at one of the bed-and-breakfast establishments in Roker, a mile or so up the coast, while she looked for somewhere to live, but time had been of the essence, as she couldn't afford to remain there for long. But the landlady had been a dear soul, offering to take care of Joy while Esther went out each day, which had been a great help. Her husband had been a different kettle of fish, though, eyeing Joy with a pursed, disapproving mouth and a tight face, and making it quite clear he considered Esther a loose piece.

Shrugging off the memory, Esther said now, 'I know it's tiny, but it's clean and warm, and it will do for the present, Mrs McGuigan.'

'Can't he . . . Joy's father' – Eliza refrained from calling him Esther's husband – 'give you something each week? He ought to, lass. He's well-oiled, isn't he?'

'I don't want anything from him, not a penny.'

Esther's voice was so vehement that Eliza said no more on the matter. 'You know best, lass. Now, I've come with an idea to put to you, an' hear me out before you say anything.' Eliza knew only too well how independent Esther was, from bits that Caleb had said. And it was to the lass's credit, she'd give her that. Esther certainly didn't intend to take Caleb for every penny, like some lassies would have done in the same circumstances; in fact, according to her son, Esther had told him that until she was legally divorced and everything was settled, she felt she had to provide for herself and Joy with no help from anyone. Mind, Eliza thought to herself, she still felt that husband of the lass's should stump up something.

'An idea?'

'Aye, lass. Now Caleb tells me you've got the chance of a job as receptionist in a hotel in Roker, not far from where you've been staying. Is that right?'

Esther nodded. She had seen the job advertised in the *Echo* and taken herself along to the hotel in question, to find out more about it and how to apply, not knowing if she would even be considered for the post, never having worked in a hotel before. As she had been talking to the present receptionist, who was leaving to have a baby within the month, the manager of the hotel had passed by and heard the conversation. Pausing, he had hovered for a minute or two and then made himself known, asking Esther if she would like to accompany him to his office.

Mr Dimple was a wily individual, and had immediately seen the advantage of having someone who spoke and conducted themselves like Esther, in the front of the hotel. She was a cut above, he told himself, and the impression that guests would receive – either over the telephone or speaking to Esther in person – would do the reputation of his establishment no harm at all. After a kind of interview, he had offered her the position then and there, at a starting wage of three pounds per week until she was fully trained: three shillings more than she had been earning in the last year as a member of the Land Army, after the powers-that-be had raised the wages to two pounds and seventeen shillings. Of course, at the farm her bed and board had been provided, and there had been no nursery fees for Joy. Nevertheless she had accepted the position gratefully, telling herself that she'd manage until she completed the training. The next day she had come across the room in Ripon Street and, because of the awful state of it, the landlady, Mrs Birch, was only asking three shillings a week, and had offered to cook a hot meal ready for the evening, if Esther provided the ingredients, which would be an enormous help.

'I've no doubt you'll be robbing Peter to pay Paul over the next little while,' Eliza went on. 'I had years of that, when the bairns were young.' Not that she could compare her circumstances with that of Caleb's poor lass. 'Now Stanley's home and earning again, an' Caleb an' all, my days of hiding from the rent man are over, thank the good Lord. But to tell you the truth, lass, I miss them times now, in a funny sort of way. I used to have to take in washing to make ends meet, and I was on me feet from dawn to dusk with the little 'uns an' the house to look after, but now' – she paused to take a breath – 'the days stretch on and on when the menfolk are at work.'

Esther stared at Caleb's mother. She had no idea where this was leading. Remembering her manners, she gestured towards the one small armchair the room contained, which she'd purchased when she had bought a new single bed that she and Joy would share. She and Caleb had got rid of Mr Mason's bed and chair. They'd stunk of urine and other unmentionable things. Then they'd scrubbed the walls and ceiling and floorboards with carbolic soap to get rid of the smell, before Caleb had whitewashed the ceiling and painted the walls. She'd made curtains for the window and a matching cover for the bed. Then Caleb had fetched the bed and chair and a fairly new and clean clippy mat for the floor, with the help of one of his pals, while she had gone out for bed linen, towels, a kettle and a few other essentials. It had all bitten a hole in her precious nest egg, but it couldn't be helped. Caleb had tried to press some money on her, but she had refused so strongly that he hadn't tried again.

'What I'm trying to say, lass,' said Eliza, 'is that I reckon we can do each other a good turn. I could look after the bairn while you're at work, and that'll save you paying out; and I'll have company in the house again. A bairn is always a pleasure, and your little one took to me straight off, didn't she?' She sat down in the armchair, which was placed at an angle to the little blackleaded fireplace in which a coal fire was burning, as they both glanced to where Joy was snuggled up fast asleep in the bed she shared with her mother. A month off her third birthday, the little girl still needed a long nap for an hour or so each afternoon or there would be tears before bedtime.

Esther perched on the end of the bed facing Caleb's mother. Not mincing her words, she said quietly, 'Did Caleb ask you to do this, Mrs McGuigan?'

Eliza smiled. 'Would it be so terrible if he had, lass? But no, as it happens, he knows nowt about it. I wanted to see you meself first, and get your take on it.'

The wind taken out of her sails, Esther didn't know what to say. 'It's very kind of you, but . . . '

'No, no buts; an' it's not kind, not really. I've told you how it is and I'm not soft-soaping you.' Eliza didn't mention here that she hadn't told her husband of her intentions, either. She'd had to do a lot of work on Stanley when he had found out that Caleb's lass wasn't white – however she looked on the outside – and that Esther had a black bairn; furthermore, she was a married woman and in the process of seeing about getting a divorce. Stanley had been angry and upset, stomping about the house and saying all sorts of things she'd known he'd regret later, and the upshot of it all had been father and son having a row that had rocked the house to its foundations. It was only when Caleb had begun to pack his things, saying he was moving out, that Stanley had seen reason. It was Caleb's life, she had told Stanley, and they couldn't live it for him. He was big enough to make his own decisions and, although she had felt exactly the same as Stanley at first, once she had met Esther and the little bairn she'd changed her mind. And he would too. Stanley had given her a look that had said it'd take hell freezing over before that was the case, but at least he had said no more and an uneasy peace had descended on the household. He had yet to meet Esther, but she'd told Caleb not to force the issue. Now that the lass had moved to the district, it would happen in good time.

'So, lass, what do you say?' Eliza smiled at Esther. 'You could drop the bairn off in the morning an' I'll have her ready when you call by, come evening.'

'I . . . I couldn't ask you to do this, Mrs McGuigan.'

'You're not asking me. I'm offering.' Heaven knew what the neighbours would say, but if Caleb was serious about this lass – and she knew her lad well enough to know that his heart and soul were set on her – then the busybodies might as well start their gossiping sooner rather than later. That la-di-da lass had been right: she could have lost her Caleb over this, and she didn't intend to let that happen. Family was everything, and the scandalmongers could go take a running jump. This line of thought prompted Eliza to say, 'Your friend – Priscilla, wasn't it? Has she finished at the farm too?'

'She was getting ready to leave a few days after me.' Esther did not elaborate, but in truth she was worried about Priscilla, who had been beside herself as the time had got closer for her to leave Yew Tree Farm. Kenny had not spoken one word about a future for the two of them. Although the Battle of Britain had ended his participation in the war, a longer and more harrowing battle for Kenny had begun the night he was burned beyond recognition, and no one was more aware of this than the man himself. He never complained, even after one of his many agonizing operations, but his true opinion of himself surfaced in jokes, and his wit then was savage and caustic. With this in mind, Esther had taken Priscilla aside the evening before her departure from the farm and given her some advice. 'Cilla, I know you see him in a different way, but you have to think about how he sees himself. Those jokes about gargoyles and such are only part of it. He must be worried about how he is going to earn a living, with his hands still so bad, and you know how proud he is. He's not going to ask a lovely young woman to commit her life to him, however much he loves her – or maybe because he does love her so much. The asking has to come from you.'

'Me?' Priscilla had looked at her, horrified. For such a modern, feisty young woman, she could be very traditional at times.

'Yes, you.' Esther had smiled gently. 'If you love him and want to be with him, ask him to marry you.'

'Esther, I couldn't.'

'Then you will lose him, because he loves you too much to ask you. Think about it, okay? And, besides his injuries, don't forget he's a working-class man and you are up there in the higher echelons of society. When it comes to keeping you in the manner to which you are accustomed, he doesn't stand a chance, does he?'

'But Kenny knows I don't care about all that.'

'Cilla' – Esther had put a compassionate hand on her friend's arm – 'perhaps *he* cares.'

She had been hoping to have word from Priscilla over the last few days, after she had sent a postcard with the address of her bed-and-breakfast establishment, but to date there had been nothing, and this morning she'd posted off her new address.

Shaking her mind free of Priscilla and Kenny, she now said to Eliza, 'I'll make us a cup of tea, shall I?'

'That'd be nice, lass.'

Eliza sat and watched as Esther filled a small black kettle from a large jug of cold water and then placed it on the hook that hung over the fire from an iron bar fixed to the wall. At the side of the fireplace was a small steel shelf on which reposed the kettle and a saucepan, and on the opposite wall a long wooden shelf held mugs and plates and utensils. Under the bed she could see a wooden trunk, and she assumed that was where Esther stored their spare clothes and linen. It was a sparse set-up, Eliza thought, and for a lass who'd been used to servants and what-have-you it must be hard. Mind you, Caleb had said it was no picnic at this farm where the lass had worked – like the Dark Ages, he'd remarked – but the food had been good and plentiful, unlike in the towns and cities. Likely that'd be an added burden for the lass now: rationing, with all its frugality. No one had expected rationing to be done away with immediately, but now the government seemed to be saying things were going to get worse, and not better. It was a rum do.

Once the tea was mashing and Esther was sitting on the end of the bed facing the armchair, Eliza said quietly, 'Well, lass, what say you?'

Esther looked at the round, homely face. This woman was Caleb's mother and dear to him, and if she and Caleb were ever to have a future together, then her relationship with his mother had to start off on the right foot. And the right foot was total honesty. 'Mrs McGuigan, it's incredibly kind of you, but . . . ' She paused, biting her lip.

'What? Spit it out, lass.'

'You know my story and it's true – every word of it – but to the world I look like a white woman who has clearly misbehaved with a black GI. Having Joy all day when I work would cause problems for you with your neighbours and friends, or at the very least awkward moments. I . . . I don't want to cause trouble for you, and I don't think you've thought this through, much as I appreciate the offer. And I do, I really do.'

Eliza, her head leaning back against the armchair, looked at Esther, and at this moment her feelings were mixed. If she were to speak the absolute truth, then she would have to admit she would have preferred her lad to pick a lass with whom it would have been plain sailing. But he hadn't. And in spite of herself, she'd grown accustomed to the idea. And she liked the lass, and the little bairn was as bonny as a summer's day. If things went the way she thought they might, Joy would be calling her Grandma sooner or later, and Stanley, Granda.

Leaning forward, she put out her hand and Esther reached out hers. 'Look, lass, you and the bairn are part of our family now, that's the way I see it. An' folk can say what they like. While they're talking about us, they're not pulling some other poor blighter to pieces. An' when you're free to wed our Caleb – an' if the good Lord blesses you with bairns – then folk'll see the truth, won't they?' It said a lot for Eliza here that no hint that this was the thing driving Stanley up the wall came through in her voice. But as she had said to him the night before, when they were lying in bed discussing the situation for the umpteenth time, he was a bigoted so-an'-so and she was having none of it. He had fought a war against the Nazis because they thought exactly like he was thinking now: that the colour of someone's skin, or the stock they came from, or whether they were physically or mentally all there mattered. There would come a day, she had hissed at him, when the world would be a melting pot of different colours and races all mixing together, and it couldn't come soon enough for her, and he ought to be ashamed of himself.

'Any bairns of a mixed marriage – be it race or religion or what-have-you – have it hard, Eliza. You don't need me to spell that out for you. Is that what you want for our lad's bairns? Is it?'

She had known he was glaring at her in the darkness, even though she couldn't make out his face.

'No, truth be told, I would have liked it easy for him,' she had retorted, 'and his bairns, but Caleb has chosen what and who he wants, and that's that. And what are you saying at heart, Stan? That Catholic and Protestant should never mix, or black and white, Arabs, them Chinese folk and the rest? Love don't take account of such things; only hate does that. And fear.'

He'd grunted, then muttered, 'You've changed your tune. When Edith Ryland's lass got mixed up with that lad from the Arab quarter, you were as against it as anyone in the street.'

'Aye, I was, an' I'm not proud of it,' she had replied.

'But that was nigh on seventeen years ago, an' folk were more set in their ways. *I* was more set in me ways, I admit it. But the war's changed everything and it'll keep changing, you mark my words. And Stan' – she had turned on her side towards him – 'if you're right and there's stormy times ahead for them, Caleb is going to need us in his corner more than ever. Edith and Leonard didn't stand by their Constance; threw her to the wolves, they did, and it's them that has missed out. Their Cedric got killed in the war, and him with no children and Constance their only other bairn. I hear she's got five lovely bairns now, but Edith's never seen them. I couldn't bear that.'

He'd grunted again and then turned his back on her, but she had lain awake for a long time praying that he would come round to her way of thinking. It would be different if he would meet the lass, she was sure of it. And the bairn could charm the apples off the tree.

Looking at Esther now, she squeezed the hand in hers as she said, 'So, it's a deal then? When do you start at the hotel?'

'They wanted me on Monday, but I said I'd let them know, because of Joy.'

'Well, you tell 'em the bairn is settled, all right?'

'But I must pay you, Mrs McGuigan.'

'Wouldn't hear of it. You're family now, lass.' And then, as Esther's eyes began to fill up, Eliza murmured, 'Now, now, no tears, and no more worrying about the bairn. We'll be as happy as pigs in muck, me an' her.'

'You . . . you're so kind. I don't know how to thank

you.' Esther felt like a great weight had been lifted from her shoulders by this little woman, and it went some way to easing the hurt of her estrangement from Rose. Not that they had actually fallen out. No, it had been very civilized, the parting of their ways, but Rose hadn't hidden her disapproval regarding Caleb, and had been icy-cold and tight-lipped about Esther's decision to send Monty away on Christmas Eve. Nancy Holden had hugged her on the day she and Joy had left the farm for Sunderland, whispering in her ear that she mustn't worry and that Rose would come round in time. It was only because Rose wanted the best for her that she was so upset, Nancy had murmured. Esther hadn't replied, but had simply hugged the farmer's wife and left it at that. There was no point in saying she was amazed that, knowing how Monty had behaved when Joy was born, Rose could seriously think he *was* the best for her. It wasn't even as though he had had a change of heart on the fundamental issue. But Rose stubbornly refused to see this, and Esther had got tired of banging her head against a brick wall. In the last few weeks she had realized that her old relationship with Rose was over, and she had mourned its passing. Then she'd accepted it and looked to the future. It was all she could do.

Esther and Eliza sat and drank their tea without saying anything more, and a quietness settled on the little room, but it was a comfortable quietness. The sleeping child in the bed, the glow from the small fire and the howling from the wind outside the house all added to the feeling of peace that slowly seeped over Esther's tired mind. She had Caleb, and now she had an unexpected friend in his mother. It was more than she could have hoped for. Very soon, now that she was in the town, she would have to set the wheels in motion regarding the divorce, but for the moment it was enough just to sit here and know that she and Joy were not alone in this strange new world she was entering.

Chapter Twenty-One

The next weeks were more difficult than Esther could have imagined, and she had a constant ache in her heart when she thought about the farm and Priscilla, and especially Rose. She was still rising at five o'clock, as she had done every day in Yorkshire, but now it was to wash and dress Joy and get herself ready, before they had a breakfast of bread toasted over their small fire with the long-handled toasting fork she had purchased, the toast spread with a scraping of butter or, if the ration of two ounces per week was used up, margarine. Babies and younger children had an allowance of concentrated orange juice and cod-liver oil from the local welfare clinic, together with priority milk, and she made sure Joy always started the day on a full mug of warm milk and ended it with her juice and oil.

Breakfast over, they would dress for the bitter outdoors and make their way on snow-packed pavements to Caleb's house, where Eliza would be waiting. After a quick cup of tea with Caleb and his parents at the kitchen table, Esther would leave for work and arrive just before seven o'clock. She had settled into the job quicker than she had expected and she knew that Mr Dimple was pleased with her progress, because after four weeks he had increased her wage to three pounds and ten shillings. She still had to be very careful at managing her money, because their room needed to be kept warm for Joy and the little fire ate a surprising amount of coal, and with food to buy and other expenses every ha'penny was precious, but she was getting by – just. Rationing, something she had never really come into contact with at the farm, she now realized, was a total headache. Two ounces of butter, cheese and tea per week didn't go far, nor did the allowance of four ounces of bacon or ham and eight ounces of sugar. One packet of dried eggs per month and one shell-egg per week – if available – made her think longingly of Mrs Holden's wonderful breakfasts, and although the monthly points system allowed the odd luxury of one can of meat or fish, or two pounds of dried fruit, it didn't go far. She was enormously grateful to Mrs Birch, who seemed to be able to magic an appetizing dinner for herself and Joy from the meagre ingredients she gave the landlady each day; and the fact that Eliza insisted on feeding Joy from the family's rations at lunchtime was a great help. But most days she found herself lunching on the bread and dripping she took in to work with her.

However, it wasn't coming to terms with rationing or her job, or the fact that she missed Joy dreadfully each day, even though she knew her child was in good hands, that was the hardest thing. It was Mr McGuigan, Caleb's father, and his stiff attitude to her and Joy that caused Esther to lie awake some nights, with Joy's tiny body curled into hers, snug and warm. She could see that his father's stance was winding Caleb up like a spring each morning, but at least when she collected Joy just before six o'clock each evening the menfolk hadn't returned from work, and she always made sure she left immediately. But it didn't bode well for family life in the future, and she knew, whatever Caleb said about it being only the two of them and Joy that mattered, that a rift with his father would grieve him deeply. Their life together would begin under a cloud.

The other thing that kept her awake at night was Priscilla. She had received a letter a week after she had moved to Ripon Street; a tear-smudged, unhappy letter. Priscilla had written that she was temporarily back at the family home while she looked for a job of some kind – against her parents' wishes, she'd added, as they thought the only job for a girl was marrying well. Kenny, she believed, had returned to Scarborough shortly after she and the other girls had left the farm, and was at present living with his parents while he awaited another (and hopefully final) operation on his damaged hands, to remove a mass of scar tissue and replace it with skin grafts that would be taken from the inside of his leg. And no, she'd said, she hadn't asked Kenny about the future, or led their last conversation round to marriage. He clearly didn't feel about her the way she felt about him, or he couldn't have let her go without saying something.

For the first time in their acquaintance Esther had been furious with her friend. She had sat down and written a letter reiterating all that she had said previously to Priscilla, and more besides, and she hadn't minced her words. She had posted it immediately, without giving herself time to wonder if she was doing the right thing, and had regretted it ever since. She had been too hard on Priscilla, she'd told herself wretchedly, when days had gone by and she had heard nothing, but it was too late now to take back what she had written. Not that she believed she was wrong; she didn't, but she should have couched it differently.

But now it was the middle of May and at last the long northern winter had given up its icy grip – the snow of March and the vicious wind and hail of April giving way to a spring that seemed to have come overnight. At the farm Esther knew pink-and-white blossom would be loading the boughs of apple and cherry trees, and the scent of wild flowers would be competing with the less desirable smell of the pigsties and cow sheds. Here in the terraced streets of Monkwearmouth there wasn't a tree to be seen, but the last two Sundays she and Caleb had taken Joy to Mowbray Park in Bishopwearmouth, where the beech trees were unfolding soft, silky leaves and the oaks were decked with dazzling green and gold. They had sat together holding hands and watching Joy play, and Esther had tried to ignore the covert (and sometimes not-so-covert) glances that had come their way. With the warm sunshine on her face and Caleb at her side, things like rationing and the daily struggle seemed shelved for an hour or so. But she knew it wasn't only her who was finding their circumstances trying. Once the euphoria of victory had faded away, it had become clear how much the war had cost. Britain was utterly exhausted and the country needed to be rebuilt for peace. But there were bright glimmers up ahead, for those who searched for them. Work was plentiful for the men returning from active service, for one thing.

'It needs to be,' Caleb had said dourly, when Esther had said as much to him. 'It's "Thanks very much and now clear off – you're on your own, chum." A civilian suit, a hat, a shirt, two collars and a tie, a pair of shoes, socks and underpants, and two studs and a pair of cuff-links, all packed in a flat cardboard box, aren't much to show for years up to your eyes in muck, sweat and bullets, in my opinion. Oh, and a mackintosh – I mustn't forget that, must I? And some men scarred or crippled, or aged beyond their years. We're the only country among the Allied nations who fought the war all the way through from 1939 to the end, but to hear some lassies talk, the GIs won it single-handed. And what about the poor devils who come home and find another man's been sleeping with their missus? A suit don't do it for them, does it?'

This had happened to a school friend of Caleb's, who had ended up in court for grievous bodily harm after he'd given his rival a good pasting.

'That's what people think about me,' Esther had said soberly. 'Or that I call myself "Mrs" when really I'm not married.'

'No, they don't, of course they don't,' Caleb had protested, knowing he had put his foot in it.

But they did, Esther thought now, as she remembered that conversation as she walked home from work on a soft May evening. Children were playing their games in the streets while housewives chattered on their front steps, the smell of dinner cooking wafting through open doors, and it seemed as if all was right with the world. But her world would never be right until she was free of the past, once and for all. She had gone to see a solicitor in Fawcett Street in Bishopwearmouth, shortly after she and Joy had settled in at Ripon Street. She had kept a portion of the nest egg she'd painstakingly saved for this very purpose.

Mr Hopper of Hopper & Sons had been polite, but she had detected a coolness in his manner as she had left that hadn't been apparent when she had entered his establishment. But then, she couldn't blame him. Mindful of Monty's threat to claim his rights, where Joy was concerned, she had told Mr Hopper that her husband was not the father of her child. When he had quietly enquired who was, she had steeled herself to lie convincingly. 'A black GI. He knows nothing about the baby. My decision.'

'And so your daughter exhibits proof of this in her . . . er . . . her physical appearance?'

'Unmistakably.'

The solicitor had promised to set the wheels in motion,

after he had asked her a host of personal questions, noting down her answers with an expensive-looking pen on a sheaf of papers in front of him. But he had asked her twice if, in view of the fact that her husband did not want a divorce and had offered to bring the child up as his, she was sure about what she was doing.

Quite sure, she had told him on the second time of asking. She would not countenance her daughter being shipped off to a remote boarding school somewhere and hidden away, which would surely be the case if her husband had his way.

Mr Hopper had made no comment. She had sensed the man's sympathies were all with Monty and had had to restrain herself from getting up and walking out. Mr Hopper was indicative of his profession, and she doubted another solicitor would be any different. As she had left the office, he had warned her that if her husband proved obstructive to the divorce going through, it would be far from plain sailing and possibly expensive.

Esther paused at the corner of Bright Street, looking up into the sky above the rows of terraced houses. Cotton-wool clouds were sailing in an expanse of blue, and a couple of seagulls wheeled in the air currents, giving their haunting cry. For a moment she longed to go back in time to when she was a young innocent on the verge of womanhood, and life was safe and secure and straight-forward. And then she shook the brief melancholy away.

She wouldn't change anything, she told herself fiercely. If things had been different, she wouldn't have her precious baby girl; she wouldn't have met Caleb – dear, dear Caleb – or Priscilla and Kenny and the others. And then, as though her last thought had conjured her friend up, she heard her name being called and saw Priscilla running along the pavement towards her.

Esther found herself hugged to within an inch of her life as Priscilla murmured incoherently, but she managed to make out, 'Thank you, thank you, thank you, darling' through Priscilla's tears, before she eventually loosened her grip.

'So?' Esther smiled at her friend. 'Do I take it you and Kenny have finally made the big decision?'

Priscilla held out her left hand, where on her third finger a pretty little engagement ring twinkled.

'We've come to tell you in person; Kenny's waiting inside with Caleb's mother but I wanted to see you by myself first.'

'Oh, Cilla!'

'Your letter did it; especially the bit where you said what did I have to lose but a smidgen of pride, whereas Kenny had lost so much, and he deserved to have someone love him like I loved him. So, I plucked up my courage and went to see him, and . . . well, everything was all right.' Priscilla found that moment too precious and intimate to share, even with Esther.

When she had reached Kenny's parents' house in a little back street in a less-than-salubrious part of Scarborough, she had stood outside on the pavement, unable to move for a minute or two, her heart pounding fit to jump out of her chest. And it was something else Esther had said that encouraged her: if she didn't go and see Kenny and ask the question, she would wonder for the rest of her life what he really felt about her. 'Every day,' Esther had written, 'you'll wonder what he is doing and who he's with, if he's sad or happy, laughing or depressed, and at special times – Christmas and so on – you'll know he's out there somewhere, living a life that doesn't hold you in it.'

And so Priscilla had knocked on the door and it had been Kenny himself who had opened it, staring at her as though she was an apparition. All her carefully rehearsed words had gone out of the window at seeing his dear, scarred and (some would say) grotesque face again. He had closed his eyes and then opened them again, as though checking she was real and not a figment of his imagination. And it was then that she had said, 'I couldn't stay away. I have to tell you' – her breath had caught in a sob – 'I have to tell you how I feel.'

Kenny had pulled her into the narrow dark hall, still without speaking, and shut the door, and his voice had held a painful, level tone as he'd said, 'Come into the kitchen. Everyone's out, and it's warmer in there.'

She had followed him down the hall and, once in the kitchen, had held out her hand, but he hadn't taken it, nor had he touched her. His face drained of colour – apart from vivid red patches from the last skin grafts, so that it resembled a patchwork quilt of different textures – he had said grimly, 'You shouldn't have come here, Priscilla. We said our goodbyes in Yorkshire.'

It was only the look in his eyes when he had first seen her standing outside that had given her the courage to go on. She had drawn in a long breath and let it out on a soundless sigh and now, as she looked at him, her gaze was steady and her voice soft, but firm. 'Yes, I should have come. I should have come weeks ago, but I was too frightened that you might not love me like I love you: in a forever way. But now, not knowing if there is a chance for me has become unbearable.'

'A chance for you?' He had been incredulous. 'You must know how I feel, Priscilla, but look at me. *Look at me.* You are young and beautiful, and you've your whole life in front of you. You could have any man you want—'

'I want you.'

'No, you are grateful to me for saving you from that fiend Peter Crosse, and I suspect you feel sorry for me too. But pity and compassion and gratefulness are not enough for a marriage. I'm never going to look better than I look now, not much anyway, and my hands' – he held them out in front of him – 'they're all but useless. That's the truth of it. Every morning you would wake up and look at the gargoyle next to you . . . '

'Don't say that. I hate it when you say that.'

'And every night you would feel these hands fumbling over your flesh and try not to cringe. I can just about feed myself again, if my meat is cut up for me and everything is bite-sized, that is. Dressing myself takes an age and—'

'I love you, Kenny. I love every inch of your poor face,

and to me it's the most precious face in the world. And your hands' – before he could stop her, she had taken them in hers and now she raised first one and then the other to her lips, kissing them gently, before she went on – 'are a witness to your courage and sacrifice, my darling. Don't you understand what I see when I look at you? I see a giant among men, a truly noble human being who is dealing with what life has dished out, despite its unfairness.'

'You don't understand what you would be taking on.'

'I'm not a stupid woman, Kenny. A dizzy one at times perhaps, but not stupid.'

He looked into her face and said from deep in his throat, 'I can't let you do this. You'll regret it one day; resent that you could have flown high like a bird, and instead you are held bound by someone who has clipped your wings.'

There was a light dawning in her face, a brightness in her eyes that had been missing since the last time she had seen him. 'Without you I have no wings at all, my darling. Don't you see? I've been wretched, without hope, and that's a terrible place to be.'

'I know.'

It was a whisper, but it was enough. She leaned against him, her arms about his neck, and as he murmured the words of love she had ached to hear, his arms crushed her to him in an agony of need that spoke more than words. Time stood still, the world faded away and the little shabby kitchen became heaven on earth.

'I take it, from your face, that Kenny convinced you he loved you.'

Priscilla came back to the present, to find Esther grinning at her. Blushing hotly now, she murmured, in true Cilla fashion, 'And how!'

'Good.'

'We're getting married next week. Special licence. Kenny wants Caleb to be his best man, and of course there is no one on earth but you and Joy that I want there. I know you work Monday to Saturday, but we've found a perfectly delightful vicar who will marry us on a Sunday. Kenny's family are coming, but mine' – she wrinkled her nose – 'have disowned me. Marrying a common working man is the last straw, according to Mother. If I'd known they'd react like that, I'd have found a common working man years ago and saved myself a lot of bother.'

Esther grinned. Priscilla was back on form, and it was *so* good to see her.

Arm-in-arm, they walked down Bright Street, Priscilla chattering away nineteen to the dozen. They were going to start married life living at Kenny's parents' home, but that wouldn't be for long, she confided, because she'd already got a job as a sewing machinist at a nearby factory and the money was good, even if the work was monotonous. But with government agencies setting the pace, jobs for women were opening up as never before, and she didn't intend to stay at the factory forever. For the time being, though, they would save every penny they could to furnish a small one-bedroomed flat somewhere, so they could rent their own place. With clothes, petrol and food on ration, there was precious little to spend any money on anyway. Once Kenny had had the operation on his hands, they'd see how he was and what sort of work he could do, because he was determined he wasn't going to sit at home all day. Priscilla stopped talking as they reached the house and hugged Esther tightly again. 'I can never thank you enough. You know that, don't you? I wouldn't have gone to see him, if it wasn't for you, and my cowardice would have ruined both our lives.'

'Not cowardice.' Esther touched her friend's cheek briefly. 'You were just deeply in love, and that makes you vulnerable.' As she knew only too well; and she wasn't thinking about the past and Monty. Caleb had an attractiveness – a magnetism – that was nothing to do with looks, and all to do with a maleness that drew women's interest like bees to a honey pot. She had seen the way girls looked at him: those bright, eager young things with a modern outlook and no baggage that she had imagined him dating in the past; and although she trusted him, it frightened her. The damage that had been done when Monty had cast her aside surfaced now and again in moments of self-doubt and panic, and try as she might, she couldn't quite overcome them. It didn't help that Mr Hopper had emphasized that, with nearly 50,000 service divorces still outstanding in the courts, even uncontested divorces were taking their time, let alone ones that one partner – as in the case of Monty – might object to.

'Come on, come and see Kenny.' Priscilla pushed open the door she had left on the latch and pulled her into the house. 'He wants to give you a big hug too.' Then she stopped dead in the hall and hugged Esther for the third time. 'I'm getting married next week,' she said, with a note of wonder in her voice. 'The war is over and I'm getting married, and I'm going to give Kenny a wedding night that will put a smile on his face for a week!'

Oh yes, Priscilla was definitely her old self.

Chapter Twenty-Two

Priscilla's wedding day went like a dream. The weather smiled on the happy couple, and the bride looked beautiful in a silk two-piece suit with a vertical scalloped edge to the front-buttoned top and a central pleat to the skirt. It was a suit Priscilla had had before war broke out, but with some modification it fitted her perfectly; and as she had only worn it once before, for a cousin's wedding, and the colour was a soft ivory, it looked every inch a bride's ensemble. A small bunch of pink rosebuds just below her shoulder, and a spectacular pink hat with a huge brim turned up and folded into a sail-like shape above her hair, which she had recently had cut short and curled, completed the outfit, but it was her beaming smile all day that everyone remembered. Kenny was like a dog with two tails and, as he turned to look at Priscilla as she walked up the aisle on the arm of his father, the look on his face brought a sea of handkerchiefs fluttering into play.

Everyone went back to Kenny's parents' house for the wedding lunch, and his mother – with the help of friends and family pooling their rations – did them proud. There were several small children for Joy to play with, and the afternoon sped by, before everyone waved the couple off to their hotel on the sea front where they were spending the night.

On the train home, Joy fell asleep on Caleb's lap and Esther sat with her head on his shoulder. She wouldn't have admitted it to a soul, and she felt more than a little ashamed of her feelings, but she had found the day bittersweet. She was thrilled for Priscilla and dear Kenny, and didn't begrudge them one drop of their happiness, but their wedding had brought home how far-off her own to Caleb was, and the battle that lay ahead with Monty, and probably Theobald too.

Caleb's voice rumbled softly above her head as he murmured, 'Are you awake?'

'Yes, I was thinking about the day and how happy everyone was. Especially Cilla and Kenny, of course.'

'Me too.' There was a pause before he added, 'Don't take this the wrong way, because I couldn't be more pleased for Kenny. He's a great bloke and he deserves someone like Priscilla who is head over heels in love with him and not afraid to show it. But . . . well, I was as jealous as hell too. I want to ask you to be my wife; I want to give you a ring, and for us to be man and wife and be together all the time.'

'I'm so glad you said that.' She sat up so that she could see his face. They had been fortunate enough to secure a compartment to themselves, and now she reached up and kissed him. 'I'd been thinking the same sort of thing, and I felt horrible for being so mean.'

'Then we're mean together.' He grinned at her. 'But our day will come, sweetheart. If I have to bump Monty off so that you're a widow and the way is clear, so be it.'

He was joking, but Esther had thought more than once that if Monty had died in the war, everything would have been so much simpler, and she felt awful about that too. But it wasn't as if she actually wished him dead, she hastened to reassure herself for the umpteenth time. She didn't. It was just that everything was such a tangle . . .

Caleb walked her home from the train station, Joy still fast asleep in his arms, but as they turned the corner into Ripon Street, Esther stopped dead. Caleb had taken a step or two before he realized she wasn't at his side, and as he turned saying, 'What is it?', Esther couldn't answer for a moment. A car was parked outside Mrs Birch's house – an unusual event in itself – and in the thick twilight it looked very much like Monty's. Her heart began to pound like a sledgehammer.

Caleb's gaze followed hers. 'Is it his?'

'I think so.' Monty would have received the divorce papers by now, and it had to be about that. Her face had lost its colour and when she said, 'Give me Joy and you go home. It's better I see him alone,' Caleb shook his head.

'If you think for one moment I'm going to let you do that, then you don't know me very well.'

'He's quite capable of dragging you into all this and trying to blacken your name.'

'My name, such as it is, can withstand anything he throws at it, sweetheart. Now listen to me' – he smiled at Esther – 'and don't look so tragic. This was always going to happen sooner or later. I knew Monty wouldn't give up without a fight, and so did you. Whether Theobald is urging him on is neither here nor there. We face this together, as we are going to face everything in the future, all right? You might not wear my ring yet and have the protection of my name, but in my heart you have both.'

'Oh, Caleb.'

'He won't threaten or bully you, with me around. Or at least he'd only attempt it once,' Caleb added grimly. 'He might still legally be your husband, but he lost every moral right to call himself such, the day he abandoned you and Joy. Keep that clear in your mind, whatever he says.'

Esther nodded, but silently she was praying there would be no unpleasantness. She and Joy were settled in Ripon Street for the time being, and Mrs Birch had turned out to be a good-natured woman and a fair landlady. But one of the things Mrs Birch often mentioned was that she was a respectable woman and ran a respectable house. Her eyebrows had lifted the first time she had seen Joy, but Esther's quiet demeanour and the fact that she obviously came from a privileged background had won the landlady over. 'Everyone makes mistakes,' she had said, clucking Joy under the chin, 'and I dare say you were taken advantage of. Them GIs had silver tongues, all right.'

Esther had not disabused her, merely saying that she was in the process of getting a divorce from her husband, but that Caleb was prepared to marry her, and be a father to Joy, when she was free.

Mrs Birch had pursed her lips slightly at this. A Catholic, she didn't hide her displeasure at the way society was going. 'It's as easy to get a marriage licence as to buy a dog licence, these days,' she'd commented stiffly, 'and even easier to get a divorce.'

Esther had bitten her lip and remained silent, and the moment had blown over, but she knew if there was a ruckus of any kind between Caleb and Monty, Mrs Birch would not be so tolerant.

Esther opened the front door with her key and then stood, hesitating, in the hall. Mrs Birch had made it clear when she had taken the room that no gentlemen callers were allowed over the front doorstep, come hell or high water, but she could hardly ask Caleb to wait outside, in these circumstances. The next moment the door to Mrs Birch's kitchen opened and the landlady said, 'Oh, there you are, Mrs Grant' and instantly Esther knew Monty had been working his charm on the woman. 'Your *husband*' – Mrs Birch placed a slight emphasis on the last word – 'has called to see you.'

As she spoke, Monty appeared behind her in the open doorway, a mug in his hand and with no overcoat or hat on. He had clearly been made very welcome. Fighting back her resentment, Esther said composedly, 'Thank you, Mrs Birch. I saw the car.'

'Hello, Esther.' And as Caleb stepped into the hall, with Joy in his arms, Monty added, 'Caleb,' and nodded at him.

Caleb's eyes narrowed. What was this? Monty was too affable, too friendly. He was up to something.

Mrs Birch, who had well and truly made up her mind on which side of the fence she sat in this *ménage à trois*, cleared her throat. 'I think perhaps it would be better if Mr McGuigan left, Mrs Grant.'

Esther looked her landlady straight in the eye. '*I* don't, Mrs Birch.' Blow the rules; she would find somewhere else if she had to. She wouldn't have Caleb treated like this.

'Oh.' Clearly affronted, Mrs Birch turned to Monty. 'Mr Grant . . . '

'It's all right, Mrs Birch,' said Monty smoothly, before looking at Esther. 'I've come to tell you that your father has had a stroke, Esther. A bad one. And he is asking for you.'

Esther stared, wide-eyed, and for once she did not correct Monty about the form of address. 'I don't want to see him.'

'He's very ill – very ill indeed – and he wants to make his peace with you,' said Monty, so reasonably and gently that Caleb wanted to punch him on the nose. 'Would you deny him the comfort that would bring?'

It was a trick. Caleb's jaw worked. Ten to one, this

was a ploy to get Esther back into the fold and away from him, but she wouldn't fall for it, would she? Not his Esther.

'He wanted nothing to do with me, or Joy; you know that yourself. You heard him – you were there. If . . . if he could have struck me dead when the baby was born, he would have.'

'That was then, and shock played a big part in his behaviour. Surely you can appreciate that?'

'What I appreciate is that it has been three years, and he has never tried to see me.'

'Now that's not quite true, is it? I told you some time ago that he was willing to let bygones be bygones.' Monty handed the mug to Mrs Birch and came to stand in front of her. 'He's dying, Esther,' he said softly. 'Surely you can find it in your heart to see him one last time? If you refuse, you may regret it in the future and it will be too late then.'

'Enough of that.' Caleb spoke for the first time, his voice harsh. 'Don't blackmail her. That man has never been a father to her, in the true sense of the word.'

Monty turned his gaze on the man he saw as his rival, and his manner was autocratic as he said coolly, 'I disagree, and I feel I am in a better position than you to make a judgement. Theobald gave her everything from the moment she was born, and denied her nothing.'

'Everything money can buy, you mean. What about love and support and understanding when she needed them most?'

Monty shrugged his shoulders, his eyes diamond-hard as he looked at the other man. 'I would be very careful about throwing the first stone,' he said evenly. 'You haven't met Theobald, so I repeat: I am in a better position than you to judge his motives. He wants to see his daughter and granddaughter. Is that too much of an extreme request to deny a dying man?'

Esther felt she wanted to be sick. The thought of going back to her childhood home was stomach-churning; seeing Theobald again was ten times worse. And yet, if he really was dying, could she refuse? It was true what Monty said: like it or not, Theobald had given her a privileged upbringing and, although that had been by default, nevertheless she had benefited from it. 'Are . . . are you sure he wants to see me?' she murmured, her head bowed.

Caleb saw the flash of satisfaction sweep over Monty's face, before the gentle mask came into play again. If he hadn't been holding Joy, he knew he would have had Esther's husband by the throat before now. 'Esther, you can't seriously be considering doing what he wants? What either of them wants? This is a ruse of some kind, you must see that?' He glared at Monty. 'You've had the divorce papers, haven't you? That's what this is really about.' If Esther went back with Monty, somehow she would be persuaded to stay and take up her old life, he thought desperately.

'Caleb, I need to go home, just this one time,' she whispered. 'Please try to understand.'

Home. She had used the word 'home'. Already the

tentacles were tightening. Fear made his voice cold as he said, 'I'm sorry, but I don't understand. You owe Theobald nothing.'

'If he's dying—'

'*If.*' He cut off her voice harshly. 'That's the thing, isn't it? You've only got his word for it.'

'You can telephone the house,' Monty interjected smoothly, 'and ascertain the facts, or Dr Martin. You would trust him to tell the truth, wouldn't you?' he said to Esther.

'Shut up!' Caleb's face was burning with fury.

'Caleb, please.' Esther turned imploring eyes to him. 'I . . . I believe Monty. He wouldn't lie about something like this.'

Caleb stared at her, terror making his insides tremble. He was going to lose her. What could he offer her, compared to the kind of life she would have as Monty's wife and Theobald's daughter – the kind of life she had been used to, until the last few years? It was familiar to her, far more familiar than existing in one small room and working all hours, and the pull of it would be strong, he knew that. And Monty wasn't stupid; he would point out every benefit in his oily, silky voice, using Joy as a lever too, no doubt, and listing the advantages that wealth and social standing would open up for Esther's daughter in the future. 'Don't go,' he said softly now. 'Please, Esther, don't go back.'

'I have to. I'm sorry, but I have to. But it won't be for long, I promise.'

Monty knew what was going on in Caleb's head, and felt a deep satisfaction in watching him squirm. Theobald's stroke couldn't have been more opportune if he'd planned it deliberately, but it was genuine enough, and it had had the effect of reinforcing in the old goat's mind his obsession with carrying on the family name. That, and the divorce papers, which had arrived a little while ago. From Theobald's reaction to them, Monty had realized that his father-in-law had never really expected Esther to go that far, and it had been a shock to him. In fact Theobald hadn't really been well from the morning they had arrived, but it had been his desire for young flesh that had tipped him over the edge.

Monty thought back to the early hours of the morning when he had been woken out of a deep sleep by one of his father-in-law's regulars pounding on his bedroom door. His initial reaction had been that it was the final straw, and he would follow through on his desire to find alternative accommodation. But when he'd opened the door, the girl had been in hysterics, saying that Theobald had 'gone all funny'. He had paid her and the child – because the second girl had been little more than a child – and got them out of the house before calling Dr Martin, and then made Theobald as comfortable as he could until the doctor arrived, but several times he had thought Theobald had breathed his last. Thinking of this now, he murmured, 'Time is short, I fear, Esther.'

Caleb stared at Esther for a moment more, without looking at Monty again, and then thrust Joy into her arms. 'Do what you want to do,' he said flatly. 'I can't stop you.'

'Well!' Mrs Birch's voice trickled like petrol on naked flames into the taut atmosphere. 'What an attitude, I must say.'

Caleb shot the landlady a glance of such venom that she shut her mouth with a little snap, and then he turned and stepped down into the street. He didn't bang the door behind him, but left it wide open, and as he walked away part of him was waiting for Esther to call him back. But she didn't. He didn't pause or slow down until he had turned the corner of the street, and then, when he was out of sight of the house, he began to shake. Leaning against the brick wall of a butcher's shop, he ran his hand over his face, cursing Monty under his breath.

He hadn't meant to leave Esther that way. He straightened, turning to retrace his footsteps, before stopping once again. Should he go back? He took a step forward, paused and swung round in a semicircle as a maelstrom of different emotions had him groaning out loud. He didn't know what to do, for crying out loud. If he went back to the house there was a damned good chance he would punch Monty in the face, and he had enough sense left to know that would play directly into the other man's hands.

And she had made her choice. He shut his eyes. He knew that. But he didn't want her to think he didn't understand.

Did he understand? he asked himself in the next

moment. And when the answer came, he muttered, 'So why go back, then? What good will it do?

How long he stood there he didn't know. It was dark now, the May night cool but not cold, but he was oblivious to his surroundings as his mind whirled and spun. And then, faintly, he heard the sound of voices and a car starting up. Walking to the corner again, he looked down the street just in time to see Mrs Birch hand Joy to Esther, who was clearly sitting in the back seat of Monty's car, although he couldn't make her out very well.

She was going right now. For a moment he almost ran down the pavement, but checked himself just in time. What a fool he would look, with his awkward gait and hobbledehoy bearing. Why give Monty more ammunition with which to prove to Esther that he was the better man?

Mrs Birch shut the car door and stood back on the pavement, and the next moment the car was drawing away. And in that second Caleb bitterly regretted not calling out or trying to see her. He stood in the shadows, calling himself every name under the sun, his hands bunched into fists at his side and his body tense. And then the sound of the car faded, the street became quiet once more and he was alone. In fact he had never felt so alone, not even when he was lying in a rat-infested trench in France, with his body lacerated with shrapnel and his best friend's body, minus its head, stretched out at the side of him.

Chapter Twenty-Three

Theobald lay back against his heaped pillows, watching Dr Martin pack his black bag after the doctor had examined him. He wondered if the doctor was aware that he wasn't as ill as he was pretending, but he rather thought not. The man was a fool, he thought dismissively. All quacks were. So full of their own importance it was easy to pull the wool over their eyes. And of course he *had* had a stroke; it just hadn't incapacitated him as severely as he was making out.

It had frightened him, though. He shut his eyes as though he was too weary to keep them open, but behind the closed lids his mind was racing. And it was a warning to get his house in order, and that meant Esther returning to live as Monty's wife. He found he didn't want to leave this earth childless, and although Esther wasn't his, with Monty's agreement the Wynford name would be carried on. He wouldn't simply turn to dust and be forgotten in a few years – not with his name alive. For a moment the panic that any thought of dying brought was strong, and as his heart began to race he silently told himself: *steady, steady*. He intended to live for a good few years yet.

'I understand Mr Grant has gone to fetch your daughter, Mr Wynford.'

Theobald opened his eyes and nodded at the doctor, saying weakly, 'I feel the need to be reconciled to her.'

'Well, that's good, that's good.' Dr Martin smiled briefly. 'If there's one thing the war's taught us, it's that life is too short to hold grudges, and family is all-important. I shall tell your housekeeper the correct dose of tincture, and so on, and I'll return tomorrow morning. Try and get a good night's sleep, Mr Wynford.'

Once he was alone, Theobald sat up straighter. The stroke had affected his left side, with the corner of his mouth slightly stretched upwards and the skin around his eye dragging a little, but he had more movement in his left arm, hand and leg than he had let on to Dr Martin. He wouldn't put it past Esther to check with the doctor how serious his condition was. He felt rough, he told himself, in justification of what he was doing, but not like some of the poor devils he'd seen who had been taken by a stroke. The doctor had wanted him admitted to hospital, but Theobald was having none of that. He could string Dr Martin along; the hospital specialists were a different kettle of fish. His speech had been slurred initially, but already that was improving, so he'd have to remember to be careful about the way he spoke. All in all, it could have been a lot worse. He inclined his head at the thought. He'd got a mite too excited about what he was doing to Mabel's little sister, that was the truth of it. It wasn't often he got his hands on one as young as her: nine years old, but already being coached very ably by Mabel. He understood there were two more sisters – twins, of seven years old – and he'd promised Mabel a small fortune if he could be the first. The parents didn't care, according to Mabel, not as long as their offspring brought home the money for their drink and drugs. Scum, the lot of them.

Theobald let himself relax against the pillows again; he mustn't think of Mabel and her sisters for the time being. The stimulus was causing his heart to race, and Dr Martin had said that he had to rest and not exert himself in any way.

The doctor had given him a spoonful of the medication he was going to leave with Mrs Norton, before he had left the room, and now Theobald began to feel the powerful sedative taking effect. He shut his eyes, a feeling of well-being stealing over him, despite the circumstances. Esther would accompany Monty back here, he was sure of it. Women were a different species from men; they set store by deathbed reunions, and the like. It would take a hard woman to refuse the wish of a dying man, and although Esther was headstrong and difficult and contentious, she wasn't hard. Or she hadn't been, when she was growing up anyway. Too emotional and fiery by half of course, but at the time he had attributed that side of her personality to his own mother, who had been something of a tartar behind closed doors.

His lips compressed at the reminder of how completely he had been fooled, and then he shrugged mentally. No matter. He could still accomplish what he wanted, if he played this stroke card to its fullest potential. Esther back here, where he could keep an eye on her; her child deposited in a boarding school – a good boarding school, he wouldn't stint on that, but he would make sure it was where she would be out of sight and mind, Switzerland perhaps, or Italy – and Monty jumping through whatever hoops he needed his son-in-law to jump through.

Theobald smiled to himself. He would see to it that this divorce idea was consigned to the past within weeks, or his name wasn't Theobald Wynford.

He must have slept, because it was late evening when Dr Martin left and, when he next opened his eyes, Osborne was gently shaking his shoulder and saying, 'Mrs Wynford-Grant is here, sir, and waiting to see you. They arrived last night, but it was decided not to disturb your sleep.' Bright sunlight was streaming into the room.

'What time is it?'

'Half-past seven, sir. Mrs Norton dared not leave giving you your medication any longer. Dr Martin was most specific that it must be given exactly to his time-table.'

Theobald would have told his butler exactly where the good doctor could insert his timetable, but, remembering the part he was playing, he murmured weakly, 'Thank you, Osborne,' causing his butler's mouth to drop open for a moment. In all the years he had worked for Theobald Wynford, he had never been thanked for one service that he had done for his master. As he said later to Mrs Norton in the privacy of her sitting room, 'Long may the master be ailing, if this is the result.' Neither of them was blind or deaf to what they termed 'the master's shenanigans', either, and much as they would have liked to leave Theobald's employ, they were both aware that at their age another position would be almost impossible to come by, especially with the sort of reference Theobald would be likely to give them. But maybe there would be an end to all that now, they agreed. And not before time.

It was twenty minutes later when Mrs Norton showed Esther into the room. Theobald had been washed and shaved by Osborne, and was sitting propped up in bed, looking as pathetic as he could manage. He had purposely refused any breakfast, although he was starving, knowing this would be duly reported back. He'd also refrained from adding a good measure of whisky, from the bottle he kept on his bedside cabinet, to his morning cup of tea, as was his custom. It wouldn't do for Esther to smell alcohol on his breath.

As though it took tremendous effort, he murmured breathlessly, 'Esther, m'dear. You came.'

Esther stared at the man she had never liked, even when she had believed him to be her father. One of her earliest memories was of Theobald barging about the house shouting and swearing and bullying the servants. He had been feared by every member of his household, including his wife, but his blistering verbal assaults and ranting and raving had never intimidated her. And he had known this. It hadn't stopped him trying to break her spirit, however, on a number of occasions when she had lived under his charge. But he had never succeeded.

The thought brought her head up and raised her chin, and she looked every inch the grand lady, despite the ordinary clothes she was wearing, when she said coolly, 'Yes, I came. I am sorry to find you so unwell.'

'Come ... come and sit by ... me.' Theobald was careful to gasp and mumble his words.

Esther hesitated. She didn't want to approach the bed; in fact she didn't want to be in the same room as Theobald, but she could hardly refuse such a simple request. And he did seem a shadow of his former self. Quietly she sat down in the armchair next to the big four-poster bed. 'Are you in pain?'

'Pain?' For a moment he wondered what to say, and then decided to tell the truth. 'N-no. Ju-just tired. Very tired.' With a gasping breath that he was proud of, he slowly murmured, 'Wanted to s-see you. Make things' – he shut his eyes and opened them on a rasping sigh – 'right between us.'

Esther wanted nothing more than to get up and run out of the room, and keep running until she was far from this place she had once called home. There was no doubt that he was ill, but something – and she didn't know what – was making the hairs on the back of her neck prickle. Perhaps it was the spectre of death that she was sensing? she asked herself. Certainly something disturbing. She had questioned both Osborne and Mrs Norton before coming into the room, and both individuals had reiterated all that Monty had told her.

'Dr Martin says he could go any time, ma'am,' Mrs Norton had whispered, as though Theobald was capable of hearing her, downstairs in the breakfast room. 'You can never tell with cases like this, he said. Some linger, and some go out "poof!" – like a light. Mind, some get better an' all, ma'am, as I said to Dr Martin. My sister-in-law was told to let the Co-op know – they'd got a savings card with them, for their funerals – that our Bart was on his way out, when he had his stroke, but two months later he was back on his milk round. Mind you, he couldn't hold the reins in his left hand like he used to, but old Tess, the horse, she knew the way round them streets without any encouragement. Lovely gentle thing, she was.'

Osborne had coughed discreetly at this point and so the story of Mrs Norton's brother had ended, but it had left Esther uneasy. She had been told by Monty that Theobald was dying, and she wanted to make her peace with him and leave; nothing more complicated than that.

Theobald had thought very carefully about his next words and he had got them off pat. Slowly, his halting voice little more than a whisper, he murmured, 'I'm sorry for the way I was when the baby came. It' – he took a seemingly laboured breath – 'it was the shock, and then Harriet saying what she did knocked me for six. The thing is' – another tortured breath – 'if I ever loved anyone, it was you. You . . . were my pride and joy, and to find out I wasn't your father . . . ' He forced moisture into his eyes. 'But now I understand it isn't just the conception of a child that . . . that makes her yours. It's the looking after when they're . . . here in the world. And I did that, lass. I looked after you.'

Esther swallowed hard. She felt completely out of her depth. This wasn't the same man who had bellowed and bullied his way through life. Helplessly she shook her head. 'It's all right.'

'You're my daughter.' Theobald was gratified to find he could squeeze out a tear. 'In . . . in every way that matters.'

'Don't upset yourself.' She couldn't bring herself to touch him, but her voice was soft.

'I need to . . . to make you understand.'

'I do understand.'

'And . . . and do you forgive me?' he asked pathetically.

What else could she do but say 'yes'? 'Yes, I forgive you, and I know it must have been hard for you to hear the truth, but I do believe Mother thought what she did was for the best. She knew how much you wanted a child.'

Theobald closed his eyes, worried they might reveal his true feelings. 'I know, I know and' – feebly he looked at her again – 'she wouldn't have wanted us to remain estranged. Esther, will you stay until . . . until it happens?

I . . . I don't want to die without my family around me, and you are my daughter; that's how I feel.'

This was awful, *awful*. What if he lingered, as Mrs Norton had said? In turmoil, she finally murmured, 'I can only stay for a little while. I have a job – responsibilities.'

'Thank you.' Closing his eyes again, he said, 'I'm tired, so tired,' and pretended to drift off to sleep.

He heard Esther stand to her feet after a couple of minutes and knew she was looking down at him. He wasn't aware of her walking across the room, but he heard the door open and then close, and when all was silent for some moments more, he cautiously opened his eyes. She had gone.

So far, so good, he said to himself. Osborne had told him she had brought her brat with her, so the next time she came into the room he'd win her round further by asking to see it. When he thought of Esther's child, it was always as an 'it'.

The bedroom door opened and Monty came tiptoeing in. Theobald waited until his son-in-law was standing by the bed before he said, 'She's staying for a while. Did she tell you?'

Monty's eyes widened for a moment. Theobald had spoken in a stronger voice than he had expected. He was further surprised when his father-in-law levered himself into a sitting position in the bed, using his left arm as well as his right. According to Osborne, Theobald hadn't been able to eat anything and was as helpless as a kitten, and Esther had seemed to think the same. 'Are you feeling better?'

Theobald ignored this. 'I said: did she tell you she's agreed to stay?' he asked irritably.

'Esther? Yes, yes, she mentioned it when she came downstairs.'

'Good. Now listen to me. We can use this to our advantage, but I don't want you messing it up, understand? She's here, and that lout she's taken up with is miles away, so now is your chance to win her round. Don't rush in like a bull in a china shop, but woo her. Do you hear me?'

Monty stared into the swarthy face as realization dawned. Theobald might have had some kind of seizure, a small stroke perhaps, but he was not at death's door as he had led everyone – including him – to believe. Stiffly he said, 'How ill are you exactly?'

'To hell with how ill I am. I'm as ill as I need to be to knock this divorce business on the head, and get Esther back here where she belongs. If you come up to scratch, there's no reason why you can't be living as man and wife in the near future.'

'She'd never agree to that.'

Theobald ground his teeth. If ever life had thrown up an ineffectual sop, it was Monty. Tersely he bit out, '*Make* her.'

Monty blinked. 'How?'

'For crying out loud!' The man needed a red-hot poker up his backside to get him energized. 'She was barmy about you once, man. Like I said: woo her, promise her the earth, make her believe she's the centre of your universe. Court her, like you did before.'

'She's a different woman now.'

'Then adapt.'

'I tell you, it won't work,' said Monty in a level tone.

'It had better.' Theobald's eyes were as hard as iron. 'You do all right out of me, and don't you forget it. Where else would you live in luxury and get paid an inordinate amount for doing precious little? A trained monkey would do a better job than you, and we both know it. This isn't 1846; it's 1946, and the days of the idle rich lording it over their estates are fast coming to an end. You were born at the wrong time, Monty; and don't forget the only thing you have left of value is your name, and the doors it opens for me. But I can do without you, if I have to.'

Monty's face was white, but he said nothing, as Theobald had known he wouldn't. The two men stared at each other for a moment more, contempt in Theobald's face and something approaching hatred in Monty's. Then Theobald said softly, 'Now go and do what you're told. And the next time you come in here, bring Esther and your daughter with you. Start acting like a husband and father, and you might just make her believe you can manage to be one.'

It was later that evening when Theobald saw Joy for the first time since her birth. Dr Martin had paid a visit that morning, privately expressing his surprise to Esther and Monty – once he had left the sickroom and come downstairs – that his patient was still with them. 'It must be the boost of seeing you again, m'dear,' the doctor said to Esther. 'It's amazing how the mind can heal the body, and I know he was anxious to set things right. He's more than holding his own now, which I wouldn't have thought possible yesterday. Of course he is still a sick man, and with things of this nature one never knows if the same problem might happen again, but for the present I am encouraged. Yes, indeed.'

Esther had taken Joy to the estate farm that afternoon. Monty had told her one of the sheepdogs had had puppies, which the little girl might like to see. As Esther had sat in the barn where the bitch and puppies were, watching Joy play with the tiny animals, Dr Martin's words had resounded in her ears. *Encouraged.* She supposed she ought to be pleased that Theobald might not die, but at the moment all she could think of was the delay in getting back to Caleb. That and the fact that she couldn't rid herself of the notion there was a dark presence brooding over the house.

But she was being silly. She nodded mentally at the thought. Of course she was going to feel strange, coming back to the home where she had lived for the first seventeen years of her life before joining the Land Army and which she had finally left in such traumatic circumstances, once and for all, after Joy's birth and the shocking revelations by the woman she had always thought of as her mother. On the way here she had hoped that, in returning, she would be able to lay to rest the ghosts that had been with her since that time, but she doubted that now. She felt more perturbed, if anything. And somehow, being back in the place where Harriet had told her about her real parents, the longing to find her roots, and the people she had come from, was growing stronger. She hadn't had time to think about that side of things too much before now; not with the war and her work as a Land Girl, whilst also being a mother, then meeting Caleb and, recently, moving to Sunderland. But this afternoon the longing to know more was so strong it made her chest ache.

Monty had come to join them after an hour or so, when he had finished talking to Neil Harley about certain farm business, and the three of them had walked back to the big house together in the warm May sunshine, with Joy swinging between them as they strolled along. Anyone observing them would think they were a young couple out for an afternoon walk, without a care in the world, Esther thought, glancing at Monty's handsome face. He caught her glance and smiled at her, the sunshine turning his fair hair into a halo. And it could have been like this, but for Harriet unknowingly throwing a time-bomb into their midst, a time-bomb that was inside her genes and which had manifested itself when Joy was born. Esther had no doubt that if Joy had been white, then the truth would never have come out, and

Harriet would have taken her secret to the grave. But fate had cast the dice instead.

They had almost reached the house when Monty had murmured, 'Theobald wants to see his granddaughter, if you have no objection?'

'She isn't—' Esther had stopped. Her voice had been too shrill. More quietly she'd said, 'You know she isn't his granddaughter, Monty, any more than I am his daughter.'

'Nevertheless, it would please him.'

And now they were on the landing outside Theobald's suite of rooms, and Esther found she didn't want to take her daughter inside. She glanced down at Joy, who was holding her hand, and Joy smiled up at her, her limpid green eyes with their thick lashes dancing as she said, 'Poorly man, Mummy. Shush!'

'Yes, darling. Poorly man, so we have to be quiet.' She had told Joy this when she had explained to the child that they were going to see the man who owned this house they were staying in. He was someone Mummy had known when she was just a small girl, like Joy was now, she had continued, when her daughter had stared at her, wide-eyed. And because he was poorly, Mummy had decided to pay him a visit.

'To help make him better?' Joy had asked trustingly. Her mummy always made a cut finger or a grazed knee better for her.

'Perhaps.' Esther had smiled down into the beautiful little face. 'We'll have to see.'

'Seeing you will certainly help,' Monty said, over-heartily, behind them. If Esther had but known, he was experiencing a similar feeling to her. Now that they were standing outside Theobald's door, he regretted persuading Esther to bring the child to Theobald. They had taken afternoon tea together, when they had got back from the farm, and he had kept up a gentle but compelling argument on Theobald's behalf, but suddenly he had the desire to tell Esther everything: that Theobald wasn't as ill as he was pretending to be; that the old man was using his indisposition to blackmail Esther into staying; that she couldn't trust a word he said.

Esther turned to look at Monty. 'Are you sure it's the right thing to do, to take Joy in to see him? It won't be too much for him?'

Now was the moment. She had given him the perfect excuse to knock this on the head. And then the memory of Theobald's face as he had spoken earlier that day – his eyes like chips of black lead, and his voice deadly with intent – filled Monty's mind. Theobald was quite capable of carrying through on his threat to cast him to the wolves; he knew that. And all he was doing was letting an old man see his granddaughter, or the nearest thing he'd got to one. There was no harm in that. He and Esther would be with the child, after all. Joy would be perfectly safe.

He didn't allow himself to pursue this last line of thought; it was too uncomfortable. Instead he leaned past Esther as he said, 'I told you: he wants to see her, and I'm sure he's strong enough to cope with it,' and opened the door to Theobald's room. He was careful to take Joy's other hand, so that the three of them entered together, with the child between them.

He had to play by Theobald's rules.

Chapter Twenty-Four

'I tell you, lad, there's somethin' here that don't sit right. I don't pretend to know the lass as well as you, but I'd stake my life on the fact that she wouldn't just disappear for this long, without getting in touch. What if she's being held against her will? You hear about these things, and don't forget the gentry think they can do whatever they like. The war hasn't changed that.'

Caleb was sitting hunched up at the kitchen table, poking at the meal in front of him with his fork. He didn't raise his head or look at his mother when he muttered, 'Leave it, Mam.'

Eliza cast a pleading glance at her husband, who was sitting eating his dinner, and after a moment Stanley said, 'I think your mam's right, son.'

'Oh, aye?' Now Caleb did raise his head to look hard at his father. 'And what would you know about it? You hardly said two words to Esther whenever you saw her, so how can you have an opinion about what she might, or might not, do?'

Stanley didn't fire back, as he might have done just a few days ago. He knew his son was beside himself; he'd never seen Caleb in such a state. He wasn't eating enough to keep a sparrow alive, and every night he and Eliza could hear Caleb downstairs in the early hours, pacing around until dawn broke. His voice quiet and steady, he said, 'I trust your mam. If she says Esther wouldn't let you stew, then she's right.'

Caleb continued to look at his father for a moment more, before saying in a slightly defensive tone, 'Right or wrong, I can hardly turn up at this mansion she was brought up in and demand to see her. They'd set the dogs on me,' he added bitterly.

'And that would bother you?'

No, it wouldn't bother him, not if he knew Esther wanted to see him, but that was the rub, wasn't it? When a whole week had crawled by and he had heard nothing from her, he had taken the bull by the horns and looked up the telephone number of the Wynford estate in the telephone directory. An officious-sounding servant had answered the phone – a butler, no less – and when he had asked to speak to Esther, the man had requested his name. After he had waited so long that practically all of his change was gone, a woman who declared herself to be the housekeeper had told him she was sorry, but Mrs Wynford-Grant was not taking calls. When Caleb had asked if that meant from anyone, or just from him, the woman had said again – but this time with a note of sympathy in her voice – that she was sorry.

He had put down the receiver and left the telephone box, ignoring the angry glares of the small queue that had formed outside; and then walked for miles, his stomach churning. It was only the fact that he walked so far that his stump had become raw and bleeding that had driven him home that night. That had been eight days ago. She had now been gone fifteen hellish days in all, and he felt he was losing his mind.

'Caleb, why don't you write another letter?'

Wearily now he said, 'There's no point, Mam. And get the idea she's been abducted, or something, out of your head. She went to see this Theobald Wynford of her own free will, and with her husband, don't forget. It was her choice. I've phoned the house and I have written to her. I cannot do more.'

'You mean you won't do more.'

'No. I won't.' He rose to his feet, pushing his plate away as he said, 'I need some fresh air. I'll be back before dark.'

'You've always been a stubborn so-an'-so.'

In spite of himself, Caleb smiled at his mother. 'Wonder where I get that from?'

'Oh, you!'

When Caleb had left the house, both Eliza and Stanley stopped eating and stared at each other. 'This might be for the best, lass,' Stanley said softly.

'*No, it's not*; and it'll crush the life out of him if she doesn't come back, you mark my words. Her and that bairn mean everything to him – can't you see that?'

'All right, all right, don't shout.'

'And I blame you for some of this. If you had made the lass feel welcome here, she might not have gone back.'

'Me?' Stanley reared up as though he had been prodded in the backside. 'It's not my fault.'

'Well, if I was you, I'd be feeling ashamed of meself. That's all I'm saying on the matter.'

Stanley swore, before he too stood to his feet. 'Let me know when I do something right, because since I've been back I can't so much as open me mouth in my own house.'

'That's not true, and you know it.'

'Oh, to hell with it. What was I supposed to do? Clap me hands and dance a jig, because me only son has got himself mixed up with a married woman who already has a bairn?' Stanley grabbed his cap from its peg on the kitchen wall, stuffing it on his head as he growled, 'Don't wait up,' and then marched out of the kitchen, banging the back door behind him.

Eliza watched him walk across the yard and then out into the back lane, indignation in every line of his body, and after a moment the silence of the house settled on her. She glanced at the two plates of food the men had left – one hardly touched and one half-eaten. And then she burst into tears.

Miles away, in Chester-le-Street, Esther would have welcomed the relief of being able to cry. The solid, cold lump that had lodged permanently in her chest over the last few days stopped any tears from falling, her desolation too great. She had written four letters to Caleb over the last two weeks, the first one just after she had arrived at the Wynford estate, but he had not replied to any of them. Not even a postcard or a few lines. He was angry with her and she couldn't blame him, but the thought that he might have washed his hands of her for good was more than she could bear.

Her despair over Caleb wasn't helped, either, by the feeling that she was being held fast in a kind of sinking sand, in the present circumstances. She felt she was slowly but inexorably being drawn into a bog of guilt and confusion, plus a hotchpotch of poignant memories from the past, of happier times. Every time she visited Theobald in his rooms, he seemed to bring up Harriet and how devoted she had been to them both. He had been utterly devastated by her untimely death, he murmured; he still was, he supposed, but Esther mustn't blame herself in any way. And then he would ramble on about Christmases they'd all shared when she was a little girl; the birthday parties, picnics in the grounds and trips out, the way she had been the light of his world and Harriet's. Lots of times she had wanted to get up and run out of the room, but she had felt duty-bound to stay. And Theobald made a great fuss of Joy, saying she was the most enchanting little girl he had ever seen, and a credit to Esther. It would make his last days the happiest he had ever known if his daughter and granddaughter – and here he always added that she must forgive him, but he couldn't think of them in any other way – were close to him. And, he gently purred, dear Monty adored them both. She knew that, didn't she?

Esther sighed. She was standing gazing out of her bedroom window, and the familiar scent of the climbing roses that covered the wall of the house was both comforting and disturbing. Comforting because she had smelt the same heady perfume every summer while she was growing up, and disturbing for the same reason. She didn't want to feel she belonged here, that she was home. She had mentally said her goodbyes to this house, and her childhood and youth here, in the pain-searing days after Joy was born.

The gardens, which had been neglected during the war when Theobald's gardener and his lads had been called up, were back to their former glory, and everywhere the essence of summer was evident. June had arrived on the crest of a warm spell, and gone was the freshness of a northern spring. Now clusters of creamy-white blooms were displayed upon dogwood and elder, and the spring-sown crops that Neil Harley's labourers had sown were pushing upwards: ears of barley and corn were appearing and thrusting their various shades on the landscape.

The house and its grounds, and the farm, were a lovely place to live, Esther acknowledged, but without Caleb even the finest house and the most perfect views were a barren desert. She and Joy had walked down the previous day to the crystal-clear little stream that ran through part of the gardens, and Joy had spent a happy hour or two gathering forget-me-nots and other wild flowers, presenting her little bouquet to her mother with great pride. Esther glanced at the flowers Joy had picked, which were sitting in a small vase on her dressing table. They were already wilting, their small heads downcast and drooping, which was exactly how she felt about staying here, she thought. It might be a wonderful place to bring up a child, as both Monty and Theobald constantly dropped into any conversation that she had with either of them, but to her it felt like a beautifully gilded cage.

She sighed again, shutting her eyes as she let the soft summer breeze ruffle her hair. She had to admit Theobald hadn't said one word out of place since she had been here, and he seemed to genuinely dote on Joy. From the first time she had brought Joy to see him, she had made it clear that Theobald was not to tell Joy he was her grandfather, or they'd both leave immediately; and although he had greeted this warning with a trembling mouth and moist eyes, rather than the harsh words she had expected, he had adhered to her demand. She couldn't prevent him showering little presents on the child, though, which she knew full well Monty obtained for him, and of course Joy thought this was perfectly wonderful. The sweet ration, which had been twelve ounces a month during the war, had recently been halved, but this didn't seem to prevent Theobald and Monty acquiring whatever they liked. Chocolates in fancy boxes, little lollipops and crystallized fruits all made their appearance, much to Joy's delight; along with a child's tiny silver bracelet with exquisite little charms, a beautifully dressed doll very much like the one Monty had destroyed at Yew Tree Farm, a nursery-rhyme book and various other little gifts, all designed to appeal to a small child.

She had told Monty more than once that she wanted it to stop, but each time he had made her feel crass and insensitive. 'You won't allow him to call her his grand-daughter,' he had said reproachfully the last time she had brought the matter up, 'so surely you can allow him this small pleasure? And Joy adores him – you must see that?'

She had replied that Joy adored the presents, which was a different matter, and the lure of a new surprise would entice any small child to its giver. And thereby a new problem had reared its head. Twice now, she had caught her daughter on the landing outside Theobald's room; once when she had thought Joy was having her afternoon nap, and another time when the little girl was supposed to be helping Cook make pastry in the kitchen – something Joy loved doing. Now Esther found herself watching Joy like a hawk, and the more she told her daughter she was only to visit 'the poorly man' with her or Monty, the more Esther wondered why she had the strangest feeling every time she watched the child with Theobald. He was every bit the doting grandparent, and yet there was something not quite right.

She frowned to herself, turning back into the room and smoothing her frock in preparation to go down to breakfast. She didn't want Joy to form an attachment to Theobald, or Monty for that matter; but in the former's case, it was because of more than just the difficulty this would cause in the matter of the divorce.

Glancing round the spacious room with its beautiful furnishings, the thought came that if someone had told her a few weeks ago that she would be longing for her little garret in Sunderland, she wouldn't have believed them. She'd probably have to look for another job when she got back; she'd told Mr Dimple she would only be gone for a couple of days initially, and he had agreed to that, but as time had gone on she had felt it only fair to say that if he couldn't keep her job open for her, she quite understood. She had left this message with one of the staff when the manager was out, and had heard nothing, although she'd given Theobald's telephone number, so she assumed Mr Dimple had taken her at her word and hired a replacement receptionist. But that didn't matter. She would find something.

Taking a deep breath, she opened the door and stepped onto the landing. Theobald had requested that she visit him alone after breakfast, although she didn't know why. She did know he had called his solicitor to the house the day before, and that the man had stayed for more than two hours, but she doubted that had anything to do with herself. Theobald was probably going to ask her to stay for another week, but she had already made up her mind she would refuse. He was getting stronger, anyone could see that, although he still insisted he couldn't leave his bed; and his recovery could go on for some time, according to Dr Martin. She couldn't – she *wouldn't* – stay here indefinitely. Monty was putting pressure on her to withdraw divorce proceedings, despite her telling him over and over again there was no future for them, and the whole thing was getting ridiculous. She bit down hard on her bottom lip as every fibre of her being called out for Caleb. If she could just see him – even hear from him, and see his handwriting – she would be all right.

When Mrs Norton had brought Esther her morning cup of tea and biscuit at eight o'clock that morning, Joy had been wide awake and clamouring to go downstairs. Esther had insisted that her daughter sleep with her while they were at the house, even though a separate room in the nursery had been prepared for the little girl. The housekeeper had smiled as Joy had bounced on the bed, her golden-brown curls dancing and her jade-green eyes shining with the delight of a new day. 'I'll take her with me, if you want, ma'am,' she'd offered. 'Cook is making a batch of singin' hinnies, and you like helping her with those, don't you, Miss Joy?' she added to the child. 'And she likes eating them fresh from the girdle with a dollop of butter too. It'll give you a chance to drink your tea in peace and get dressed, ma'am.'

After quickly dressing the little girl, Esther had watched her go off hand-in-hand with the housekeeper and then had drunk her tea. Joy seemed perfectly happy here, she had thought to herself, which had set off a whole train of thought that had resulted in her present state of mind. She didn't want Joy to get used to this house and its occupants, she thought now as she walked along the sunny landing, looking towards the end of it, where the master suite was. And two weeks was a long time in a little girl's life.

She didn't know what made her pause at the top of the wide, winding staircase. No noise had disturbed her. There was a discreet murmur of voices and the sound of rattling crockery downstairs, and she presumed breakfast was ready in the dining room, but somewhere deep in her psyche an alarm bell had rung. She stood for a moment more and then quietly walked on towards the door of the master suite. When she reached it, she pressed her ear to the heavy wooden door, but she could still hear nothing – not until she cautiously opened it the merest crack. Then she heard her daughter's voice, shrill and slightly alarmed, saying, 'No, I don't want to. I want to go and see my mummy.'

'You can in a minute, my sweet.' Theobald's voice was odd; thick somehow, excited. 'And you like your new present, don't you? I told you I had got you something nice, didn't I? Our secret. Like me being your grandfather is our secret. You like having a grandfather, don't you? One who buys you nice things.'

'I want to get down now. No more bouncing. Let me go.'

Esther flung open the door and stepped into the room, the blood rushing into her ears. Joy was sitting on Theobald's lap and his thin, bare legs were dangling over the side of the bed, his nightshirt up to his thighs. The shock of her entrance caused him to let Joy slip out of his grasp, and for a second Esther saw the gross erection that his bobbing the child up and down on his lap had caused, before he grabbed at the bedspread to cover himself. Joy had been holding a teddy bear, but now she dropped this as she ran to her mother saying, 'I don't want to play the bouncy game any more, Mummy. I don't like it. Tell Grandfather I don't like it.'

'He is not your grandfather, darling.' Somehow she stopped herself from screaming, aware that if she reacted in the wrong way, this incident could imprint itself on Joy's young mind for a long time. With a calm that she was amazed at afterwards, she took Joy by the hand, saying, 'I came to find you for breakfast, so come along now. I thought you were helping Cook?'

'I was.' They were out of the room now and on the landing, and as Joy skipped along beside her, Esther tried to control her own shaking. 'But I remembered Grand-father—'

'No, not Grandfather, darling. Remember?'

'I remembered the poorly man had said he'd got an extra-special present for me, but it was a secret, and I had to go and get it by myself.' Joy stopped abruptly. 'I've left it, Mummy. My teddy bear.'

'I'll get it later, after breakfast.'

How she didn't fall headlong down the stairs she didn't know, her legs were trembling so much, but somehow she got Joy downstairs and into the dining room, where they found Monty already sitting at the table, a newspaper propped against the milk jug and a half-eaten plateful of bacon, sausages, steak and eggs in front of him. He looked up, smiling, and then his face changed as he took in Esther's deathly pallor. 'What is it? Are you feeling unwell?'

As he stood to his feet she shook her head, motioning at Joy, and then addressed the new housemaid who was standing ready to serve them. 'Teresa, could I leave my daughter with you for a little while? I need to talk to Mr Grant. And, Teresa, you keep her with you until I get back, do you understand? You don't let her out of your sight, no matter what.'

Teresa was what Mrs Norton scathingly called 'a modern young thing', and she tried the housekeeper's patience daily, but as it was becoming increasingly difficult to obtain the services of staff for below stairs, Mrs Norton had to bite her tongue most of the time. Teresa now displayed what Mrs Norton called her 'forwardness' when she said, 'Are you all right, ma'am? You look like death warmed up, if you don't mind me saying so.'

'I'm fine, Teresa. Just take care of Miss Joy, and keep her in here until I return.' As Teresa sat the little girl down at the table, Esther turned to Monty. 'I need to talk to you *now*.'

Once in the hall, she shut the door to the dining room and took hold of Monty's arm, marching him along towards the door that opened onto a corridor leading to the kitchens. 'What are you doing?' He tried to swing her round to face him, but she resisted. 'Esther, what is it?'

'Wait.' She knew Mrs Norton, Osborne and Cook

would be having their breakfast, and when she said what she had to say she wanted them all together, where she could see their faces – especially Monty's. Theobald was a pervert, a pervert of the worst kind, one who preyed on little ones; and the older staff had worked for him for practically a lifetime. She needed to know if they knew and, if they did, whether they had mentioned it to Monty. She couldn't believe he would allow Joy to be in the house if he had known, but she needed to be sure, and the only way to prevent half-truths and lies was to confront them all together and watch their reaction.

She was shaking, she could feel it, and she wanted to be sick, but as they entered the corridor she ignored Monty's questions. She had to find out what they all knew, before she saw Theobald again. Her fingers tightened on the sharp steak knife that she'd slipped into the pocket of her dress from the dining table. She didn't think Theobald had managed to do anything to Joy – the child's demeanour had been too normal and happy for that, after her initial words when Joy had first seen her in the doorway – but the fact that he had been pleasuring himself by using her baby's innocent little body was beyond endurance. She would kill him, she would. The filthy, dirty beast.

Like Monty and Teresa, the rest of the staff stared at her in concern when they entered the kitchen, but before anyone could say a word, she said, 'Sit down, all of you; you too, Monty, and listen to me.'

'Dear, you're not well. Let me—'

'*Sit down, Monty.*' Her composure had slipped, and now she took a deep trembling breath before she said more quietly, 'Please.'

Mrs Norton, Osborne, the cook and her sister and the new kitchen maid, who had been employed at the same time as Teresa, sank down into their seats. And as Monty took a chair to one side of the table, Esther said, 'I just found my daughter in Mr Wynford's room. He had her on his lap and he was sexually aroused.' It was deliberately bald and unadorned. 'Who among you is aware that he is depraved and sick in this way?'

For a moment no one spoke or moved a muscle. Shock registered on every face.

'You must be mistaken.' Monty stared at her. 'He wouldn't with a child so young as Joy.'

Mrs Norton and Osborne exchanged a glance – a swift momentary glance, but Esther caught it. 'Mrs Norton?'

'Ma'am, it's not my place to say.'

'He was using my daughter for his sexual gratification, and it is only by the grace of God that I got there before things got out of hand. Do you understand?' She glared at them all. 'Do you?'

'Esther, calm down.'

She swung round on Monty so quickly, and with such fury, that he visibly jumped. '*Don't tell me to calm down. Did you know he is that way inclined? With children?*'

Monty's denial was just a fraction too long in coming and held no weight. Esther stared at him. 'I don't know you,' she said flatly. 'I have no idea who you are – who any of you are.'

'Ma'am, please.' It was Fanny Kennedy, the cook, who spoke now. Of all the staff, she was the one who was quite besotted with Joy. Never having had children of her own, she had been delighted when the little girl had taken to her so readily. 'It's not like you think, not really. The thing is, as the master's got older he's started to' – she cast a glance at Mrs Norton and Osborne, but they seemed transfixed – 'become inclined towards . . . well, women of the night, if you get my meaning, and . . . ' Fanny didn't know how to continue.

'And?'

'Well, they've got younger. The . . . the girls who come to the house.'

Esther felt she was in the middle of a nightmare. 'Come to the *house*? You mean here? This house?'

'In the past, ma'am, aye. Not since he was took bad of course, but before . . . ' Again Fanny glanced at her fellow servants for help.

This time it was Osborne who said flatly, 'We've been aware of what has gone on, ma'am, but it's not our place to object. None of us' – he inclined his head towards Mrs Norton and the cook and her sister – 'are getting any younger. The young 'uns could get something else, no doubt, but we're used to our going-on here, and the thing is' – he took a deep breath – 'and begging your pardon, ma'am, the master is a spiteful man. If we said a word out of place, we'd be out on our ear even though we've given him good service for years.'

Esther was holding onto the back of a chair now, for she needed its support. Turning to Monty, who had got to his feet when she had shouted at him, she said, 'And you? Wasn't it your place to object, either? And don't tell me you haven't been aware of what he was doing, and with whom. You are living here. You have been living here for some time.'

Monty's mind was racing. The last few days he had felt he was on the brink of breaking through Esther's reserve and wariness, and he had begun to hope that perhaps Theobald was right and they could persuade her to take up residence here permanently. Osborne had followed his instructions that any letters Esther wrote were not to be posted, but given to him; and likewise that she was not told about any telephone calls to the house that might be made. It had been fortuitous that when this Caleb fellow had called, Esther had been out in the gardens with Joy. Osborne had also lain in wait for the postman each morning, and brought any letters addressed to Esther straight to Monty, whereupon he'd burned them, telling himself it was for Esther's own good. Here, under Theobald's roof, she could take up her rightful station as a lady; with that working scum, she would be reduced to little more than a menial.

Quietly, and in a tone that aimed to remind Esther who she was, he said stiffly, 'Come along to the drawing room, and we will discuss this in private.'

'I think not, Monty. I want the truth, and I want it now.'

'I refuse to—'

He got no further before she swung round, saying, 'Then my daughter and I are leaving.' *But not before she had given Theobald his due.*

'Wait.' He caught her arm. 'Yes, I knew your fa—' He corrected himself, 'I knew Theobald availed himself of a certain type of woman, but so do a great deal of men, Esther. Surely you know that? Especially ones in your . . . in Theobald's position, who have no wife. It is indelicate to say this, but a man – even an elderly one – has certain needs.'

'With children?' She disengaged his hand from her arm.

'Of course not. I'm not saying that.'

'But you knew the way he was inclined? No' – as Monty went to speak, she held up her hand – 'don't lie. You knew, and you let me bring Joy here.'

Looking straight at Fanny Kennedy again, she said, 'How old were these girls? Please, I need to know. You won't lose your job, I promise you, but I need to know.'

'We've thought as young as nine or ten, ma'am,' Fanny whispered, tears now running down her face. 'Maybe younger.'

Mrs Norton was also weeping, but Esther's eyes were fiercely dry. Looking at Monty again, she said, 'I hate you. I shall hate you to my dying day.'

Even knowing it was the end and that he had lost her

for good, he tried one last time. 'He wouldn't have hurt Joy; she's little more than a baby.'

Pushing him away, Esther ran out of the kitchen and down the corridor into the hall. Taking the stairs two at a time, she flew upstairs and burst into Theobald's room.

Theobald's initial shock and anger at being discovered in a compromising position had given way to a determination to convince Esther that she had been mistaken in what she had seen, and the longer she was in coming to see him, the more he persuaded himself that she had perhaps noticed nothing at all.

He would not let her take Joy away, he had been telling himself in the last few minutes. From the moment he had seen the child he had burned for her; he could think of little else. She filled his days and caused him tormented nights. If only he had known she would grow into such an enchanting creature, he would never have sent Esther away. That was the thought that haunted him. He could have had Joy here, under his roof. Watched her. Played the grandfather. Picked his moments.

Now, as Esther stood panting in the doorway for a moment, before slowly approaching the bed, he followed the stratagem he'd decided on, despite her white face and burning eyes. 'Hello, my dear.' He was sitting propped up against the pillows, and his voice was weak and breathless. 'That was a fleeting visit earlier.'

When Esther was a yard from him, she stopped, her hand tight on the knife in her pocket. 'You filthy, dirty old man.' She was bending slightly forward, and her voice was not loud, but a low hiss.

'Wh-what?' Forcing indignation and fury into his voice, he raised himself up a little.

'You will never touch her again. Do you hear me? *Never*.'

'I don't know what you're talking about.'

Monty had come running after Esther and now he stood just within the doorway, and as he said, 'Come away, Esther', Osborne, too, appeared behind him, wheezing slightly from taking the stairs faster than he had moved in years.

Esther ignored the two men behind her. Her eyes fixed on the swarthy face surveying her with feigned outrage – a face she had always disliked, but which now repulsed and sickened her – she stepped closer. 'You're unnatural,' she said, her voice deep and guttural and not sounding like hers. 'Depraved. Evil and sick.'

'What is this?' Theobald appealed to Monty. 'What's happened to her? She's gone mad.'

'I'm not mad.' She was at the bedside now; the faintly sweet, musty smell that surrounded him these days assaulted her nostrils and caused bile to rise in her throat. 'And you're not, either. If you were, there would be some excuse for your wickedness. But no, you're sane and in full possession of your senses. All those presents – the hours you've spent playing the sick invalid – all for one purpose: to harm my little girl.'

'You *have* gone mad.'

'I should have known. As a mother, I should have known, but then who would think such a base, terrible thing?'

'Monty?' Again Theobald appealed to his son-in-law.

'He's told me. About the girls that have come here. Children, I should say.'

Theobald's face was red now and all trace of the feeble, infirm patient was gone. 'You need a doctor,' he ground out through clenched teeth. 'You're insane. There are places that deal with women like you – institutions where you can be taken care of.'

Esther pulled the knife out of her pocket, standing over him and putting it to his throat before he realized what she was doing. 'One move and I'll press down,' she said with a softness that was more threatening than any shouting. 'I swear it.' As Monty said her name, she added, 'And you come any nearer, and I'll do it. It's over his artery – he'll be dead in minutes.' She didn't quite know if this was true, but the threat worked because the two men behind her were perfectly still.

'Admit what you were doing.' She looked down into a face that, for the first time since she had come into the room, was showing fear. 'You admit it, or so help me I will slit your throat right now. I mean it, and you know I mean it, don't you? I can see it in your eyes.'

'You've got it wrong.' And then as she pressed down into the flabby skin, so that the tip of the serrated blade pierced the skin, bringing a spot of blood, Theobald's bravado crumpled. Whimpering, he said, 'I didn't hurt her, I swear it.'

'No, but you would have. Maybe not today, or even tomorrow, but you would have, wouldn't you? Like you hurt those children you have had here. Little ones you had brought to this very house.'

'You don't understand – they like it. Some girls are born that way.'

The urge to do what she had threatened was so strong she could taste it, but then she would be locked away, and Joy would be left alone. And she couldn't take a human life. Even one as vile and sick as Theobald's. But neither could he be allowed to carry on doing what he'd been doing.

'Listen to me, Esther.' Theobald's voice was a whine. 'I wanted to see you today, and it was to tell you I have changed my will. You inherit everything. *Everything.* If you and Joy stay here – if you agree to staying on as my daughter and granddaughter, as far as the world is con-cerned – then it's all yours. Think of it. Joy would be set up for life. Look, on that table over there. It's a copy of the will, signed and witnessed. My solicitor will confirm it's genuine. It shows I mean what I say, doesn't it?'

'I wouldn't stay here for one more day for all the money in the world, but before I leave, I'll see to it you never harm another little girl. I'm going to the police – do you hear me? And whatever it takes, I'll see this through. I'm going to make your name a byword in these parts, and however you try to wriggle out of it, mud sticks.

Remember that. Mud sticks, and you'll have so much sticking to you that the smell will be with you forever.'

She had withdrawn the blade pressed against his throat and now, as she stepped back a pace, Monty came and took the knife from her, his face as white as a sheet. He still couldn't quite believe that Theobald would have tried to molest Joy; she was only three years old, for crying out loud. And yet . . .

They had turned to leave the room when Theobald reared up in the bed, letting out an unintelligible roar that caused Monty to push Esther protectively behind him.

'You stinking half-breed!' Spittle was spraying from Theobald's mouth as he snarled the words, and he appeared possessed as he lunged forward. 'You: to threaten me with ruining my name. You! You're scum, fathered by scum. Your kind litter the waterfronts looking for trade with men who aren't too particular what they take, and your brat's the same. Ready for breaking in already, she is. A ready-made little whore.'

Esther was struggling with Monty now, and Osborne had sprung forward to hold back Theobald, who was attempting to scramble off the bed, spewing out curses and threats as he did so. And then suddenly he collapsed, gurgling, on the covers, losing control of his bodily functions as his face and body twisted and contracted.

'He's having a fit, sir,' Osborne said urgently to Monty, who was still having his work cut out to prevent Esther reaching Theobald.

It wasn't until Monty had managed to bundle Esther

onto the landing, where Mrs Norton and Fanny Kennedy were standing, their hands pressed tightly to their mouths, that he dared to let go of her. Pushing her into Mrs Norton's arms, he said, 'Take her downstairs, both of you, and keep her there by force if you have to.' And then he turned back into the room, shutting the door and turning the key in the lock.

Osborne was leaning over the figure on the bed and, as Monty walked towards them, the smell of human faeces was so strong it made him want to retch. He knew what had happened. Theobald had had another stroke – a major one this time – and from the inhuman sounds coming from him, he was fully aware of what had happened.

As he helped Osborne drag Theobald further back up the bed, he looked down into the distorted face, which was demoniacal in its malignant helplessness, saliva trickling from the twisted mouth that had stretched upwards to meet the dragging skin from the left eye. And he realized, with a little stab of shock, that he felt not the slightest shred of pity.

Theobald lasted another forty-eight hours, and during that time he was unable to make anyone understand what he was trying to say through his rasping grunts, his body as helpless as a newborn babe's. Only one person understood, but Monty wasn't about to call the solicitor to the house with regard to the will.

He owed Esther that.

Chapter Twenty-Five

After knocking on the door, Esther took a deep breath, holding Joy's hand more tightly as she heard footsteps inside the house.

'Why, lass!' For a moment Eliza just stared at the two of them, and then she beamed, reaching out and pulling Esther into the hall as she said, 'Well, you're a sight for sore eyes, an' no mistake. By, we've been that worried about the pair of you. I'd got it in my head you were being held prisoner, and all sorts.'

Theobald had breathed his last that morning, and only Osborne had been sitting by the bed when it had happened, Monty having gone to his room for a nap after remaining with his father-in-law since the stroke. It was strange, Esther thought now, as she allowed Eliza to usher them through the house into the kitchen, but she had felt she had to stay until she knew he was dead. Only then could she be sure Theobald wouldn't revive and recover. Everyone had told her that was impossible, but the Devil looked after his own, and if anyone had sold his soul to the Devil, it was the man she had once thought was her father. She had to know he was in a place where he couldn't hurt any more little girls. She'd had a long chat with both Osborne and Mrs Norton, in the hours when they waited for Theobald to die, and the housekeeper had admitted through her tears that many times after one of the 'master's escapades', as they'd called them, the bedclothes had been blood-stained.

'We felt awful, ma'am, we really did, but what could we do?' Mrs Norton had sobbed. 'It was Mr Monty's place to say something, not ours.'

Esther had made no comment to this. All that good people had to do, to allow evil to abound, was to do and say nothing. Mrs Norton and the others knew this well enough and were clearly feeling wretched.

When Osborne had come downstairs to tell them the news, Esther had telephoned for a taxi immediately, before going to wake Monty and tell him she was leaving. He had offered to drive her back to Sunderland, but she had declined. They would go on the train, she'd said coldly. And she would like to take with her the divorce papers, which he had been sent recently – duly signed by him. Monty had agreed without demur. In the immediate aftermath of Theobald's seizure, while they had waited for the doctor, knowing that it was truly the end of any hope of reclaiming Esther as his wife, Monty had confessed about Caleb's telephone call and letters. Esther had listened and then left him without a word, her silence more condemnatory than any spoken rebuke.

'So what's been happening?' Eliza said now, lifting a smiling Joy up into her arms and giving the child a kiss. 'Caleb's been going out of his mind, when you didn't write. You know he phoned the house one day?'

Esther sank down onto a kitchen chair. Now that she was here in Eliza's kitchen the normality of it, after what she had left, was such a relief it was weakening, and she didn't want to cry in front of Joy. Her face must have given away the fact that she was at the end of her tether, because suddenly Eliza became briskly busy, settling Joy on the clippy mat in front of the range with some toys and a biscuit to eat, before she put the kettle on for a cup of tea. It was only when the two of them were sitting with a cup of tea and a slice of rice cake in front of them that Eliza gently reached out her hand and took Esther's. 'So?' she said softly. 'Tell me.'

And Esther told her. Apart from Eliza's 'The dirty beggar!' when Esther got to the part about Theobald and Joy, Caleb's mother was silent throughout, and she didn't let go of Esther's hand. When Esther finished speaking, they continued to sit quietly for a few moments, before Eliza murmured, 'Drink your tea, lass.'

It was a good job the old man had died, Eliza thought grimly, because when Caleb found out what had gone on, he wouldn't have rested until he'd got his hands on Theobald. She just hoped her lad wouldn't try and settle the score with this Monty bloke, because no good would come of it. But Esther could talk him out of that, especially now the divorce was under way. Caleb would see the sense of not doing anything to get in the way of that. Heavens above! Eliza mentally shook her head. Whatever next? But it wasn't the lass's fault. Nevertheless, trouble seemed to follow Esther wherever she went, bless her.

'And so you haven't been back to your lodgings yet?' she said, once they had both drained their cups and eaten their cake, with Joy now stretched out on the thick rug, fast asleep.

'I came straight here. I – I wanted to see Caleb, to put things right.'

Eliza nodded. She could understand that. Looking at the clock on the shelf above the range, she said, 'He'll be home in an hour or so, lass. Have another cuppa, an' try and relax now. You're still as tense as a coiled spring, aren't you?'

Esther smiled weakly, a small deprecating quirk to her mouth as she said, 'Is it so obvious?' She wouldn't be herself until she saw Caleb, until she knew things were right again between them. She had gone away against his wishes, and then he had heard nothing from her. What must he be thinking?

It was exactly an hour later, at six o'clock, when the back door opened, but it wasn't Caleb who walked in, but Stanley. He stopped dead at the sight of Esther sitting with Eliza, who now had a wide-awake Joy on her lap.

Esther stared at Caleb's father anxiously. He hadn't hidden the fact that he didn't approve of her, and although she could understand why he would have preferred a girl with no messy past for his son, it didn't make communicating with him on a day-to-day level any easier. She opened her mouth to say hello, but it was Joy who got in first, sliding off Eliza's lap and running to Stanley as she gabbled, 'We're back again, see? We're home.'

'Aye, I see, hinny,' Stanley said and, as the little girl held up her arms, he could do nothing else but bend and pick her up.

And then to Esther's surprise and embarrassment, once Joy was in Caleb's father's arms, she said, 'We went to visit the poorly man. He said he was my grandfather, but Mummy says he isn't. He was telling a fib. That's naughty, isn't it? But I want a grandfather. Are you my grandfather?'

There was a moment of charged silence. Stanley didn't look at the two women. He didn't look anywhere but at the small, innocent face staring into his. And then gruffly he murmured, 'Aye, hinny. I'm your granda all right.'

Joy beamed, before turning to look at her mother for confirmation. Esther couldn't speak, the lump in her throat was too big, and it was Eliza who stepped into the breach, saying, 'And I'm your grandma, pet. So you've got a grandma *and* a granda, see? That's nice, isn't it? But let your granda take his coat off and have a sup tea, there's a good little lassie.'

Esther had just finished telling her story again – this time to a visibly shocked and amazed Stanley, while his wife kept Joy occupied and out of earshot – when the back door was thrust open once more. Esther's heart jerked in her breast. Caleb stood where he was in the doorway, his gaze fixed on her, as though he was scared to blink in case she was a figment of his imagination; and such was the look on his face that, before Esther was aware of it, Eliza had bustled out of the kitchen, taking Stanley and Joy with her, saying they had something to do in the front room.

Esther felt she was going to cry and was forbidding herself to do so. The last two weeks had exhausted her, mentally, physically and emotionally, and now the feeling that swamped her at the sight of his dear face made her faint. She had never felt so tired and yet so alive.

'Esther?' He took a step towards her, and perhaps because he too was at the end of himself, he stumbled, almost going headlong, as he had that night when they had first spoken under the stars outside the village hall. The sound of frustration that he made at his own inadequacy brought her across the kitchen and into his arms, which opened wide to receive her, before closing with an intensity that seemed to take the breath from her body. His mouth on hers, they kissed with a frantic urgency that took no account of time or place, murmuring endearments and words of love, and straining into each other as though they needed to consume and be consumed.

How long it was before they were sated enough to pull slightly apart, Esther didn't know, but it was Caleb who first spoke coherently, his deep voice rueful as he murmured, 'I think this is the first time I have ever witnessed my mother voluntarily taking a child into her hallowed front room. None of the grandchildren are allowed in there, not even on high days and holidays. We're honoured.'

She breathed in the nearness of him, and it was as intoxicating as any alcohol. 'I didn't know, about you phoning the house – and the letters. And they took mine to you. I should have gone into town and posted them myself, but I never thought for a moment—'

'Hey, hey, slow down, it's all right.' He stopped her gasping words by the simple expedient of kissing her again. When the tears welled from her eyes, he sat down on a kitchen chair, pulling her onto his lap. 'Okay, from the beginning. So you didn't get my letters, and I didn't get yours. Call me old-fashioned, but am I right that Monty and Theobald play a part in this somewhere?' Kissing the tip of her nose, he said gently, 'Come on, no more tears. We're together again and I tell you right now: nothing is going to separate us, for as long as we are both alive. That's a promise. I shouldn't have let you go, I know that now; but I was a jealous fool and by the time I realized what an idiot I was, you had gone. The thing is, I know you're too good for me.' And when she would have protested, he put his finger on her lips. 'It's true, but I'll never let that hinder me again. I'm going to take what God has sent me and say, "Thank you very much, and keep it coming."' She was laughing now, as he had intended she should, and after a moment or two he whispered, 'Okay, sweetheart, tell me.'

For the third time that afternoon she related the sorry

happenings of the last few days. Eliza had been saddened and aghast, Stanley amazed and shocked; but Caleb was so blazingly angry she was frightened. In that moment she thanked God that Theobald was dead, because she knew without a doubt that Caleb would have found him and meted out his own rough justice, even if he had swung for it. As it was, when he muttered, 'And Monty stood by, without lifting a finger to stop him? And if Theobald was confined to bed, who took the letters you wrote to me, before they could be posted?' she knew a moment's deep fear.

'Listen to me.' She took his craggy face between her hands. 'Monty is a broken man. No, don't jerk away like that. He is, Caleb. He lost everything during the war. The family home and his wealth and prestige; his social standing with his peers; and even his health. His hands are poor things, and he wasn't trained to do anything but fly. But more than that, it has changed him, deep inside. He is a shell of his former self and will always be so. His self-respect is all gone.'

'You're sorry for him?' he growled incredulously. 'After how he treated you and Joy?'

'Yes, I suppose I am. He's got nothing and no one. He knows I despise him as much as I once adored him, and that must be hard to take. He is one of those people that the war has left in a kind of time-warp; he wants what has gone forever, the old privileged life he was brought up in, and he can't adapt.'

'Or won't.'

'Maybe.' She nodded. 'Yes, maybe; but whatever the case, he has nothing, and we have everything in each other. Can't you see that? Don't be bitter about him, Caleb. It'll only hurt you and me in the long run. He's agreed to the divorce; he even told me he will admit to some affairs that he had, in the months after Joy was born, if it helps to quicken things up.'

'That's big of him,' Caleb muttered with scathing sarcasm.

Esther smiled, she couldn't help it. He sounded like a sulky little boy.

Seeing the smile, Caleb had the grace to grin sheepishly, before his expression sobered. 'I hate the fact that you once loved him,' he said quietly. 'That's the truth of it. And Joy is his. You have a child that you share.'

'No, we don't,' she said sadly. 'We never did. If she had been white, Monty would have loved her as she deserves to be loved; and he only still loves me because I don't look half-black. But I am. More than that, I am proud of it. From the little I know, my parents defied everyone for their love, and that's a mighty heritage to live up to.'

'Don't cry, love.'

'My mother gave me up because she wanted a good life for me, and she had been put in an impossible situation by her family, but I believe she and my father are together somewhere. I want to find them, Caleb. I want to know who I come from and see their faces, hear them speak, *know* them.'

'We can do that.'

'My eyes have been opened to prejudice and bigotry and all kinds of things, in the last three years, but as I speak right now I can say I wouldn't change a thing. What does the colour of someone's skin matter? Or their social standing, or religion or culture? I know now that I walked through the first part of my life with my eyes shut, but no more. And much as I hate the thought of Joy coming up against narrow-mindedness and discrimination, I can see it has to be, if the world is going to change. The black GI Priscilla dated for a while told us such terrible things about what went on in his country, and that's what my father must have lived under. It's horrible, Caleb. Unbelievable in a civilized world, and yet it's happening.'

He drew her close again, soothing her with words of love as he promised her the moon. He had begun to believe she had gone from him, over the last weeks, and he knew now that if that had truly been the case, his life would have ended. He might have still continued breathing and walking and talking, but essentially he would have been dead. But Esther was here with him now; moreover she loved him, and the threads to her previous life were cut at last. She wanted to find her mother and father, and by all that was holy he would make it happen. He didn't know how right now, but that didn't matter.

'I love you.' He lifted her chin with the tip of his finger so that he could gaze into the depths of her chocolate-brown eyes. 'I always will – in this world and the one to come. I promise you that, sweetheart.'

For a moment the memory of the evening Joy was conceived was vivid; Monty had said much the same thing, after they had made love for the first time. He had promised her the forever kind of love. *But Caleb meant it.*

She looked into the rough-hewn face, every feature of which declared his roots, and she smiled. They would never have much money, and life wouldn't be a bed of roses, but they would have love pressed down and spilling over. That was riches indeed.

Chapter Twenty-Six

Much to Esther's surprise and relief, she found that Mr Dimple had kept her job open for her, when she went to the hotel the day after she'd arrived back in Sunderland. Within a short while she'd slipped into the previous routine, and the nightmare of the preceding weeks faded as the busyness of her working life took over. Until, that was, she discovered Theobald hadn't been lying about making her the sole beneficiary of his will.

She hadn't given his declaration a second thought, sure that it was just some clever ruse to keep her under his thumb. But no; according to Theobald's solicitor, as Theobald's daughter and sole heir she was entitled to the proceeds of the estate, his many enterprises and any monies, bonds and shares that he'd accrued.

'It's all yours, m'dear,' the solicitor had assured her, when she and Caleb had visited his offices in answer to a letter she'd received. 'Lock, stock and barrel. And may I say there are plenty of barrels, in this case.'

He smiled an oily smile, and Esther thought she quite

understood why this particular individual had suited Theobald.

'And because, I understand, you are in the throes of a divorce, your husband, Mr Montgomery Grant, has informed me that he wants to make it plain he relinquishes any claim to your late father's estate.'

The solicitor kept his voice expressionless and did not glance at Caleb at this point. This lady was a very wealthy woman now. He did not wish to offend her by letting his avid interest in her private life show.

Esther and Caleb left the plush offices in Chester-le-Street with their heads whirling, a short time later. Eliza was taking care of Joy, and so they went for a meal in a nearby hotel before they caught the train to Sunderland. Once the waiter had taken their order for drinks, he left them with the menu, with a promise to return shortly.

It was Caleb who spoke first, raising his eyes from the embossed card as he murmured, 'Life with you is never dull, that's for sure.'

Esther had been unable to determine what he was thinking, when they had been talking to the solicitor, and now she said, 'Are you upset? About the inheritance?'

'Truthfully?'

She nodded.

'It's going to take a bit of getting used to, and I'm damned glad we met before I knew I'd bagged myself a rich heiress.' He smiled. 'Don't look so tragic. You've just been told you're a very wealthy woman.'

'I'll say I don't want a penny, if it's going to cause a problem between us.'

His smile widened. 'I believe you would.'

'Nothing is more important than us, Caleb.' She reached forward and took his hand across the table. 'And I think Theobald was trying to use this as a form of blackmail, to keep me and Joy with him. He would probably have changed the will as soon as he had got what he wanted. Who knows?'

'Who knows indeed.' He squeezed her fingers. 'What are you going to do?'

'We'll decide together.' The waiter was returning and, as she disengaged her hand, Esther glanced down at her menu, saying, 'Look at the price of the chicken.' Poultry, which had been almost unobtainable for town-dwellers during the war years, had become more available in recent months, but the price had increased in the shops to an unbelievably high two shillings and sixpence a pound, and the menu reflected this. 'Who on earth can afford these prices?'

'You, for one,' said Caleb drily.

Esther glanced quickly at him, but he was smiling again. She smiled back, relieved he was taking it so well. She had been among his kind long enough to understand that the working man was quite different from the gentry and upper-class, when it came to marrying a woman better off than he was. The working man saw himself as the provider, and until the war many wouldn't have dreamed of letting their wives work outside the home –

Stanley being one of them. And he wasn't alone. Ida, Caleb's sister, had recently had an almighty row with her husband shortly after he'd returned from the war, simply because she wanted to continue working as a conductress on the buses.

The time of women having to 'do their bit', because the men had been called up, was over, he'd told Ida. He was home now. Things could get back to normal. When Ida had declared she had no intention of returning to what he called 'normal', they hadn't spoken for a week, according to Eliza.

It was the same everywhere. There'd been an expectation by the male sex that women would leave their war jobs to make way for the home-coming soldiers, but although some had been happy to comply, others – like Ida – weren't willing to sacrifice their new status. Working-class women had tasted independence, and for many there was no going back.

They ate the mediocre meal quickly, when it came. While Caleb settled the bill, Esther went to the ladies' room. She had no wish to use the facilities, but she needed a few moments to herself. Entering one of the two cubicles, she stood with her back pressed against the door and her eyes shut.

This inheritance was going to change everything. She had watched Caleb's face when the solicitor had been speaking and, whatever he said to the contrary, he hadn't liked it. She pressed her hands against her cheeks. He definitely hadn't liked it. While he might be a little more liberated than his father, with regard to a woman's role in life and marriage, Caleb was a man of the people. In his world, the man was *always* the breadwinner – simple as that. In certain circumstances it might be permissible for a woman to marry into money, although even then she didn't doubt that those less charitable would attach certain labels to the unfortunate girl. But for a man to do so?

Opening her eyes, she shook her head slowly. What was she going to do? Even if she gave everything away, it wouldn't help now. If they found themselves struggling in the next years and things were tough, Caleb would blame himself that she was in that position, when she didn't need to be. If she kept her inheritance, it would drive a wedge between them, she knew it. And she didn't want to live in her old home and play the lady of the manor; she was as far removed from that Esther as the man-in-the-moon. And there was Monty too. In spite of everything, she couldn't see him penniless. She didn't want him in her life, or Joy's for that matter; but he needed help to start a new life of his own and, now she was in a position to provide that help, she couldn't pass by on the other side of the road. But Caleb wouldn't see it that way, and she couldn't blame him.

Leaving the cubicle, she washed her hands at the small basin in the outside area and then looked at her reflection in the long, spotted mirror attached to the cloakroom wall. She was wearing a Utility dress that she had bought with her coupons in the last year of the war. The square-shouldered frock was serviceable at best, and her brown wartime coat was cut without fastenings, to be wrapped around the body and held in place by a tie belt. Economy, and making do. And Eliza and Caleb's sisters wore similar clothes, like all working-class folk. This was her world now and she had adapted to it, and in the last three years she had come to know that Joy didn't need fancy schools and a nanny, and servants and beautiful clothes, to grow into a happy little girl – just love. Queuing at the baker's shop, now that bread was on ration, along with cakes and flour and oatmeal; asking Caleb to resole her shoes, because she couldn't afford new ones; making a penny stretch to two – this was normal life. And she liked it. She liked it because it was Caleb's world, and she wanted to be part of it with him.

He was waiting for her in the foyer when she left the cloakroom, slipping her arm through his as they left the hotel, as though there was nothing wrong. But there was. And they both knew it.

The train ride was a short one and they were in a carriage with other folk, so it wasn't until they were back in Sunderland and making their way to Bright Street that Esther said, 'What shall we tell your parents? About the will, I mean.'

'The truth, of course.'

They had just turned into the back lane of Bright Street and now, in the middle of a hot July, the privies in the back yards were stinking to high heaven in one or two of the houses, where the occupants were less than particular. As they passed one yard two small children, as naked as the day they were born, were playing in an old tin bath that their mother had filled with water, while an elderly dog snoozed at their side in the late-afternoon sunshine. Esther glanced at their little faces; they were alight with the joy of the moment. Stopping, she said, 'Caleb? If we tell them, it becomes real.'

'What?' He walked on a step and now he turned to face her.

Softly she whispered, 'I'm frightened. We're happy, and I don't want it all to go wrong. I don't want to lose you.'

'You couldn't lose me if you tried.' He took her in his arms and kissed her, before saying softly, 'Hey, sweetheart, there's nothing to cry about. Look, from the moment I met you, I knew you were unique – a one-off – and that's part of why I love you, I suppose. And let's face it, we were never going to be your average family, were we?' He lifted her chin and smiled into her tear-drenched eyes. 'Even before you open your mouth, it's obvious you're a cut above. That's just the way it is. And I'm' – he shrugged – 'as working-class as old boots. Then there's Joy, and any children we might have, to be added to the mix. We were always going to stick out like a sore thumb and be the subject of speculation. I came to terms with that a long time ago, and I don't give a damn what people say or think; it doesn't matter, as long as we're together. The thing is, love: the way I see it, we make our own world, a new world, like a good many others will have to do. Wherever it is – be it here in a house in one of these streets, or somewhere else – once we shut the door at night, it'll be us and our family, and the rest of them can go to hell as far as I'm concerned.'

With a sigh that swept the tenseness from her body, Esther relaxed against him. He meant it, she could tell. It probably wasn't the moment to say what she was going to say, but she needed to say it nonetheless. Quietly she said, 'I was thinking on the train, and I want to sell everything, Caleb: the house, the businesses, and the rest. I couldn't bear to live in that house now, not knowing what I do about Theobald. And . . . and once things are settled and we know how we stand financially, I'd like to settle an amount on Monty. Enough for him to make a new start somewhere.'

Grimly Caleb said, 'He doesn't deserve such generosity.'

'He is who he is; a product of his parents, as much as I am of mine. His father was a weak man too. I used to feel sorry for him, having a wife like Clarissa, but I think, looking back, that Hubert liked being led by the nose. He was somewhat helpless.'

His voice was stiff when he muttered, 'And you think Monty is helpless too? Do you still care for him?'

'Not in the way you mean.'

'He's a spineless excuse of a man, and I don't want him in our lives.'

'He won't be, but he is still Joy's father, Caleb.' He didn't reply, and she went on, 'She might want to contact him when she's older, because I can't keep the fact that he's her father a secret. There have been enough secrets and enough damage done, as it is. But believe me when I say I know Monty, and he won't want visiting rights or anything like that. At the bottom of him, he's still embarrassed by her.' She swallowed hard. It was difficult to say. 'By her colour.'

'Oh, my love.' Again Caleb gathered her to him, and for some moments they stood entwined, oblivious of the mean little lane with its smells and poverty. Sometimes, because he didn't see Joy's colour, just the enchanting little girl she was, he forgot Esther worried about how her daughter was going to fare in a world where children, as well as adults, could be horribly cruel. But he would make sure Joy had a childhood filled with love and happiness, where home was a sanctuary and family was everything. The child might not have come from him in a biological sense, but he was her father in every way that mattered, and Joy would grow up sure of that. 'Do whatever you want about Monty,' he murmured into the silk of her hair. 'I don't mind.'

Eliza and Stanley sat staring at Esther and Caleb, who had just finished telling them what the solicitor had said. Their faces were a picture. Stanley's mouth had fallen open in a gape, and Eliza was pop-eyed. It was Caleb who said, 'Well, say something. Don't just sit there.'

'I . . . We . . . ' Eliza took a steadying breath. 'We thought it was likely something to do with the divorce.' She glanced at her husband, who was still clearly in shock. 'I can't believe it. Are you sure this solicitor fellow has got it right?'

'It's a will, Mam.'

'Aye, I know – I know it's a will, you said, but he could still have made a mistake.'

'There's no mistake, Mrs McGuigan,' said Esther softly. 'At least not as far as the will is concerned. Whether Theobald ever intended it to be permanent, I don't know. He had an obsession about his name being carried on, and I think he thought he could persuade me to resume my position as his daughter and Monty's wife, by the bribe of his fortune.'

'Did he indeed? Didn't know you that well then, did he, in spite of bringing you up?' Eliza shook her head. 'Well, I never; you don't know what a day's going to bring, do you? So it's a lot, is it? What you're getting?'

Esther nodded.

'Well, lass, we're pleased for you. Aren't we?' she added to Stanley. 'To my mind, you had a raw deal from that so-an'-so when the bab was born, and this makes up for it.' She shook her head again. 'This'll change things, though, won't it?' Her gaze moved to Caleb, as she realized it perhaps wasn't the most tactful thing to say, and then back to Esther. 'I mean, you won't have to stay in that room now,' she added hastily. 'You'll be able to please yourself where you live, and what you do.'

'*Mam!*'

'I'm just saying . . . '

'I know what you're saying, Mrs McGuigan, and

you're right, of course. I can look for somewhere nicer for Joy, but as for the rest of it, we haven't decided yet, have we?' Esther turned to Caleb. 'The main thing, as we see it, is to get the divorce through, so we can be married.'

Eliza looked hard at the girl who had taken her son's heart. And then her face took on a tenderness that was unusual. 'Aye, I see. Well, don't stand there, the pair of you. Take the weight off, and I'll put the kettle on. Prudence has taken Joy to play with her two for a while; she should be bringing her back soon.'

Stanley spoke for the first time. His voice gruff, he said, 'You're a good lass, an' no mistake. Caleb's a lucky fella.'

Caleb looked at his parents and didn't know whether to be amused or resentful. Had they really expected that Esther would give him the old heave-ho, because she'd come into a fortune? Clearly it had crossed their minds. He glanced at Esther and she met his gaze, and she had a small quirk to her mouth. It said: *I've passed the test, haven't I? So be pleased and let it alone.*

And he did let it alone.

Chapter Twenty-Seven

The winding-up of the estate and all the financial threads connected to it took time, but Esther was content to wait. The Wynford name had died with Theobald, and she felt a great weight had been lifted from her shoulders because of it. To her, his name personified darkness and sick perversion, and to cut if off for all time gave her great satisfaction, along with the fact that no blood of his ran through her veins or that of her child.

By the middle of October, when the newspapers and wireless were buzzing with reports of the execution at Nuremberg of ten top Nazi war criminals, along with the more alarming news to most folk that new research linked smoking to lung cancer, the Wynford house and farm had been sold to a rich London businessman who wanted a country retreat, and the various enterprises Theobald had built up had also been disposed of, mainly to wealthy locals. The bank in Bishopwearmouth, where Esther had opened an account, treated her with a deference that caused her many a wry smile as she walked back to her humble room in Ripon Street. She could have moved to wherever she liked, but she wanted her next home to be one she shared with Caleb from the first day. Besides which, knowing that she wouldn't be remaining long in her cramped surroundings, the little room had taken on a cosiness that made it bearable, and Joy was happy there.

The six months between a decree nisi and a decree absolute had been cut to six weeks in August, mainly to accommodate the tidal wave of divorces that had swept Britain, primarily due to the war. Many of the broken marriages were those between servicemen and their wives, the victims of too-lengthy separations or too-hasty marriages. So it was that, at the beginning of November on a bitterly cold Monday morning, Esther received an official-looking envelope in the post, which made her tremble. She and Caleb had been to look at a house on the outskirts of Southwick at the weekend, a large establishment set in its own extensive grounds, which she had noticed advertised in an estate agent's window during the week. She hadn't told Caleb much about the property, and she could tell he was surprised and uncomfortable at the grandeur of the house and the largeness of the grounds surrounding it.

Once they had finished and had made their goodbyes to the estate agent, who had manfully tried to hide his surprise at the odd and, he thought, ill-matched couple, they had walked back into town, refusing a lift in the estate agent's car. It was then, with her arm tucked in

Caleb's, that Esther had said, 'What do you think about the house? Do you like it?'

She could tell he was considering his words carefully when he said, 'What was there not to like. But isn't it a bit big for the three of us? I mean, I know you were brought up in a place like that, but for me . . . ' He swallowed. 'I thought we'd get somewhere smaller. Less . . . grand.'

She stopped, turning her face up to his and putting her gloved hands on his chest. 'I want to talk to you about that. I've been thinking, over the last weeks, about the girls Theobald used so cruelly—'

'Don't. Don't think about it.'

'Them, and all the babies and children who are being abandoned in the last little while.'

Although some 60,000 war brides had set sail in a steady convoy of ships across the Atlantic, to join their husbands in Canada and America since the beginning of the year, there were many girls who had been left to bring up illegitimate babies alone, by their exotic boyfriends who had returned home. Not only that, but servicemen returning to find either their wives pregnant or a new baby in the house, fathered by someone else, were sometimes insisting that the wife make a choice between the child or them; and in cases where there were other children in the family, the cuckoo was often being given up into the care of the authorities. For every smiling, waving girl with a baby in her arms standing on the deck of a ship bound across the ocean, which had become the cliché of Pathé and Movietone newsreels, there was another who was in a less-than-happy position. And it was the children who were suffering most, some of them abandoned at the doors of government buildings or convents; others given over personally to the authorities by their mothers.

Esther took a deep breath. 'I want us to make that house into a children's home.'

'What?'

'I want us to run a children's home. Oh, Caleb, I know we can do it.' She stared into his astonished face. 'We'd have to employ staff, of course, and there'd be all sorts of regulations and rules to understand and take into consideration, but to think of Theobald's money being used for good would be so wonderful. And we could make it a real home for them – not an institution, like so many are. A big family. I was thinking Prudence might like to come and be the matron, with her nursing experience; she could live in with her children. I know she gets lonely at nights, and in a children's home there'd always be someone to talk to and something to do. And there's Priscilla and Kenny. Since his last operation he's longing to do something – have a real job – but Priscilla says he'd been turned down so often it's depressing him. He could manage the home, or something; he's bright enough. Work with his head rather than his hands.'

Caleb was utterly taken aback. 'I don't know what to say. How long have you been thinking like this?'

'Only lately.' She didn't tell him that it had begun

when she had seen the photograph of an abandoned little girl in the newspaper in the summer. The tot had looked so like Joy they could have been sisters, although the little girl in the paper had darker, curlier hair, obviously inherited from her black father. The photograph had hit her like a punch in the stomach, and for a moment it had been almost as though it was Joy who had been left at the doors of the orphanage, with a label tied around her wrist that read, 'Her name is Katy and she's eighteen months old.' That was all. Someone's baby, and all she had deserved were nine words on the sort of label you would tie on a package. She would tell Caleb about it one day, and how it had affected her, but for the moment she didn't want him to think she was using emotional blackmail. This was his life too, and if they went down this road it was a huge commitment forever.

They had walked slowly back to Caleb's house, where Eliza was looking after Joy, discussing the pros and cons of Esther's proposition, until they reached the others, whereupon they had acted as though the viewing of the house had been merely with regard to a family home.

Esther looked again now at the envelope she was holding. She knew what it was. Her decree absolute. And when Caleb had left her and Joy at the door of the house in Ripon Street last night, his last words had been that they would think about her idea, when her divorce came through. Esther didn't think it was coincidence that the very next morning it arrived in the post. It was a sign, she told herself, as she nervously slit open the envelope;

an indication that they should pursue this. If, of course, the contents of this envelope *were* her decree absolute.

And there it was, in black and white. As she stared at the official authorization stating that her marriage was over, she felt a sharp stab of pain. It was unexpected. She glanced over to where Joy was still curled up in their bed, fast asleep, and bit her lip. Who would have thought it would end like this? She had loved Monty with all her heart and had been over the moon when she knew she was expecting his baby, even though it hadn't been planned. She would be twenty-three years old in a few days' time and already she was a divorced woman, and her child would grow up without her natural father. Nothing in life was certain; it was like those mirrors they had at the fairgrounds, which distorted the image of the person looking into them and turned them into something macabre and strange. She had trusted and loved Harriet, and believed she was her daughter, and all the time it had been a lie. And somewhere in the world her real mother and father had got on with their lives, without her. When she had returned to her home, had her real mother thought about the little baby she had given away, or had she secretly been glad to be free of the burden of an illegitimate daughter?

Thoughts as dark as the night swept in, and for a few minutes Esther was powerless to do anything but let them swamp her mind and emotions. From somewhere deep inside, the cry of a child rose, saying that she wanted her mother; she wanted the woman who had borne her to love her and hug her, and tell her everything was going to be all right; that she hadn't been cast aside for convenience's sake, and that she was loved and thought about often. And it was in that moment that Esther realized the children's home wasn't just about wanting to help little ones less fortunate than Joy; it was about herself too.

She stood with the letter hanging limply in her fingers, and tears pouring down her face for long minutes – grief for what had been lost paramount. Joy had been the catalyst for finding out the truth, and because she'd had a tiny baby to care for by herself, combined with Monty's rejection and Harriet's death, she had never allowed herself to grieve for her mother and father. She had just got on with life. But now pain and sorrow were uppermost, and she was powerless to prevent their onslaught.

It was Joy beginning to stir that brought her back to her senses. Scrubbing at her face with her handkerchief, she took a great shuddering breath. She had to pull herself together. Joy mustn't be upset. Brushing a few strands of hair from her damp cheeks, she reached for her handbag and stuffed the letter inside it. And as she did so, she saw a little square of paper that Caleb must have slipped inside it at some point the previous evening, before he left her on the doorstep, as Mrs Birch decreed.

Opening it, she read:

Sweetheart, whatever you want to do is all right with me, and a children's home sounds good. We'll have to look into it, and it won't be plain sailing, I'm sure, but together we can conquer the world, so this is nothing. And I like the idea of it being a family thing, with Prudence and her bairns, and Priscilla and Kenny. Maybe even my parents can get involved? Bairns need grandparents. Anyway, I love you, and the minute you get that certain piece of paper I want to know, because I have something to say to you: okay? Sleep tight, my darling.

Your Caleb

He was; he was her Caleb. Her world stopped fragmenting and she shut her eyes tightly, whispering, 'Thank you, God. Thank you for Caleb.' And she knew she had to get Joy up and dressed quickly, because she intended to catch Caleb before he left for work.

'Esther, lass, you're early the day.' Eliza stared at Esther's face; the lass had been crying, if she wasn't mistaken. What now? she thought. She couldn't understand why the lass continued to live in that poky little room and had carried on working at the hotel, when she could buy and sell half of Sunderland if she'd a mind. Caleb had told her Esther wanted to keep everything the same for Joy, until they got the divorce through and could get married, so the child only had to cope with one set of changes, but she thought that was daft. Why work if you didn't have to? But at least they'd begun to look for a house – that was something. But now it looked as though something, or someone, had thrown a spanner in the works. Brushing her thoughts aside, Eliza said, 'Come in, come in, lass, it's bitter this morning. They're saying we're in for a packet this winter, and I reckon they might be right. That's all we need, on top of rationing and the rest of it. All through the war we went without bread and flour being rationed, and what happens? We win the war and things get worse. Can't work that one out, meself.'

Esther was only listening with half an ear. Joy immediately went to Eliza, for she was used to having a cup of weak tea and a teacake as soon as she arrived at her 'grandma's' in the morning, and as Caleb's mother lifted the child into her arms, Caleb walked into the kitchen.

He started to say what his mother had said: 'You're early.' And then stopped abruptly. 'What's the matter?' He couldn't quite fathom the expression on Esther's face, and although it was clear she had been weeping, there was something – an expectation – that made his heart kick against his ribs. Without waiting for a reply, he said, 'We're going in the front room, Mam. Look after the bairn for a minute.' And before Esther could speak, he had taken her hand and pulled her out into the hall and then into what the family irreverently called 'The holy of holies': Eliza's front room, which was her pride and joy. As he shut the door, neither of them noticed the faintly musty smell that pervaded the mausoleum. Their senses were immersed in each other. Softly Caleb said, 'It's come?'

'This morning. Mrs Birch brought it up first thing

after the postman had been. Joy was still asleep and—'
Her words were smothered as Caleb took her in his arms
and kissed her until she was gasping for breath.

Only then did he loosen his hold and press her a little
way from him. Looking down into her face, he murmured, 'At last. I've been waiting for this day all of my
life.'

'You've only known me for the last bit of it.'

'No.' He was deadly serious. 'I was born loving you.'
He gently traced the soft outline of her lips with the tip
of his forefinger, the expression on his tough face causing
her eyes to mist. 'You're the other part of me, Esther. The
best part. Why you love me I'll never know, but I thank
God every night that you do. Wait here a moment.'

To her surprise, he whirled round and was gone, shutting the door behind him. She stood where he had left
her as she heard him climb the stairs, his footsteps
unmistakable because of his leg. Her heart was racing
now, anticipation of the moment she felt sure was coming causing her to tremble.

She was glad she had made her peace with Monty
before this day. The thought came out of nowhere.

Once Theobald's estate had been wound up, she had
sent Monty a substantial cheque – enough to see him live
comfortably for the rest of his life, if he invested the
money wisely. She had written a letter explaining how
she felt, and she had shown both the letter and the
cheque to Caleb before she had sent it. The letter had
been short and to the point:

Monty, I don't want to embarrass you, but I feel it's right you have the enclosed cheque. Thank you for making the divorce easy. Caleb and I will marry as soon as the decree absolute comes through, and he'd like to officially adopt Joy at that time. Will you give your consent to this? If you refuse I won't press the matter, but I would like her to have his name.

Best wishes for the future, Esther.

Monty had replied by return of post, thanking her for the cheque and saying that once the decree absolute was issued, he would have no objection to Joy taking Caleb's name, nor would he be pressing for any contact with her. It would be far less upsetting and confusing for the child that way.

She had stared at this letter for a long time, angry and sore of heart, while telling herself she was being silly and irrational. It was so much better that Monty was willing to step out of their lives completely, considering how he felt about Joy, she knew that. But it still hurt. Illogical and unreasonable maybe, but it hurt that he didn't want his own child.

And then all thoughts of Monty went out of her head as she heard Caleb returning.

Caleb's heart was thudding so hard it actually ached, as he opened the door and saw Esther standing there, waiting for him. He had pictured this moment for so long; had dreamed of it, played it out in his mind, during the long night hours when his body had burned to have her at his side so that he could make love to her until dawn. Now the moment was here, and he was terrified it wouldn't be perfect for her. He had bought the ring – a half-band of diamonds that had taken most of his savings – a few weeks ago and had been thrilled with it; now he was worried she might not like it. He didn't doubt that Monty's ring (which Esther had sent back to her then-husband just after Joy was born) had been a splendid thing, and that Monty had proposed in style: a fancy dinner maybe, or a drive into the country. Certainly it hadn't taken place in a rather dismal, stiff front room that smelled of mothballs. He wouldn't even be able to go down on one knee, damn it.

'Come and sit down.' He drew her to the sofa of the three-piece suite, which was ten years old now, but had only been sat on a dozen times, if that. It was upholstered in a green paisley pattern and Caleb had always hated it.

Quietly he took her hands in his and, when he felt she was trembling, it actually gave him the courage he needed. 'I love you with all my heart and mind, and soul and spirit,' he said softly, 'for now and eternity. Will you marry me, Esther?' He let go of her hands, reaching into his pocket and bringing out the small leather box. Opening it, he revealed the ring nestling in its bed of blue velvet.

She had thought she would cry when the moment happened, but now she looked at him with shining eyes, her face alight. 'Yes, yes, yes.' And as he slipped the ring on the third finger of her left hand, she murmured, 'It's so beautiful. Oh, my darling, I love you. You have no idea just how much I love you.'

Chapter Twenty-Eight

They were married in the midst of the worst winter the country had experienced in decades. The freezing weather began before Christmas, but the inhabitants of the northeast were used to severe conditions now and again. They would have been less complacent if they'd known what was going to follow: a long spell of ferocious cold – the worst of the century – was about to descend, with heavy snowstorms and sub-zero, arctic temperatures for weeks on end, bringing Britain to its economic knees.

On the last weekend of January the temperatures all over Britain plummeted. Snow fell continuously, accompanied by raw gale-force winds from the east, and it was this Saturday that Esther and Caleb had chosen for their small, quiet wedding. The house in Southwick was ready to move into and was waiting for them to begin their married life, and after the service the guests – consisting of Caleb's parents; his sisters and their families; Priscilla and Kenny, who was Caleb's best man; Vera, Lydia and Beryl and her Yorkshire boyfriend, who was now her fiancé; along with a few other friends and relations of Caleb – were driven through the whirling snowstorm to Esther and Caleb's home, where the wedding reception was being held. But Esther and Caleb didn't care about the terrible weather; it was their wedding day, and they couldn't have been happier.

When Esther walked into the register office on the arm of Stanley, radiant in a simple cream dress with a matching fur-lined cape with a sweeping hood, she was beautiful enough to take Caleb's breath away. Joy, who was sitting on Eliza's lap, stole the show when she clapped her hands, shouting, 'Pretty Mummy, pretty Mummy', especially as the little girl was dressed in a miniature version of her mother's outfit.

Esther had written to Rose and Farmer Holden and his wife, inviting them to the wedding and offering to put them up for a day or two at the house. She'd received a letter from Rose saying that although they would have loved to attend, everyone at Yew Tree Farm was working from dawn to dusk seven days a week, and no one could be spared. It was a valid excuse. Esther was aware of the government's emphasis on the growth and increasing self-sufficiency of British agriculture, and of the threat held over farmers by the retention of wartime disciplinary powers of enforced supervision and, ultimately, dispossession, if government targets weren't met. Yew Tree Farm had been in the Holden family for more than a century, and it would have broken Farmer Holden to lose it. Rose had promised that she and Nancy would visit in the summer, when circumstances permitted, and with that Esther had to be content. Their relationship would never be what it had been, but at least some contact had been maintained.

Esther and Caleb had hired a fleet of taxis to drive their guests to the house and, wrapped in Caleb's arms in the leading car, Esther didn't even notice that the snow was coming down thicker than ever. She was Mrs McGuigan at last. A dream come true.

As though he'd read her mind, Caleb murmured between kisses, 'How does it feel to be Mrs McGuigan?'

'Wonderful.'

Caleb smiled. Tonight he would make her his, in body as well as mind; and if he'd had his way, he would have packed everyone off home the minute they'd eaten, rather than make a day of it. One thing troubled him, and he had been pushing it to the back of his mind for some time. How would Esther feel when she saw the stump where his leg had been? Repulsed? Embarrassed? Nauseated? Worse – pitying? He didn't want her to feel sorry for him; he wanted to be her lover: vigorous, masterful and manly.

Taking her hand, he kissed the finger where a gold band now sat beside his engagement ring, telling himself it would be all right. Esther had never seen him as a cripple, he knew that, and he was grateful. Nevertheless, he'd be relieved when that hurdle was over, and he couldn't help how he felt.

Blazing fires in the drawing and dining rooms greeted

the guests as they walked in from the cold, and in the kitchens at the back of the house, Fanny Kennedy and her sister were busy finishing the hot and cold wedding buffet. The new owner of what had been the Wynford estate had offered to keep all the resident staff on, but when Esther had approached Fanny and her sister with the proposition of running the kitchen and catering for what was to be a children's home in the future, they had been thrilled. They had moved into their quarters in the house the week before.

The day sped by and it was a happy one, and when the taxis arrived to transport the guests to their homes – those who weren't staying overnight at the house – Esther and Caleb stood entwined on the doorstep to wave them off, with Joy perched on Caleb's shoulders. Everything was covered in a mantle of white, but the clean, pure vista somehow suited the day. The world was bright and new, and that was how Esther felt later that evening, when Joy was asleep in her pretty pink bedroom and she and Caleb were alone in the master suite.

She looked at him as he shut the door and, as he took her in his arms, she murmured, 'Are you sure you didn't mind, about having to get married in a register office?' She would have loved a church wedding, but as a divorced woman it hadn't been possible in the parish church.

Caleb smiled. 'Do I look as though I mind?' he said softly. 'We had everyone we care about there, and it has been a wonderful day, but I'd have been just as happy to get married in a coal hole, as long as it meant we were man and wife.'

Esther giggled. 'You're a heathen.'

'I know it.' And then, as he drew her over to the bed and they sat down, he gave her an envelope. 'My wedding present.'

'Wedding present?' she said in surprise. 'What is it?'

'Read it and see. It only came a couple of days ago, and I wanted to give you it at the very start of our life together.'

The envelope had already been opened, and now she said, 'Caleb?', an inexplicable nervousness filling her.

'Read it, sweetheart,' he said again, his voice husky and filled with love.

Slowly she drew out the letter the envelope contained, along with a smaller envelope, which was unopened. She read:

Dear Mr McGuigan,

I was very glad to receive your letter. I think I have been waiting for it for a long time, without realizing it. Ruth Flaggerty was my sister, and before she died she entrusted me with a letter, which I now enclose.

Esther gasped, dropping the letter as though it had burned her, and again she said, 'Caleb?', reaching for him blindly.

'It's all right, darling.'

'Who . . . who is this person?'

'Your aunt. Look, I'll explain everything, once you've read what she has to say.' He handed her the letter again. 'Read it, Esther,' he said for the third time, his voice soothing.

Her hands trembling, she took the letter from him. Her aunt wrote:

> As you will see, Ruth's letter has not been opened.
> She never told me who she gave her baby girl to, only
> that it was a kind gentlewoman of good birth, rather
> than the nuns at the convent she was bound for,
> before the shipwreck. As you know, my parents
> forced my sister to make that journey; and what I
> now have to tell you makes for harrowing reading,
> and for that I am sorry. The only thing I would ask is
> that you do not judge my parents too harshly. They
> were products of their time – a time which,
> thankfully, is changing. I must explain their
> backgrounds before I go any further.

Esther shut her eyes for a second, unable to take in that this was her *aunt*'s handwriting – that this woman was her mother's sister. And she said what she had to tell was harrowing. With her heart thumping hard against her ribcage, she opened her eyes. And her mother was dead; this woman had said so. She would never meet her now. Pain gripped her, but her eyes were drawn again to the letter:

My mother's and my father's parents emigrated to America from Ireland at the height of the potato famine, as newly married couples. Those men and women who pursued this path only did so because they knew their future in the country of their birth would be more poverty, disease and terrible English oppression. They left Ireland on ships that were so crowded, and with conditions so dire, that my grandmother always referred to them as 'coffin ships'.

When the boats docked, for those who'd survived the journey, life was going to get worse. Hundreds of men known as runners – harsh, greedy individuals devoid of pity or basic human kindness – swarmed aboard the ships, grabbing the immigrants and their bags with the purpose of forcing them to tenement houses, where they would then exact an outrageous fee for their services. Both my grandfathers were barely sixteen years old, and their poor wives were even younger. They had no idea what was happening to them or whom they could trust, and they were treated cruelly. Almshouses were filled with hundreds of immigrants who begged on every street corner, and their position in their new country was one of shame and even more poverty. My grandmother told us that no group was considered lower than Irishmen in America during the 1850s, and she was terribly bitter about that to her dying day.

Both couples tried to get work, in spite of all the advertisements for employment that stated: 'No Irish need apply'. My grandparents were proud people, Mr McGuigan. Can you imagine how they must have felt? They were forced to live in a cellar in a kind of shanty town, with no plumbing or running water, and these conditions bred sickness and early death. I understand that my paternal grandmother lost her first baby a day after it had been born, when they had only been in America six months. She went on to have ten more, and only my father and one other sibling, a girl, survived. On my mother's side, she and two sisters lived, out of nine children born to my grandmother, but my mother's sisters were apparently always ailing and died in early adulthood.

Understandably, the Irish became a close-knit community, to help each other survive the new life. My grandmother said they prayed and drank and worked together when they could, forming a militant church that fought not only for their souls, but for their human rights. My grandfathers were cousins and they took any jobs they could and, for the reasons I have explained, the work was always what the Americans disdained as beneath them, fit only for slaves and servants. For this reason, the black population resented and hated the Irish newcomers, feeling they took work that could have been theirs, and the feeling was mutual. You would have thought the Irish and the black people would have joined together in a common purpose, wouldn't you, Mr McGuigan, and hated their oppressors, rather than each other? But that was not the case. Such is human nature, I fear.

I know my grandparents were terribly bitter about having competed with African Americans, who were freed slaves, for the most menial jobs and poorest housing, and they instilled their hatred in their children. Many Irish immigrants at that time were driven to despair and drink and crime, but my paternal and maternal grandparents stuck together. They were determined they would not sink under the morass of intemperance and degradation that prevailed, and they did not. Together, after some years, they moved south and bought some land. They built a fine plantation, with their blood, sweat and tears, and they rose in the world. But their past had moulded their characters and their outlook on life. They were four of the most hard, unforgiving, bitter people I have ever met, and cruel. Terribly cruel to their black workers. I think even my parents were terrified of them. I know us children were.

And now I must speak of my sister, Ruth.

Esther's eyes were full of tears. 'I'm frightened to read on,' she whispered. It had been a bitter blow to find out that her mother was dead, but what else was she going to discover? And yet she needed to know. She had lain awake so many nights thinking about the part of her that was shrouded in mystery, and this woman who was her aunt could provide the answers.

Caleb drew her to him and kissed her. 'I know, love. That's why I wanted to give you this when I could be with you all the time, holding you, loving you, being here.' He'd had so little to go on when he'd begun the search, just a name, and the fact that the family might have lived in Cincinnati or Albany, and that Ruth's father had been a member of the Democratic Party and possibly elected to the city council; that was all Esther had known. But then he'd uncovered all this, and he'd wondered if he should ever have started.

Esther read on:

There were four of us: two older brothers, me, then Ruth. She was born to my mother late in life. I think if my parents loved anyone, it was Ruth, so it made it all the more unthinkable for them when they discovered she was expecting a baby at the age of fifteen. A dreadful time followed. Ruth admitted that the father of her baby was Michael – one of our plantation workers – and I think my father lost his mind for a while. That is the only excuse I can give for what happened.

Ruth was sent away to have her baby, as you know, and Michael disappeared the same night. The story was that he had run away, but I fear I don't believe that. He would never have left Ruth. My father and my brothers disposed of him, I am sure of it, and I think my mother knew it. Certainly it was what Ruth suspected when she came home; and from the day she walked through the door, she simply faded away. Within three months she had died. One of my brothers was killed in a riding accident shortly afterwards, and the other one died in his fifties without having married, as I have not. I believe a curse was put on our family the night Michael disappeared, although some would say that is fanciful.

Before she died, Ruth gave me the enclosed letter, in the hope that one day her daughter would read it. That is the story, Mr McGuigan, and I am glad that out of it all, my poor sister's child is alive and well. I fear I am in ill health myself and suffering from a heart condition, but if Ruth's daughter can find it in her heart to forgive our family, I would dearly like to hear from her.

With very best wishes,
Catherine Flaggerty

Esther sat for a moment, staring at the smaller envelope. There was no writing on it. She turned it over. Her mother had touched it; her fingers had caressed the paper, and she had been thinking of her daughter when she had sealed the envelope.

'All right, darling?' Caleb put his arm round her and she leaned against him for a moment, unable to speak because her throat was blocked and aching.

After a long, shuddering sigh, she straightened. Gently, almost reverently, she slipped the tip of a nail under the edge of the envelope. The old paper gave without protest immediately, the ancient glue so brittle it had no hold.

Esther unfolded the two sheets of notepaper within, but she had to wipe her eyes again before she could focus on the words:

My darling beautiful baby girl,

It is my prayer you will read this some day and know how precious and infinitely special you are. I don't know what you will be told about me and your father. It is true that our love conceived you out of wedlock, but it *was* love, my darling. Believe that. Your father was the most sweet-tempered, tender, wonderful man in the world, a giant among men, even at the age of eighteen. He would have made a difference in the world, if he had been allowed to live, I know that. But I am going to be reunited with him and so I cannot be sad, except for the fact that I would have so loved us to be a family together.

Your father's name was Michael, and his grandparents were brought to America in shackles in the hold of a slave ship – torn from their village and peaceful way of life by men who were brutal and without mercy. The slaves on our plantation are allowed no surname, but Michael's parents have told him his is Bamogi, and that his grandfather was a chief in his own country and greatly respected for his wisdom and compassion. His spirit lives on in his grandson, or did before other men with white skin, equally brutal and without mercy, took his life. But you are his daughter, my darling, and I believe he lives on in you.

We love you, my sweet baby, your father and I. We will always love you. Death cannot quench love. I believe that from the bottom of my heart, and in the last few days I have felt your father very close, as my time on this earthly vale draws to a close. Men would say we committed a sin in our coming together, but only God is the true judge, and I am content to put my trust in Him.

I did not want to give you up, but I knew Harriet would be a loving and good mother and would protect you when I could not. There has not been a moment since you were born when you haven't filled my heart and soul, and I pray that God will give you a good and long life with much happiness and joy – like your name. I pray also that you will see a time when man's inhumanity to man will be a thing of the past, and each man, woman and child will stand on who they are, and not on the colour of their skin or the culture from which they have sprung. Michael believed that would happen one day, and because he believed it, I have to believe it too.

My sister, Catherine, is the only one I can trust with this letter. I am virtually a prisoner in my room, and nothing I have is sacrosanct, as far as the rest of my family is concerned, but I know she will keep it safe for you. My arms ache to hold you and tell you how much you are loved. Always remember that. Be strong, my darling.

I love you, so much.

Your Mama xxxxx

It was more than she could have hoped for, and yet at the same time the sense of loss was so acute that it was unbearable. When Caleb drew her close, Esther's body shook them both with the force of her weeping, and she cried for some minutes. But when at last she straightened, taking the handkerchief he gave her and mopping her eyes, a sense of peace had stolen over her, without her being aware of it.

'She loved me,' she whispered, turning to look at him. 'And I was right; they are together somewhere.'

Caleb's response to this was not to speak, but to put his hand gently to her cheeks and stroke away the last of her tears. He hadn't wanted to spoil their wedding night, and he hadn't known how Esther would deal with hearing from this aunt, but he felt that to keep the letter – especially the one from her mother – from her for one more day was wrong. He'd known she would be upset, and that was why he hadn't given her the letter before their wedding day. As he had said to her, he could be with her twenty-four hours a day now, talk through anything that needed to be talked through and make sure she was all right. They had both left their jobs after Christmas, to prepare for their marriage and begin planning for the future and the huge project of the home.

'Thank you for finding her.' Esther smiled shakily. 'I don't know how you did it, but thank you. You will never know what it means to have my mother's letter. It's a dream come true, Caleb.'

'No more tears, sweetheart.' He pulled her to him again. 'I didn't want to make you cry, especially on this night of all nights.'

'I needed to know,' she whispered, brushing away the tears. 'And they're happy tears, in a way. I knew in my heart they were good people and that they cared about me, but this puts all the pieces together. It's just hard to hear they were treated so cruelly. And they died so young.'

'But they live on in you, and in Joy, and any bairns we might have.'

'That's true, but I want them here, *now*, seeing it all.' She shook her head. 'I want it all and I know I can't have that, but I'd give ten years of my life to feel my mother's arms around me and for her to kiss me.'

'You'll have to make do with me,' he said softly, 'and all the other people who love you.'

'My mother did the only thing she could, in giving me to Harriet, I see that; and Harriet did love me as her own child. It can't have been easy for her, married to Theobald . . . '

They talked on in the quiet of the room, the snow falling outside the window and the world hushed and silent. And later, in the early hours of the morning, they made love, and Caleb's fears were laid to rest.

*

They settled into married life as ten-foot drifts of snow transformed the landscape, turning the countryside into a huge, white maze, and as the cold tightened its grip in London the River Thames froze over. Non-stop blizzards crippled the roads and railways as effectively as Hitler's bombs had done, but this time it was the whole country that was hit. Almost no coal got through to power stations, factories and homes, and major roads became impassable, cutting off the north of England from the south.

The crisis soon meant that the forces of winter succeeded where the Nazis had failed, invading the British Isles and holding it in an iron grip. By the end of the first week of February, when Emanuel Shinwell, the Minister of Fuel and Power, was forced to announce drastic measures and declare that power to industries was to be cut off altogether, and householders had periods of being without electricity for hours on end, Caleb had stockpiled a huge mountain of logs from trees that he'd cut down in the area of woodland on their property. Hundreds of coal trains were unable to battle their way through the twenty-foot-high snowdrifts that had developed as the weather had worsened, which meant that many homes had no heating at all. Not only that, but shipping in the Channel had stopped, creating a new threat to food supplies, and in some villages whole families were literally starving in their cold, dark homes.

Snow fell every day and Esther felt guilty that, far from finding the isolation and difficulties that the winter had caused untenable, as so many people did, she was enjoying the time cut off from the outside world with her new husband; and Joy was as happy as a bug in a rug. Fanny Kennedy and her sister still managed to provide hot food, courtesy of Caleb's logs in the range and, after he'd made himself a toboggan to fetch supplies from the town, they wanted for little. With no electricity most of the time, they relied on candlelight once it grew dark, and to save burning too many candles they went early to bed and rose when it was light. This meant many warm hours snuggled up to Caleb in the privacy of their big bed, the logs crackling in the small fireplace and sending flickering shadows on the walls of the bedroom, as they made leisurely love and explored each other's bodies. They talked for hours, getting to know each other intimately in a short time, which could never have happened in the usual way. Together they drew up plans for the alterations to turn the house into a children's home. It was a magical interlude.

At present Fanny and her sister occupied the old servants' quarters, situated off the kitchen and scullery at the back of the house. These were very comfortable, having recently been modernized by the previous owner. There were five bedrooms, a large communal sitting room, and a bathroom and a separate toilet. Esther thought Prudence and her children could have the remaining three bedrooms. Fanny and her sister were motherly sort of women, and she felt Prudence and her little ones would settle in well there. A small cottage in the grounds, which had been the home of the previous gardener and his family, was designated by Esther and Caleb for Priscilla and Kenny. It only had two bedrooms at present, but an extension would take care of that and would also enlarge the living space downstairs.

The main house already had fourteen bedrooms, and they intended to knock down walls to make two large boys' dormitories and two for girls, with separate bathrooms and toilets. Each dormitory would sleep eight, and a separate bedroom-cum-sitting-room at the head of the rooms would house a permanent member of staff, of which there would be nine, besides Priscilla, Kenny and Prudence. Downstairs, a sitting room, games room, dining room and library would be for the older children, while in the east wing babies and children up to the age of six would have their own bedrooms, nursery, play area and dining facilities, with attendant staff. The west wing would be a separate entity with its own front door – a house within a house. This would be Esther and Caleb's family home, comprising a kitchen and three rooms downstairs, and four bedrooms and two bathrooms upstairs.

It was an ambitious undertaking, involving a lot of building work, but that was fine. Officialdom would need to be consulted and a hundred and one obstacles overcome, but Esther knew it was the right thing to do. She had never been more sure of anything in her life. The home would be just that – a home; not an institution, but a place where children would grow up loved, and knowing they were part of a big family, with grown-ups who cared about them.

With inches of snow every night, even Esther was glad when at long last, on the ides of March, the thaw began. But the ice and snow melted into torrents, the rivers overflowed and a great storm in the middle of March spread the floodwaters far and wide. The small, tinkling stream that ran through the grounds near the woodland area turned into a vast lake, which flowed right to the steps of the house, but mercifully not inside it, although Caleb sat up all one night making sandbags in case things became dire. A harsh winter had been followed by a cruel spring, but by the time food rations were cut in June, as the government warned of a new economy drive, a gloriously hot summer brought some relief to Britain's beleaguered citizens.

All over the country, with the housing shortage now acute, it was a time of reconstruction, as the government attempted to put a roof over the heads of those made homeless by the Luftwaffe. Caleb and Esther's plans for the home were approved by the powers that be, and with the production of prefabricated houses taking prece-dence everywhere, they eventually found a small building firm to take on the work, with Esther and Caleb helping out where they could. Even Joy had her own tiny wheel-barrow and did her bit. Stanley and Eliza, Prudence and her sisters and their families came at weekends to lend a hand, and as they all took a break in the hot sunshine, Fanny and her sister would bring out a picnic lunch for everyone. For the first time in her life Esther felt she was experiencing what real family life was like, and it made even the hardest, most exhausting days wonderful.

By the third week of November, when Princess Elizabeth, the heir-presumptive to the throne, married Prince Philip, the Duke of Edinburgh, at Westminster Abbey in a glittering ceremony such as the nation had not seen for decades, the work at 'Blessings' – as Esther had decided to call the home – was all but finished.

Prudence and her children moved into their quarters at the beginning of December, after Prudence had worked her notice at the hospital, and immediately settled in well with Fanny and her sister. Priscilla and Kenny were installed in the cottage in the grounds the same week, although any work to extend their accommodation would not begin until spring the following year. Kenny was already proving a huge asset in his role of manager, taking the load off Esther and Caleb's shoulders whenever he could. And, as Priscilla confided to Esther when they had a quiet moment alone, he seemed to have grown a few inches in the process. Priscilla was the home's secretary and in charge of the office; over the summer she had learned to type and even take shorthand.

At the end of the autumn Esther and Caleb had advertised for the other staff required to run the home, when it opened its doors officially in the New Year. They had chosen those applicants who, although not necessarily the highest qualified, would fit in best with the relaxed family atmosphere that already prevailed.

A few days before Christmas the dormitories and nursery had been painted in warm colours and the brightly patterned bedspreads and curtains were in place. Wall-to-wall carpeting covered the floor, rather than the linoleum that was usual in most establishments of this nature; but, as Esther had said, she didn't want little feet to get cold, and who cared about practicality anyway. The east wing's playroom was full of toys and books and cuddly teddy bears, and the games room for the older children was equally stocked with items appropriate for their age, including table tennis, dartboards and board games.

A little extra meat, sugar and sweets were made available by the government for Christmas, warmly welcomed by the populace, as it had been a difficult year, with bad weather lasting to the spring and shortages of many foods. Some nuts had come onto the market in December, but cream was still unavailable, and in their weaker moments Esther and Priscilla reminisced longingly about Mrs Holden's creamed rice pudding. Nevertheless, the valiant Fanny did her best with butter icing, and was a dab hand at turning the much-reviled whalemeat into something edible. Fanny always finely minced the meat before cooking it, mixing it with strong flavours, and her hamburgers and goulash were delicious. Whalemeat was not rationed; most people grimly declared they knew why, but in Fanny's hands it was tasty enough.

Knowing it would be the last Christmas before the home was up and running, Esther decided that Christmas

Day would be a party for everyone who'd had a hand in preparing for the big event, as well as for friends and any relatives of Caleb who wanted to join them and the new staff they had employed. Fanny and her sister enjoyed a tipple, and had made several gallons of cider in the summer from the apples in the orchard close to the woodland, along with bottles of elderberry, blackberry and cherry wine; and these, together with the beer that Stanley and Ida's and Clara's husbands contributed, ensured the party went with a swing.

Fanny made a huge vat of her celebrated goulash for the grown-ups, along with hamburgers and what she called her 'eight-minute doughnuts' for the children. The doughnuts were fairly flat, like a fritter, as there was insufficient fat to fry a thicker mixture due to rationing, but they tasted delicious, especially the apple ones. They'd had a bumper crop of apples that summer, and Fanny had stored hundreds on brown paper in the attics of the house. This was reflected in the apple croquettes and apple sponges that also appeared on the table. It wasn't the traditional Christmas fare, but no one minded, and as their guests were all sleeping over and no one had to turn out into the bitterly cold night, the party continued into the early hours of Boxing Day.

It was gone two o'clock in the morning when Esther and Caleb climbed into bed. The room was lit only by the glowing fire flickering in the grate, and by the light from the white world outside the windows. It had snowed thickly all day, and that afternoon their guests had helped the children create an army of snowmen and snow-women – and even some snow-dogs that stood, sentry like, on either side of the long, curving drive leading to the house.

Esther snuggled into Caleb's side, one arm across his chest. It had been a wonderful day, and in a short time, at the beginning of January, the first of the children were due to arrive. Every place had been taken, and they could have filled the home ten times over, if they'd had the room. Their life was going to change – quite how much Caleb wasn't yet aware of, but Esther had been keeping a special Christmas present for him for some days.

'It's been the best Christmas ever,' she whispered, burying her nose in his neck and then kissing him softly.

'Grand,' he agreed sleepily.

'Can you think of anything that could have made it better?'

He shifted slightly, turning to face her. 'Not a thing. It was perfect – like you.'

'Nothing?' she persisted.

'Esther, you did everyone proud. Stop worrying.'

'I'm not worried.' She kissed him again, this time on the lips. 'Quite the opposite, in fact.'

'Good.' He pulled her closer, his body responding to hers, as it always did. She was more intoxicating than any drink or drug, he thought drowsily. He couldn't get enough of her.

'I've got something to tell you.'

There was a note of something in her voice that made

him fully compos mentis. 'What is it?' He couldn't see her clearly in the soft shadows, but her eyes, bright and glittering, smiled at him.

'You're going to be a father,' she whispered. 'I'm expecting our baby.'

Epilogue

1976

It was Esther and Caleb's thirtieth wedding anniversary, and they were celebrating with a family get-together at home. After lunch, the grown-ups had sat and chatted while the children played, but now the long January twilight was deepening and Esther had got up to draw the curtains and shut out the frozen white world outside the sitting-room windows.

She stood for a moment, looking out into the grounds where the last of the home's children had just been rounded up and taken indoors for their tea. So many little ones had passed through its doors since it had opened, and the face of each child – even those who'd gone out into the world years ago – was etched on her mind. Of course, many of them came back at regular intervals for a chat and a cup of tea, some bringing their own children to meet Esther and Caleb and the rest of the staff. Esther often felt as though she wasn't just the mother of four children, but of hundreds, and each one was special. They came with their own particular problems, and from diverse backgrounds and circumstances, and some were harder to reach than others, but once they walked over Blessings' threshold they were loved and cherished no matter what had gone before.

Esther turned, looking over the room where her family were assembled. Caleb was sitting in his armchair close to the fire with Joy's youngest child on his lap. He was pretending to understand her gabbled baby talk, nodding and making the odd comment much to the little girl's delight. At two years old, Christina was the image of her mother, although her skin was as fair as her father's. Joy had married Prudence's oldest lad, Arnie, twelve years ago, and they'd had three children, all girls, and each one was quite spectacularly beautiful like their mother.

For a moment, Esther felt a stab of the old sadness that Monty had never attempted to get in touch with Joy through the years, or to see his grandchildren. Joy didn't know, but Esther had written to Monty when each of Joy's little girls were born, telling him of their arrival and their names, but he had never responded by so much as a card or a little note. His loss, as Caleb always said when the two of them were alone, and she agreed with that, but nevertheless she found it hard to understand.

Monty had settled in London after the divorce, and had apparently risen to the upper echelons of the Civil Service, although she had no idea what he did. He had never married again, and Esther found it even more strange, in view of this, that he was content to lead such an insular life and have no contact with his only child.

But perhaps it was for the best; Caleb certainly thought so, and as Joy adored Caleb and looked on him completely as her father, she hadn't missed out, which was all that mattered.

Esther and Caleb had three children of their own: two boys and a girl. Cyril, the eldest, had married a local girl and had five-year-old twin boys who were as dark-skinned and dark-eyed as their handsome father. Desmond, their second child, was as different from his brother as chalk is from cheese, having the palest of skin, which burned if the sun so much as looked at him, and eyes as blue as cornflowers. He'd married Sarai, a lovely gentle Indian girl he had met at university, and they had a little boy called Thomas. Sophie, the baby of the family at twenty-one, had recently got engaged at Christmas to a Chinese lad, whose parents had a restaurant in the town. At the engagement party, Joy had jokingly remarked that their family resembled the United Nations, and Esther had replied fervently that she did hope so.

Esther's gaze wandered over each one of her precious family, taking in the different shades of colour in their skin and hair and eyes. Each of her children was a strong-minded, determined and resilient individual, and they all liked nothing more than a family get-together like this one. Everyone laughed and chatted and teased each other, along with having the odd argument, but that was family. She was so blessed, she told herself, her heart full to bursting. She watched as Chan murmured something in Sophie's ear, which caused her daughter to smile and reach up and stroke his face, and the gesture seemed to encapsulate the feeling in the room.

Esther's eyes moved to the mantelpiece. There, framed and in pride of place, stood her mother's letter. It was her most treasured possession. So softly that her words were merely the faintest of breaths, she murmured, 'The colours of love are here in this room, precious one.'

They were in the blue of Caleb's eyes; in the white, honey, brown and ebony shades of the skin of her children and their partners and her grandchildren; in the silver-blonde of little Christina's hair and the tight black curls of the twins. And – most of all – in the fragile, yellowing paper of her mother's letter, its charcoal smudged in places with the salt of Ruth's tears as she had written to the baby girl she had loved, and lost, so many years ago.

'Love has won, my darling,' she whispered. 'Love has won.'

The Colours of Love

Rita Bradshaw was born in Northamptonshire, where she still lives today. At the age of sixteen she met her husband – whom she considers her soulmate – and they have two daughters and a son, and six grandchildren. Much to her delight, Rita's first novel was accepted for publication and she has gone on to write many more successful novels since then, including the number one bestseller *Dancing in the Moonlight*.

As a committed Christian and passionate animal-lover her life is full, but she loves walking her dogs, reading, eating out and visiting the cinema and theatre, as well as being involved in her local church and animal welfare.

BY RITA BRADSHAW

Alone Beneath the Heaven
Reach for Tomorrow
Ragamuffin Angel
The Stony Path
The Urchin's Song
Candles in the Storm
The Most Precious Thing
Always I'll Remember
The Rainbow Years
Skylarks at Sunset
Above the Harvest Moon
Eve and Her Sisters
Gilding the Lily
Born to Trouble
Forever Yours
Break of Dawn
Dancing in the Moonlight
Beyond the Veil of Tears
The Colours of Love